WRAITHWEAVER

THE MELDERBLOOD CHRONICLES
BOOK 3

E.A. WINTERS

To those who have survived betrayal and come out the other side stronger than you once believed you were.

SOCIAL MEDIA

Connect with me on social media! [1]

- Website and newsletter: eawinters.com
- Facebook: facebook.com/eawintersnovels
- TikTok: @eawinters
- Instagram: @e.a.winters

---

1. Warning: connecting on social media may lead to exclusive content, behind the scenes snapshots, and joining a community that is way more fun than your daily to-do list. Engage with caution.

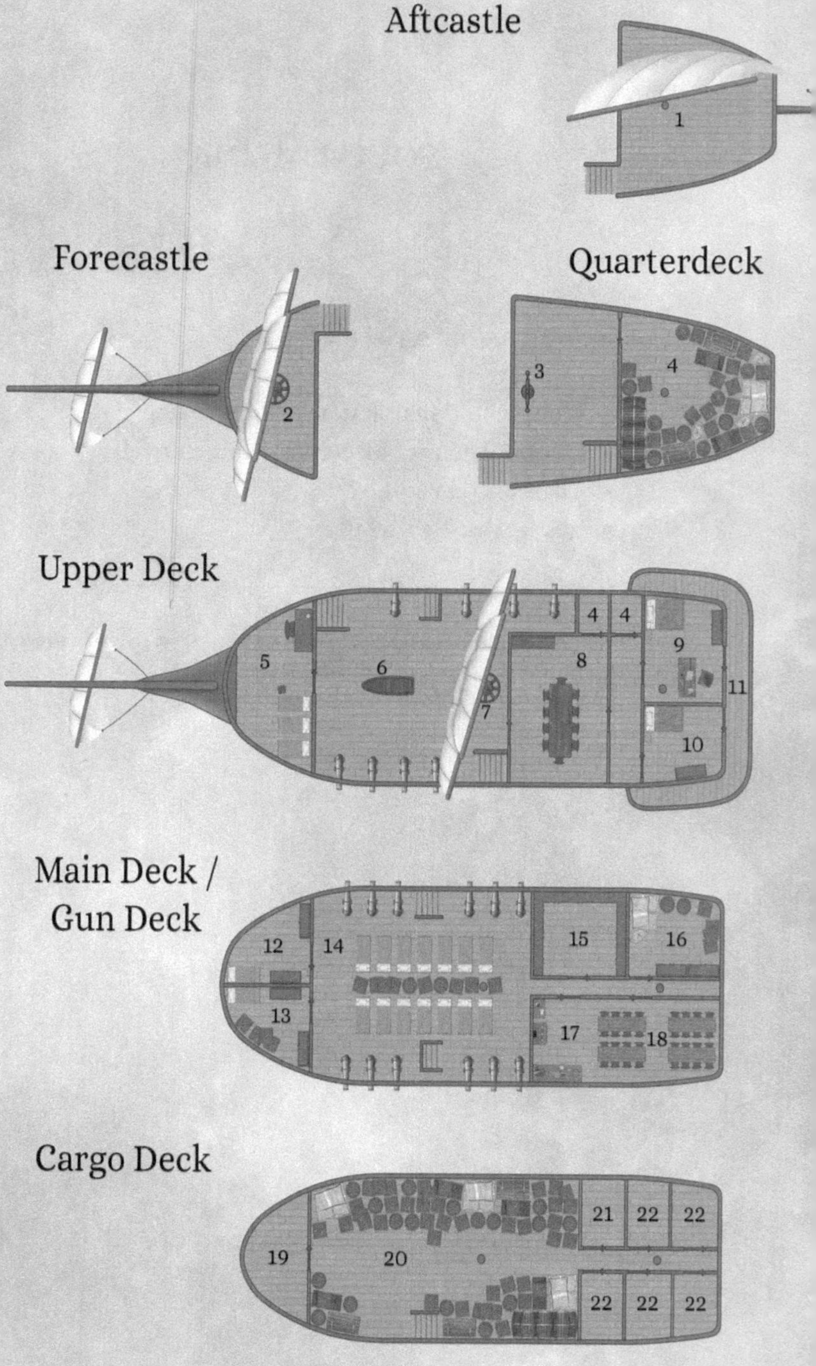

Aftcastle
Forecastle
Quarterdeck
Upper Deck
Main Deck /
Gun Deck
Cargo Deck

1 -	Mizzenmast	12 -	Sai's room/cannon locker
2 -	Foremast	13 -	Durga's room/storage locker
3 -	Helm	14 -	Crew quarters
4 -	Storage	15 -	Armory
5 -	Infirmary	16 -	Pantry
6 -	Rowboat	17 -	Kitchen
7 -	Main mast	18 -	Mess hall
8 -	Officer's Mess	19 -	Sails locker
9 -	Shiva's room	20 -	Cargo hold
10 -	Aviama's room	21 -	Guard room
11 -	Gallery/balcony	22 -	Brig

1

"I'll drag her out now. Call the men. It's time to set the stage for what we're up against."

Aviama lurched awake. That silky-smooth voice had once pulled her in, but now she'd rather be doused with icy water. She'd even rather hear it in her frequent nightmares than face the man himself in real life. Her princeling fiancé, the confidence in his voice bolstered by last night's victory but hardened with resolve in the wake of Aviama's deception.

Ex-fiancé, actually. At least, that was her best guess about what they were, considering her last words to him were that she'd never marry him, and he'd responded that he couldn't care less. More specifically, he'd said, *It no longer matters.*

But the words that followed had chilled her to the bone. *I will get what I want by other means.*

Aviama tugged the blanket up tighter around her, as if its thin barrier could protect her from Prince Shiva's wrath. She hadn't faced him since last night. She shut her eyes tight, but the ship still rocked from side to side, and the wooden bed built into the wall still creaked in one corner when she rolled. Sailors called to one another from the main deck, and the smell of sea salt in the air mixed with the oak of her room. She heard a rustle through the wall she shared with the captain's quarters.

Metal rattled in the lock at her door. She braced herself, shifting away from the entrance, startling as the clink of chains followed her movement. She'd hoped last night had been nothing but a horrible dream, another nightmare from which to awake. But the shackles on her wrists were real, and the red marks developing on her skin combined with the chafing pain where the metal had rubbed gave more proof that last night had been no dream.

The door flung open with a bang. Heavy boots marched closer and closer until they stopped just short of the edge of the bed. "I know you're awake. You can sit up on your own, or I can drag you out by your hair."

Aviama moaned and sat up, squinting against the sunlight pouring in from the circular window at the back of the room. How long had she slept? She pursed her lips. "Good morning to you too, sunshine. All pretenses gone today? No more 'Lilac' nonsense, or waxing on about working together and making the world a better place while you destroy my homeland and plot the murder of my family?"

Prince Shiva looked no worse for the wear of last night's bitter battle on the dock, where Aviama had nearly escaped Radha—Shiva's kingdom full of melder haters—with Chenzira. He'd gone to the black market to cut a deal for passage on a ship, but wouldn't they know it, swindlers and gangsters couldn't be trusted. The man, Onkar Dhoka, took their exorbitant fare and the ridiculous "rush fee" he demanded and skipped off, leaving them high and dry.

That's how Aviama and Chenzira had found themselves alone on the dock with no one to meet them. From there, Shiva and a slew of Radhan soldiers had converged by the water, and at the same time, a group of extremist magic melders attacked from the other side. Both sides suffered losses, but in the end, chemical warfare won the day. Konnolan boomed from a small cannon, incapacitating the melderbloods while those without magic swept through and slaughtered them right there in the sand.

Shiva's dark eyes bored into her like daggers, and his jaw clenched. "Says the woman who aligned herself with genocidal maniacs. Word on the street is that if it weren't for our little show last night, my family and I and the entire court would have been dead by nightfall tonight."

She winced. "Yes, well, I only just found out about that, and I wanted to stop it."

"And yet, when I fed you the lie that we already knew where the Shadow was hiding, you scampered off to warn them, didn't you? Led us right to them." Shiva seized her by the elbow and wrenched her to her feet as her heart plunged to her toes. He'd played her like a fiddle. Again.

Shiva half-escorted, half-dragged her out the door, eyes fixed straight ahead. "They were right to want you dead. You might have thought you could play both sides, but you never thought what a plague you'd be to radicals and royals alike. Total opposites, and you made them both hate you. It's a skill, truly."

The rough-spun wool tunic dress and pants she'd stolen from a clothesline last night itched against her smooth skin. She could only hope the owner didn't mind the wildly expensive gown she'd left in its place. Besides, they would never want it back now. Not with the bloodstains smattered across it.

Mostly not hers, but still.

Aviama opened her mouth to retort, but then they were through the door. She'd thought they were on the main deck —or whatever it was; she wasn't a sailor—but instead Shiva marched her through a narrow hallway, past a door on the right, past some stairs, and past a sailor whistling a jaunty tune as he washed a stack of plates in the corner. The rattle of plates and place settings and splash of water followed them as Shiva tugged her through the room with its long, empty dining table and through a door on the far side.

A flurry of activity met them as they walked out into a covered space, then out under the morning sun. Three cannons lined each side of the deck, since they apparently were on the upper deck level. A rowboat sat in the center, tied down to a series of hatches and surrounded by several barrels and crates. Seamen ran this way and that, one carrying a barrel, another reaching for one of the lines running up to the main sail. A pair of scowling sailors scrubbed bloodstains from the deck. They looked up as the prince passed by, dragging his bedraggled melderblood fiancée with him. Between the wrist shackles and the common clothing, no one could have imagined she was a princess.

Except for the jeweled headpiece still attached to her tangled hair from the night before, the pendant dripping down her forehead, and the fact that she was blonde and of the skin tone that got scorched in the sun for no good reason. Everyone else on the ship looked like the sun really did bless them the moment they were born. House of the Blessing Sun, indeed. Aviama stuck out like a sore thumb. Everyone in Radha had seen her paraded through the streets with the elaborate pomp of the Tanashai family, celebrating her engagement to their crown prince.

But she felt more like a street urchin wearing a lie—and instead of the stolen rough cloth against her skin, it was the headpiece that felt like deception. *I am not one of you. I am not Radhan. And I will not marry your prince.*

Shiva's grip on her elbow tightened as the eyes of every

man on the ship turned to watch the royal pair. He marched her from the rear of the boat toward the front, up the stairs to a landing with the frontmost mast, two more cannons, and the Tanashai family's sharp-nosed melder puppet, Durga. Her mouth twisted into an ugly sneer as her gaze fell on Aviama, but she dropped into a curtsy to acknowledge Shiva.

Prince Shiva glared at her. "Whom do you serve?"

Durga pulled back, as if she could possibly be affronted by the question.

"You, Your Highness. Crown Prince Shiva of the glorious kingdom of Radha."

Considering the girl spied on both Aviama and Shiva back at the palace, spilling her guts to the queen every chance she got, Aviama thought the innocent performance was sickeningly well acted.

Shiva pursed his lips. "Don't forget it. My mother isn't here. Play your part, or you'll wish I never let you on board."

Durga clenched her jaw, but nodded. Aviama's breathing quickened as Shiva shoved her to the rail overlooking the ship. Four masts graced the vessel, unfurled sails bound up tightly. Across from them, up the stairs from the upper deck, back toward the rear of the ship, Captain Samud manned the wheel. Shining gold buttons glinted from his embroidered teal coat, and streaks of white mottled his full beard. Gold bordered his matching teal hat, a turban wrapping up to a brim, the skull figurehead of the Wraithweaver reimagined in gold in the center of his headpiece. He glanced up from the compass in his hand, and Shiva gave him a nod.

Samud turned to one side and jerked his head at the man in an embroidered navy jacket standing by his side. The man slipped down the stairs to the upper deck and disappeared under the overhang of the quarterdeck.

Shiva squared his shoulders and raised his voice. "It's a

fine day to be at sea with such worthy sailors! There is no crew I'd rather be sailing with than you."

Seamen poured onto the upper deck, pressing in to hear the prince. Aviama's stomach lurched. The deck hardly contained everyone who wanted to listen. Men stood shoulder to shoulder around the rowboat and crowded over the rail of the raised quarterdeck by the wheel toward the stern. The man in the navy jacket pushed his way to the stairs, shook his head, and gestured to the rest to stay where they were. How many men were on the ship?

A half-dozen men carried out a long rectangular box made of thick glass, the sea of sailors parting before it as if escaping some infectious disease. Aviama held her breath. The box was filled high with water and barred across the top. Inside, a pewter fish tail reflected silver like the moon in every direction, its bright scales transitioning to the smooth skin of a woman's waist. A one-shoulder, seal-pelt top clung to every curve; white hair swirled in the water, and lavender eyes cut them to pieces with her penetrating glare.

Makana, the siren mermaid. The mermaid who had dared to trust Aviama. The mermaid Aviama had failed to save.

The men gawked open-mouthed at the mermaid, equally entranced by her stunning womanly features as they were terrified of the danger she posed as a siren. Makana pressed her hands to the glass and stared down the sailors surrounding her, then turned to look up at the railing of the forecastle. For a moment, her gaze locked on Aviama, and something in Aviama's chest broke.

Another captive, another hopeless soul. Another exotic display under Shiva's exclusive control. Her cheeks flushed hot as the sailors followed Makana's eyeline up to Aviama—hands shackled, pressed up against the railing, Shiva's strong hand never leaving her elbow. Makana turned her attention from

fall and righting him again. When he regained his balance, his eyes lit with victory.

Fear gripped her by the gullet, and Aviama took a step back. What had she done? Shiva was obsessed with his image, with his presentation of authority. She'd physically defied him in public. He would be incensed.

Except he wasn't. He was triumphant, a wicked sneer painted across his face as he stalked back toward her.

But I pushed him away. I showed him up. I made him look bad...

It didn't make sense.

And then the cannon went off.

2

Boom.

The effects were instantaneous. Weakness hit Aviama like a sledgehammer. Nausea rocketed through her stomach, and she collapsed to the wooden planks of the ship's forecastle. Her muscles screamed at her. Her head exploded in pain. She wavered; the onslaught of airborne konnolan reached to every fiber, every filament of her body.

Through the railing she saw that several crew members had fallen too. The man in the navy jacket strode through the crowd. Working with four other men, he seized the hand of every sailor who fell, ripped a knife from his belt, and slashed open the man's palm.

The crew fell away from the exposed melderbloods in their midst, gasping in horror. But Durga still stood behind Shiva. Unaffected, though she was a windcaller like Aviama. Aviama sucked in ragged breaths, still woozy from the substance in the air. Weight pressed in on her chest as hopelessness began to set in.

Shiva was doling out the antidote to melderbloods on his side. Durga must have taken it right after protecting Shiva from Aviama's strike. Aviama swallowed hard against the burn of bile in the back of her throat and lifted her chin to drill Shiva with a death stare.

At least, that's what she'd hoped it would be. In reality, it probably felt more like the pitiful grimace of a frail, disappointed grandmother as she struggled to sit up. In contrast, while Aviama looked like a thief from the slums of Waif's Garden, Shiva looked every inch the majestic royal. Almond skin glistening in the morning light, the cords of his strong arms visible up to the place where his sleeves were rolled up just above his elbow, Shiva was born for this. His too-perfect sculpted face and muscled chest and arms made him an intimidating specimen for men and women alike—women because they wanted him, and men because they wanted to be like him.

Aviama had learned her lesson the hard way. A pretty exterior sometimes only hid the rot. But now the truth of his character was exposed. She knew Shiva was a master schemer and manipulator. How had he outwitted her again?

He'd outmaneuvered her yet again, provoking her on purpose with the forced kiss. He'd wanted her to lose control, to use her powers against him. Shiva wanted to put on a show, to demonstrate his dominance and total control. And she'd played right into his hands.

Not only that, but he'd used it to identify any unknown melders among the crew. There would be no surprises on this voyage.

Aviama felt sick. And this time, it wasn't from the konnolan.

Shiva reached down and yanked Aviama to her feet beside him. She wavered, gripping the railing for support.

"Their power is mine to command," he said. "On my

whim, I can allow it or take it away. Tell me, if that is true, who has the greater power?"

A hush fell over the crowd. Another wave of dizziness washed over Aviama, but she leaned on the rail until it passed.

Shiva spoke again. "Did you know which of your colleagues were melderblood? How long have you known them? And yet I have been with you for twelve hours, and now I know every melderblood on board. I have knowledge you need. You have proficiencies I need. We will work together. For those of you who are melderblood, know that my engagement to Princess Aviama of Jannemar has been real. My plan has been and continues to be to marry her. It is only her rejection of me, her personal prejudices, that have caused the problem you witnessed today. Not the other way around.

"The elimination of melderbloods is no longer a goal for the kingdom of Radha. Times have changed, and we will change with them. Instead, we will ensure the safety of our people by other means—through channeling that power toward productivity and progress rather than chaos and destruction, and removing it for anyone who cannot correctly handle its responsibility."

Aviama groaned. What a pretty way to say everything was her fault and melderbloods can either fall in line with Shiva's commands or suffer konnolan exposure or magna. Konnolan would be worse, incapacitating magic melders. Magna, though it muted magical essence and the ability to use powers, didn't cause pain; it temporarily suspended powers for melders entering a room lined with the substance, or for any who ingested it.

Shiva's fingers dug into the flesh of her arm. Her arm had started to go numb. She clamped her mouth shut. There were too many people, his authority too strong, to go against him publicly again. Not now, anyway. What good would it do?

"You feared melderbloods, and I have resolved this issue for you. You feared sirens, and I have one in a cage. She is no goddess, but a creature that can be caught, that can bleed, like anything else. Using her song will be useless, as any sailor who comes to her will not fit through the bars at the top and would never drown. Neither can she escape to the open sea. If she tries anything, she will be punished. Severely." He leveled a cool stare at Makana. "And I think she knows how severe I can be."

Makana clung to the bars at the top of her box, drawing a breath where there was just enough room for her head to emerge between the bars and the water. If she had any reaction to what Shiva had said, she gave no indication of it.

"But I, as severe as I am to those who threaten my kingdom and my people, generously reward those who prove themselves. Show me your dedication, show me your loyalty, and you will not go unnoticed. Melderbloods, report to the infirmary. Your hands will be bound up, and your name written down. If you prove yourselves, unique opportunities and rewards await you as well.

"In the meantime, stay away from the siren. She may not be able to drown you with her death lullaby, but make no mistake, your murder is her deepest desire. Don't listen to a word that comes from her mouth. Secondly, keep your hands off Princess Aviama. Anyone who touches her answers directly to me."

Aviama's stomach soured. Considering that the ship was full of coarse seamen, a part of her was relieved for the protection, since Shiva had removed her means of protecting herself. At the same time, she hated herself and Shiva for putting her in such a position.

Shiva released Aviama's arm—blood rushed back into its aching muscles—and he spread his hands wide to address his minions. "We have a long voyage together. Ask me your questions. Learn from me, and I from you. Know that we have a plan. That this particular siren is not a nobody. And that this adventure we are embarking on will make history. You will tell the stories of your valor to your children and your children's children. Bards will sing of our travels."

Aviama called the wind in vain. The konnolan was too strong. Nothing happened, but a natural breeze wafted through her hair, mocking her.

Prince Shiva smiled. "Men of the sea—sailors, warriors— let's conquer the world. To the Gorge!" Shiva threw his fist in the air, and the crewmen roared in response.

"To the Gorge!"

"Onward!"

"To Lady Mistress!"

This last shout drew boisterous laughs and a few whoops and hollers before the crew broke out in a sea shanty, half on key and half along for the ride, as they dispersed across the deck to their various duties.

> *Heave away, haul away*
> *On to my lady mistress*
> *Heave away, haul away*
> *On to my lady mistress*

Shiva turned to Aviama, and she swallowed hard against the nausea still battling for pre-eminence in her throat. Aviama straightened to look him in the eye, but her hand clutched the railing to keep her on her feet.

His gaze flicked to her knuckles, white on the rail, and the corner of his mouth quirked up. "You should know. Sai is on the ship. I know you think she betrayed you, that you were friends. But she betrayed me last night too. She spent the night in the brig as recompense. And if you cause trouble, I'll cut her to pieces and turn her into chum."

Aviama's jaw dropped. Aviama had known that Sai, one of the three handmaids assigned to her at the palace in Radha, had been Shiva's spy. But they'd also begun a friendship of their own. She shook her head. "You're a monster."

Shiva shrugged. "You're the one who gave me the konnolan idea. Thanks for that, by the way. If it wasn't for you, none of this would have been possible. Who's the monster now?"

Tears pricked at her eyes, and blinking them back hard, she turned away from him to look out over the water. Durga stood on her other side. Aviama felt stifled, trapped, hemmed in by the sea, by the railing, by people she hated and people who hated her. An empty chasm opened up in her chest, the ache in her heart only deepening at the sight of the sparkling water reaching out to the horizon in every direction.

A school of flying fish leaped out into the air before disappearing below the surface once again. The tune of the sailors' shanty danced through jovial notes, exiting a verse about drinking and moving on to something about harlots and sirens. Pure blue sky made way for the sun's ascent toward its zenith as yet another day of her life progressed under the thumb of Shiva, Crown Prince of Radha. New location, same old captivity. On sea or on land, she was never free. Not anymore.

Never again.

And between the massive anti-melderblood crew, melders like Durga under Shiva's control, and konnolan and magna on board, there wasn't a thing Aviama could do about it.

3

—————

Shiva handed Aviama a flask, and she glared at him.

He rolled his eyes. "It'll help."

Aviama turned back to the side rail, away from Shiva, away from the prying eyes of seamen sneaking glances up at the forecastle. She bumped into Durga, sent her a cold look, and brushed past her toward the prow. "I don't care. I don't want anything from you."

The brass figurehead looked out to the sea, its wavy locks pouring out from beneath its helmet. How a skull had hair, she'd never know. If she leaned over, she could see the breastplate fitted to the ribcage at the top, and a hatch at her feet dropped down inside the skull behind the eyes as the thing leaned out over the water.

Shiva cleared his throat, and Durga turned and swept off down the stairs, offering some small relief in the absence of her arrogant, prickly presence. The prince approached slowly, stopping several paces behind her.

He lowered his voice. "It's magna. It'll help lessen the effects of the konnolan. It's already impacting your system, so I'm not sure if all your symptoms will go away. But I have a lot to do this morning, and I can't have you trying anything stupid. So if you don't drink it, I'll force your teeth open with a wooden spike and dump it down your throat myself, in the sight of everyone on board."

Aviama spun, opening her mouth to retort, but the swiftness of her movement sent her stumbling along the rail. She snatched the edge of it as the weakness in her bones ebbed, the swirling world stabilizing. Shiva arched an eyebrow.

Biscuits. He was horrible. She snatched the flask from his outreached hand and took a sip. She handed it back to him, but he shook his head.

"More. I know how much you had at the banquet, and it wore off by the time you got to the dock."

Aviama eyed him, lifted it to her lips, and swallowed.

He nodded. "Better."

She passed him the flask, her only victory the secret knowledge that she hadn't ingested any more the second time. And maybe the solace of some strength returning to her body. Her balance seemed better, and though the weakness was still there, the dizzy spells seemed less overwhelming.

Shiva looked her up and down, and Aviama ran a hand through her hair to get it out of her face as another breeze ran through it. Her fingers caught in the tangles barely a third of the way through her hair. She winced. He pursed his lips.

"Your lowlife tunic is disgusting, not to mention bloody and dirty and otherwise reprehensible. I'll have the men look through trunks for women's clothes. I think a band of gypsies or dancers or something entertained the men on board recently."

"Gypsies?" Gypsy clothing wasn't her style. Not that her current garb was particularly spectacular either. Aviama reached up to scratch at her neck where the coarse cloth itched against her skin.

Shiva ignored her. "It'll be a good cover for you and the other girls—for who you are and what you're doing on board —if we run into anyone unfriendly."

"Who would we run into? We're going to a place where everyone dies. The closest nation on the other side of it is Jannemar. If you drop me off there, I don't care what they think I am."

"You're hilarious. You're obviously not going home. I'll have clothes sent to your room, and when I do, I expect you to put them on and take the headpiece off. You look ridiculous. Go wait for me there."

Aviama made a face. *Go wait for me there.* He was revolting. How dare he?

Because he holds all the cards, idiot.

With wind in her knotted, messy tresses, and a measure more steadiness in her feet, Aviama lifted her chin and pushed off the railing toward the stairs. She nearly tripped on the way, but didn't dare look back to see if Shiva noticed. Down the stairs she went.

Not because he sent her. But because she'd take any excuse to get away from him. Who knew where she might go after she got out of sight?

At least that's what she told herself as she left the forecastle, crossed the deck, and walked in exactly the direction he had dictated.

The sailors climbed up the rigging to the beat of their own lively music. Aviama tried not to look at them as she maneuvered around the rowboat. A man arranged coils of ropes and another returned to washing blood from the deck—blood that had since multiplied, what with Shiva's thoughtful melder identification tactic.

The siren sang her song

And she nearly got my soul

Aviama disappeared under the roof of the quarterdeck, pausing just before the door Shiva had led her through earlier. Speaking of sirens, where would they take Makana?

But the whisper on the wind
Said her love is deep as shoal

She left the door behind, keeping under the shade of the roof, and crept to the other side. The seamen cast a few curious looks her way, but largely ignored her. It was the best reaction she could have hoped for.

Aviama stepped around a stack of barrels and poked her head out the other side. Now that she was closer to it, she saw that the glass box Makana was in had long poles attached to either side for the men to hold on to for transport. Makana's silver tail curved along the bottom of the box, her upper half floating in the remaining water, staring out at the sailors as they went about their duties.

The first of the great sails unfurled at the mast. The wind rippled through it and tugged at its billowing bulk as the men worked. Aviama's chest tightened. Shiva hadn't even let them let out the sails until after she'd been dosed with magna. He'd thought it all through, three steps ahead of wherever she was at any given time. What hope did she have?

Aviama leaned out from behind the barrels for a better look up at the masts, and her hands slipped on the edge of the top barrel. The barrel tipped, and her heart lurched to her throat as it toppled and fell. She lunged to catch it, but a wave of dizziness hit her at her jerking movement. She stumbled.

Crash.

The barrel hit the deck, spilling apples in every direction.

Makana whipped her head toward Aviama and rushed to the surface beneath the bars. Someone bellowed an order from the quarterdeck overhead, and a dozen men swarmed the siren's box cage. Across the ship, Shiva turned from the rail with a glowering expression that raised the hair on the back of her neck.

Biscuits. She was already in trouble. What was the difference now?

The dozen men picked up Makana's cage, six on each side, grunting under the weight of the water-filled box and its mermaid. Makana pressed her palm to the glass on one end of her confined space, her lavender gaze piercing Aviama through. Her lips parted as if to speak, but no sound escaped her lips.

Aviama ran forward, scattering the apples at her feet further across the deck and backward toward the stairs. *She has to know. I didn't want this. I don't want this. I...*

Her mind was spinning, and her thoughts were only half-formed by the time she threw out her palm to meet the siren's through the glass. She remembered the gesture. *Tabeun sister.* Makana and Aviama were both creatures of tabeun magic—natural magic—different species, yet two of a kind. Two captive souls held by the same monster.

The sailors lifted the box and drove forward, pushing Aviama backward. Tears pricked at her eyes. Makana pressed both hands to the glass, and Aviama shook her head, swallowing hard at the lump in her throat.

"I'm sorry. I'm sorry, I didn't know. I didn't know."

The siren reached up and gripped the bars over the opening of the box, the defined muscles of her upper arms flexing as she pulled herself up to stay above the surface of the water as the men sloshed the water this way and that, the cage swaying between the sailors as they marched out of the sun and back toward Aviama.

One of the sailors tripped over an apple, and the corner dipped, splashing water over the side and dousing two of the men at the back. Makana spit water out of her mouth as the water level straightened out again. She turned to face Aviama and moved her hands along the bars to stay as close to her as she could as the box was carried away.

"Key and sea. He will kill. My family, one. Your family, two." She lifted a fist, holding up first one finger and then a second. "Key and sea. Key and sea!"

Down the deck, Shiva was barking orders. Two sailors left the rigging and angled for the shaded space where Aviama was standing. A third man, still washing blood off the deck, ignored Shiva's order. Shiva kicked at him as he passed, shouting again. "Are you deaf, sailor?"

Makana sent a sidelong glance at Aviama as the men carried her away, awkwardly maneuvering to take the bulky cage down the stairs to a lower deck. She pointed to the sailor still scrubbing the deck a handsbreadth from Shiva's boot. "Spear man."

Spear man?

Aviama turned to look, and her stomach dropped like a stone. She'd wondered if he'd gotten on board. When she'd seen him last night, he was in the shadows of the dock, as Shiva carried Aviama's limp body up from the sand and onto the *Wraithweaver.* She'd dreamed of him sliding around the far side of the hull, just before they boarded. She'd dreamed he stayed with her, instead of escaping Shiva once and for all, and running for his life as Darsh and the other melderblood extremists scattered.

It would have been his best chance. It would have been a

good chance. He said he had connections at the border. He had to have known he was forfeiting his life if he boarded the ship.

But Aviama was selfish and cruel at heart. She must be. Because all through the night, as she'd tossed and turned, she had hoped and dreamed and wished that Chenzira had not abandoned her to Shiva's wicked whims.

The sailor kneeled on the deck, a blood-stained rag in his hand and a hat pulled over his brow. Warmth flooded her body. He was here. He came. He hadn't left her.

And then a chill ran down her spine, chasing the warmth away as if it had never been. It didn't matter. What good did his presence do here on the sea, under Shiva's thumb, with konnolan and magna on board?

The floorboards of the quarterdeck over Aviama's head creaked. She flinched at the sound, and a shadow blocked the cracks of light coming through the slats as a figure passed overhead. Heavy boots landed squarely on each stair three paces in front of where Aviama stood. In front of her, the two sailors Shiva had called to picked up their pace as they strode toward her.

She had to see what was going to happen. She had to know if it was really him. She had to—

Shiva ripped his sword from its scabbard at his side. Flashes of dead bodies cycled through her mind's eye, from her father's body on the ground in the wake of the explosion at Shamaran Castle, to the knife in her mother's chest at the gala, to Liben's glassy eyes in the outer ward, and the massacre of melders and Radhan soldiers on the sand at the dock just last night.

She couldn't bear Chenzira's face added to the wheel of death her nightmares replayed for her each night. Shiva struck the man on the face, and he fell to the deck. His cheek hit the wooden planks, facing Aviama. His face was paler than it should have been. Sweat beaded on his brow, and though his broad shoulders and large frame were what she remembered, his muscled arms looked hardly capable of holding him up. Konnolan still coursed through his body, but it was him—Chenzira, runaway prince of Keket, newly revealed as an enemy of Radha and an associate of the criminal melderblood extremist Darsh Mushkil.

At least, that's what Shiva would see. Traitor. Enemy. Fugitive. Murderer. Previous friend who bit the hand that fed him.

Chenzira's eyes locked onto Aviama. Weight slammed into her chest like a thousand pounds of shackles dropped from the heights. Captain Samud's boots descended the stairs, and his teal coat swept forward with him toward the altercation on his left, passing by the pair of sailors headed for Aviama.

Shiva's lip curled, and he raised his sword.

Aviama moved before she could think. She darted to the other side of the barrels, ripping a second barrel down behind her as she went. Her feet slapped the deck as she sprinted for Shiva. Magna was still in her system. She had no power. No windcalling ability. No weapon. Nothing but sheer impulse and a weakened body made of easily sliceable flesh and vulnerable vital organs.

Shiva's sword swung down.

Aviama dove for Chenzira beneath the blade.

4

Shiva swore, diverting the blade just shy of Chenzira's chest. A stinging bite ran up Aviama's arm, the sword grazing it as she slammed into Chenzira on the deck. Chenzira grunted under her weight, her body shielding his as she twisted to look up at Shiva, arm extended out toward him in defense.

"Coward!" Aviama screamed. "You can't face him unless he's sick, is that it?"

"Hello to you too," Chenzira mumbled.

Shiva reached down and seized her by the arm, ripping her off Chenzira. His eyes were fire, his voice a snarl as he yanked her to her feet beside him. "How many lives do you think you have?"

Aviama clenched her jaw. "How many wars can you afford?" Chenzira was a prince, after all. Was there any chance Keket would still defend him if Radha dispatched one of their royals?

Captain Samud crossed his arms and laughed. "She's a little more fiery without all the dead bodies around her, isn't she?"

Aviama's cheeks flushed hot. She lifted her chin. "Shiva has never faced me directly without blackmail or magna or konnolan. Usually it's a combination."

"Maybe I haven't needed to because you're so easy to manipulate."

Samud glanced between Shiva and Aviama and chuckled. "What a pity you two lovebirds didn't get married. It would have made for such a peaceful kingdom! But perhaps she had another man on her mind..." His gaze drifted to Chenzira, still weak from the aftereffects of the konnolan. "He's a melderblood, then? How did no one notice him when the cannon went off?"

Shiva adjusted his grip on his sword. "He was already on the floor, I suppose, and didn't fall. And the girl calls me a coward."

Chenzira's chest heaved, and another bead of sweat ran into his hairline from his brow. "I have never had to threaten a girl to get her to marry me. And I've never slaughtered innocent people."

"By *innocent civilians*, do you mean a criminal militia with the power of the Origin Wellspring and all the control of a three-year-old? You fled your own home."

Chenzira drew a ragged breath, but the corner of his lips quirked up into a smirk. "Isn't that what you're doing now, now that your father doesn't trust you to run the military, and you've fallen from the favor of your mother?"

Shiva released Aviama's arm, lunged forward, and pressed his sword to Chenzira's throat. Aviama squealed, then clapped a hand over her mouth. Neither of the men looked at her as they stared each other down. After a moment, Shiva nicked Chenzira on the neck, a trickle of blood escaping the cut he left behind. But just as he was about to step back, Shiva lunged, snatching Chenzira's wrist and slicing across his palm.

"Pretty words are all you ever had, Chen. Pretty, empty words."

Aviama jutted her chin up at Shiva. "That sounds familiar."

Samud clucked his tongue and gave Shiva a long, knowing look before turning his ire on Aviama. "Careful, strumpet. Disrespect spreads like gangrene on a ship this size, and konnolan isn't the only punishment we could come up with. If His Highness decides to make you fair game to the crew for even a day, you'd never say another word."

Aviama's lips parted, and the breath left her body. A sailor on the netting over Samud's shoulder waggled his eyebrows at her, and she staggered backward. Chenzira clenched his fist and launched to his feet, blood dripping from his injured palm.

"Never fear, Captain." Shiva raised his sword, pressing the point of the blade into Chenzira's chest. "I will escort our overzealous princess to her quarters myself. And when I emerge again, we will not have any more problems."

Ice shot down her spine in a violent chill. He wouldn't. Shiva's iron grip clamped down on Aviama's elbow, and she winced. Shiva gestured at Chenzira and glanced at Samud. "If you'd like to turn this one over to the crew, you're more than welcome to. Do what you see fit, and I'll get your report when I return."

Samud pursed his lips, but stepped forward to block Chenzira's way as Shiva dragged her to the back of the ship, under the quarterdeck, through the door, and back through the officers' dining area. Two doors led to two adjacent rooms at the rear of the vessel on this deck: the one on the right was hers. Shiva bypassed it and shoved through the door on the left.

The room was easily twice the size of hers. A table and

chairs sat on a crimson rug in the main section. A stack of books and an unrolled map lay on one end next to a bottle of wine and an empty goblet. Shelves lined with books, fresh candles, and small crates filled the wall on the right, the one adjacent to Aviama's room. Light poured in from large windows across the back of the ship, and a door led out to a rear balcony. But beyond this main room, through an open door, next to a cannon facing potential enemies to the side of the ship, dressed in red and draped with exotic furs, was a large bed. Aviama's mouth went dry.

He wouldn't. Would he?

Shiva slammed the door behind them, dragged her behind him to the wall of windows at the aft, and shoved her up against it. "Do you understand what the captain would recommend I do to keep you in line?"

Aviama swallowed, eyes wide, the edges of the window biting into her back as she pressed hard against it to get as far away from him as she could.

"You can stop looking at me like that. I'm not going to do it. If I needed female company, I wouldn't beg or force to get it." Shiva ran a hand through his hair and stepped away. "I'm not that kind of man."

Right. You just murder people. But this was not the time to be quippy, so she kept her mouth shut. She'd clearly fulfilled her quota for the morning of all that he could handle.

He turned away, then slammed his open hand down on the table. Aviama jumped, stifling a scream. He spun. "Do you understand how tenuous our situation is? I have a fleet. They'll be meeting us at coordinates I already set. But these sailors are more loyal to Samud than they are to me. If his ship is not being run with the decorum he requires, he can overrule me. It would come with consequences, but he could do it.

I have to keep him happy so we can work together. Do you understand?"

Aviama gaped at him.

Shiva stretched out his hand and stared down at it. His fingers shook, and he curled his hand into a fist and looked up at her. "You're sick of me. You hate me. That's your prerogative. I don't care. But if you want to survive this cursed voyage, you'll keep the status quo. Because I promise you that if there are problems on board, Samud won't think twice before sending you down to the depths. I'm the only one who wants you alive. The only one that *matters* who wants you alive. Chen is just as likely as you to cause enough issues to get himself killed. He'll be lucky if all he gets is a beating for what happened just now."

She'd never seen him so on edge. He strode to the shelf and grabbed a bottle of wine. It was early, but she wasn't about to mention it. Shiva popped the cork, poured himself a goblet, and drank.

Aviama pursed her lips, pushed off the wall, and walked to the far side of the table. Something told her having a large object between them was a good idea, even if he currently seemed more unraveled than violent. "What happened with you and Chenzira?"

"He arrived several years ago. Said he was in a bad state, his family kicked him out or something. We agreed to house him in exchange for information on Keket and the potential to put him on the throne and secure our interests in the north-west. But even with a friendly relationship with Keket, trade routes would take twice as long avoiding the Gorge and other less savory areas of the Aeian Sea."

"Have you gone to war with the Iolani before?"

She regretted the words the instant they escaped her lips. Shiva snapped his attention from the rim of his goblet to Aviama's face, his expression cold as flint. The tension in his shoulders had just begun to ease, but all sense of calm fled at the mention of Makana's people. Shiva set the goblet on the table and ran a finger along the map. Aviama craned her neck, but she couldn't tell if he was pointing at anything in particular or just sort of idly dragging his hand along the parchment.

"It's been many years. Many, many years. The Iolani have since fallen into myth, and with their legendary status came paralyzing fear like any of the great ghost stories men tell late at night to set a shiver in the bones of less judicious companions. The problem is, if even half of the myth is true, they have reason to be afraid." Shiva brushed his chin with his thumb and quirked an eyebrow at her. "And then we found Makana."

Found was a generous term. Based on Makana's interactions, *fished for* and *captured* seemed a more fitting description. But Shiva was saying more about political dealings than ever before, and she wasn't about to stop him. Even if she couldn't trust that all he said was true.

Shiva tapped his finger along the map somewhere in the Aeian Sea. "She was real as rain. Fierce and deadly. Callous as poison. A brutal beast, comparable with cirabas and zegraths, killing anything in her vicinity. And then there was you."

His fingers stopped, and he tilted his head to scrutinize Aviama. "What's so special about you?" Shiva shook his head. "It's like you open people up. You make them believe you're such a pure soul, even if you're plotting to knife them in the back the next day. You look so innocent, and you sound so—so captivating. People *want* to like you. Apparently, even killers of the ocean. You are the key to the siren."

Aviama's heart stopped. Ice flooded her chest and seeped through her veins. What had Makana said? *Key and sea...*

Today wasn't the first time Makana had tried to tell Aviama this. The memory of the two of them in the menagerie, the first time Makana had truly spoken to her, came to the forefront of her mind in a rush.

"You are melderblood key. I am sea. They cannot come to use both."

Aviama hadn't understood it then. But after Shiva wanted her to train an elite melderblood force as weapons for Radha, after the war between Darsh's radical melders and Shiva's soldiers and melders of his own, like Durga—if Shiva had melders working for him, he might have a chance against the Iolani, the mer people in the Aeian Sea.

Maybe. Maybe before, when Shiva was going to force her to marry him, and large numbers of melders were going to flock to him to serve under his command rather than die for their melder blood. But Shiva said he no longer needed her to marry him to get what he wanted. So what was the point of having her on board at all? Why not kill her and be done with it?

"I am Iolani. My father must not treaty. You must not marry."

Could melderbloods really hold a candle to a civilization of merpeople? Of sirens? Of myths and legends come to life?

How many Iolani were there? Did konnolan impact them the way it impacted other tabeun-magic creatures? Konnolan had impacted the dragons in Jannemar. The two dragons had fallen from the sky, and her dragonlord sister-in-law Semra had been incapacitated along with them. Semra nearly died that day. And Aviama hadn't even been on site to help. Not that she could have done anything if she *had* been there. It was before The Return, and Aviama's nonmagical skills included curtsying, singing in her room, and drawing little sketches. Her chest constricted.

Never again.

But with magna and konnolan on board the ship, and nothing but water for miles around, Aviama's lack of nonmagical skill was a knot in her stomach that grew with each passing second.

Shiva ran both hands over his face and shook his head as if to clear it. He frowned. He opened his mouth to speak when a knock came at the door.

Aviama jumped. *Biscuits.* She had to stop doing that. Did she have to *look* as fragile as she felt?

Shiva eyed her and strode to the door. When he opened it, no one was there—but a large wooden trunk had been left just beyond it. Shiva grabbed the trunk by a metal handle on one side, dragged it into the room, and shut the door.

"I think the men have brought us wardrobe options."

Shiva unlatched the lid and opened it, then cocked his head at the contents.

Aviama groaned. "What?"

Shiva dug through the trunk, tossing scanty options this way and that.

Aviama's eyes widened. It wasn't normal for Jannemar women to show their midsection, and this one looked like it would. "I'm not wearing that."

"What was it that made you think it was a suggestion?"

Aviama glared at him, and he sighed and dug through the trunk. Halfway through, he snorted and pulled out another outfit.

"You could wear this one instead. The men might have a harder time following my order about you, though."

Shiva held up a top on one finger. The thing had hardly enough material to cover a child, though it was clearly designed for someone with a much more substantial bosom than Aviama possessed. It appeared to be part of a two-piece dancer's outfit, dripping in gold. The baubles on it jingled as he spun it on one finger.

Aviama made a face. "No."

"They were probably feeling hopeful, poor idiots. I don't need people misunderstanding your role here, so you'll wear the first option. It's decent, looks like you have at least decent birth, and even is styled somewhat Radhan. I will *not* have you wearing what you're wearing now. You might not want to marry me, but you're still associated with me, and I'm burning that thing the instant it's off your body."

She glanced down at her filthy, bedraggled, blood-stained tunic. It looked even worse than it did when it was clean, which was saying something. "Fine. But I'm washing up in private."

Shiva rolled his eyes. "I've ordered a bath set up in your room. Don't get excited. The water is probably tepid, and the bath is little more than a big tin, and you won't be enjoying them every day. Or *enjoying* them at all, really, if you're hoping for what you're used to in Radha or at home in Jannemar."

That was almost nice of him. As far as nice went, for murderous people. Aviama pursed her lips. "I want to see Chenzira. And Sai."

"She should have been released from the brig already. Bhumi is here too."

Aviama's jaw dropped. All three of the maidservants she'd had in Radha were on board, then. Durga, the queen's wind-caller informant, had turned into Shiva's lapdog. Sai, another windcaller, had been working for Shiva but had hidden her abilities. Had Shiva found out about her with the konnolan, or had being in the brig protected her from detection? And Bhumi, the young girl who'd found a way to serve the princess of Jannemar, the supposed future queen, the one Darsh wanted as the face of his militant melderblood revolution. Bhumi had been Darsh's informant, though Aviama doubted Shiva had figured that out yet.

The last time Aviama had seen Bhumi, they were in the

palace, and Bhumi still thought Aviama was going to work for Darsh and marry Shiva. She'd even thought Aviama would be noble for doing it.

A glint in Shiva's eye told Aviama she shouldn't have reacted so strongly upon hearing Bhumi's name, and she snapped her mouth shut with a grimace. Shiva flipped the lid shut on the trunk and tossed the chosen outfit at Aviama.

"We brought her with us, and if you want her to live, you'll encourage her to be good and not rock the boat. Figuratively or otherwise—as of this morning, we know she's melderblood. We also know where her brother is, and we've made sure to remind her of that."

More threats. More blackmail. But Bhumi was a melder, and melderbloods he had leverage over were a rare commodity.

"Get out of here. We'll speak again. And remember, Chenzira, Sai, and Bhumi are all more valuable to me as expendable leverage for your behavior than as anything else. Keep your head down. Stay away from Chenzira. Don't make the captain angry. And don't be stupid."

Aviama offered an exaggerated curtsy in response, lifted her chin, and swept out of the room. But Shiva was no idiot. They both knew the truth.

Doing something stupid was Aviama's specialty. And seeing Chenzira was first on her list.

5

The bath was just as lukewarm and underwhelming as Shiva had promised, but feeling clean again was worth it. It took Aviama ten minutes to untangle the jeweled headpiece from the matted mess of her hair and another fifteen to yank the comb she found through her tangles. By the time she was done, the comb carried nearly as much hair as her head.

Aviama placed the comb back in the drawer where she'd found it, in a wooden chest of drawers against the wall, and stared out the windows at the rear of the ship. A balcony wrapped the aft, and a door led out to it. She tried the knob. The knob turned, but the door wouldn't open. It was stuck. Aviama stepped back, turned the knob sharply, and rammed her shoulder into the door.

Biscuits. Her bare shoulder smarted where she'd hit it against the door. But now she knew—it wasn't just stuck; it was secured. Maybe from the outside.

The outfit Shiva had given her to wear was like nothing she'd ever seen in Jannemar, and the pants portion was certainly reminiscent of Radha, though she hadn't seen anything quite like it there either. It was odd to set aside gowns or even tunics for a two-piece ensemble. A thick green band with a floral design wrapped around the bulk of her torso, with a maroon-and-gold panel laid over it from the base around her ribs up past the green band to her neck, leaving her shoulders and arms bare. A sliver of her midriff was exposed too, which she'd seen in Radha, but never at home. Having her midsection exposed to the air was strange. It felt weird. And absolutely too Radhan for her tastes.

Still, she had to admit it was also beautiful. The bottom portion was a maroon-and-gold waistband flowing out to a green-and-floral skirt. In the front, the skirt met together only at the waistband before falling to either side, revealing long green-and-floral pants to match the top. Aviama eyed herself in the small mirror on the wooden desk. It reminded her a little of the outfit she had designed for her sister-in-law. It had been a bit of a shock to the Jannemari court, but apparently Aviama hadn't invented the idea.

She couldn't see the entirety of herself with such a small mirror, and she already missed real gowns and full skirts, but the pants were amazing. Aviama ran her hands over the soft cloth. Excellent quality, and a far cry from the rough, itchy commoner garb she'd stolen last night. She felt supremely comfortable.

Her hand disappeared through a hidden opening in her pantleg behind the coverage of the skirt, and she squealed. Oh, this design was far superior to hers! They'd added pockets!

She needed to go find Chenzira, but if she found something to tie her hair back first, maybe she wouldn't spend all night ripping her hair out with the comb later. Aviama pulled open the drawers of the chest in her room. The top drawers were empty. The bottom drawer contained a long brown man's cloak and an extra blanket for the single bed on the opposite side of the room. The desk contained a writing kit, two books on maneuvering galleon vessels, and one book on navigation by the stars.

Aviama sighed and turned away. She bumped the edge of the desk as she went. Something rattled. But there wasn't a drawer. She ran her hands along the edges of the desk and shoved the desk again. The oil lamp shifted on the desk, but the sound came again too. A rattle.

What was that? She searched the desk, but nothing else opened. This was taking too long. She had to find Chenzira.

Aviama braided her hair quickly in the mirror and held the edge of her braid to keep it from unraveling while she looked for something to tie it. The room held nothing useful, so she headed out the door, sped down the corridor past her door, with Shiva's only a few paces down, and angled for the kitchen she'd been through earlier. Off-key singing—at least, she assumed it was supposed to be singing—bludgeoned her ears from the other side of the door. Something about pranks to pull on drunk sailors. She couldn't help but smile. For all Shiva's threats, and all their fears, at the end of the day, the men on board were regular men going about their regular jobs.

Maybe if she was more careful, she could get them to like her. Enough to not want to kill her, but not the kind of attention Shiva had implied. Her stomach twisted at the memory of the sailor's face from the rigging, wiggling his eyebrows at her. No, thank you.

Aviama pushed through the door into the kitchen, and the screeching singing choked to a stop. A broad-shouldered man with a long graying beard grinned sheepishly at her from the corner where he stood stacking crates. She offered him a smile and a nod and, still holding the end of her braid, walked past the table, past the sink, and out onto the deck.

A coil of rope lay by the rail on one side. Keeping under the shade of the quarterdeck above her, she pulled on one of the threads from the rope's frayed edges and snapped off enough to tie her braid. Her heartbeat ticked up a notch. She had a lot to do today. Find Chenzira. Avoid Shiva. Find Makana. Avoid Samud. Find Sai. Avoid creepy sailor from the rigging.

Lots of finding and avoiding. And lots of information gathering: like what exactly Ghosts' Gorge was; how Shiva planned on killing or taking over the Iolani; and how she could stop him from any and every plan he put in place.

Aviama scooped up a fallen apple from behind the coil of rope and took a bite as she stepped out into the sun. Across the deck, two sailors adjusted the lines to the mainmast. The forecastle was empty, but four men strode out from underneath it, and Aviama had no interest in a place where so many seamen might be gathered.

"Oy! I've been waiting for you."

Aviama jumped at a deep voice coming from just over her shoulder. She spun. Samud stood behind her, arms crossed, feet planted a shoulder's width apart. He arched an eyebrow. "You cleaned up."

She swallowed, but it didn't ease the tension. "It wasn't for you."

"I should hope not. You're not my type." He gestured at the apple. "That's mine."

Aviama pursed her lips. "I thought it was for the crew."

"Are you part of the crew?"

"I'm as much at the mercy of the sea as anyone else. I'm stuck on the boat like everyone else."

"It's a galleon."

"Fine. Whatever it is, I'm stuck on it. And since it was Shiva's idea, I'd take up the issue of my meals with him."

Samud frowned. "I thought princesses had better decorum. So far, you've demonstrated impulsive violence when you had no hope of success, rebellion against the native royalty, caused a scene that put a target on your back for quite possibly the entirety of the voyage, and stolen my food from my barrels on my ship. What's next?"

"I'm not sure. But at least I've bumped starvation off the list." She took another bite.

"Your nescience knows no bounds."

Aviama blinked at him. Samud plucked the apple from her fingers, took a bite, and strolled past her into the sun, his shoulder ramming into her as he went.

Her stomach growled. She watched him go, walked to the stack of barrels she'd knocked over earlier, and opened the lid of the apple barrel. Aviama snatched another, replaced the lid, and dashed out into the sun and up the stairs to the quarterdeck while Samud still strolled toward the bow. A cannon stood on each side of the quarterdeck with a square hatch in the floor between them. Stairs went up one more level to the aftcastle from there, with doors going somewhere underneath it. And there, at the rail of the aftcastle, just beyond the helm, stood Chenzira, talking and laughing with a sailor.

Laughing?

Aviama knit her brows together as she studied him. His face was still two shades too pale, probably from the lingering effects of the konnolan blast. He hadn't had any magna, as far as she knew. But as Chenzira gestured at the mizzenmast over Aviama's head, pointing out this or that and throwing his head back at whatever joke the sailor made, Aviama's gut wrenched. He looked unburdened. Comfortable. Far more comfortable than he'd seemed in the palace, even when he was free to roam as a respected visiting dignitary with all the luxuries afforded a man of his station.

Forgetting Chenzira's royal blood was easy. Pulling off an air of ease like Chenzira did was hard. He'd done it with the black market cheat Onkar Dhoka, and with Darsh, and with this sailor. She gazed at his face, trying to remember the last time she'd seem him look so himself. Had she even had the chance to know him? To really know him, instead of just trying not to die together?

Chenzira laughed again at something the sailor said, and then his eyes drifted down the mast and landed on Aviama. The smile froze on his face and slowly slipped away. The sailor beside him followed his gaze, grinned, and elbowed Chenzira in the ribs. He grimaced, and his knuckles whitened as he clenched the rail behind him.

The sailor descended the stairs to the quarterdeck and tipped his hat at Aviama as he passed. Aviama gave a half-hearted smile, went up the stairs, and—

Her heart stopped. Chenzira turned away. He walked up a final set of stairs to the aftcastle, the highest part of the ship at the rear of the vessel, away from the helm and completely unoccupied. The furthest away from her he could get.

Aviama's stomach squirmed. It was the encounter on the main deck earlier. He hated her for it. He must. But she was only trying to help. She kept Shiva from killing him. Bitterness bubbled up in her chest, and her throat tightened. He had no right to be angry, and she'd been right to stop another sense-less killing.

She spun the rings on her fingers, the one part of her ensemble that never changed. Aviama shifted her weight and bit her lip. Chenzira leaned heavily on the rail, his face entirely shielded from her now.

No. This was stupid. He didn't get to be angry. If anything, she should be angry that he was angry! Because she hadn't done anything wrong. And if he was going to be ridiculous, she was going to point it out.

Aviama marched up the stairs and planted her feet behind him. She crossed her arms, stuffing the apple under one arm. He didn't turn around. She took a deep breath and stepped up to the rail instead, sliding in and resting her forearms on the railing beside him, mimicking his posture. She cleared her throat.

"You seem mad. That's not fair."

Chenzira didn't even stiffen as her words hung in the air. Her mind whirled. *Biscuits.* Must she accuse him of something every time she wound them up in trouble? It was a mercy he'd put up with her this long.

She breathed in the tension like a douse of ice water. He was here in the first place because of her. Just like he'd been in the arena because of her. And if he rejected her now, she'd be one melderblood against an army—with a Radhan fleet on its way to join them.

6

———

Chenzira had already been staring out at the ocean, and when she spoke, he didn't move. He only stared harder.

Aviama hesitated. Maybe she should walk it back, be more diplomatic. "How come every time you get mad at me, it's for trying to save your life? Do you have a death wish or something? Or do you just hate me generally?"

Okay, so diplomatic was out the window. But the words gushed out before she could stop them.

A shadow passed over his face, and his jaw clenched. Aviama waited, but still he said nothing. He'd never felt so impenetrable. He'd never been so silent. *Because he hates you. Backpedal, before he runs away.* Aviama stifled a groan and sucked in a deep breath instead.

"What does nescience mean?"

Chenzira frowned. "Why? Who said it?"

"Samud."

"You're an idiot."

"Thanks."

The corner of Chenzira's mouth twitched. "No, that's what it means. Clueless. Ignorant."

Aviama winced. "Spectacular."

But her chest exploded. He'd almost smiled. And then, as quickly as it had come, that glimmer of a smile disappeared.

"You shouldn't have jumped in front of me. It was stupid."

Aviama gripped the apple with one hand, running her thumb over the stone on her ring with the other. "Glad to see you and Samud have something to bond over."

She stared out at the water, and this time it was Chenzira who turned to look at her and Aviama who looked away. She could feel the heat of his gaze on her face and couldn't stop the lump from rising to her throat. "Maybe you should stop telling me what to do."

"Aviama," he said. "I boarded an enemy ship with two hundred men under the command of someone I betrayed. Respect is life. Respect is currency. Without it, I am nothing. Without it, I'm a dead man."

"There are *two hundred* men on board?"

The *Wraithweaver* really was a big ship. But two hundred? How could she stop Shiva if it was her against two hundred men? Two hundred men and Durga, who was a windcaller like her. Aviama scanned the deck. Sailors moved to and fro, but the bulk of them must be on lower decks at any given time. And beyond the rails, beyond the borders of their little wooden island, lay nothing at all but sparkling blue waters.

Ocean spread out in every direction as far as the eye could see, from horizon to horizon. If she got Makana overboard somehow, if she set her free, it would be the last thing Aviama ever did. Saving herself wouldn't be possible. At least, not here in these waters, where any ship that came would be Radhan. Down below, so small she almost missed it, a fish jumped out of the water. What did Makana's world look like from the other side of the surface? Were there Iolani down there now, looking up at her?

"Focus."

"Right, sorry."

"I was challenged. Tested. I don't think he was going to kill me. I think he wanted to know what I'd do. Then you jumped in front of me, and my value became entirely wrapped up in being a leverage item to make you do what they want. I'm expendable, the weak guy saved by the woman who couldn't stand on his own two feet. Who couldn't fight." Chenzira sighed. "My first impression with Samud, with the crew, is as an incapable enemy not even worth disposing of. It's the worst kind of enemy to be."

Aviama chewed the inside of her cheek. "You don't know he wouldn't have killed you."

"You don't know he would have."

"But—"

Chenzira slapped the rail. "But nothing!"

Aviama jerked her head sideways to look at him, startled.

His eyes were flint. He shook his head and lowered his voice.

"You don't get it. Shiva is, at least for now, protecting you." He waved his hand at her new clothes. "You'll drink magna from his flask, you'll wear clothes he tells you to wear, you'll eat food he tells you to eat. Not me."

Aviama's cheeks flushed hot. The nails of her hand bit into the flesh of the apple. Beads of juice ran down her fingers. "How dare you? You have skills. Actual skills. When konnolan turns the magic off, when magna slashes your plan to bits, you're still the best fighter. You can fight with an axe. You can fight with a sword. You can apparently make excellent friends with sailors you only just met, despite just having been made the worst kind of enemy."

A seaman caught her eye two decks down, and she lowered her voice to a whisper. Aviama leaned in, glaring daggers back at Chenzira, and stuck a finger in his face. "Shiva is all about appearances. If I ruin the status quo this early on, I'll be shackled to the bed and useless until he's ready for another konnolan demonstration. If he doesn't feel like I'll play the game, I'll never be able to beat him at it."

She sank back onto the railing, staring down at the bruised apple in her hands. "I can play, or I can die. It's just that my survival options are different than yours. You survive, apparently, by hoping that the people threatening to kill you won't really kill you, and then dueling people with swords. If I dueled people, I would die. So yes, sometimes I wear a dress I'm handed."

He opened his mouth to speak, but Aviama's cheeks still burned, and her hands were shaking. And she wasn't done. "I need a plan to fight. I need to stop him before he uses Makana. And I need him not to know I'm doing it."

Chenzira eyed her, and she stopped, chest heaving.

"So that—"

"And this wasn't the only clothing option," she added in a rush. "It was just the only one I wouldn't be caught dead in. They're—they were, um, er, dancers' clothes or something."

He arched an eyebrow.

She winced. Why she felt the need to add the last bit, she didn't know.

"Are you done?"

"Maybe."

"Do you think you can act a little less erratic when you talk about treason, so as not to attract attention?"

Aviama shrugged. "Do you think you can stop insulting me all the time?"

"If you didn't do dumb things so often, it wouldn't be so easy to do."

A sliver of a smirk slid onto his face, and her jaw dropped. She swung at his face with the apple still in her hand. In a flash, he captured her hand in his own, his fist wrapping around her hand and the apple together, stopping it in midair. The rest of him hadn't even flinched.

"Where'd you get the apple?"

Aviama ripped her hand free and grinned. "Oh, no. Find one yourself, mister strongman. I wouldn't want you to be accused of getting help from a woman."

Chenzira reached out to snatch it, but Aviama danced away. She took a bite out of it and waved it in front of his face.

He reached for it again, but as she pulled it out of his reach, he seized her free hand and pulled it toward him. Warm tingling shot up her arm, and her stomach twisted in knots at his touch.

He looked up at her, the levity gone from his face, then he glanced down again and brushed a thumb lightly over the scrapes and bruises covering her knuckles. She winced and tugged her hand back, but he held it fast. "What's this from?"

"Nothing. It's not from Shiva or anything, if that's what you're worried about."

"No, it looks like you're beating up the walls of your room."

"It's from two nights ago. When I ran from the palace, through the tunnels. When I thought I was warning the Shadow that they'd all be slaughtered by midnight. I got to the end of the tunnel, and it was a door all boarded up. I was screaming and beating the door." She bit her lip. "For a while."

Chenzira traced the lines of her hand with one finger, up over her knuckles, and along her wrist. His softness surprised her. She shifted her weight. He flipped her arm over to expose the soft skin of her forearm. More scrapes. He looked up at her expectantly.

She shrugged, trying not to think about the warmth emanating from his gentle touch against her skin. "Durga had me high in the air last night. She dropped me. I fell. The sand wasn't friendly."

Chenzira rotated her arm again, inspecting the redness encircling her wrists. "And this?"

He brushed the inside of her wrist with his thumb. Goose-bumps fled up her arm, and he froze. His eyes bored into her then, deep pools of cinnamon with flecks of gold. Aviama's stomach dropped. Her mouth went dry.

"Lovely day for a cruise."

Aviama gasped and jerked backward as a man strode up the steps of the aftcastle.

Chenzira released her, and the two of them turned as one toward the newcomer. It couldn't be...

The extravagant black-and-gold jacket was missing. The gold buttons and exorbitant flaunts of wealth were erased in all but the cocky confidence he wore. But there before them, in a plain white tunic with sleeves rolled above the elbow and paired with brown-stained, flour-dusted trousers, stood Onkar Dhoka—the swindling cheat who'd taken their money and left them to die.

He winked. "Hello, darlin'."

7

———

Aviama stiffened. She dropped the apple overboard behind her back and reached for the wind, but the magna still dampened her magic.

Onkar's gaze flicked to the free hand at her side, and he cocked his head. "I thought we had a gentleman's agreement. I suppose that doesn't apply to ladies."

Chenzira started forward, then rocked back on his heel and leaned back against the rail instead. Probably wasn't a good idea to start a scene on such a visible part of the ship. Aviama grimaced. *Another* scene, anyway. Chenzira's jaw clenched.

"Sand and sea, what part of our *safe passage* agreement did you uphold, exactly?" she asked.

"I like you. I see what Rookie sees in you." He gasped at himself and held up his hands in mock shock. "Excuse me. Her *Highness,* that is."

Aviama groaned. "Biscuits. You've got to be kidding me."

Onkar waved her off. "I never kid. No, that's a lie. I do kid, and rather often, but I never go back on a deal. It's a good thing you paid that maladroit incidentals fee. Because the situation you've found yourselves in now..." Onkar shook his head and clucked his tongue. He swept his hands toward the galleon and the wide-open sea stretching beyond it. "Well, this is quite the incident, wouldn't you say?"

Chenzira pulled himself up to his full height and bored the man through with a dagger glare. "Give me one good reason not to rip you apart where you stand."

Onkar pursed his lips and glanced at Aviama. "I might be changing my mind. He's rude, isn't he? Does he ever treat you this way? Oh, never mind." The man rerolled the sleeve of one arm where it had started to fall below the elbow, then spread his hands. "You ask for one reason. I'll give you three. One, because you're both still affected by the konnolan, and you, my enthusiastic friend, don't have the benefit of magna to mitigate its effects. You're still unsteady on your feet. Hence, you're staying close to the railing like a child with his blanket. Not to mention the beating you took while Rookie went to play dress up—that couldn't have helped matters."

Aviama glanced at Chenzira, and the whites of his knuckles ebbed as he released the rail. Chenzira avoided her gaze and folded his arms, but his movements were stiff. Her brow knit together, and her stomach soured. What had they done to him? But Onkar wasn't done.

"Second, because I am a magnificent ally, a phenomenal strategist, and one look at my luscious shining hair will bring hope to the saddest soul—I'm sorry to say I can't help you with yours, Taug; it's all genetics, I'm afraid."

Aviama steeled herself to keep her expression neutral. Onkar was still using Chenzira's alias from Boar Tooth Tavern, but at their first meeting, he'd seemed to know Chenzira's true identity. At the very least, he'd known Chenzira was a man of station. Better not to confirm any suspicions he had.

Onkar strode to the railing, leaned against it with his back to the water, and crossed his arms and ankles. "And third, I never broke my part of the deal. You wanted passage on a ship. You wanted out of Radha. Here you are on a glorious galleon, and here am I, going above and beyond to usher you there!"

"Ha!" Aviama threw her hands up. "You've got an interesting definition of *safe*. I was dragged onto this ship, shackled all night, and made a spectacle of this morning. And Taug was beaten."

The man sucked his teeth, an irritating sound that set Aviama's own teeth on edge. "You didn't outline the specifics of what experience you wanted on board. Perhaps you should have. As for the spectacle of this morning, I think you did a fine job of arranging that yourself."

"You're insane."

"I don't disagree with you, but it's a lot more fun than being boring. Speaking of which, it looks like we've got a long voyage ahead of us. If you get bored, I could use a few extra hands in the kitchen."

Chenzira laughed. "You're a cook?"

Onkar grinned, a glint catching in his eye. "I'm *the* cook, thank you very much. My esteemed position allows all sorts of access with almost no supervision. But the position is filled, so if you had your eye on baking a mean sourdough, you'd be doing it under my purview."

Aviama wrinkled her nose. Stuck in close quarters with the criminal who ditched them, and a laundry list of chores? "Not interested."

"Suit yourself. Just thought I'd offer." Onkar shoved off the railing and headed toward the steps, then paused. "By the way, have you noticed Sunboy keeps a map in his pocket? No sailor has one like it. Any chance you've seen it?"

Shiva? Chenzira and Aviama exchanged a quizzical glance, and Aviama shook her head. "No. What is it?"

Onkar waved her off. "Oh, probably nothing. Feel free to get back to flirting or bickering or whatever you were doing. If you get hungry, you know where to find me. Main deck."

The swindler swept off down the aftcastle to the quarterdeck and down again before disappearing from view. He wasn't wearing it, but Aviama pictured his ostentatious jacket blowing in the wind behind him as he went. Aviama turned to Chenzira.

"Isn't the main deck that one, where the rowboat is?"

Chenzira stared after Onkar Dhoka for a moment, leaving her question hanging in the air. He pursed his lips and then turned back to her. "No. That's the upper deck. The main deck is below it. Also called the gun deck, with the bulk of the cannons."

"Oh." Aviama glanced out at the water, then back at Chenzira. "How hurt are you?"

He shifted against the railing and grunted. "Fine. We should split up, so we don't get seen together all the time. I'll try to find out more about Ghosts' Gorge."

Aviama eyed him. But if he wasn't interested in telling her about his injuries, there wasn't much she could do about it. After a long moment, she nodded. "Okay. We need more eyes and ears too. Sai and Bhumi are here somewhere. I need to find them and see if they're with us or not."

"That's not a bad idea. Find the mermaid while you're at it. Try to avoid dying."

"Haven't you heard? Death-defying feats are my specialty." She grinned and turned on her heel, leaving him at the railing behind her as she skipped off down the steps. A lightness threatened her doomed reality as she hit the quarterdeck, passed the ship's wheel, and descended to the upper deck. Because just before she'd turned away, she'd seen a quirky smile sneak onto Chenzira's face. And she was the one who had put it there.

Across the deck, on the far side of the ship, Samud conversed with several of his men. The group of them stared at her as she landed on the deck. Ice ran down her back, snatching the smile off her face. Could a smile earn Chenzira another beating? Had she worsened his situation somehow by talking to him?

Samud nudged one of his men and jerked his chin in her direction, and two of his men split off toward the aft of the ship. Aviama's heart lodged in her throat. She ducked under the quarterdeck and plunged down the stairs to the gun deck. To her left, a corridor split the rear of the ship in two. She ducked down it and started into the first door she found.

Four men sat at a long table, looking up from their work sharpening a collection of swords. Spears, axes, bows and arrows, and maces lined the wall behind them. Two of the men looked her up and down with interest, as if drinking in the sight of her. A squirm in her belly told her to get out, and she wheeled around just as the oldest man shot her a glare and dragged the whetting stone in a long motion across the edge of his sword, and another rose halfway from his seat.

Aviama spun, but even now she could see through the slats of the stairs where she'd come—sailors' boots thudding down to the gun deck after her. She sucked in a breath and stretched out her fingers. Wind bumped gently against her palm. Too gently.

Two hands reached out and yanked her back by the elbows, through the door opposite the armory and out of the hall. Aviama stumbled into a large kitchen, four times the size of the small one outside her room.

Onkar Dhoka raised an eyebrow. "Miss me so soon?"

On the other side of her, a young girl, perhaps two years

her junior, wrapped her arms around Aviama's waist. "You're here! You're okay! Oh, when I saw you last night, just hanging there, I thought—"

Aviama blinked. "Bhumi. You're here." She hadn't been sure whether Shiva was telling the truth before. Did Shiva know Bhumi was part of Darsh's Shadow? Aviama looked her over, but there were no apparent injuries. Bhumi released her and nodded, dropping into a curtsy. Aviama seized her elbow, brought her up, and gave her a look.

Not here.

Bhumi swallowed, nodded her understanding, and bounced back into her excitement. "Yes, yes! I'm here to serve you, of course, as always. But the prince said you wouldn't need me today, so Aakar invited me to help him here."

Aviama scooted away from the door and dropped her voice, eyes narrowing. "You mean Onkar?"

Onkar glanced out the door, blocked it with his body, and handed her a large wooden rolling pin. "No, Rookie. You must have me mistaken for someone else. Aakarshak Devesh, at your service."

Aviama took the rolling pin and ducked down under the nearest table as the sailor Samud had sent passed by. Four long tables graced the room further toward the back of the galleon, with two shorter ones on this side, surrounded by four crewmen rather than by rows of chairs. They glanced up, but said nothing, and returned to beating and rolling long slabs of meat with rolling pins like hers.

A moment later, Onkar dropped an apron on the ground and knelt beside Aviama underneath the table to retrieve it. "It's clear."

Aviama stood up, slid to the end of the table, and rolled her pin along a slab of meat staged there—perhaps one Bhumi had been working on. "Aakarshak? Handsome?"

Onkar grinned. "Glad you noticed."

She rolled her eyes and kept her voice low. "I didn't say you *were* handsome. Doesn't that name mean 'handsome'?"

"If the shoe fits."

"It doesn't."

"Oh, but it does. And as an added bonus, it sounds a lot like what rookies might call me when they forget themselves."

Aviama ignored him and turned to Bhumi. "Did you see where they took the mermaid?"

Bhumi shook her head. "No. But the brig is on the cargo deck, directly below us. That's where Sai was, last I saw her."

Onkar reached over Bhumi's head to retrieve a sack of something from a row of shelves and set it on the table. "Cargo hold is down there too. What valuable substances might they store down there, do you think?"

Aviama met his gaze. He gave her a long look, then turned his attention back to his work as if nothing had happened. The other four men in the kitchen ignored Aviama and Bhumi's conspicuous presence, and for a moment, Aviama stood awkwardly at the table, rolling pin in hand, with a surprisingly pleasant sense of invisibility.

Her relationship with Bhumi was clearly no worse for wear after the events on the dock, and her involvement with the Shadow would suggest she wanted Shiva's downfall as much as Aviama did—even if they had had differing opinions on how to get it. But Aviama still needed to find Sai and Makana.

Aviama pulled Bhumi into a hug. Bhumi hesitated, but hugged her back. Aviama leaned close and whispered in her ear. "I'm glad you're okay. Keep an eye on ... Aakar. I'll find you later."

Bhumi nodded and returned to the slab of meat in front of

her. Onkar didn't look up as Aviama slipped past him, but his voice followed her out: "Later, Rookie."

She turned left out of the kitchen, quickly passing the armory. On the other side of the stairs, large barrels and crates ran down the center, dividing the hull into two sides filled with beds and cannons. On the right, five sailors perched on barrels, playing dice on the lid of a cask. On both sides, several men tried to catch up on sleep. Perhaps they worked the night shift. Raucous laughter went up from the men playing dice, and one of the sleeping sailors lifted his groggy head just high enough to chuck an empty bottle at the noisemakers.

Aviama skipped the stairs leading up and took the second set leading down from the gun deck to the cargo deck. Bhumi had said the brig was right beneath their feet. She turned toward the back of the ship, where the kitchen had been on the main deck. Barred cages lined the aft of the cargo deck, three on her right and two on her left, next to a small room with a closed door on the side nearest her, probably a guard-room or office of some kind.

An aisle split the cages down the middle, and light was scarce without the main deck luxury of windows. A narrow shaft of light made its way to the cargo hold from the stairs, aided only by needle pricks of sunlight that snuck down through a hatch in the center of the ceiling. Its scant rays filtered through the hatch above it and snuffed out every time anybody walked over the hatches on the upper two decks. An oil lamp swung from its place outside the guardroom, but it was unlit. Oil, fire, and wood were a bad mix to leave unsuper-vised on a ship.

But it wasn't the lack of light or the cells of the brig that sent Aviama's stomach plunging to her toes. It was Durga— and the knife in her hands, pressed up against Sai's throat.

8

Durga's blade was little more than a glint and a wink of light, but Aviama knew every angle of a steel knife. She knew it from her memories. She knew it from her nightmares.

For a moment, Mother stood there between the galleon's brig cells, looking back at her with wide eyes. She was gorgeous as always, the only sign of nerves her twisting a sapphire ring on her finger. The galleon dropped away then, replaced by the great hall in Shamaran Castle. Colorful jugglers' balls made a high arc overhead, dancing over the heads of the couples on the floor. Aviama's feet skipped lightly through the steps, soaking in the familiar movements, the solace of the dance.

She spun in a turn and looked for her mother as she whirled back into place—but she was gone. Shouts. Chaos. Blood. So. Much. Blood. Queen Sharsi, a knife in her chest. Such mindless, rote destruction. Another day, another death.

Weight bore down on Aviama's chest, but the weight burned like fire in her heart. Instead of the dark cloud she'd walked through before, inside the cloud a match was lit. No more the paralyzing fog that held her captive so long. No more the demure, helpless princess.

Fury seized Aviama by the gullet. Feral cry trapped in her throat, she launched forward on wings of rage, slamming into Durga with twice the force anyone her size should have been able to leverage. Durga hit the steel bars with a metallic *clang* and dropped like a stone, the knife skittering away from her. Aviama scooped it up in one swift motion and plunged her knee into Durga's sternum as she lay, stunned, on her back.

Sai stumbled to one side, but all Aviama could see was red. The pretentious look on Durga's stupid face finally replaced with fear. Fear of *her.* Maybe even respect. The girl's saucer-wide eyes and open mouth stared up at Aviama through shades of crimson, shades of blood. Blood Durga was ready to spill.

Aviama's lip curled. She pressed the cold steel against Durga's neck, where warm blood pulsed ... beckoned ... begged. *You know you want to. You know she deserves it.* Aviama pressed the blade harder into Durga's skin, a trickle of red seeping out and crawling down the girl's smooth skin.

Another memory assaulted her then. Knives flashed from Semra's nimble fingers, flying steady and true, hitting their mark more perfectly than if the most powerful windcaller had guided them. A knife between the eyes. A knife to the heart. A knife sinking into the soft flesh of an exposed throat. Dead bodies everywhere, as Semra escorted Aviama to safety—the useless princess who didn't know how to fight, and the assassin girl who barely thought twice before dispatching a problem.

But Semra was good. And Zephan, Aviama's brother, was good, though he was a soldier. A warrior.

Was this war? Would Durga's blood be a battle casualty?

Durga's sneering face outside the queen's library sprang to

mind. The strength of her wind as the girl slung every ounce of power she could muster at Aviama's slim frame. The look in Durga's eyes as she raised her hands, lifting Aviama high into the air over the bloodbath at the docks. *She deserves this. She earned it.*

Aviama's fingers shook as she adjusted her grip on the knife handle.

Who are you?

The thought stopped her cold. She shoved it down deep, clenching her jaw to keep it from quivering. Durga's eyes narrowed. Aviama was losing control.

Aviama kept her right hand close on the blade on Durga's throat, balled her left hand into a tight fist, and slugged Durga in the stomach. The girl grunted, but said nothing. It hadn't been hard enough. Aviama spun the knife and slammed the butt of the handle into her chest.

Durga gasped in pain and struggled to escape Aviama's grasp, but Aviama only dug her knee harder into her chest.

Aviama leaned forward until she was nose to nose with Durga and dropped her voice into a low hiss. "The next time I see you touch Sai. Or Bhumi. I will *end* you." The girl stared up at Aviama, but Aviama wasn't finished. "You think you can play in the wind once and be big and bad? You couldn't even keep me in the air last night. You *dropped* me. That's not a victory, that's a loss. You have no control. Just like you had no control on the terrace, when I left you in the dust after saving your life. You went over the railing that day. *I* brought you back. Consider what I might do if I was bent on ending your life instead."

Durga swallowed, and her eyes hardened. "You don't have any power here. Prince Shiva has konnolan and magna. You wouldn't dare."

"And yet here I am with the knife, and here you are on the

floor." Aviama flicked the blade again and drew blood along Durga's neck on the other side. "I know how you care about appearances. Now you're symmetrical. Stay away from us."

Aviama rose, turned, and caught Sai's elbow as she went, pulling her down the corridor. Opposite the brig, barrels, crates, and boxes filled the cargo deck, divided into sections, all the way down the deck until darkness swallowed them. Did Shiva store the konnolan somewhere in this maze? Where was Makana?

Sai clutched Aviama's arm as Aviama drew her out from the brig, up the stairs, and—Aviama hesitated. Where could they go without being seen? Durga was in a foul mood on the cargo deck. Onkar and Bhumi were in the kitchen, and the rest of the gun deck was filled with bunks for sailors. The upper deck held her own room, but it was next to Shiva's, and to get there, they would have to pass through the smaller kitchen meant for officers.

The rolling dice of the men's latest game rattled along the top of a barrel among the bunks behind them, and the smell of spices wafted to them from the main kitchen, joined with the mess hall. Aviama groaned.

"Biscuits. I thought privacy was hard to come by at the palace."

Sai nodded. "I know. Come with me."

Now it was Sai's turn to lead Aviama. Aviama tucked the blade of Durga's knife tight between her forearm and her torso as Sai drew her away from the kitchens and down past the gambling seamen, past rows of empty bunks and the occasional snoring sailor, toward the bow of the ship. Crates and barrels stood in stacks down the center. Did any of *those* contain konnolan?

All the way at the end, two doors led to small rooms at the front of the ship. Sai opened one and pulled Aviama inside. A window faced the front, showcasing the base of the brass wraith skull figurehead leading the *Wraithweaver* across the sea, and two small cots lay together between stacks of crates.

Sai shut the door behind them and spread her hands. "Home sweet home. Prince Shiva says this is where Bhumi and I will sleep. Durga is next door. We can't lock the doors, though, because the seamen need access to the storage."

Aviama pursed her lips. "Comforting."

Sai shrugged. "I haven't slept in here yet, but I assume it's better than the brig."

"I'd imagine so. Though Durga is too close for comfort."

"I think the prince separated us to ensure we didn't murder each other. But again, no locked doors, so she could get in if she wanted."

Aviama wiped the blood off her knife and wiped her fingers clean on the dark wood behind one of the crates. "And vice versa. Let's make sure she remembers that part. She needs to stay away."

"No, her door locks."

Aviama hesitated. "Her door locks?"

Sai nodded.

"Isn't that room for storage too? What's in it?"

"I don't know."

"We need to find out. But first..." Aviama lifted the lid on one of the crates. Cannonballs. She lifted the lid on the next one. Powder. Aviama glanced up. "They trust you with extra ammunition, but they lock Durga's room?"

"Those are heavy. It's not like I can throw them."

"You're a windcaller."

Sai winced. "Not with magna. Durga made me take some this morning. She said she'd dose me with it every day."

Aviama looked down at her hands, willing the wind to come to her palm. A soft eddy of air circled in the palm of her hand. Power was returning. She needed to find a way to stop the magna doses or avoid taking enough to last long. Like this morning, when she'd only taken a partial dose from Shiva.

But first and foremost, she needed to know who was on her side. "I started training you in the palace. I told you I wanted to trust you."

Sai stepped further into the room and leaned heavily against a stack of crates in the corner. Her brow knit together as she stared out the window at the open sea, and Aviama's heart wrenched. Sai wore a similar outfit to Aviama, perhaps from the same trunk Shiva had found. In the light of day, with her arms bare, the bruising on her arms stood out more than before. Three fading stripes marked her upper arm, and a yellowed area marked the soft skin on the underside of her wrist.

The girl's round face was deceptively gentle, considering her wiry, muscular arms and fiery spirit. She may be slender, but she was strong. And in more ways than one, Aviama guessed. But here, in the midday light on a hostile voyage, what was hidden stayed hidden no longer. Nightmares and reality collided.

Sai worried her lip and stared down at the crate on which she leaned. She drew a trail in the dust with one finger. "Why would you trust me? Chenzira doesn't. He trapped me, and for good reason. I showed the prince—I told him where you were going. I saw you enter the tunnel."

Aviama tilted her head and leaned over across her own stack of crates to see Sai's face better, but she turned it away toward the window. The girl's chest rose and fell faster than it had before, and her fingers started anxiously tapping on the edge of the crate.

It wasn't new information. But even when Sai had admitted it when Aviama ran into her in their flight, when the squads of soldiers descended on Waif's Garden and the cries of the dying rattled the silence of the night, she had said it with tears. She hadn't wanted to do it. But she had.

"Why did you do it?"

"My parents are old, and my father is ill. My mother cares for him full time, and we don't have other family. Without me working to support them, they couldn't afford the medicine my father needs. We can barely afford it on my pay as it is, much less enough food to keep them healthy." Sai ran her finger along the end of the crate. She took a breath. "I can't get another job. I know things. I'm in a useful position for them. They would stop me from working anywhere else. They would hurt my family. They *have* hurt my family."

A lump rose in Aviama's throat. "And the bruising?"

Sai shrugged again. "The cost of my family's health."

Aviama frowned. "Your health must suffer to pay for theirs?"

"I'm young. I can take it." Sai let out a mirthless laugh. "And I'm not innocent, either—I betrayed you, didn't I? Better me than them."

Aviama scanned Sai again, taking in the strange pattern of bruising on her arm, the strength of her upper arms, the scar on the underside of her chin that she'd never noticed before. She looked at Sai, but Sai's eyes brimmed with tears, and she stared down again. Aviama took a slow step forward, lifted her hand, and gently pressed her fingers along the three marks on Sai's upper arm.

Sai looked up at her then. Her lip quivered.

Aviama spoke softly as she looked intently into Sai's face. "I think the cost is too high. You deserve to be safe."

"What if I don't?"

Aviama gritted her teeth. "Who was it?"

"Doesn't matter."

"It does." Long fingers of fear reached through her stomach, threatening to turn it inside out. Perhaps she couldn't say because the person was on board. Perhaps Aviama had been engaged to the man.

As if reading her thoughts, Sai grimaced and shook her head. "They're not here."

Aviama frowned. "Was it the queen? Did Satya do it?"

"No. She's threatened me before, mostly to get information on you or on Prince Shiva. But the prince usually handles it when she tries to get to me, and she left me alone after a while."

Aviama's mind spun. Shiva protected his informant from his mother. So who could be hurting Sai if she was under his protection? Who knew how to blackmail her? Who was higher than the prince, than the queen?

Her jaw dropped. "No."

Sai swatted at an unbidden tear and stared down at the lid of the barrel. "He told me he just wanted someone to talk to. That the queen was too harsh, too unforgiving. And then he wanted more, and sometimes, if he'd had a bad day, he took out his frustrations on me. But with the war afoot ... well, he had more bad days."

Aviama wrapped her arms around Sai's shoulders. A lump formed in her throat, and tears sprang to her eyes. Heat rushed to her chest and flushed her cheeks as her heart broke and rage poured out of the chasm. Each tear might as well have been made of steam as Aviama's muscles tensed, encircling Sai as if the gesture could take it all back—could shield her from what had happened in the House of the Blessing Sun.

House of Curses. House of Evil. House of King Dahnuk Tanashai and his despicable wife and bloodthirsty son. The family deserved each other. No wonder they were all so twisted. But context was no excuse, and the bruises the king had left on Sai reached far deeper than the skin. Sai let out a soft whimper, and Aviama pulled her in against her shoulder. For a moment, nothing happened, the two of them frozen in wordless turmoil.

And then the tears flowed. The two of them stood together, speechless, holding each other as if an embrace could hold together the fragile threads of sanity. Aviama told herself she would be strong, that she would let Sai weep into her shoulder until all her tears were spent, that she would be a firm rock to hold on to in that moment. But as images spun unbidden in her mind of the abuse the king had exacted, and the pain of her friend—because traitor or not, she couldn't help but think of Sai as a friend—her own eyes welled with tears and overflowed down her cheeks, dampening Sai's hair.

Aviama didn't know how long they stood there. She only knew that when she'd spent the night crying in her room after her father's death and had gone to Semra for solace, Semra hadn't been in a hurry. That sometimes *being* was better than speaking.

When at last Sai pulled away, Aviama's golden braid tangled with Sai's shining black hair. The two of them laughed as they separated their hair and smoothed it back, then wiped their faces.

Aviama shrugged helplessly as she looked into the deep wells of Sai's auburn eyes. "I didn't see it. I didn't stop it."

Sai dragged a finger under her eye and pulled in one last sniffle. "You did see it. You asked. You prodded. I didn't answer your questions. Because there was nothing you could have done that wouldn't have gotten you killed."

"I'm thoroughly sick of that." Aviama let out a sigh, a whoosh of air that pulled her shoulders down and eased, if only a little, the knot in her chest. She lifted her hand, pulling the wind in the room around them in a gentle breeze that played in their hair and sent the dust on the lid of the crate dancing up into the air, sparkling in the rays from the window. Aviama dropped her hand, and the wind dissipated.

"I can't do anything. I understand now why Semra always ran toward danger. If danger is assumed, it's better to run toward it than away from it. At least, it is when running is only a delay and not a real solution." Aviama glanced up at Sai. "I need to know whose side you're on. I know Shiva knows about your family. I know he could hurt them, and so can the king. So can the queen. But I also know that whatever Shiva is planning to do at Ghosts' Gorge will kill not just one family, but many. He wants control of the sea. He's planning to either manipulate or kill the Iolani, and if he does that, his path to Jannemar will be clear. Sai, Radha isn't enough for him. I don't think he'll settle for a king's throne. He won't stop until he's an emperor."

Sai's eyes widened, but she nodded. She knew Shiva was ambitious. And they both knew how far he would go to get what he wanted.

"You know, I always wanted to be on your side."

"Yes. But you haven't always let yourself be on my side. If you aren't all in, the best you can do for me is allow me to keep you at arm's length. I don't want to, but it would protect us both."

Sai swallowed. "I gave Chenzira magna. On the dock, before the konnolan went off. Durga and I were both given magna, and when the horn blew, we were to take it to protect ourselves from the effects. I told Prince Shiva that Chenzira stole mine, but he didn't buy it. That's why I spent the night in the brig."

Aviama nodded. "I wondered if that was it."

"I want to be with you. I want you to win. I just..." Sai bit her lip and stared down at her hands.

Aviama's chest tightened. "Take a little time and think it over. But I don't want to be at odds with you. I am for you. I hope you know that."

Sai gave a weak smile and dipped her head.

It was time to go. Aviama took a deep breath and crossed to the door, stopping just short of it and turning back to Sai. "Don't feel bad about believing a lie. About believing you deserved what happened to you. We all believe lies sometimes." It didn't sound right. It didn't convey everything she wanted to say. But it was something. Aviama reached for the knob and hesitated. "I once believed Shiva might be good. But I was wrong."

9

By the time Aviama headed out of Sai's room, seamen were streaming toward the mess hall. Aviama's stomach grumbled, but the thought of that many strangers staring at her after the debacle of that morning made her nauseous. So up she went to the upper deck, aiming for the officer's mess outside her room instead.

She pushed open the door. Only one sailor occupied the space—an older man with a graying beard and a long scar down the side of his face. Aviama breathed a sigh of relief.

The man nodded at her and waved a hand at a dozen steaming plates of food along a counter against the wall. "Hungry?"

Salted beef, cheese, and bread adorned every plate. Aviama's mouth watered, and her stomach growled in answer before she could speak. The sailor laughed and handed her a plate, followed by a knife and fork. She took it, glanced around the space, and sat at the long table across from the sailor. "Thanks."

"Too scared to go to the mess hall?"

"No." The lie soured on the way out of her mouth. Aviama replaced it with a chunk of beef.

The man chuckled. "I'm Peg."

Aviama arched an eyebrow. "Lose a limb?"

Peg spread his hands. "Guilty as charged."

She cut off another piece of meat and speared it with her fork. "What do they call everybody else who loses a leg? Peg the Second?"

"Not my problem, kid." The man laughed, then froze. He glanced up from his plate to look at her, realizing his mistake mid-chew.

Aviama winced and waved him off. "Don't bother. I'd rather be called *kid* by somebody friendly than any formal title by someone who isn't."

Peg grinned. "Whatever you say, kid."

Aviama stuffed another bite into her mouth and swallowed. "How does the crew feel about Ghosts' Gorge?"

"You don't want to know how they feel about you?"

She made a face. "I assume it isn't good, so no, I'm not sure I do."

"You should. And you should try to change it." Peg ripped off a piece of bread with his teeth.

The knot in her chest tightened. "Why?"

Peg shrugged. "I guess I don't think spearing fish in a barrel is sportsmanlike."

"It's that bad?"

The man ran a hand across his mouth, knocking crumbs in every direction. "Elite girl with chaotic powers that could influence the wind in the sails or explode cargo on board? Girl who sets the captain on edge? Samud isn't ruffled easily, but he doesn't take kindly to disrespect. He hasn't been sharing sparkling impressions of you."

Aviama blanched. So Samud was less than excited to have

her on board, and spreading the sentiment to the men. She took another bite. "I can't make things explode."

Peg eyed her for a moment before shoveling another gulp down his gullet. "Shame. We could afford for things to get shaken up a bit."

The tightness in her chest eased just a hair at his words. "And the Gorge?"

The door shoved open and Samud himself strode in. Any respite she'd experienced from Peg's casual, friendly demeanor dissolved in an instant.

"The Gorge is every sailor's nightmare, Princess. And every sailor's challenge, at the same time." Samud snatched a plate off the counter and swung himself into the chair at the end of the table, three seats down from them. "A mystery to solve, a conquest to master. The only redemption for probable death."

Peg flared his eyes wide at Aviama as if to say, *Isn't he a plum?*

Aviama choked on her beef, shoveled the last of it into her mouth, and snatched the bread from the plate. Samud drilled her with a cool stare as she gathered her plate and silverware, walked to the counter, and placed them in the bucket of soapy water she found there. "Thanks for the lesson, Captain. Thankfully for me, probable death is practically an old friend by now."

She lifted the bread in salute to Samud and slipped out the door. With a row of full plates still steaming on the counter, it was only a matter of time before others joined Samud, and Aviama felt sure they would share his sentiments about her— the same sentiments Peg had warned her about. But what was she supposed to do to change that?

Three sailors hummed a tune on their way past her as she stepped out from under the quarterdeck and into the broad daylight of afternoon. The sun warmed her skin, the natural breeze toying with her braid as she crossed the deck to the railing. A rustling caught her ear above her to the right. Aviama turned to see Shiva stuffing a painted cloth into the pocket of his jacket. She jerked her gaze forward. It was too late to avoid him, but she didn't have to let on that she'd seen him, either.

The sparkle of the water winked up at her as it lapped lazily against the hull of the *Wraithweaver.* If it weren't for the name of the ship, or the prince commanding it, she might have believed with days as fair as these that their voyage could be to any place at all—somewhere nice, maybe. A vacation home, perhaps, or an allied nation. An adventure where adrenaline only came from exciting new places and foods, and not from an ever-present risk of death.

Aviama glanced down at the sapphire ring on her finger, nestled by four white stones above and four white stones beneath. She wore other rings, too—slender gold bands, and an opal that reminded her of Semra. But it was the sapphire that she could not part with, no matter how desperate she got. She traced her finger over the four stones on top of the sapphire, breathing in and out to steady herself as she counted them over and over. *One, two, three, four.*

Boots hit the steps to her right, descending toward her from the quarterdeck. *Thud, thud, thud.* Aviama stiffened. She spun the rings on her fingers. Counted the stones again. *One, two, three—*

"You've been busy this morning."

Aviama cringed at the sound of his despicably silk-smooth voice. After all, a spider would go hungry if not for its silken web, and Shiva was well practiced at building his.

She gripped the rail and lifted her chin. "I was shut up long enough in the palace. I get restless."

"Does it count as being shut up if you find your way out every other night?"

"Do you fault the fish when it tries to escape its net?"

Shiva propped his elbow on the rail beside her, and his gaze fell heavily on her face. "You are hardly helpless. And as for nets, we all have them. Other women would have died to be caught in the one you bore."

Aviama swallowed. It was true. On paper, the offer of a marriage alliance to the strongest kingdom in the region, where the groom-to-be was neither old nor ugly, but young, handsome, and charming—it was a dream come true. But after stepping into that reality, she'd uncovered the truth. Nightmares were dreams too. "I am not other women." Her gut wrenched, and her breath hitched as she stared out at the endless water of yet another lovely cage. *I am helpless. You made me helpless.*

From the pot to the fire, from the palace to the ship. Surrounded by enemies and smothered in blackmail. Dosed with magna and controlled by konnolan.

"No. No, you are not." Shiva let out a long sigh. "I thought I knew what I was getting into with the contest. But I didn't expect you at all."

Aviama wrapped her fingers around the railing and shifted her weight. Why did he have to have moments of normalcy? It was creepy. Aviama eyed him, but he was already looking at her. She snapped her head forward, staring hard out at the endless ocean before them. "The contest is over. You still failed to find a wife. And now you say you don't need one, but you still brought me on this boat headed for nightmaresville in the middle of fairyland. Did you just want to make sure that I died? Is that why I'm here?"

"Fairyland, hmm?"

Aviama shrugged. "Mox wrote fairy tales, like *Crater Wood,*

Fairies Descend, and *Ghosts' Gorge.* Fairies aren't real. Why would the Gorge be real?"

Shiva slid closer to her on the rail, until his arm pressed against hers. She fought the urge to flinch and took their close proximity as an opportunity to glance down at his pocket. The corner of the cloth he'd been studying on the quarterdeck was peeking out. Shiva looked out at the water. "Mox was a naval officer before he was a writer."

"And I like to draw. So what?"

"The difference between *Fairies Descend* and *Ghosts' Gorge* is that nobody has ever hidden from the fairies. No one has ever mysteriously disappeared near the mythical portals he wrote about. But Ghosts' Gorge has taken many a ship—and released none of them. The only one that ever got close was the *Valiance.*"

Aviama's eyes narrowed. She'd never heard of the *Valiance,* and she didn't know Mox had been anything but a storyteller. A pelican coasted through the air ahead of them, banked right, and plunged after some unfortunate fish too small to see.

Shiva straightened his jacket and cleared his throat. "As the story goes, Mox was on board the *Valiance* when she approached a seamount amid a raging storm. The top of the rocky mount crested the water, threatening to break the ship apart, but the wind and waves were so wild that they lost control. It is said that the sailors heard music in the wind. Mox had lost all hearing in one ear several years prior, and the other was ringing from the ship pitching forward and him falling on the deck and hitting his head on the stairs. When he looked up, he saw his men jumping overboard, and a half-woman, half-fish creature clinging to the rocks. They locked eyes, and they say he saw his own death reflected in her gaze.

"Mox stopped up his ears with wax, tied his first mate to

the mast, and turned the ship from the seamount. Another wall of rock stood opposite to the one they escaped, and a whirlpool opened up in the ocean gorge. Flashes of scales caught his eye at every turn. Thick fog descended until he could hardly see. He set a fuse fixed to all the cannons, fired them at once, and set an explosive in the figurehead that ripped it from the bow. It hit a great chieftain of the sea, and the storm and fog began to break apart. But he'd ignited their anger."

Aviama shook her head. She had to admit, it was a marvelous story. Ridiculous, but marvelous nonetheless. She could picture it now, the buffeting wind and mighty waves, the boom of the cannons, the thick fog. Impossible. But interesting.

The pelican circled and dove again into a sea of glass, then came up with its catch wriggling in its mouth.

"The sea rose, and the ship began to sink. Mox climbed the mast and swore to send more ships in his stead if they saved the *Valiance* and returned his men. The wind died down and the most beautiful creature Mox had ever seen appeared at the rail of the ship. She gestured for him to unplug his ear to make a deal. Mox agreed, took out the wax from his deaf ear, and approached the siren..."

Shiva's voice trailed off. Aviama looked at him. "And?"

Shiva scanned her face and smiled.

She pursed her lips. Okay, so she wanted to know what happened in the story. That didn't mean she believed it.

"Mox was captivated. The sight of her alone was enough to make him wonder if perhaps death at her hands was not more desirable than life without her. He removed the wax from the other ear and reached toward her." Shiva turned toward Aviama, and his hand brushed hers on the rail. Aviama's stomach dropped, and she leaned back. "Her lips moved in song, and he was rooted to the deck, staring at her perfect face, her lips, her neck."

Aviama knew how Mox felt. Except it wasn't allure that froze her in place, but fear. And one small hope...

She dropped her hand from the rail, lifting it gently between them, palm up, as a warning. But even as she did, her own lips parted with a sigh like the siren in the story. Her gaze was hard at first, but as she looked deep into the endless umber of his eyes, she softened. Shiva lifted one hand slowly and brushed her neck with the back of his hand. His thumb brushed over her mouth, and he stepped closer until she couldn't smell anything but the musky oils he always wore.

His breathing quickened, and his eyes locked on hers. "Her song cut through the wind, and the storm calmed. He knew she was his destiny."

Shiva pressed into her right hand so that his chest met her open palm, and she did nothing to stop him. Her left hand brushed the edge of his jacket. Her heart stopped, and the world halted. His next words flew toward her in a low rumble.

"Just as you are mine." He seized her then, his hand wrapping around the nape of her neck and pulling her in.

The moment broke as alarm surged through Aviama's body with an ocean of adrenaline. Aviama gasped, and wind whipped between them like a wall. She wrested herself from his grasp, but just as she turned to run, he caught her around the waist.

And then a dark blur knocked her sideways.

10

———

Aviama stumbled to one side as Chenzira came flying out of nowhere like an arrow from the string. His fist connected with Shiva's nose, and Shiva's head snapped back. Chenzira lunged, clasped Shiva behind the neck, and yanked him forward. Shiva's arms flailed and latched onto Chenzira, but with a lightning-fast dip down and burst upward, Chenzira wrapped Shiva's body across his shoulders. With one arm around Shiva's and the other around the man's leg, Chenzira spun and chucked Shiva flat on his back on the deck, where he gasped like a fish out of water.

Chenzira rolled to his feet and glared down at Shiva, his eyes a burning fire. "Leave her alone."

Shiva clutched at his chest and curled his lip. "You're insane!"

Aviama stepped away, staring back and forth between the men. What game was Shiva playing at that he still tried to make moves on her? There was no audience to perform for. No servants or dignitaries. No hopeful crowds. Here, he'd publicly used her as a tool to prove his control over melderbloods and made it clear he had no further need of her as a fiancée.

What did he hope to gain? Why would he care if she trusted him again, if she kissed him again?

And what had possessed Chenzira to brawl with him on the upper deck for the second time in one day?

Chenzira tugged his shirt back into place from where it had slid up his torso in the takedown. "She pushed you away."

Shiva glanced behind them and made a gesturing motion. Aviama whirled to see Samud and two henchmen heading their way. Her stomach soured. She stuffed her hands in her pockets and extended her fingers, knocking over a barrel in their path as they marched toward Chenzira. The first man tumbled straight over it, plowing into the wooden deck with his face.

"With wind she shouldn't have had." Shiva gathered his feet and turned an intense gaze on Aviama. "But she also stood still when she could have left. She leaned into me."

Aviama gaped at him. "No, I didn't."

"You did. I've seen that look on your face before. I know it. I know you."

Chenzira turned to look at her. Aviama set her jaw and shook her head at Shiva. "You don't know me at all. I don't know why you want me alive. I don't know why you're doing what you're doing. But whatever the reason is, I can only assume that by the time you're finished, I'll wish I was dead."

I won't let you marry him.

The phrase surged to her memory, taking her off guard. A fierce expression had darkened Chenzira's face as he'd said it, in the dark, when Arjun had gone on ahead and they were sending her back into the palace. Back to the wolves. That promise had kept her going, kept her believing she might make it out of Shiva's clutches after all.

The same expression was painted on Chenzira's features now. Fury rolled off him in waves, his arms tense as he stepped in front of Aviama.

"They're not coming for *me*, dummy," she whispered. "Let me."

One hand slithered out of her pocket and angled up toward Samud and his men, who had already recovered and were closing the distance.

Chenzira clasped her wrist in his large, warm hand and squeezed. "Don't show off. Let them take me."

His gentle hold surprised her after the strength of his attack on Shiva. His palm swallowed her whole wrist. He let go, and Aviama swallowed. "I thought you didn't want to make yourself an enemy early on in the voyage."

"I didn't want to look weak. But this time it was him who was weak—he went down like a feather. Besides..." Chenzira grinned and glanced at her with an impish look in his eye. "It was worth it."

Shiva bored daggers at them both, and the ire in his eyes sent a chill down Aviama's spine. He was right. He *did* know her, at least to some extent. And she knew him.

She knew he would stop at nothing to restore an impenetrable reputation. That nearly everyone was disposable. And that he really believed at least part of his story about Mox. He'd been so exhilarated when he'd spoken of it. His entire frame had lit up. A dangerous man pursuing a dangerous passion.

Shiva put his hand on the hilt of his sword—a little late to be of use—and squared off toward Chenzira. "I'll up her magna dose. Yours too, unless you'd prefer konnolan."

Samud strolled in between the men. "Play nice, boys. What idiocy has come over the island rat now?"

Chenzira stood taller than the others, except perhaps for

Samud. Chenzira rolled his shoulders back, spread his hands, and flashed a smile. "To the brig, gentlemen? Want to get a few shots in first?"

Shiva glowered at him and jerked his chin to one side. "Get him out of my sight."

Samud swept his hand in an arc toward the stairs down the deck with the flair of a man who had just issued an invitation to a grand ballroom.

Chenzira gave a mock bow to Samud and his men and headed back under the quarterdeck, the two sailors on his heels. Aviama's chest tightened. If this was the first day of their voyage, how would the rest of the trip go?

Aviama slipped sideways away from Shiva and Samud, watching Chenzira's strong frame as he crossed the deck. After three more paces, he turned and met her gaze—but his voice was bold, meant for all to hear. "Mox kissed her, as the story goes. The siren. You know what he did after that? He drew his dagger, held her at knifepoint until he was safely out of the Gorge, and then slit her throat when he was free. Still sound romantic?"

Shiva strode forward, but Chenzira only held up his hands and swept off under the shadow of the quarterdeck and down the stairs, flanked by Samud's men as they escorted him to the brig. Samud gave Aviama and Shiva a long look, turned on his heel, and headed up toward the helm. Aviama flattened her lips in a tight line and sidestepped away from Shiva, hurrying to reach the shade of the quarterdeck and be shielded from Shiva's boring gaze.

Afternoon sun kissed the oak planks underneath her feet, landing on the polish with a glinting sheen. She passed out of its path into shadow, shielded from the heat that beaded sweat upon her brow and from the eyes of any sailors working on the upper deck. She breathed in deep and let out a sigh of relief.

Now the question was, did playing the part of an enraptured schoolgirl pay off? Or should she have sent the prince reeling against the side of the ship when he tried to get close to her?

Aviama ducked to the left, into the alcove next to the kitchen, and pressed her back flat against the wall behind a stack of crates. Her hand shook as she reached into her pocket and pulled out a painted cloth. The light of one of the circular windows spilled onto the cloth in her hands: a map. And from the rock formations creating a narrow passageway, the varying hues of blue surrounding them, and the lightning, rain, and wind symbols across the center, it wasn't just a map. It was Ghosts' Gorge.

Notes and numbers splayed across the map. Some of it seemed to be guessing at the precise location of the Iolani, sketching out where they might live, and some of it could have been the headings to take to get there. But the rest looked like little more than chicken scratch, and less decipherable.

"Lovers' quarrel, Rookie?"

Aviama yelped and snapped her head up, inadvertently slamming the back of her head into the wall behind her.

"So sad. So sweet. It makes the soul feel alive, even if a little upside down, doesn't it?"

Mock sympathy knit Onkar Dhoka's brow together as he leaned against the crates. He clucked his tongue, then dropped the pitying look and craned his neck at the map in her hands.

Her heart raced. *Biscuits.* She stuffed it into her pocket.

Onkar's brows soared. "Did little Rookie just play two men against each other for personal gain? And to cover a lift, no less." He pressed a hand to his heart. "My dear, you've restored my faith in the young."

Aviama folded her arms. "A lift?"

"Yes. A lift." Onkar snapped his fingers in front of her face. "Pay attention, Rookie. But make sure you pay attention to the right things. Otherwise, you might lose something ... valuable." He lifted his free hand and dangled the map in the air between them.

She gasped and snatched at the map. "Give me that!"

"Ah, ah, ah!" Onkar wagged a finger at her, tossed the cloth to his other hand, and nudged her with his elbow. "It's as much mine as it is yours. I'm only grateful I got to see you get it. I must admit, it was deeply satisfying. Sunboy certainly has a way with people, wouldn't you say? The kind that makes you want to see him swim with the fishies."

Aviama set her jaw. She had to get that map. With a twirl of her fingers, Aviama sent a vine of wind around Onkar's ankle and yanked hard. The man stumbled and fell against the opposite stack of crates, and Aviama lunged for the map. Her fingers sank around its folds, but Onkar wouldn't let go.

The swindler's strong arms encircled her, lifting her from the ground as he pried her fingers off the prize one by one. Aviama bit her lip to keep from grunting with the exertion as she threw an elbow up at Onkar's nose and swung to reclaim her hold on the cloth. She sent another gale of wind, but they were in close quarters, and the best it did was knock a crate against them both so they fell into the wall.

Onkar shoved the crate back in place and wrested the map from her fingers once and for all. By the time he stepped back and she straightened, he'd stashed it somewhere, because his hands were empty and his expression was smug.

"Listen, Rookie, I was impressed by the lift. You have good instincts for timing. But brute strength is not your strong suit."

Aviama ground her teeth. "I need that map."

"Yes, you've made that clear." Onkar examined the cuticles of his nails and then held up a finger as if he'd been hit by a sudden stroke of genius. "How about a deal?"

"Our last deal resulted in a bloodbath at the dock, my kidnapping, and ultimately my looming death as we set course for a fairytale death trap."

The man waved her off. "Semantics. You asked for a ship, and wouldn't you know it, here you are on a ship! And because you wisely paid your maladroit incidentals insurance, I will see to it you make it off this ship alive."

Aviama scoffed. "Easy for you to say. Dead people can't come to collect refunds."

"Astute, Rookie. Though not exactly diplomatic. Aren't you a royal? I'm not sure you and Islander know how to be royal. You seem better suited to chaos. That said, I will offer you a chance to earn back the map."

Warning bells set off in the back of her mind, but she only pressed her lips together. "How?"

"Come work for me in the kitchens, and I'll teach you what it takes to steal. Better yet, I'll teach you not just how to steal from lovesick puppies, but how to steal from a thief. I swear on Islander's life, I'll keep the map on me at all times, just for fair play. If you can take it, it's yours." He grinned.

Aviama blinked. "You want me to steal it back?"

"I want you to *earn* it back. I want you to think with more than your ego or your muscles. If you can do that, you'll be better off than most, and a worthy opponent."

"What's the catch?"

"No catch. I'm feeling generous."

Aviama rolled her eyes. "Please."

Onkar held up his hands in defense. "I really am feeling generous. I even paid you for the map. Check your pocket."

Aviama screwed her face up in a skeptical grimace, but when she slipped her hand into her pocket, sure enough, she withdrew a coin: one gold Radhan dhan. Her lips parted. How had he done it?

Onkar winked. "By nightfall tomorrow, I want you to give it back to me without me noticing." He wiped a dusting of flour off his trousers and tipped an invisible hat in her direction. "Lessons start at dawn."

And then he was gone.

11

———

Afternoon wore on into evening, and Aviama hid in her room for the bulk of that time, trying to give herself reasons not to show up the next morning for thievery lessons with Onkar. She wandered out of her room shortly before dinner and found Peg setting out meals. Gratefully, the man gave her a nod and a clasp on the shoulder and sent her off with a plate of her own, beyond the reach of prying eyes or angry captains.

Aviama tried to open the door at the back of her room again, but whatever was jamming it from the outside had her soundly sealed inside her room and blocked off from the balcony. She took her hair down from its braid and brushed it —or rather, fought it—with the comb. The tangles were better contained than before, but still significant. How hair managed to knot itself up even when tied back, she'd never know.

Chenzira was in the brig. Sai had gotten out just that morning. Bhumi was working in the kitchens with Onkar. And Makana was still hidden somewhere on the ship. The cargo deck made the most sense. Aviama had already walked the other decks of the ship, and though it was possible Makana was somehow stashed behind barrels or something on the gun deck, or in the guardroom, it seemed unlikely they would place a siren near weapons or a deck full of curious sailors.

Options were slim, so the cargo deck would be the place. Would she be guarded? Would the guards stuff their ears with wax, like Mox did in the story, or did Samud and Shiva decide the risk was low since no sailor would be able to fit through the bars of her cage?

Aviama knew what it was like to be in a cage. She sank into the chair at her desk and shivered. She'd been stuffed in a cage opposite Makana in the king's menagerie. With Chenzira.

They'd bickered about whether Aviama was to blame for their situation. They'd talked through how Aviama had broken into the king's office. And they'd each confessed something to the other.

Makana had witnessed it all.

Aviama stood up abruptly, knocking the desk. Something rattled in the drawer. What *was* that?

She shook her head, folded the chunk of cold meat and half a roll she'd saved inside a napkin, thrust it into her pocket, and headed for the door. All was dark as she slowly turned the knob, opened her door, and crept through the small kitchen or officer's mess. A bushel of apples sat next to three unidentifiable sacks. Aviama snatched one and stuffed it into her other pocket before proceeding out the kitchen door and under the quarterdeck.

Moonlight spilled onto the billowing sails, a thousand stars offering their silver light to join the moon through the blanket of night. Water lapped at the hull of the ship. Sails pulled at their lines, giving wood and rope a soft creak here and there as the *Wraithweaver* made her way through the sea.

A silhouetted figure stood on the far side of the ship, up on the forecastle. His shoulders drooped and his head hung low as he stared out at the silver dancing along the gently rocking waves.

Aviama watched him for a moment from the safety of the shadows. Then she stole down the stairs to the gun deck. Men snored or talked softly. Someone sneezed. Aviama rounded the stairs and took the last staircase down to the cargo deck two floors beneath her own room at the aft of the ship.

An oil lamp swung from its place outside the guardroom, but the man inside was slumped over the table, sound asleep. The barrels and crates didn't concern themselves with late-night roamers, so there was only one thing left to do.

Aviama took a step toward the cells, out of view of the guardroom, and stopped. She bit her lip. This was a bad idea. Chenzira had gotten into two major scrapes today, both because of her. On the first day of their voyage. The voyage he was only on because she'd been captured.

She shifted her weight. Maybe she should go. But should she leave the food somewhere? Or would that get him in more trouble somehow?

"Aviama?" His voice was gentle. Surprised, but soft. She walked forward, but the dim lamp light only illuminated a couple of meters of the aisle, and little of the cells themselves.

"Chenzira? Where are you? I can't see anything."

"Last one on the left."

Aviama stuck her hands out to keep from hitting her nose on the wall and crept forward.

"Five more steps forward. Now three to your left. Don't scream. I'm going to put my hand out."

Aviama prepared herself and swung her arm to find him, but she still sucked in a breath when his hand bumped into her side. He guided her forward with a hand on her arm, then released her, pulling his arm back through the bars.

"Wait." Aviama reached out and grabbed at his arm, but

got his hand instead. She dropped it, heat flooding her cheeks, and stuffed her hands in her pockets. "I brought you ... um."

Biscuits. The roll was broken apart and squished into the meat. At least the apple was still what it was supposed to be.

She sighed and handed it to him anyway. "It's not much. I wasn't sure if they'd feed you down here. Sorry, it's kind of crushed."

Chenzira took it, and a rustle told her he'd sat down. "Thank you."

She followed suit, settling into place on the floor. "Oh, you know." She gave a halfhearted smile before remembering it was too dark to see anyway. "What are friends who get tossed into cages together, and fight to the death, survive, and then drag you into deadly adventures for?"

Crunch, crunch.

Great, the bread was hard too.

Chenzira ripped off another piece of roll. "Believe it or not, you're the first friend of this kind I've had. I guess I don't know the rules. I don't have much to compare it to."

Aviama laughed. "Good. Then you'll have to take my word for it when I tell you I'm doing a fantastic job filling the role."

"Ah. Excellent. And what about me? Am I doing as splendid a job?"

Aviama swallowed. Her chest tightened, and she winced against the sudden pain in her throat as a lump the size of her fist lodged itself in her esophagus.

Without Chenzira, she'd be dead. Many times over. She would have been caught snooping in the king's office. She would have been killed in the arena. By the trolls, if not by him. She didn't even know what strings he might have pulled with Darsh.

I won't let you marry him.

Her eyes burned with unshed tears. She turned her head

away and wiped an escaped tear from her cheek, thankful for the dark once again. "You're doing fine. Just don't get a big head about it."

"I will absolutely get a big head about it."

Aviama laughed. How could he make her feel light when she felt so low?

She crossed her legs on the wood floor next to Chenzira's cell and chewed her lip. What were they going to do now? Samud hated her. Shiva was as snake-like as ever, and threatening to kill Sai and Bhumi if she didn't behave. Peg had told her to make herself more likable to the crew, and her latest stunt was unlikely to have helped matters.

Aviama let out a long sigh and leaned over her legs to prop her elbows on the floor and her chin on her hands. Crisp night air had made its way to the cargo deck, but without any of the warm breezes tempering the cold on the upper deck. She shivered.

"Next time you get tossed in a cell, can you do it someplace warm?"

"We *are* someplace warm. The Aeian Sea this time of year is about as warm as you could get without traveling quite a way."

"Maybe I need a bigger dress."

"You look nice in what you have on."

Aviama blinked back at him in the dark. He could see her? "I thought you hated it."

"I hated that *he* got it for you."

"If I'd been swimming in options, he wouldn't have had to. I didn't have much choice." Aviama pulled her legs up to her chest, wrapped her arms around her legs, and rested her chin on her knees. "You think I ... look nice?"

"You look good in everything."

Aviama's stomach flopped. Was he making fun of her? But

her eyes had begun to adjust to the dark, and Chenzira looked straight at her—solemn as the grave. She opened her mouth, then shut it. "Even in purple?"

Chenzira wrinkled his nose. "I just might burn every purple cloth I see."

Aviama grinned. "Good. I'll light the match."

After Shiva, she wasn't sure she'd ever be able to wear purple again. Certainly not lilac.

Chenzira folded up the empty napkin and passed it back to her through the bars. She put it back in her pocket and ran her hands up and down her arms, hugging herself as her arms circled her legs in a tight ball. Aviama leaned her head against the bars. The cold of the metal bars sent a chill through her body, so she scooted back and leaned against the planks of the wall instead, with the bars touching her arm on one side and the rear of the ship at her back.

"Sand and sea, you really are cold."

Aviama arched an eyebrow and lifted one arm as proof, hair standing on end as goosebumps ran the full length of her arm. "Does this look like a joke to you?"

"I don't know. It's dark. I can't see that well." Chenzira shuffled closer to the bars, and Aviama stuck her arm through.

"See?"

Chenzira touched her arm. Warmth flooded her body. He closed both hands around her forearm and felt the goosebumps up and down between her elbow and wrist. "I'm sorry. I thought you were going to show me your arm. This is an icicle."

Aviama rolled her eyes in the dark. "I told you! It's cold!"

"It's not cold. You're ridiculous."

No witty comebacks presented themselves. "You're ... ridiculous..."

Chenzira moved to the edge of his cell, his throaty laugh igniting the air between them. "I'm always warm."

He slid his arms through the bars, encircling her as best he could. Aviama gasped and leaned closer toward him. "Are you made of lava?"

"Not that I know of."

"This can't be normal."

"Maybe you're the weird one who's cold on the Aeian Sea. If we sail west, it'll only get warmer from here."

Aviama hesitated, then pressed her icy fingers against the heat of his skin. He flinched when she first touched him, but didn't pull away. He adjusted his position against the bars, and she pressed into the circle of his strong arms and body heat. The muscles of his arm flexed and relaxed under her fingers as he shifted. She fought the urge not to trace the outline of the rope-like veins in his arm, and the two of them sat there together, unmoving.

Down the hall, the lantern swayed outside the guardroom with the gentle rock of the ship. Dim light cast down to the floor around it, but the light fell short of the two of them by several paces, leaving them in the dark. Aviama rested her head back against the hard steel bars and let out a long breath. His cheek pressed against the back of her head through the bars, and her shoulders dropped as she relaxed into Chenzira's soothing presence and calming warmth.

"I remember the first time I saw you," he murmured against her hair. Aviama's heart skipped a beat. He cleared his throat. "You walked out on your balcony, and I was in the courtyard below. You were wearing a light blue dress. Your hair was damp, but shining, and it fell down your shoulders. No hairstyles, no makeup. No jewelry, except for the rings you always wear."

Aviama turned her head. "You remember that?"

"Mhmm." His arms tightened. "It's my favorite image of you. Not done up. Not done up *for* anyone. Devastatingly beautiful."

Her mouth went dry, and heat flushed her cheeks. She rolled his words over in her mind, and they shot warmth down to the tips of her toes. "Really?"

"Yes." Chenzira paused. "You were solemn. No fake smiles. You thought you were alone. And then you saw me, and I guess I scared you."

Aviama laughed. "I'd just found a threatening note hidden in my food. I thought maybe you were planning on murdering me."

"What?"

"How was I supposed to know? I didn't know anybody. I'd been in the palace less than twenty-four hours!"

"So that was your first impression of me?"

Aviama hesitated. "You were staring. Kind of intense. Maybe you hated me. Maybe you wanted me dead. And then you were half-naked, so, you know ... that was surprising."

"It was evening. I thought I was alone."

"You were in a common area. Wearing a jeweled collar."

Chenzira shrugged. "In Keket, a schenti and jeweled collar are typical for the royal family. We are an island nation. And it's warm there."

"If you're used to everything being warm, shouldn't you be cold in other places?"

"I don't know. But I'm not."

"Obviously."

"What were you doing wandering the palace when I met you after that?"

Aviama grinned in the dark. "Secret meeting with a threatening stranger who had access to my food supply."

Chenzira moaned. "Your tally of stupid things might be even longer than mine. I was expecting to win that contest."

"Winning too much isn't good for your ego. I'm here to help."

"Can you let me win sometimes, when the alternative is you dying?"

"Biscuits, I'm not dead yet."

"It's not for lack of trying."

"Takes one to know one."

Chenzira paused, then laughed. "Sand and sea, I guess it does."

Aviama let herself lazily trace the veins on his arms with one finger. He didn't react. She bit her lip. He'd called her beautiful. He'd saved her life. He was the safest person for miles around. Should she share what she really thought of him?

Her hand stopped moving. She opened her mouth, then closed it. Then opened it again, her stomach bursting with knots. And then the words spilled out.

12

"I don't think I've ever met anyone like you. I thought of you in the courtyard ... um ... sort of often. You're..." Aviama cringed at her own awkwardness. "Biscuits. Well, you're nice to look at, okay? And then when I met you, you were so surprising, and clever, and frustrating."

"Nice to look at, hmm?" She couldn't see his face, but she could tell by his tone that he was smiling.

Her stomach flopped. "And frustrating. Don't forget that part."

"Frustrating. Of course."

"Yes, frustrating. And then you were everywhere, and I thought about you all the time, and it was highly inconvenient."

"The nightmares weren't of me, I hope."

Aviama stilled. She'd woken screaming from nightmares many nights in the palace. Everyone had known she had them. "No."

Chenzira's tone sobered. "Sorry. I didn't know." He paused. "I imagine, if I dreamed of you, I'd sleep soundly every night."

Aviama's lips parted. She'd had someone compliment her

before, tell her she was beautiful before. But she'd never wanted to believe it as much as she did right now. "Do you often talk to girls like this late at night, or only when you're locked up?"

"Maybe loneliness pries me open."

"Maybe I'll get you in trouble more often, so you get lonely more."

"If you'll come to visit me, maybe you should."

Aviama pressed her lips together to keep from smiling, but a big stupid grin crept over her face anyway. She stared down at the sapphire on her finger and rotated the stone. "I guess it does the same to me. Last time we were locked up together, I told you I was a melder."

"Do you still have nightmares?"

Aviama shifted, and his arms loosened. Images filed in through her mind, one after another. She shut her eyes hard. Her heart hammered in her chest.

Chenzira's hand slipped off her arm, down to her wrist, and flipped it over. He pressed two fingers to the inside of her wrist and waited. Aviama tilted her head, distracted by his movement. He was taking her pulse? Did she seem that crazy? But she let him do it.

"Yes. Not every night, like I used to have. They used to just be of different deaths. Over and over, death." Aviama sucked in a breath and let it out slowly. "My father. The explosion, the debris. Someone's arm flying, detached, in front of me as I ran out to find him. My mother, smiling, and the next moment, lying on the ground in a pool of blood with a knife in her chest. The man I killed at my Awakening."

"What happened?"

Aviama shuddered, and the familiar weight returned to bear down on her chest once more. "Whirlwind windstorm. I didn't know I'd been the one to cause it. The gale took off half the roof to the smithy. Liben was just doing his job. One of our servants. A hammer got caught in the wind and smashed him in the head."

Chenzira was quiet for a moment. Aviama wiped the tears from her face, and his hand slipped from her wrist to let her do it. He waited until she resettled before he spoke. "This is why you hate killing. You relive all the deaths you've seen. Unnecessary deaths."

Aviama nodded. "Yes. Death. Sometimes, I dream of Zephan and Semra dying. It hasn't happened yet, but it will if Shiva gets what he wants. And I dream of Shiva. Of him killing people I love. Of his lying mouth, and his voice in my ear."

Her voice shook as she said it, and a tremor rocked her body. She thought of the melderblood face-down in the pool at the palace, ripped to shreds by the queen's hyena. The body she'd thought was Chenzira's. Shiva's threat to kill Sai and Bhumi. Words she believed more than any compliment the man ever gave.

Shiva approached her in her mind's eye, cornering her against some dark wall. Her muscles tensed as he stared her down. He drew a sword, never removing his gaze from her face. Somewhere in her mind, she knew he wasn't really there, but even in this waking dream, he seemed as vivid as her nightmares.

The konnolan you gave me will give me all of Jannemar. And your blood will give me the sea.

Makana appeared behind him, illuminated by some unknown light, caught in Aviama's imagination. *"Key and sea,"* she said. *"Key and sea..."*

"You really are scared of him."

Chenzira's voice cut through her internal vision, and she gasped at the interruption as the reality of the *Wraithweaver* brig returned to her. Wooden slats beneath her, cell bars behind her, Chenzira's arms around her.

She swallowed. "If I can count on Shiva for anything, it's that he will use anything and anyone to gain power. I don't know why he still toys with me, if he says he doesn't need our engagement. But I need a way to be free of him, even while I'm still stuck." Aviama twisted the ring on her finger. "I'm going to work in the kitchens with Onkar. Earlier, when Shiva was with me ... I don't know why he got close; I don't know why he kissed me, but I let him do it to take the map in his pocket. It's something about the Gorge, something that isn't on normal maps."

Chenzira stiffened and started to speak, but Aviama cut him off. "Onkar stole it from me. I need to get it back. He says he'll teach me. I'm going to find Makana. I'm going to learn from Onkar. And I'm going to build allies. There are two hundred men on this ship. They can't all love the prince of Radha."

"Why don't you keep your head down until they let me out? I'll come with you. Keep an eye on you."

Aviama shook her head. "I don't know how long Shiva will keep you down here. If I step out of line too far, he's got three people I care about on board to kill. You're top of the list. I can't wait."

Chenzira pulled back, and Aviama twisted to look at him. His mouth twisted up at the corner. "I'm top of the list, huh?"

She rolled her eyes. "Don't let it go to your head."

"Too late."

Aviama did her best to suppress another smile and leaned back again.

Chenzira sighed. "I don't trust Onkar."

"You trusted him well enough when you dragged me to his

hidey hole and landed me on this boat. Thanks ever so much, by the way."

"Says the woman on the *outside* of the bars."

"But I came to see you, didn't I?"

"You did."

"Add it to my tally of stupid choices."

The two of them sat in silence from then on, ruminating over the night's conversation, and the next day's dangers. The ship rocked from side to side, and the oil lamp went out, neglected by the sleeping guard. Aviama's eyelids grew heavy, and with every lull of the ship, she gave up the fight a little more—until sleep won out, and she slipped into the deepest, dreamless sleep she'd had in weeks.

Aviama lurched awake to shouts and the thundering of a dozen heavy footsteps. She pushed herself up off the planks of the floor and squinted in the dark. Chenzira stirred on the other side of the bars, from the position on his back where he'd apparently sunken during the night.

"Find her."

The voice cut to the quick of Aviama's consciousness, and she leaped to her feet. Chenzira rolled away from her and popped upright on the far side of his cell. He jerked his head toward the stairs. "Get out of here."

He didn't have to tell her twice. Aviama crept down the hall and peered into the guardroom. The poor sot was just waking up. She could get by the stairs and hide in the cargo crates until the sailors passed.

Aviama dashed past the guardroom toward the stairs, but boots descended before her eyes. *Biscuits.* She skidded to a halt and receded back into the dark of the brig. Wind pooled in her palms. Every ounce of magna from the day before had left her system. Power raged through her blood.

She could fight. She could protect. She could do all the

nuanced, controlled motions that windcalling offered. She could do anything.

Aviama backed against the wall. Her sight was adjusted to the dark. She had a few seconds before the sailors' eyes would adjust. She glanced sideways at Chenzira, palm up, eddies of wind swirling before her and wafting her hair back over her shoulders. He shook his head.

Don't do anything stupid.

If Shiva found her with Chenzira, there was no telling what he might do. But if he found her actively running from the sailors or blowing a hole in the ship...

Aviama winced. Her heart pounded. The first footsteps landed at the base of the stairs. With a flick of her wrist and a pull of her fingers, Aviama sent tendrils of wind darting into the lock of the cell door opposite Chenzira's. The door swung open with a click. She slipped inside and closed the door.

Chenzira gaped at her, eyes wide—horrorstruck. Aviama grimaced and drew a straight line in the air with her finger. *Tally,* she mouthed. He pressed his lips in a flat line, and they each backed away from each other to the recesses of their respective cells as half a dozen sailors landed at the base of the stairs and spread out.

A pair of footsteps ran down the cargo deck toward the bow, and two more men rushed into the guardroom. *Smack.* Aviama flinched at the sound of an open hand on someone's skin—probably the guard's face.

One of the men walked down the aisle of the brig, and Aviama slid into a crouch, making herself as small as possible in the shadows.

Chenzira stretched and strolled to the bars. "Morning, Bhavin. Captain worried about me already?"

The sailor shook his head. "Looking for the melderblood girl. She's not in her room, and something's gone missing."

Aviama's stomach dropped. The map. Their characterization of her was interesting, too—all her life she'd been relegated to nothing more than a princess. A shell persona of frills and dances and fake smiles. Now, the princess part was secondary to a more sinister persona: *melderblood.*

A second sailor dragged the guard out of the guardroom and slapped Bhavin on the back of the head. "Keep your trap shut, Bhavin. It's none of his business. Get some oil and light the lamp."

Bhavin rubbed the back of his head. "Cool it, Parth. There's nobody down here but him, and he's locked up. Who's he gonna go tell?"

Parth was unimpressed, and Bhavin grumbled something under his breath as he went to fetch the oil.

Voices called out from down the cargo deck.

"Cargo starboard, clear."

"Cargo port, clear."

"Siren?"

"Accounted for."

"Guards?"

"Present and alert."

So Makana *was* on the cargo deck. And guarded.

The guard drooped in the grip of the second sailor. Present *and alert.* Maybe one of the brig cells would be reserved for *him* for the day.

Bhavin returned with the lamp, and Parth gestured him down the brig aisle.

Chenzira leaned his elbow on a crossbar. "Day two, and the prince is turning the ship upside down after a girl? Is this the same one who embarrassed him yesterday?"

Parth leveled him with a glare. "Same one you punched him over. How'd that go for you, again? I'd watch your tongue if I were you."

Chenzira shrugged. "Just seems like if he's this obsessed over the melderblood girl, and uses all the captain's resources every time she slips out of sight, maybe he isn't stable enough in the head to lead you all into death at the Gorge."

Parth's face turned to flint, and Aviama wondered if Chenzira had struck a nerve. "Above my pay grade."

"Ah, yes." Chenzira ran a hand through his neatly trimmed beard and offered a sympathetic smile. "Expendable men are never at the right pay grade for the stuff that dictates their fate."

Bhavin lifted the lamp by Chenzira's cell and peered into it. Chenzira gestured inside. "You're welcome to come in for tea if you'd like."

Bhavin ignored him and moved on to the other cells. Aviama's breathing quickened. The light flickered over her cell. She pulled her feet in close, the light falling a handsbreadth from the edge of her garment. He turned away.

Parth eyed Chenzira and turned back to Bhavin. "Wait." He grabbed the lamp and thrust it up against the bars of Aviama's cell. Aviama threw a hand up against the light. Her gut wrenched. Parth smirked. "Call the prince."

Bhavin disappeared, and the sleepy guard blanched. The man started edging toward the stairs, but Parth seized him and threw him down to the floor. "Don't you move." He turned back to peer at Aviama. "Raisa's sails, how'd you get in there?"

More shouts came from the upper decks, and a flurry of heavy boots heralded the coming of the prince of Radha, the royal in charge of commissioning the voyage. The man who paid their salaries and had convinced their captain to sail to Ghosts' Gorge.

A dozen sailors packed like sardines into the aisle of the brig, but they parted when Shiva swept down the stairs and strode down to stand between the cells. He marched down to

Chenzira, glared at him, and then spun to Aviama. A note of surprise flickered across his face to find her *inside* the cell. A cell he was supposed to have control over. Across from yet another man he had thrown into yet another cage.

The fear of him balled up in her stomach, but she shoved it down. If she could smile at galas and curtsy to murderous dignitaries, she could fake strength in front of Sunboy. The Blessing Sun, indeed.

Besides, the sailors were watching. Chenzira wanted them to see him as strong, and Peg had warned her that she would need to earn their good favor too. Collapsing on the deck for Shiva's demonstration hadn't been the best first impression of her, and causing a scene over a kiss on the upper deck yesterday probably hadn't helped matters.

Aviama squared her shoulders, uncurled the fists at her sides, and offered Shiva a coy smile. "Good morning."

Shiva drilled her with a cool stare. "Morning it may be, but good it most certainly is not."

"Speak for yourself."

Chenzira tossed her a firm look from over Shiva's shoulder, but Aviama ignored it. She made one infinitesimal imaginary mark in the air with her finger at her side, without moving her gaze from Shiva's face. *Tally.*

Shiva took a step forward. Aviama stepped forward to mirror him. He clenched his jaw. "You stole from me. I know it was you, and you're going to give back to me what is mine."

Aviama cocked her head at him. "Do I strike you as a thief? Isn't it more probable that you misplaced it? Big ship."

He didn't answer, and for a moment none of the twenty or so people crammed in that tiny space dared to breathe. Shiva reached into his jacket and pulled out a knife. Aviama swallowed.

Durga's knife. She'd forgotten it when she left last night. They'd tossed her room.

"You had a run in with Durga." Shiva's expression flattened. "She didn't tell me."

Aviama lifted her chin. "Servants don't often brag about their failures. I'm the one who ended up with her knife. I'll let you guess how it went."

Someone shifted their weight, and a sailor coughed.

Shiva examined the knife in his hands, twisting the end into the tip of his index finger until a trickle of blood ran down the blade. "I know the magna has worn off, so why don't you come on out and join us."

The knot hardened in Aviama's stomach as she watched the blood run down the length of the blade and drip to the floor. She forced another smile. "I rather like it where I am. I'm considering spending more time in here. Do you think I could hang up a tapestry or two?"

Shiva sighed and turned to Parth. "Give me the man on duty last night. The sleeping guard."

Parth gripped the man by the neck and tossed him to the floor in front of Shiva. The guard lifted his hands. "Sir, my name is—"

"My title is Royal Highness."

"Your Royal Highness. My name is Sona. Forgive me, I don't know what came over me. It will never happen again."

"No, it won't." Shiva seized the man's hand and turned it over, revealing a bandage across the palm. "You're melderblood. Aren't you the same man who set fire to the pitch in the cargo deck?"

Sona's face paled. "I have a wife and three daughters."

"That doesn't answer my question." Shiva flipped the knife in the air and caught it with the other hand. "A melderblood without control. A *fireblood,* no less. And a sailor without discipline."

Shiva's expression changed in an instant, and Aviama saw death in his eyes just before he struck. She'd seen that look before. Knuckles white on the grip of the knife, Shiva's arm drew back.

Aviama's heart flew to her throat, and she lunged, palm out. Wind tore through the cargo deck as she sucked air from the upper decks to do her bidding. She slammed into the cell bars as she lurched toward Shiva and Sona. The blast dashed half the seamen against the wall and snuffed out the lamp.

Darkness enveloped the cargo deck.

13

———

"Light!" Shiva growled the order, and a great scrambling and shuffling followed.

Aviama jutted her fingers in the direction of the cell-door lock, and the door swung open, clocking someone in the head as they moved. Grunt, stumble, stumble. Aviama slipped through the opening and shut the door again behind her just as the flickering light of a fresh oil lamp appeared over the guardroom door.

A gasp ran through the brig, and Aviama nearly jumped out of her skin herself to find herself nose to nose with Shiva and surrounded by seamen. Sona groveled on the floor behind her, and Shiva himself was startled to find her suddenly so close. Shiva swore. Music to her ears.

Aviama's mouth went dry, and she swallowed. "You wanted me out of the cell, and I'm out of the cell. You want to show everyone how big and bad you are, and I want Sona to live. Why don't you tell me to go to my room, or lock me in the brig, or make me go without food, and we can all move on?"

Sailors gathered their feet, gawking at Aviama with renewed interest. Chenzira, to Aviama's chagrin, also picked himself up off the floor of the cell beside them. She hadn't accounted for how the wind might spin in such close quarters.

Shiva lifted a hand toward her face, and she stepped back, nearly tripping over Sona. Shiva dropped his hand. "I've got time for all three. But I can't ignore the danger Sona poses. You should know better than anyone what can happen when a melderblood is out of control. And the *Wraithweaver* isn't carrying us to just any location. We are headed to Ghosts' Gorge. This voyage is for the best of the best, and we must be precise, or die. I'd rather lose one than two hundred any day."

Aviama raised her hand and unlocked the cell next to Chenzira. The door clicked open. "So punish him, and let him learn from his mistake."

Shiva caught the door as it opened and slammed it shut again. "Give me what belongs to me, and maybe I'll be in a more forgiving mood."

"I don't know what you're talking about." Aviama spread her hands, patted herself down to show no lumps or hidden spaces, reached into her pockets, and pulled them out. "I've got an empty napkin. Is this what you were missing?"

Shiva jerked his head to one side. "Move. I'll deal with the sleeper first, and then you."

A chill ran down her spine, but she did not move. Sona sobbed quietly behind her feet. She lifted one palm.

Shiva rushed forward to one side, and she lunged after him. A gale whipped through the small space, but she crafted it narrower this time, avoiding the sailors and ripping the knife from the prince's hand. Aviama floated the blade to her own hand and spun back to face him, but he was already past her.

In one smooth motion, Shiva drew his sword and slit Sona's throat. Aviama screamed. The sound carried through the brig on the wings of the wind, amplified through the confines of the cargo hold, and then cut off abruptly as a wet cloth covered her mouth and nose. Strong arms wrapped around her, stuffing her face more securely into the cloth. A sickly sweet scent assaulted her nostrils.

Her head swam. Shiva wiped his sword clean on Sona's shirt. He was talking, and sailors were moving, but she didn't hear a word he said. Aviama sagged in the arms of her captor, and whoever it was lowered her to the floor.

Somewhere above her, Chenzira's outline pounded against the bars of his cell. An incessant thudding crashed against her temples like a hyperactive drum. Through the haze descending on her mind, a thought came to her like a dream. *It's your heartbeat, idiot.* Her breath caught in her chest, and every muscle screamed in protest at the konnolan fumes flooding her senses.

The man who had held her left her on the floor and stood over her. Parth. Convulsions racked Aviama's body as she stared out in front of her—straight into the glassy eyes of Shiva's latest kill. Sona's unblinking orbs offered her no sympathy. Just a promise of another face for another nightmare. His blood seeped toward her across the treated wood of the floor, but she had no strength to avoid its path.

The crimson pool crept closer, and her heart crashed against her ribcage like waves in a raging storm. Red silhouettes of people reflected the room around her in the liquid. Men came with a large blanket and lifted Sona onto it to haul the body away. Buckets and rags filled the space where Sona's corpse had been, mopping up the blood. The sailors disappeared, one by one. And then Shiva knelt before her, snapping his fingers in front of her face.

Aviama winced through the pain and struggled to focus on Shiva's intense glare, ice-cold eyes lit with fire. He leaned down until his face was inches from hers.

"You can't handle blood. Women aren't meant for battle. Powers are wasted on you." He tugged on a strand of her hair, and let it fall. "You couldn't save Sona. Look at you, you would have done anything to save him. And you didn't even know him. But now, his wife and daughters will have no one to provide for them. Because of you."

Aviama gasped for air. Nausea roiled her stomach, and it was all she could do to muster the strength to swallow. She convulsed again, and her gaze fell from Shiva's dark eyes to the oak planks of the floor.

Shiva smiled. "I really must thank you for the konnolan idea. Without it, I wouldn't be half as productive. Did you know you are also the reason Sai's parents are dead?"

Dead? Aviama raised her eyes to meet his again.

He shrugged. "A pity, really. We released volleys of konnolan as tests in the slums before you ever found your way out of the palace. The first volley exposed her father as a melderblood, but his body couldn't take it. You're lucky you're so healthy, because condensing the konnolan like this the way we did today—well, we weren't exactly sure what it would do to you. It's all experimental. The shaking is an interesting effect. We'll note it in our observations. But Sai's father wasn't quite so lucky."

Shiva ran a hand through his hair and examined the cuticles of his fingernails. "He was old and ailing. Konnolan sent him into a heart attack. Her mother wasn't melderblood, but when the soldiers came, she attacked them in a rage. You know how insurrections build. We couldn't have that. The soldier defended himself. Outbursts only ever make things worse. And that's all you ever do. Tantrum and outburst."

He stood and brushed the dust off his trousers, as though the dirt of the floor might somehow strip him of his elevated status, and surveyed Chenzira in the cell behind him and

Aviama still convulsing on the floor of the brig aisle. "This is nice. I do hope you both remember it. Between konnolan, magna, cell bars, and rash decisions, the two of you may well be made for each other. But with all that melderblood in your veins, you're still weak. Weaker even than those of us with purer blood. And for all your straining, every time you act out, you only heap pain on each other."

Shiva heaved a heavy sigh. "I'd require a response, but under the circumstances..." He gave a mocking bow and flashed her one last smile. "I'll see myself out."

And with that, he turned on his heel and swept off down the corridor, leaving Aviama convulsing on the floor in his wake.

14

Tears ran silently over the bridge of Aviama's nose and down her face as she lay on the oak, as if to form a new pool to replace Sona's blood. Dizzy spells alternated with nausea as minutes ticked by, but the muscle weakness and the ache in her body remained constant companions. Crushing weight drilled straight through her chest like an impaler's stake.

She'd handed him konnolan on a silver platter, and that slip had already caused dozens of lives, if not hundreds. How high would the death toll rise once the Radhan army reached Jannemar?

Two hundred sailors manned the *Wraithweaver*. How many would die in the Gorge because of Shiva's belief that konnolan could protect him from any tabeun powers? Would it even work, or would the Iolani rip the galleon to shreds and send them all to the depths?

"Aviama."

The word was urgent, but she liked the sound of her name in Chenzira's mouth. She tried to push herself up, but fell back. Still, her arms could move, if not bear weight. That was an improvement.

"Aviama, can you hear me? I've been calling over and over. The shaking seems to have stopped. Reach your hand out, and I'll pull you."

Aviama craned her neck. Chenzira crouched on the other side of the bars, hand outstretched toward her. He could have been a hundred meters off, and it wouldn't have made any difference. She rested her head on her arm and squeezed her eyes shut against another bout of dizziness.

"Come on, Avs."

The wooziness lifted, and with it, some of the weakness ebbed. Aviama coughed and pushed up on her elbows. "Avs is my sister, Avaya."

"Noted. How do you feel?"

Aviama tested her limbs. "I think maybe it hits harder and then wears off faster. The way he used it this time."

Chenzira nodded. "Good. I think he meant that it was experimental—I don't think he meant for whatever they did with the konnolan to have such a strong effect. I think the shaking scared him a little."

Possible. But if Shiva was frightened, it wasn't because he'd hoped for a kinder alternative. It was because he wasn't in *control* of the outcome.

And he wanted her alive for some reason. Bargaining chip? Experimental dummy? Maybe he just wanted to watch her die on his own terms when the timing was right.

Aviama groaned and pulled herself up, then flung an arm out to stabilize herself as another rush to the head threatened to knock her sideways. "I guess they didn't want to light powder on fire below deck."

"Or they're worried about their supply."

Her jaw dropped. She hadn't considered that. "You think they might not have enough?"

Chenzira reached for her again, and this time she managed the distance. His hand closed over hers, and he tugged her toward him. He shrugged. "Maybe. I don't know. Now let me look at you. Did you hit your head or anything when you fell?"

Parth stepped out from the guardroom with a grunt. Aviama jumped. She hadn't known he was there. Even Chenzira was startled. Parth beckoned Aviama with one hand. "That's enough gab out of you. Once you're recovered enough to move, you're to go upstairs."

Aviama pursed her lips. "I'm not recovered."

Parth folded his arms. "You look more alive than dead, and you're talking. That counts. Get up, or I'll toss you over my shoulder."

Ire burned in her chest, but Chenzira tapped her on the shoulder and shook his head. "No more tallies for today. You'll be fine. Up you go."

"You'll be fine?" Aviama grimaced as she pulled herself up, then wavered before pitching sideways into the bars. "Biscuits. Easy for you to say."

Chenzira caught her arm, but her torso rotated so she hit the bars hard. Pain lit up the back of her skull, and lights danced across her vision. Chenzira swore. "A little help from the free man?"

Parth gripped her by the arm and yanked her free of Chenzira. Her heart sank as they broke contact, and Parth half-led, half-hauled her down the aisle and up the stairs to the gun deck.

The sailor released her at the top of the stairs, sending her careening into a stack of barrels. "I don't care where you go from here, and I'm not a bodyguard. Just don't count on visiting the brig anytime soon."

Aviama had a feeling she might very much count on visiting the brig as long as Chenzira was down there. Especially after last night. The memory of his arms around her, his warm cheek against her hair, filled her with a lightness and freedom that made no sense. Not on the *Wraithweaver*. Not while Shiva still pulled the strings.

She leaned heavily on the nearest barrel and moaned against the splitting headache only now beginning to ease. "It's been a pleasure."

Parth pulled a flask from a pouch at his belt and handed it to her. "Dose up, Princess."

Magna. It would relieve her symptoms, but it might dampen her powers for longer. She shook her head. "I'm fine."

"Sure. You look fine, pale as the moon and walking like a drunk." Parth lifted the flask again. "Drink, and swallow, or I'll pry your teeth open myself. Prince's orders."

Aviama glared at him, took the flask, and lifted it to her lips. She threw her head back, swallowed, and handed it back. Parth took the flask and shook it, the sound of sloshing liquid betraying her.

"Try again."

Biscuits, they'd upped their game. Aviama snatched the flask, took a sip, and swallowed. Parth arched an eyebrow. "And again."

She dumped the rest into her mouth, swallowed, turned over the flask, and dropped it at Parth's feet. He bent to get it, and she turned and stumbled the few paces to the kitchen door, grateful to find it nearly empty. Nearly.

Vacant tables and chairs warned of future occupants, but judging by the gray haze through the window, the sun had not quite yet made its appearance on the horizon. And only one man had arrived so far to prepare the morning meal.

Onkar glanced up at her in surprise as she half-walked, half-fell through the door and stabilized herself against one of the long tables.

"Quite a ruckus down there, darlin'. Sunboy make any declarations of love?"

Onkar rolled out a ball of dough and kneaded it through as he watched her. Aviama's lip curled, and her stomach soured. She hesitated as a bout of nausea washed over her. Aviama grabbed a bowl off the shelf along the wall and spit a mouthful of magna into it.

Onkar jumped back as if contact with the spittle might poison him. "Hey! Watch it, Rookie. It's a kitchen, not a pigsty."

"You called Shiva a lovesick puppy before." Aviama wiped her mouth and clenched her jaw. "He's not. He hates me."

Onkar quirked an eyebrow. "Based on yesterday? Could've fooled me, Rookie."

Aviama winced. "Exactly. You and everyone else."

She leaned hard on the table and waited out another dizzy spell. It dissipated quicker than the last one, and her head grew a little clearer. How could Shiva convince so many people he was something other than what he was? How did she herself believe him, after such a short time, and want to trust him with more of herself—and more information?

Aviama thought back to what he'd said to her on the brig floor. He'd waited until the sailors were gone. They didn't need to know how he really spoke to her. What his true self was like. Killer, yes, but manipulator? Shiva didn't mind keeping that one under wraps. All in due time.

But there was something else. He'd said Sai's parents were dead. The parents Sai said she needed to protect. The ones keeping Sai from helping Aviama. Shiva had removed his leverage over Sai, and he didn't even realize the slip. He probably had too many deaths on his hands to notice the excess...

Aviama snapped her focus back to Onkar. "Whatever Shiva's up to, love has nothing to do with it. And I want to know what it is."

Onkar gave her a long sideways glance, then set a bowl and towel in front of her and held up a pitcher. "So let's give you every tool we can."

Aviama nodded. She held her hands out, and Onkar poured the water so she could wash up before handing her a lump of dough. Aviama watched Onkar's movements and copied them the best she could. "Where does he keep the konnolan?"

"Slow down, Rookie. You're not ready for that yet."

Her chest tightened, a burning eating up at her from the inside out. She hit the dough hard. "Where does he keep it?"

"Darlin', sending you after the konnolan would be like sending a sword-wielding moth to a fire."

Aviama made a face. "What does that even mean?"

Onkar sighed. "It means you're rash and stupid and you would fail."

"I can't do nothing."

"You're not doing nothing. You're rolling dough."

He formed his dough into a loaf, twisted the top into a braided design, and turned to stoke the coals in a stone furnace set behind the two worktables. Onkar glanced at Aviama's work, pursed his lips, and took it from her hands before twisting the same design into the top of hers and tossing both loaves onto the coals. "And it takes practice, just like anything worth doing. Think less like a charging ciraba and more like a chameleon with a sticky tongue. It's small, but the chameleon gets its target. And if you blink, you miss it."

Aviama planted her hands on her hips as she watched him. His easy demeanor and over-casual presence reminded her of one of Semra's other assassin colleagues—except Onkar had a bit more dramatic flair. Confident, eccentric, and lackadaisical, with a dash of slimy mixed in. But behind the blithe veil, his sharp eyes and intentional words told a different story.

"You're saying a ciraba couldn't take the konnolan."

"Brute force? No. Maybe it worked for you in the arena. Maybe it worked for you yesterday, a little. But it's predictable. *Boring.* And there are two hundred men on board this ship. You can't win by fighting like a ciraba when you have the fragile little body of a chameleon." Onkar looked her up and down. "Do you *like* getting dragged around by all the men? They're twice your size."

Aviama pursed her lips and folded her arms. "Make me a chameleon, then."

Four men strode in the door, and Aviama clamped her mouth shut and edged around the corner of the worktable she stood behind to put distance between her and the sailors. Onkar greeted them each by name and set out the bowl and towel before them. The men washed each other's hands, each man pouring water for the next.

Every one of them had the same bandaged injury on one palm. Aviama's eyes narrowed, and she glanced at Onkar. With less than ten percent of the crew being melderblood, what was the likelihood that all the sailors assigned to the kitchen would be melders?

Onkar ignored her, letting the men discover her presence on their own. The first man reached for a sack of grain on the second worktable and froze as his gaze landed on Aviama. Aviama grimaced.

The men had seen her collapse to konnolan on the first morning, push Shiva away when he kissed her yesterday, and heard her screams in just the last hour or two since Sona had been killed. She wasn't sure how long she'd spent convulsing on the brig floor, but she guessed it wasn't long enough for the sailors to forget all the trouble she brought with her wherever she went.

The first man hefted the heavy sack up off the floor and dropped it onto the worktable with a thud. He was a short, broad-shouldered fellow with a beard and long, tied-back black hair. Penetrating dark eyes examined her from a middle-aged face, the wrinkles in his sun-weathered skin betraying his age. He strode up to Aviama, and she sucked in a breath.

She stood behind one of two worktables. Onkar blocked her exit on one side, and the newcomers blocked her from the aisle between the tables. There was nowhere to run. She spun the ring on her finger just once and drew herself up tall.

But though his jaw clenched, and his muscles went taut, just when she wondered if he might strike her, he tapped the fingers of his right hand to his heart and offered a gentle bow.

"I am Umed. Sona was a friend. His wife and daughters are known to me and my family. Today we have with you what sailors call a heartmeet."

Aviama's jaw dropped, and her stomach twisted. Guilt hit her like a sledgehammer, and she stood rooted to the spot, staring after him as Umed stepped back, and the next man stepped forward.

He was younger than Umed, with an impish face set with small, sharp features, a cropped beard, and wiry frame. "I am Jignesh. *Heartmeet.*" The man repeated Umed's gesture, tapping his fingers to his chest, and stepped back just as Umed had.

The next two followed suit, a young beardless man with long wavy hair who introduced himself as Manan, and a stocky boulder of a man with a crooked nose and a head wrap named Laksh.

Aviama's mouth went dry. She bit her lip. "But I didn't do anything. He died."

Manan shook his head. "All respect, ma'am, but I was below decks this morn. I did nothing. You did something."

Laksh clapped Manan on the shoulder. "There weren't nothin' to do, boy." Laksh looked up at Aviama. "Sona was our brother, and today you were his sister."

Umed poured grain into a large bowl, and Jignesh measured water into it. Onkar tossed Umed a piece of the last batch of dough, and Umed tossed it to Aviama with a short nod. "We will work with you."

Aviama caught it, and when she did, an uneasy spark of hope caught flame in her heart. A sad sort of smile spread across her face. "Heartmeet."

Onkar's brows soared. He tossed chunks of dough to each of the men, and they murmured their agreement as Umed began mixing and measuring out new dough for the next round of loaves. The swindler settled his gaze on Aviama, then winked. And when she saw it, the spark in her chest burgeoned into flame.

The somber tone of a funeral filled the room when Onkar clapped his hands and rubbed them together, a little puff of flour escaping from his hands as he did so. "I'll hear the story later, but we have work to do. We've got an hour before mess, gentlemen. Bhumi is late, so she is our mark." Onkar waved his hand, and a gold medallion appeared between his index and middle fingers. He held it up. "Keep it moving and don't let her catch you passing it. The man—or woman—who impresses me the most by breakfast keeps the medallion."

15

———

Bhumi arrived half an hour later, anxious and flighty, reporting yelling coming from the captain's quarters and debate swirling on whether Aviama's actions had been admirable in standing up for one of their own, or fatally moronic, sending them to death. Grumbling and division spread among the men, some blaming melderbloods as a whole and advocating for any melders to be removed from the crew. Unrest was growing, and the legend of Ghosts' Gorge hanging over their heads was no comfort. Aviama took in the information, but kept her face as neutral as possible, asking no questions that could be misconstrued by her new colleagues.

By the time Bhumi arrived, the men had shown her how to manipulate the medallion with her index and middle fingers, or middle and ring fingers, for subtler motions rather than using a bulky thumb too short to dip smoothly into a pocket without being noticed. More than half the time, Aviama didn't notice when the medallion was passed, even to her. Manan or Jignesh would nudge her or glare at her behind Bhumi's back until she searched her pockets, bread dough, or the materials before her on the worktable to find the medallion already in her possession and ready for the next drop.

The day passed quickly as they prepped bread and salted beef for the morning, and took an inventory of the fish, grain, beef, pork, fresh water, and coal in the kitchen. Onkar took copious notes in a journal and set the journal up on the high shelf next to the door, explaining how much they could store at a time and what the minimum storage should be for each item before bringing more up from the cargo hold. Aviama's ears perked up at this. Onkar had somehow surrounded himself exclusively with melders, and melders who were all already pupils for pickpocketing or other questionable shenanigans. As head cook of the ship, he had full control over the food supply, came and went with little oversight from anyone else, not to mention access to the entirety of the cargo deck. Aviama could only shake her head. Genius.

The more time she spent with Onkar and the men in the kitchen, the more questions she had. If he only planned to take their money and run, why bother embroiling himself on a dangerous sea voyage with volatile killers, alongside the people he swindled? On the other hand, if he had been operating in good faith, wouldn't he have landed them passage on another vessel rather than a warship headed for Ghosts' Gorge? And if Chenzira and Aviama had only moved up their timeline on the night of their departure, how did he beat them to the ship dock with his position as cook already established?

Bhumi finally noticed the medallion when Aviama fumbled her pass to Umed, just as the first wave of crew began trickling in for breakfast. Onkar awarded Manan the medallion while the room was full, without a man outside the kitchen crew noticing the exchange. It was clear the man knew what he was doing. But what Aviama couldn't figure out was why he was doing it.

Aviama hid in the kitchen all day, avoiding any duty that would take her to the officers' mess or anywhere on the upper deck where she might run into Shiva. By the time she left, night was falling, the last of the magna had worn off, and she'd managed to roll extra beef and bread rolls in a napkin and stuff them into her pockets.

The light chill of evening nipped at her skin, but the thought of seeing Chenzira brought warmth to her bones. Right until she ran into two armed guards at the base of the stairs.

The first man stiffened the moment he saw her. "Not a chance."

Aviama cleared her throat to cover the tremor that washed over her. She waved him off. "Relax. I'm working for the cook. Just checking inventory."

"Uh huh."

The second man put a hand on the hilt of his sword. "Look, I don't care what you do. You're just not getting past this door, okay?"

Aviama peered around him into the dark. The lamp swung from outside the guard door, but its light was too weak to see into the last brig cell. A rustling noise from the darkness told her Chenzira was still imprisoned there. He could probably see her, even though she couldn't see him. She swallowed.

"I don't want any trouble. What crime have I committed except to exist in the world as a melder and visit a friend? And because of that—and because someone managed to steal from the prince, or so he says—the prince decided to kill someone. Does that make sense to you? Does that sound like the actions of a reasonable person?"

The first guard puffed out his chest. "We're not here to chat. You said you had inventory. Get to it."

Aviama held up her hands. "As you say."

She turned away from the men and walked down the cargo deck, the waning light of the oil lamp dropping away until she was covered in shadow. Aviama hid behind the first stack of crates and dug her hands into her pockets to pull out the napkin of food for Chenzira. She unwrapped the food from the napkin, stuffed the napkin back in her pocket, and waited. Three minutes. Four.

Footsteps alerted her that one of the guards walked back into the guardroom. Aviama peeked around the crates. The second guard still stood by the door. Well, her idea wouldn't break any of the rules. She wouldn't be passing the door. A thrill ran through her at her little rebellion, and she summoned trickles of air to her hand. Pulling gently from the air around her, Aviama buoyed up the ball of food in her hands and floated it over her head.

She grinned. Not bad. Aviama tested the movement of it this way and that in the air over her head. A few escaped crumbs fell on her face, but the rest remained aloft. Higher it went until the meal was just a hair beneath the ceiling. Aviama directed the air to carry it over the guard's head, down between the cells, and into Chenzira's cell at the end.

The wind followed her command with a soft *whoosh*. The oil lamp went out. The guards exclaimed, and a grunt came from the brig.

"I thought you refreshed the oil."

"I did."

Aviama winced at her mistake, but she still couldn't help the smile tugging at her lips as the guards fumbled for more oil and she slipped further into the dark of the cargo hold.

Crates and barrels filled the hull everywhere she turned. Twice she knocked into something as she walked, teaching her to slow down and keep her hands in front of her as she went. She should have thought to bring a lamp. Too bad she wasn't a fireblood.

Konnolan had no scent before it was lit, that she knew of. And with a cargo deck this size, in the dark, there was no way she'd be able to find it. Aviama had thought Shiva would have it guarded somewhere, but there were no lights for guards.

And then she saw it, down at the end. An orange flicker swaying with the ship. Aviama's heart leaped. She picked up her pace.

Something shifted under her feet, and she gasped as she flailed her feet over it in a sort of stumbling half-shuffle, half-jump. Her stomach dropped, and she froze. The guards would have heard that noise. Onkar was right. She had no subtlety.

Chameleon, Aviama. Biscuits.

But no yell demanded she announce herself. No heavy boots came marching to accost her. So she pressed onward, hands in front of her, with soft, slow, deliberate steps.

Her hands found smooth wood thicker around than her torso, rooted to the floor and rising higher above her than she could reach. The pole of one of the masts. Large barrels were stacked on either side, leaving only a narrow aisle to walk. Aviama brushed between them, the smell of salt and ale, turpentine and linseed oil filling her nostrils as she went. The air was dank, lit only by the slowly increasing orange glow of the lamp ahead.

Knots knit together in her stomach as she continued onward, the glow growing brighter with each step. Aviama felt in her pockets, but all she had was the napkin she'd wrapped Chenzira's supper in. She should have snatched a knife from the kitchens. But where would she safely sheath a knife on her body? Her arms were bare, covered only by the goosebumps gifted to her by the chill of night, and the top she wore was too fitted to hide anything. A knife would only rip up her pockets if she stowed one there, probably ripping free and dropping against her legs at the most inconvenient moment.

Still, as her heart beat in double time and her breathing quickened, she wished she had more than the wind at her disposal. The wind was strong, but if she used it, Shiva would know she hadn't downed the magna dose. Or he'd think it wasn't enough and triple it.

Aviama hugged the barrel stacks as she approached the light at the front of the ship's cargo hold. A space the width of the ship had been cleared, with several stacks of barrels on the far side. Two gently swaying oil lamps flanked the space, and a guard stood under each one. And in the center was the siren, in her watery cage, lazily twirling a long strand of her alabaster white hair around her finger.

Makana.

One of the guards glanced at their charge in her watery enclosure, and when he did, Aviama noticed something stuffed in his ears. Wax.

Was it Shiva who was so terrified of her, or the sailors themselves? Maybe Samud?

But what made them feel safer from Makana also made them dead to the world for any noise Aviama might make. Aviama leaned against the stack of crates to one side, testing its sturdiness. Yes, that would do. She slipped to the far side, as far away from the guards' line of sight as she could manage, and clambered up the crates toward the barrels hanging from the ceiling.

The wood creaked slightly under her weight. She winced. But the guards made no sound, so Aviama continued her climb. The rough wood alternated under her fingertips with the smooth metal latches fastening each crate. Aviama reached up to stabilize herself, grasping at the rim of a hanging barrel. Her foot slipped.

Aviama's heart lurched to her throat as she plummeted back to the top crate. Beyond her, water sloshed, and one of the guards yelled. Aviama froze. She hung half on, half off the top crate. Her elbow ached where it had slammed down on the wooden surface beneath her.

Don't look, idiot. If you do, they'll see you.

But if she didn't, she'd never know if they were coming for her. Aviama's mouth went dry. As stupid as it was, she couldn't bear the not knowing. She craned her neck over the top of the crate.

Makana flipped around in the water and slammed her tail against the surface of the water, dousing the guard with another splash. He put his hand on the hilt of his sword, but wasn't dumb enough to use it. He slammed his hand against the glass instead, a posturing gesture to accomplish absolutely nothing.

"By the gallows, cut it out! If you empty that box of yours, you've got no guarantees it'll get refilled. Long journey ahead, Siren."

Makana rotated and rose, reaching her hands up to grasp the bars so that her head and shoulders crested the surface. The guard stumbled back and reset his position, clenching his jaw as he scooted just a hair further from the mermaid than he had been before. As soon as his back was turned, Makana looked up at Aviama, her lavender gaze piercing through the dark. The hint of a smile played at her lips.

Aviama shook her head and smiled back. "Covering my tracks, as always. Thank you."

Makana raised and lowered herself on the bars, and Aviama marveled at the siren's muscled arms. Considering the heft of her long tail, if she didn't let her muscled fishtail assist, her arms must be strong as an ox. What had she done to maintain her strength in the menagerie, other than occasionally choking people with braided seaweed?

"Tabeun sister. What news?"

Aviama propped her chin up on her hands as she lay across the top of the highest crate, maybe a meter over the guards' heads, as she peered down into Makana's box. "Shiva's got some sort of map with information on Ghosts' Gorge, and the ship is headed there now. Actually, he lost the map. Which he's very angry about. But he seems to still have his heading without it."

Makana's eyes narrowed. "Who have?"

"I stole it, but someone else took it. I think I can get it back, but it will take time. My engagement with Shiva is off, but he hasn't killed me yet and wants me on board anyway. What do you know?"

"Key and sea. Konnolan hurt Iolani. Controlled tabeun maybe hurt Iolani. Poison ocean. War at home. I prisoner of war."

Aviama's mouth parted, and her gut wrenched. "At war with who? Radha? I thought Radha didn't stand a chance against the Iolani. Where is home? Is the Gorge home?"

Makana curled her lip into a snarl. "Gorge gateway. Protect home. Protect children. Radha rats try take children."

"He's kidnapping siren children?"

Makana leveled her a cool stare. "Try. Fail. Yet." She curled her pewter tail and rotated in the water, revealing a long scar along her shimmering scales. "Me, get. Children, no."

Aviama gasped, and a rotting, cringing feeling set in on her chest as realization hit. "He's trying to steal Iolani children. To control the sirens and have access to their power."

Makana gave a nod. "Dahnuk campaign. Many years. Many tries. They kill, but me first take."

"Of course. The king started it, and Shiva has doubled

down. So. They've killed your people before, but never managed to take an Iolani alive until now. Ugh."

The mermaid's mouth tugged down into a frown. She dropped down into the water again, resting her arms, then propelled herself up out of the water with her tail, flipping to float on her back, keeping herself afloat with the slow, constant movement of her arms and tail. Makana stared up at Aviama. "Need hope. Radha cannot have key. You are key."

Aviama nodded. "I hear you. I know. I'm working on it—a way to keep him from using melderbloods. Do you know where he keeps the konnolan and magna?"

Makana shook her head. "Not see."

"That's fine. We'll figure it out." Aviama paused. "Thank you. I'll try to come visit again." She turned away and started scooting down from the crate, when Makana's crystal voice called out again, soft and clear as a glassy sea.

"Sister?"

Aviama pulled herself back up and peered back over the edge of the topmost crate. "Yes?"

Makana winced, then took a deep breath. She rose up out of the water again, her hands holding fast to the bars above her. When she spoke, a sadness etched every line of her stunning face. "Come sing. When can."

Aviama tried to swallow, but found a lump wedged in her throat. Tears stung at her eyes. She blinked them back. "I will."

An ache set in her chest and dragged at her feet as Aviama slowly descended the crates and receded back through the darkness of the cargo hold. The loneliness Makana must feel, with no one in the world to talk to, to understand her, to be near—how ice cold her world must be. As hopeless and helpless as Aviama had felt, Makana must feel that weight threefold. And now, on a ship of two hundred men bent on destroying her people and her home, Aviama alone could take action to stop them.

But what could one girl do? Even with her powers, Durga and the other unidentified melders on board were a chaos volcano just waiting to erupt. Chenzira had strength and control, but his tabeun power was over the land, and there was no land at sea. Besides, with konnolan in Shiva's control, there was little left to be said. Her powers were worthless against it.

Resolve hardened in her heart. No, the swindler was right. It was not the ciraba that would win against this beast. It was the chameleon.

Like the Radhan queen with her secret spiders, running along her underground web to bring her news and do her bidding, Aviama would spin her own silk and make her own allies. She would find the konnolan and destroy it. And as for thieves and grifters?

Aviama would become the best of the best.

16

———————

By the time Aviama returned to her room, she'd nearly forgotten that Shiva had had her room tossed. But considering she hadn't come on board the *Wraith-weaver* with anything but the clothes on her back, there was little to toss. She righted the chair by her desk, stuffed the extra blankets and spare men's tunic back into the chest of drawers, closed the rest of the drawers that had been left haphazard, open, and empty, and collapsed into bed.

Little reason existed to leave the drawers open beyond intimidation. Nothing had been in there to begin with, so there was little shock value in finding them empty, and anything that could be rectified with ten seconds of returning the drawers to their places could not have been that bad to begin with. Empty papers from the desk floated about the room for no apparent reason. In the morning, Aviama snatched a pen from the desk, scratched out a note, and dropped it in one of the drawers.

It would be a shame if this drawer was empty twice in a row. I hope this makes searching my room feel more productive for you.

She grinned as she closed the drawer once again and grabbed another piece of paper.

Dream away, oh dream away—
There's nothing here to find today.

Aviama stuffed this one inside her pillowcase. That would do. She had more important work to attend to.

Showing up for work in the kitchens with Onkar, Bhumi, and the rest of the kitchen crew became as normal as breathing. Days wore on, and every day Aviama went to the kitchens at daybreak, avoided Shiva and Durga as much as she could, and devoted herself to the making of bread and burglary.

As it turned out, one of the other four melder sailors, Jignesh, had worked with Onkar before. He said he'd worked in Onkar's bakery before they came on board the *Wraithweaver* when a sudden illness prevented the cook that had been slotted for the voyage out of commission. Aviama tried not to roll her eyes. Black market grifter in his network on shore. Got it. She wondered if the original cook's illness had involved a knife in the back, or something more sophisticated.

After watching Aviama for several days, a sort of rhythm developed. Whenever Durga came to the kitchens, Manan would take over Aviama's duties with a soft, "Tornado comin', ma'am."

Aviama would turn away wordlessly, busying herself toward the back of the room, while the guys filled the space between her and Durga. She'd tried to peacock her puffed chest out the first day, but one look at Umed's broad muscular build blocking her path—and the slashed mark on his wrist identifying him as a melder—kept her from making any confrontation attempts in the kitchens.

Shiva started meeting Aviama in the mornings as she left

her room, delivering her magna himself and watching her take it before she started work for the day. She took it dutifully and without a word, then passed the flask back to him and headed for the kitchens. He tried speaking to her a time or two, but she only stared back at him while he was talking, and walked off when he was done. Each evening, she would take a small bundle of food down to the brig and waft it over the guards' heads and into Chenzira's cell when the magna wore off.

Since the night she'd slept against the bars of the brig with Chenzira, her dreams had started to shift. She still had nightmares some nights. Twice she woke screaming from her bed, and once Shiva had stormed into her room, hair mussed, arm raised with a sword.

She'd recovered enough to wave him off, but it took all she had not to spit back, *"Don't worry yourself. I dreamed of you."*

Of course, she also dreamed of the dead. Of her mother. Her father. Of Sona, or those on board she cared for that weren't dead yet, but might be soon. But she'd also started to have pleasant dreams. The warmth of Chenzira's arms. Snarky comments under his breath as he caught her up in his arms and whisked her away to anywhere—anywhere at all away from Shiva and Radha and the terror of causing destruction to Jannemar and the Iolani.

Aviama saw little of Sai in those first couple of weeks, but she did pull her aside to tell her the news of what had happened to her parents. Sai had bitten her lip, shook her head, and told her it was just another of Shiva's games. That her parents were fine; she had received a letter from them after those initial konnolan explosions.

"Was it in their handwriting, or did they use a scribe?"

Sai had shaken her head at Aviama's question, thanked

Aviama for telling her, and turned away—wiping a tear from her eye as she did. Aviama didn't know how to confirm something so monumental with only a manipulative snake for a source, so she let her go.

After two weeks in the kitchens, Onkar started sending them on small missions to steal little things here and there for practice. The joker of a card deck. Dice. Something carved. An extra tunic. Aviama started frequenting the upper deck for excuses to be out and about from the kitchens so her movements wouldn't seem out of place when she tried to snatch something, but the fresh air did her good too. The open sky, the ocean spreading out before her. Little brought balm to her soul but the salt of the air and the wind on her face.

Until the day she made a perfect lift.

She stood at the worktable at the height of the midday rush, when the day shift crew came in greatest numbers. Laksh passed her plate after plate, and Aviama smiled and nodded at sailors whose faces she'd come to know over the past few weeks. One of them lifted a bread roll in salute to her as he passed, and Peg winked in line after him. *They're starting to like you,* he seemed to say. She grinned, dusted invisible lint from his shoulder, and used the distraction to slip an extra roll into his pocket. As fun as taking harmless items could be, unexpected generosity was her favorite way to use her new skill.

This one was a bit dangerous, perhaps, as it might show her slippery hand, as it were. But Peg was always smiling, always humming some off-key tune, always giving her a nod and a nudge and subtly pointing out which people hated her guts and which ones were friendly. Whenever he arched an eyebrow and tipped his head at someone, she worked twice as hard to win over that sailor. As her confidence increased,

Aviama left the line to sit with sailors and talk for a spell here and there before and after the rush times, asking them about themselves and their lives, hoping to see their humanity—and for them to see hers, and acknowledge it when the time came to choose her life or her death.

Aviama scanned the room. The weekend nightshift guard was playing a betting game with the helmsman and one of the guards she'd seen with Makana. They were talking myths and legends while rolling two dice to play the game. Bhumi had her eyes set on a mark, and she was making her way over with a tray of ale. No off-duty seaman had turned her down yet.

"Daydreaming again, birdie?"

Aviama snapped her attention back to the man in front of her. His gray beard reeked of ale, and his half-closed eyelids and sagging aged skin with pits under his eyes begged for a few days' sleep. Or maybe a week's sleep and an alcohol detox.

"I don't daydream."

"Aye, you do, and I bet I know what about." He snickered at her, and she slid a plate across the table to him.

She spread her hands. "You caught me. I was dreaming someone would come and read my mind. How'd you know?"

"I got a sixth sense." The man took a swig from his flask— a marvel the thing was not empty already—and dropped it on the cord by his belt.

"Mhmm."

Laksh spun another plate of salted beef across the long table in her direction, and she caught it. "Roll!"

Jignesh threw her a bread roll from the basket across the room and she snatched it out of the air, dropped it onto the plate, and slid it to the next man in line. Umed filled a glass to the brim and Aviama passed it to the next man in line but nudged it just enough as Ale Beard lingered by the edge of the table. The glass tipped over, spilling its contents on the older man.

"Hey!"

"So sorry!" Aviama snatched two cloth napkins, dove under the table, and popped up on the other side, dabbing at the man's wet clothes and mopping up the floor. "My hand slipped."

Ale Beard swatted her away and snatched his plate off the table. "Keep yer daydreamin' for yer own time, then, birdie!"

Aviama dipped her head. "I'll be more careful, I promise."

Umed filled the gap she'd left, passing the next plates on through the line of sailors. Three tables down, the dice rolled again. Bhumi cleared an empty plate, lingering to watch the game—and the dice—an extra moment. Aviama dabbed at her face and walked over.

"Griffons and sphinxes! You're as daft as Peg. They're fairy tales."

The helmsman.

Makana's guard shook his head. "The siren's real enough. So's the Gorge, I reckon. How else do you explain all the lost ships? All the unregistered ships sailing in that direction, from the port closest to the palace?"

"Couldn't help but overhear." Aviama plopped down on an empty chair and dropped her chin in her hand, watching the dice land on a six and a three. "I thought hyland trolls were a myth too, until I saw two of them with my own eyes."

The nightshift guard's eyes bugged out. "Hyland trolls?"

Aviama nodded and raised two fingers. "Two of them."

The helmsman's eyes narrowed. "Hyland trolls aren't so new. They just aren't known in Radha. Griffons and sphinxes are different."

"Sure, of course. Hyland legends are reliable, and Mox's

fairy tales should be treated like history, but *griffons!*" Aviama put a hand to her chest. "Say it isn't so!"

The guards laughed, and one elbowed the helmsman with a smirk. Bhumi offered the helmsman a refill of ale, and when she took his empty glass, only one die was left to roll. The men didn't seem to notice.

"Aye, the Gorge is real enough, Princess." The helmsman leaned forward across the table and tapped the wood with his finger. "No arena. No boyfriend. No baby trolls from the king's exotic collection of cute little pets. Just you, the open ocean, and a cliff of rocks for the demons of the deep to dash your scrawny little body across."

The nightshift guard swallowed, and Makana's sentry shifted uncomfortably.

Aviama snapped her open mouth shut, but the concern on her face was enough to encourage the man to continue. "They want nothing more than the destruction of all human flesh. They consume humans as a delicacy, and their women prey on sailors with their death lullabies and bring the bodies back to their nests."

Bhumi floated off, and Aviama shook her head and stood, leaning forward on the table until her face was close with the helmsman. "If you know so much about sirens, tell me—what other powers do mermaids hold with their song?"

The helmsman frowned, but the other two guards were laser-focused on her face.

"They have no other powers with their song. Only to kill and destroy. Maybe to strengthen the storm of the male sirens, the whirlwinds they stir up in the clouds. Or maybe the males do that all on their own."

Aviama hesitated. She hadn't known the male sirens could cause windstorms. Death lullabies from murderous sirens paired with windstorms smashing the *Wraithweaver* against the rocks did not sound promising. "Then why did a siren save my life—twice? Why did she sing with me?"

The helmsman opened his mouth, then shut it, and paused. Aviama left him to ponder the question, turning on her heel and moving back to where Bhumi was pulling down a fresh bag of flour as the two guards broke into an argument over what she'd said.

Manan glanced at her as she passed him, his mouth only twisting with contained mirth as she squeezed Bhumi on the arm in an affectionate half-hug before offering her a hand with the flour. Aviama caught his eye and shot him a dark look, and he sobered, but she could hardly contain the thrill than ran through her own body. Biscuits, she'd really done it.

She busied herself with baking fresh bread and tidying up plates and tables, waiting until the last of the men finished lunch and sauntered out slower, happier, and several pounds heavier than they'd been when they walked in. The footsteps of the last man receded down the hall, and Onkar rapped the worktable with his knuckles.

"Pay up, friends. What do you have for me today?"

Aviama's heart beat wildly, her fingers brushing the object in her pocket ever so gently to reassure herself that it was still there as Umed produced three gold coins. Manan had been charged with an information-gathering goal, and he reported that the guard schedules would be changing every Tuesday, and dissent against Shiva's paranoid requirements was growing. Jignesh revealed a shark-tooth necklace.

Bhumi was next. Aviama's breathing ticked up a notch as she reached into her sash. She paused, then gasped as she pulled out Ale Beard's silver flask.

Onkar frowned. "The flask was Aviama's take. Yours was dice."

Bhumi stared at the flask in her hands. "I—I took dice. From the helmsman. I didn't take this."

All heads swiveled toward Aviama. Heat flushed her cheeks. Aviama reached into her pocket and placed the stolen die on the table, and silence fell over the kitchen like a blanket.

17

————

Onkar stared at the die on the table, and for a moment Aviama hardly dared to breathe. The swindler raised his gaze to Aviama, and a grin broke out across his face. "Gold and gumption, she's done it."

A cheer went up, and Jignesh tossed a handful of flour into the air. Aviama's chest filled with pride, and she let out a relieved sigh all in a rush as Laksh broke into song with the sea shanty she'd become familiar with over the past weeks. The others joined in, clapping along the rhythm, and Bhumi grabbed her by the arm and spun her in a circle. Jignesh hooked his elbow in hers, whirled her round, and passed her off to Umed, who slung her round and caught her opposite arm in the crook of his elbow in another turn as the song grew.

Heave away, haul away
On to my lady mistress
Heave away, haul away
On to my lady mistress

My missus back on shore
Told me I should stay at home
She'll knock me to be sure
But it's better on the roam

The bottom of my bottle
Made some promises to me
It told me I'd be happy
If I drowned myself at sea

Heave away, haul away
On to my lady mistress
Heave away, haul away
On to my lady mistress

Manan tossed another handful of flour in the air as Umed spun her round again and tossed her off to Bhumi. A giggle bubbled up in Aviama's throat until she full on snort-laughed at Bhumi's antics, stamping and clapping. The men joined the two girls as they clapped and sang, stomping out the beat in a circle before rushing in toward the center, making a turn, and dancing back out again as the lyrics bounced along the jaunty tune.

The harlot on the dock
Said she'd take me to the sky
But I missed my ocean blue
So I told her bye, goodbye

The siren sang her song
And she nearly got my soul
But the whisper on the wind
Said her love is deep as shoal

> *Heave away, haul away*
> *On to my lady mistress*
> *Heave away, haul away*
> *On to my lady mistress*

A peal of laughter escaped Aviama's lips as they hooked elbows again, taking turns looping this way and that. The song grew, and when she looked up again, a crowd had gathered at the door, and several men were shoving tables out of the way to make a space in the center of the room.

> *Oh, the pull of lady mistress*
> *Has a deeper call to me*
> *The pull of lady mistress*
> *Is the calling of the sea*
>
> *Heave away, haul away*
> *On to my lady mistress*
> *Heave away, haul away*
> *On to my lady mistress*

Warmth burst from her chest, and the flow of power in her veins bumped up against its magna restraints like a wave on the shore, begging to be let free, but not quite able to break the spell of the sea. She threw her head back and laughed, only barely managing to join in for the next verse of the song. Laksh sang out in a rich tenor she never would have expected from the surly man, and the men's voices rose and repeated the chorus with gusto.

The floorboards shook under their feet, and as the men drowned out the sounds of the ship, Aviama let her own voice twine through the verses, dancing through the harmonious notes she found as she went, weaving above and below the melody. It wasn't until the last chorus that she noticed the men around her singing less, and more eyes drawn to her as she sang.

The song died out, and the room erupted in whoops and hollers. Aviama threw herself down on a chair, breathing in gasps and grinning like a child. Who would have thought she'd find joy, not in the palace she'd been sent to, but as a hostage, in the kitchens of an enemy ship? She could only shake her head at the absurdity of it all.

And then Onkar Dhoka approached her, the swindler who'd had the gall to speak to her at all after taking her money and allowing her kidnapping—the black market cheat whose mere name was a lie. He mopped the sweat on his brow with a cloth, and it took her a moment to realize what he'd just done. The cloth he'd used was the map. He'd shown her the map, the reason she was learning to steal, the ultimate test and challenge of her skill, in a room full of people.

Her lips parted, but as quickly as it appeared, it was gone. How did he do it? Where had he stashed it? And most importantly, how could she get it?

She moved to the edge of her seat, but something about the blithe way he glided forward reminded her of a time and a place beyond the sea entirely. She stood on instinct, and Onkar tilted his head with a knowing look.

He tossed something shiny to Jignesh, and he caught it. "Sing a ballad, Laksh."

Jignesh played a few test notes with his mouth against a small hand-sized instrument, an earthenware item the size of his palm with holes across its surface, and Laksh nodded and suggested some tune or other to Jignesh.

Onkar bowed and offered his hand to her, the perfect cotillion to invite her to dance. "Do me the honor, Your Highness. Let's show these uncouth rascals how it's done."

Aviama took his arm, and he led her into the center of the kitchen floor. His arm slid to her upper back, and her hand moved to his shoulder, their free hands meeting together as Laksh began to sing in a language she had never heard before. Onkar moved her through the dance, and he proved to be a marvelous dancer, quick on his feet, placing her precisely where he wanted her to go—giving just enough direction that she might pick up on his intention, and flow into the motion like rose petals loosed on a gentle breeze.

He smiled, and she returned the gesture. Onkar lifted his arm, and she spun under it, sneaking a glance at his jacket as she rotated through the twirl. The man wasn't wearing a jacket like he had been in Boar Tooth Tavern. Where could he manage hidden pockets to hold the map? All he ever carried was a compass hooked to his beltloop, a coin pouch too small to hold her prize, and a simple black leather belt cinching the tunic at his waist.

Onkar spun her back to him and pulled her in so his breath tickled her ear. "You're a woman of royal birth. You learned to dance like the men here learned to brawl. You learned by *doing* until your body knew more than your head. Dance, Rookie. Dance in mystery. Dance in shadows. Become an *artist*, darlin'."

The two of them stepped and swirled through another verse of Laksh's stunningly clear tenor vibrato before he made an excuse to bring her in close again.

"Nice work today, Rookie. Now the real fun begins."

She rotated away in another spin, then whirled back to him on light feet, ducking under his arm as she moved, and—there. There, peeking out from the edge of his belt, almost hidden under the coin pouch at his side. The corner of a painted cloth. The inside of the belt somehow held the map. Was it hollow? Were there hooks holding it on the underside of the leather? How did he get it out and replace it so fast without anyone else noticing its significance?

Aviama smiled again. "Thank you." And she meant it.

"Chameleon, missy. You're changing colors, and it shows. New skills, new personas. But don't forget, true luxury is the freedom to be yourself and find acceptance under your own name. You might yet manage to do both."

Aviama cocked her head. The statement was out of place from her normal training regimen. It was something her old mentor Frigibar might have said, and Onkar was a far cry from the nobler character of the older man living on the outskirts of Ellix back home. "What acceptance have you found under your name? Your *real* name?"

Onkar let the music fill the silence between them for a measure, then sucked his teeth in a grimacing manner less gentile than the formality of the dance might have required. "None, Rookie. That's how I know it's a luxury."

Something in her gut wrenched at his words, and she stared at him, using his face as her spot to maintain her balance through a series of turns, watching the strange solemnity that settled there. What rejection had Onkar seen, and under what name?

They came together again, only for Onkar to send her spinning away from him again, hard. Hard enough that she lost her grip on him and went sailing off to one side, only barely keeping her footing as she careened off the floor— straight into a solid chest and a pair of strong arms.

"Hey there, Tally."

Chenzira caught her at the waist as she collided with him. He lifted her off her feet and whirled her in a low circle before setting her gingerly on her feet. Aviama gaped up at him. His dark beard was longer than she remembered, but not unkempt, and a clean white tunic draped his muscled frame, paired with pants that had seen better days. But his eyes—what a far cry from the harshness she'd seen in them in the pakshi courtyard beneath her balcony all those weeks ago! Deep cinnamon eyes took her in with a tenderness that melted her insides like butter.

"Sand and sea, you're gorgeous."

Somewhere in her peripheral vision, Onkar nudged Laksh, and he picked up some fresh new melody as Jignesh played the small instrument in his hands. But as she looked at him, in his arms without bars, without magic, without an arena to fight through, her mouth went dry. Her stomach dropped. She wanted to throw her arms around his neck, to hold him close, to tell him how she'd thought of him every day the last month. That today was the first day she'd *really* laughed, and that she'd wished it had been with him.

But she said nothing. Biscuits, he was beautiful. He must think her so ridiculous, gaping at him like a fish out of water.

Suddenly she became aware of the fact that sailors were crammed in the kitchen like sardines, watching them. Aviama swallowed and straightened, smoothing the overskirt flowing out from the belt at her waist and dividing in the center to reveal the loose, beautifully patterned trousers beneath. She pulled away, heart slamming into her ribs like a battering ram, but she couldn't bring herself to tear her gaze away from his face.

Chenzira bowed low, took her hand in his, and kissed her knuckles. His warm lips against her skin sent a shot of warmth through her body. She hoped no one noticed the goosebumps popping up along her bare arm.

"May I?"

Aviama only managed to nod as Laksh's song lifted through notes bold and sweet, and Chenzira led her out into the open space of the kitchen once again. He slipped his hand to her upper back, and she dropped hers lightly on his shoulder, their free hands meeting in the position of the waltz just as the verse of Laksh's ballad began to swell.

Her feet found solace in the familiar, graceful steps. Someone on the sidelines let out a low whistle as they began to move together as one, like converging raindrops, or snow drifting aloft on a gentle wind. Chenzira was a marvelous dancer, better even than Onkar or Shiva had been. A smile tugged at the corner of his mouth.

"Struck you speechless, have I?"

"Don't get used to it."

His smile widened. "I think I'd like to do it again."

Heat flooded her cheeks, and she bit her lip. Aviama dropped her voice low. "I thought you needed the crew to see you in ... a certain light..."

"I don't care."

He moved her through a turn, and they separated only for a moment before coming close together again on the next beat. Aviama swallowed. "I—didn't expect to see you."

"Because, you know, the brig."

She nodded. "Bars and such."

"I was released."

"I mean, yes. I gathered."

He grinned. "Do you always talk so much when you dance?"

"No. Have you always loved dancing?"

Have you always loved dancing? She stifled an inward groan at her inane question and wondered why she didn't ask him literally anything else relevant. Or maybe she could have just shut her mouth and danced with the man.

Chenzira pulled her in a tight circle and lifted her off her feet. A gasp escaped her, and another small smile tugged at the corner of his lips. "No, but this is my favorite dance."

Aviama landed, breathless, and threw herself into the next steps to cover her embarrassment. Her cheeks were hot, and she could only imagine how red they might look. She cleared her throat. "What? The waltz?"

"No. This one. With you."

She opened her mouth to speak, but he gave a small shake of his head, that same little smile toying at his perfect mouth, and she closed it. And they danced.

The music grew, and Chenzira moved them through more technical, sweeping steps across the delicate space, moving her away and back again, an extension of his own arm one moment, and then two bodies close together again the next. For unknown blissful minutes, she knew nothing but Chenzira's arms, the smoothness of a stunning waltz, and the penetrating gaze of the man she'd most desired to see over these last weeks.

Aviama hardly noticed when the song died out, except that she was smiling and hadn't realized it—Chenzira at last came to a stop and offered her a low bow. She dropped into a deep curtsy in answer. And the room exploded in applause.

She scanned the room. Men filled every inch of the kitchens around the impromptu dance floor, with more peering over each other at the door. The worktables were swept clean of the day's stolen trinkets, and Umed dropped something into someone's pocket. With a start, she realized it was Ale Beard. They were returning what had been stolen.

Bhumi beamed from the edge of the circle, completely oblivious to Manan's soft glance. Laksh and Jignesh congratulated each other on their musicianship, smiling and clapping. On the other side of the circle, Peg gave a toothy grin and a nod.

Aviama gulped. "So much for keeping my head down."

Chenzira laughed. "When were you trying to blend in, exactly?"

Onkar slithered beside them just as the circle converged into a mass of bodies. "In a world of snores, be an artist, darlin'." He winked. "See you tomorrow. You're ready for the next phase of lessons."

Aviama nearly squealed, restraining herself just in time. "I'll be there." Her gaze drifted again over the gathered crew. Sai perched on the edge of one of the tables. The pain etched on her face hit Aviama like a slug to the gut. Just inside the door, Durga peered in with a sneer and a black look that made her skin crawl. Aviama started to turn away, but a flash of teal caught her eye. The warmth in her chest from the dance, the joviality of her success in the take, all dissipated like smoke. Captain Samud. The teal headwrap towered over the rest of the men craning their necks into the kitchens, and his glare turned her blood to ice.

Her mouth went dry. A pit formed in her stomach, and the smile vanished from her face. Whatever advantage Onkar was willing to teach her, she was willing to learn. She'd need it.

And if she only became more entrenched with cheats and swindlers to do it? So be it.

But what did Samud think of her causing a scene? And what would Shiva do to Chenzira once he heard about it?

18

Aviama waited for the crowd to dissipate and took the stairs up to the upper deck alone. The kitchen crew decided it was better to disperse and wait for the dust to settle before reconvening to prepare for supper. Onkar, as usual, was the last to leave. But Aviama would be the first to return.

Because though the map might be on his person, what were the chances Onkar didn't have other valuables hidden around somewhere? He slept somewhere on the gun deck with the rest of the crew, his belongings as exposed as anyone else's. If he were to hide valuables, they'd be in the kitchen, where he spent most of his time. She'd just waste some time in her room first, avoiding Shiva and Samud for a couple of hours before heading back.

Her breathing ticked up a notch as she emerged at the top of the stairs under the quarterdeck and pushed into the smaller kitchen reserved for Shiva, the captain, and select members of the crew. She could feel the eyes of the sailors on her back as she slipped out of the common area of the upper deck and pushed the door open to the kitchen.

The walk through the captain's kitchen on the way to her room always made her palms sweat. This time, it was empty. She breathed a sigh of relief. The last thing she needed was to run into Samud after the commotion he'd regarded with such displeasure.

A painted cloth map lay on the table, with a mug of something steaming set beside it. Someone was coming back any minute. Aviama stared at the map as she strode through the kitchen, her steps slowing as she passed it.

She glanced down at it. The map was standard, with a small carved ship marking the *Wraithweaver*'s progress. Radha's shores, well behind them. Jannemar's coast, still two months' journey from their current position, when one factored in the detour every ship took to avoid Ghosts' Gorge. How quickly could Radha get to Jannemar if they had control of that passage? If the fear of the Gorge didn't keep them away?

A vague area was marked off with a whirlpool and lightning illustration, with no written designation at all. The *Wraithweaver* was headed straight toward it. Aviama's stomach dropped. They were far closer to it than she'd imagined. She was no sailor, but if it took them a month to get to this point—what was that, just weeks away from the Gorge? How accurate was the generic whirlpool illustration as to the Gorge's placement?

"You sure are getting around."

Aviama sucked in a breath and jerked her head up. Durga sneered at her from the door. The morning's magna dose still coursed through Aviama's veins, the windcalling magic swirling uselessly in her blood, ignoring her calls.

Durga sent a light breeze through the room, reveling in the exclusivity of her power. "You think anyone really likes you, Princess? You think anyone really *trusts* you? A dance here, a song there, and you'll escape what's coming?"

Aviama clenched her jaw. "I don't expect anyone to trust me without cause."

"What cause could you give them? The rogue foreign melderblood, the one whose family dumped chaos into our world after hundreds of years. The one who came to seek the hand of the prince in bad faith, betraying Radha." Durga laughed. "Bhumi might be stupid enough to be wrapped around your finger, but even Sai has been distant, hasn't she?"

Aviama tilted her head, ignoring Durga's wind playing with the ends of her hair. The girl was wild. If she got too upset, her lack of control could blow the door off its hinges. But then, if she *did* destroy the captain's kitchen, would Samud demand that Shiva doses Durga with magna as well?

"You're right. Sai has been distant. I don't blame her. If I had to sleep as close to you as she does, I would spiral too."

The wind rose, then Durga dropped her hand, and it cut off abruptly. Her expression hardened. "You ruined my life. Just as you ruined Sai's."

Aviama swallowed. Knots formed in her stomach, and a chill ran down her spine at the intensity of her tone. But if she was going to win against Durga, she'd have to let Durga's temper best her—and keep her own in check. Aviama ran her finger along the Jannemari coast on the map. Several circular markers sat just beyond the whirlwind illustration. Was that Shiva's waiting fleet? How many ships were there? She scooted the markers askew and rotated the carved ship a hair.

"I haven't done anything to you but save your life."

"Save my *life*?"

Aviama shrugged. "You tried to keep me from leaving the palace, and I blasted you over the terrace wall. You were about as precise with your power then as a toddler throwing a rock.

How did you survive that? Oh, that's right. Me. I saved you. I pulled you back. And I sent you back inside the palace. And locked the door. How'd you get out after that? Oh, that's right. You didn't. You had to go get a key or something, didn't you?"

Durga's face flushed red. She took a step forward and crossed her arms. "You just don't have what it takes to do what needs doing."

"Ahh. You'd respect me more if I had killed you, is that it? Does killing people make you strong, or make you too weak to manage a living person?" Aviama shook her head and pursed her lips. "The queen isn't happy with you, and now you're working for Shiva. How's that going? Do you feel happier? Safer? Have your prospects improved, or are you just another melderblood under his thumb—a toy for his very own menagerie?"

Durga lifted her chin, but the mug of steaming liquid trembled on the table as a fresh wind zig-zagged its way helter-skelter through the room. "I am to be the captain of the elite melderblood guard. *You* will end up at the bottom of the ocean if I have anything to do with it."

Aviama shook her head. "I doubt you'll have much to do with anything. You dropped me on the sand before we boarded. How do you plan on training recruits? Why would anyone want to join under your leadership? Your winning personality?"

The girl's smirk faded into a scowl. "I saw Sai just this morning. She tried to defend your treacherous actions back in Radha. I told her *you* were the reason her parents are dead. I don't think you'll be gaining friends when they realize how much blood is on your hands—including one of their own. If it weren't for you, Sona would be alive."

Aviama froze. "You told her that?"

Durga flashed a wicked grin. "Yes."

"Today?"

She twirled a strand of her hair and tossed it over her shoulder. "Just before you made a fool of yourself making a scene in the main kitchen."

No wonder Sai had looked upset. Durga had just confirmed that her parents were dead. A pit formed in her stomach for her friend's pain. And yet, satisfaction settled in her chest at Durga's stupid mistake. Aviama steeled herself to keep a neutral expression and straightened. "Thank you for letting me know."

The door opened, and Durga jumped as Samud and Shiva strolled in together. Both of their faces were flint, hardening further at the sight of the two women. Aviama stepped back and smiled.

"Gentlemen. I'd hate to interrupt your meeting, so I'll be going. But if you'd like some company, Durga is becoming quite the conversationalist."

With that, she disappeared through the door opposite the men, down the short hall, turned the knob to her room, pushed open the door—and came face to face with Sai, waiting for her inside.

The girl's face was streaked with tears, her eyes red from weeping. She stared back at Aviama, a hollowness reflected in her eyes.

Aviama shut the door behind her and rushed forward, catching Sai in her arms as the girl reached out and collapsed into her. Sai's shoulders racked with sobs as they stood together, speechless, in the space of their grief. Aviama tried not to remember when she saw her mother die, the dearest person in the world to her staining the marble with her blood. She tried not to remember the explosion and seeing her father on the ground. The chaos, the shouting.

Semra disappearing to look for the assassin, risking her

life and opening up the chance of Aviama losing yet another soul close to her. Aviama running after her father, and being shut out from entry, as they worked to save him in a small room. Aviama had run after Semra then, down the hall, down the stairs, into the catacombs. She'd found her, half-dead and trapped in an opened, defiled sarcophagus.

Liben, on the ground with the hammer lying motionless next to his glassy eyes. Hardly more than a boy. Her first kill.

Sona, father of three.

Sai. Sai, whose parents were murdered by a maniac who saw human life as chattel.

Tears poured down her face. *Death, death, death.* Every heartbeat in her chest mocked her, a reminder of a life she bore, a life stolen from her loved ones.

Sai pulled back and wiped her face with her hands. "They're dead."

Aviama sniffled and nodded. "I know."

The girl wiped her face again. She bit her lip, then the worry and pain etched in her forehead eased—and her expression dropped to stone, like a chisel had been raked across it, chipping away every line. Her eyes hardened, and she swallowed.

"Teach me."

"What?"

"Teach me. You did it once. Do it again." Sai lifted her chin. "You need allies. You have them. You have me and Prince Chenzira. And I've seen you with the kitchen crew these last weeks. Every one of them is a melder. Teach us all."

Rap, rap. Aviama was startled at the sound of the sharp knocks on the door. Her heart leaped to her throat. She ushered Sai under her writing desk so she wouldn't be visible from the door—but if anyone came in, the ruse would be up.

Aviama cleared her throat and raised her voice. "If it's Durga, and you're here for tea, I don't have any."

"It's not Durga."

Worse, it was Shiva. She winced. Aviama walked to the door and cracked it open, blocking the narrow space. "I'm not in the mood for visitors."

Shiva's eyes were ice as he glared daggers into her soul, feet shoulders-width apart, arms crossed. "You interfered with the map."

Aviama shrugged. "I bumped the table. Honest mistake. Not to mention Durga letting wind roll through the captain's kitchen. Have you considered dosing her with magna as well? It doesn't seem like the brightest move to paralyze *my* powers but let hers run wild, when she's more likely to blow holes in the ship than anyone else on board. Did you see her on the dock?"

He arched an eyebrow. "You mean when she tossed you around like a rag doll?"

"No, when she *dropped* me. By *accident*. Accidents at sea are higher risk, wouldn't you say?"

"This is not what I came for."

"Have at it, Prince. What's the latest threat?"

"I'll allow you to work in the kitchens. It keeps you busy. But you have to keep your head down."

Aviama pursed her lips. He'd *allow* her to continue doing what she was already doing without permission, would he? How kind of him. She leaned into the door, her face in the sliver of space between the door's edge and the wall.

"If you're offended by the dancing, it wasn't my idea. And the men seemed to enjoy it. Don't you think a little respite from the doom hanging over us is good for them? A little joy, a moment of levity, as we sail to our deaths for you?"

Shiva glared at her, but said nothing. He shifted his weight.

"I told you, things don't have to be this way. We could have been partners. And Samud doesn't like the unexpected. You're a liability everywhere you go."

Aviama stiffened. Somewhere in the back of her mind, caution told her to keep her mouth shut—but by the time the thought formulated, it was too late. She was already talking. "I'll keep my head down, don't you worry. If it pleases Your Highness, I will occasionally breathe air on the upper deck, and will go about the duties assigned to me by the kitchen. Biscuits, I might sing a song to myself now and then, or join others when they sing. I will eat and sleep and sometimes even blink, in between mixing dough and prepping meals for the crew. What say you, Highness?"

Shiva's mouth formed a menacing snarl, and he stabbed a finger at her face. "I say that for all your sarcasm, you know that the worst thing you have are biting words. And the worst thing *I* have are the lives of Bhumi, Sai, and Chenzira. Sona was the tip of the iceberg. And if your attitude steps one hair beyond my profound tolerance for your insolence, I will give no warning. I will simply deliver someone's head to your door."

He disappeared, and Aviama shut the door. Memories of her bodyguard Enzo's decapitated head on a platter slammed into her like a sledgehammer, and a tremor rocked her body. *Death. Death.*

Every beat of her heart heralded the impending and inevitable eternal stop to hearts around her, like a drum growing louder and louder.

"Charming. I'm shocked you didn't want to marry him."

Aviama snort-laughed at Sai's commentary from under the desk, breaking the tension. She sighed. "He'll never stop. Not until we're all dead—or wish we were."

Sai twisted to get out from under the desk and hit her head on the side. The rattling sound came again. She paused. "Did you know there is a button here?"

Aviama dropped to the floor and crawled halfway under the desk next to Sai, craning her neck at the corner she indicated. A small carved circle she'd thought was part of the construction was hidden away on one side. Sai pressed it, and Aviama pulled at the drawer. It opened, but only the normal drawer slid out. Aviama slipped back out from under the desk, feeling along the side.

A thought hit her. "Press it again and hold it down." Sai acquiesced, and Aviama tugged the drawer open again. This time, a small white object tumbled out. Aviama gaped down at it.

It was a wood-carved mermaid, with intricate designs of the four tabeun elements working their way all through the tail: wind, fire, water, and earth. She ran her fingers over its smooth surface as Sai made her way out from under the desk.

"Wow. That's lovely."

"It's for me." *And Shiva would hate it, which means it was from an ally. Someone she knew already? Or someone new?* Aviama picked it up and turned it over, but no other hints presented themselves. "I just don't know who it's from."

"And they knew about the hidden compartment in your desk."

Aviama nodded, pondering.

Sai was right. Onkar might be teaching Aviama to be a chameleon, but she had skills to teach too. And they'd need all the help they could get—because once her team of thieves could control their powers, they were going to find and destroy the konnolan. And the magna.

Aviama straightened, a small smile creeping over her face.

She'd keep her head down, all right. Because that's what chameleons did. Blend in. And the moment Shiva thought he was safe, her melderblood insurrectionists would rise.

19

———————

Aviama waited two hours in her room with Sai, teaching Sai as much of tabeun magic as one could teach without demonstrating it, as the morning's magna was in full effect and wouldn't wear off until that night. After the two hours, Aviama checked that the coast was clear in the captain's kitchen, let Sai leave first, and set out for the main kitchen.

Not knowing how long they had until meeting up with Shiva's fleet and plunging into Ghosts' Gorge, there was no time to waste. Aviama mentally rehearsed her to-do list.

Learn thievery.

Teach tabeun magic.

Find out where the konnolan is.

Find out where the magna is.

Destroy them both without getting everyone killed.

Save Makana.

Stop Shiva.

Oh, right—and search the kitchens today before Onkar got back. Because he still had the map, and she needed secrets. Leverage. Anything.

None of her goals were particularly well fleshed out. The action steps were hazy on all of them. One decision she did make with Sai was that Sai would not work in the kitchens. Aviama would give her private lessons in the evening, when her magna dose had worn off, and they would stay away from each other during the day to keep up appearances that their relationship might have soured.

And maybe she could find Chenzira some evening too. Her stomach flopped, and a warmth spread through her chest at the thought. He'd been so forward when last they spoke. His arms around her, his eyes gazing down at her as they danced...

I won't let you marry him.

These precious words had kept her going when little else would. And now, the engagement was off, but with freedom still far beyond their grasp—death looming at every turn—it was Chenzira's face she dreamed of. It was Chenzira's presence she craved. And it was to Chenzira she wanted to tell all her worries and fears and celebrations.

Aviama slipped down the stairs to the gun deck, down the hallway, and into the kitchen. All was quiet. She scanned the shelves, the crates along the wall, the sacks of flour, salt, and other preservatives. Three jars lined the top shelf on the end. It had been weeks, and they'd never used them. Hiding something in plain sight was definitely up Onkar's alley. And now, with the secret compartment in her desk, she probably needed to make a thorough search of the worktables too. Maybe even the shelves and the furnace.

Glancing this way and that, Aviama shoved a crate over to the wall and stepped on it to reach up to the jars on the shelf.

"Careful, Rookie."

Aviama gasped, nearly falling off the crate as she turned to Onkar. "Biscuits. Do you *have* to sneak up on people?"

Onkar shrugged as he leaned against the kitchen door,

arms folded, examining her snooping. "I don't have to. But it's both more fun and more informative when I do."

Aviama grimaced. "Yes, well, don't get any ideas. I'm checking inventory on salt."

"We did that yesterday. We've got enough for a week without restocking from cargo."

"Right. Well, you never know." Aviama stepped down from the crate and smoothed out her skirt. She spun her rings.

Onkar arched an eyebrow. "Next time you want to stick your nose where it doesn't belong, make sure you have a decent cover story *before* you get caught."

Aviama blanched.

Onkar laughed. "Go ahead and get the jars down, Rookie."

"The ... these jars?"

The man pushed off the door frame and sauntered to the first worktable. "The ones you're dying to know what's inside, yes. Set them here."

Heart sinking to her toes, Aviama climbed back up on the crate, carefully lifted the jars down, and set them on the table between them. Onkar gestured to the lid. "Go on."

She eyed him, but his expression was neutral. Was he mad? Amused? Mocking?

Aviama opened the jar and peered inside. A yellowish liquid sat inside. Boring. "Oil?"

He nodded. "High end too. Next."

She opened the next jar, and Onkar breathed in the sweet scent and let out a long, contented sigh. "Sun-dried spice mix imported from Curion. Rare. Expensive."

Aviama pursed her lips. "Okay, so it's all too fancy for us to use for the masses and it belongs on the top shelf. Got it. Can I put them back now?"

"No. Next."

Aviama opened the third jar and pulled out several pouches of dried roots, herbs, and spices.

"Mandrake. Myrrh. Turmeric. Medicinal items."

Disappointment settled over her like a cloud. She'd gotten caught snooping, and for what? A few spices?

"Didn't I tell you I'd teach you to be a chameleon?"

Aviama glanced up at him. "Yes?"

"Gold and gumption, I should have upped your maladroit fee." Onkar sucked on his teeth and tapped the surface of the table. "Listen, I've been waiting for you to try to poke around unsupervised. Why believe me that I said the map would be on my person? I'm a cheat, after all. And if you weren't willing to do a little snoopery, you wouldn't be worthy of my instruction. But if you're going to be my pupil, you're going to have to be better at it. I've got a reputation to uphold."

Aviama opened her mouth to retort, but Onkar held up one finger, picked up the jar of dried spice pouches and dumped them out on the table. He snagged one with muted yellow, orange, and tan-looking crystalline pebbles, sniffed it, and held it up. "This one looks almost identical to myrrh. It's mixed with some real myrrh, too, for kicks. And to maintain the smell to sell the ruse."

"But it's not?"

Onkar grinned. He took one pebble out of the pouch and held it in his hand, then grabbed an empty glass from the middle shelf and set it on the stone top of the furnace. Moving to the other side of the furnace, he tugged at one of the stones until it popped out and something fell out of a hollowed-out space inside. A container filled with clear liquid.

"There are few things as exciting as the thrill of an exquisite take. But there is one thing." Onkar opened the crate of cleaning supplies in the corner, pulled out a jug, and poured some of its contents into the glass. He added the liquid he'd taken from the side of the furnace. It looked like a glass of water.

"What's that?"

Onkar grinned. "Explosions."

He dropped the pebble from his hand into the solution. The moment the pebble hit the surface of the liquid, fire lit the surface, sparks flew, and a purple cloud filled the glass.

Aviama's jaw dropped. "How did you do that?"

"It's no tabeun magic, I'll assure you. It's not even sifal. Just chemistry."

A thrill ran through her. She snapped her head from the sparks to the swindler. "Teach me."

Onkar grabbed a glass bowl, turned it upside down, and smothered the glass on the furnace with it until the fire extinguished. "I agreed to make you a thief. Chemistry is an area of specialty. They tie in well, but I'll need something extra from you in exchange."

"More than the money you stiffed us out of already?"

"You're a risk factory if ever I met one, Rookie. I've held up my end of the bargain. And you still owe me the second half of the payment for the voyage upon safe exit from this ship, I might add."

Aviama snorted. "You think we'll get off this ship?"

Onkar crossed his arms. "That's awfully pessimistic for a girl made of impulsive decisions, siren magic, and sunshine."

"I don't have siren magic."

"Just this morning, you captivated a ship full of crude sailors with nothing but a song, a dance, and a smile. If that's not siren magic, I don't know what is."

Aviama tilted her head and frowned, hiding the small smile that almost escaped. "That sounded suspiciously like a compliment. Was that a compliment?"

Onkar dumped the solution from the glass into a bucket

and handed her the empty glass. "Your strengths are also your weaknesses. Play up your strengths. There's no room for modesty when your life is on the line—if you're good at something, use it. You can sing. You can dance. You draw the eyes of men."

Her stomach soured. "I've experienced attention from evil men. It's not the sort of attention I want to draw."

"What if it saves your life?"

"There are certain things I will never do for any purpose whatsoever."

"Noble. But while princesses can afford nobility, knaves frequently can't. You're not in the palace anymore, darlin'."

Aviama shrugged. "Maybe I can be a knave with a few scruples."

Onkar laughed. "A knave with scruples! Gold and gumption, what a thought! I hope to hear how that turns out for you one day." He shook his head in disbelief and held out the pouch of spices. Aviama reached for it, but he snatched it back. "Information. What do you know of Sunboy's involvement with the Iolani?"

Aviama's lips parted. "What does a black market trickster need with politics?"

Onkar recoiled. "Got me figured out, do you? Pegged me as a bottom-barrel jester, did you?" For a moment, the levity in his face dropped like a sheet to reveal a face solemn as the grave, hard as flint, his eyes dark as he took a step toward her.

Her heart beat fast, and she stepped back. Her mouth went dry. Was Onkar one of the evil men she seemed to attract? Why did they flock to her with every turn? Her fingers spread to call the wind, but the magna still dampened her abilities. She needed to find the magna.

But just as quickly as the shadow came, the facade dropped back into place, and the man wagged a finger at her as if she were a naughty but beloved pet who didn't know any better. "Projecting harmlessness when one is a capable killing machine is something that often takes skill. You have that part in the bag already. You're the size of a twig and as imposing as a mouse. Just as with anything, this is both a strength and a concern. Now tell me what I want to know."

Aviama swallowed. *Biscuits.* She needed to stop acting like a pushover. She had to get herself back together and be someone strong. She lifted her chin and dropped her voice low. "Tell me why Shiva's dealings with the Iolani matter to you."

Onkar leaned down until he was nose to nose with her and flashed a grin. "None of your business."

"Then I don't need your chemistry lessons." Aviama twirled a piece of hair around her finger, then released it to examine the cuticles of her nails the way she'd seen her sister Avaya do—in her most cocky, pretentious moments. She crossed the room toward the door, hesitated, then rotated back to the swindler. "I think I might store extra salt in the furnace. Maybe do some magic tricks for the crew. You know, earn their favor, play up the charm as you suggested. What do you think?"

Onkar sucked his teeth and leveled her with a cool stare. "You think any of the ingredients I showed you today will still be in place by supper?"

Aviama shrugged. "You think you'll have time in the kitchens *unsupervised* to come up with new hiding spots as good as these? Built into the ship like the furnace?"

He looked at her for a long time, then shook his head. "And the moth picks up the sword."

She smiled. "So you'll teach me?"

"Tell me one thing about the Iolani that I don't already know, on the first try, and you've got yourself a deal."

Aviama paused. It was a test. Underestimate him and offer information too simple, and she would fail. Overestimate him, and she would part with information more valuable than she should.

Makana filled her mind. Her simple request that Aviama come back and sing with her. Her sadness when warning Aviama of the dangers Shiva posed to the Aeian Sea. The treaty that must not be struck.

What did most sailors know? That sirens sang lullabies, luring them to their deaths. But since the arena, they would also know not all songs sung by a siren heralded death. Radha's cruel targeting of Iolani children seemed too sensitive to hand off to a criminal. And the details of what Makana could do with her magic—though Aviama herself did not know the extent—could be used against her.

But she only had to share *enough...*

A thought struck her then. Aviama drew in a deep breath. "Iolani do not use their magic to kill."

Onkar's brows soared. He hadn't expected that answer. "What do they use it for, then?"

Aviama spread her hands. "That's another question."

A slow smile spread across his face. He tossed her the spices. "Let's learn chemistry."

20

Onkar worked with Aviama for an hour and a half before the others showed up, talking powders, metals, and substance mixtures until her head spun. Flurin was inert, until mixed with jenakl, when it activated something or other that killed instantly and without trace. Zahar was a paralytic poison, but it took hours to kill, and if kamatlab was introduced into the bloodstream by the third hour, the person would revive. Lye was another favorite. Anything corrosive or explosive brightened Onkar's face and got him talking with his whole body, gesturing and speed-talking his way through the amounts and effects and how to modify each one.

Aviama retained maybe twenty percent of what he said any given moment.

Samud walked by twice while they were working. It set her teeth on edge. Chenzira came down next. Onkar mixed flurin into a glass of wine, took a sip, and offered some to Chenzira, talking nonsense about how such-and-such enhanced the flavor. By the time he'd taken the drink, half the ingredients they'd been experimenting with were gone from the table, and by the time Jignesh arrived, they were ready to prep the evening meal.

Days passed quickly after that. Every morning, Shiva brought her morning dose of magna, and every morning, Aviama took it without a word and headed to the kitchens for work. Chenzira joined the crew hesitantly, more interested in positioning himself close to the door and watching everyone coming in and out than applying himself to theft.

For her part, she enjoyed stealing glances in his direction. The first day Chenzira was there, she fumbled two lifts and a drop. Laksh nudged her in the ribs, and Manan waggled his eyebrows at her, and she rolled her eyes. But she also couldn't stop studying him whenever he wasn't looking—his strong arms, rich laugh, soft lips.

Chenzira's lifts were clumsy, but the guys liked him, and watching him walk in each day was Aviama's favorite moment. He scanned the kitchen, locked eyes with her, and smiled.

He had a beautiful smile. The kind that turned her insides to melted butter. But when he looked at Onkar, his expression grew stony.

That night after supper, Onkar sent Aviama to inventory the salt in the cargo hold while the others cleaned up the kitchen. Aviama gripped the wax tablet and stylus in her left hand and the lantern in her right as she descended the stairs to the cargo deck. They'd already counted the salt in cargo, but after Aviama's snooping, Onkar was almost certainly punishing her for having a terrible cover story.

Did that mean he didn't care if she told the truth, if only she was imaginative? Would any good cover story do?

Although, having the wax tablet and stylus for inventory was a decent cover in itself. Aviama lifted the lantern and took her time walking through the stacks of crates and barrels. How much magna had Shiva brought on board?

Would it all be in one place, or would he have spread it out? She tried to remember what Onkar had told her about substances. Could any of them destroy the magna without blowing up the ship?

Not that she could recall. *Biscuits.*

Aviama took her time, peering into as many crates and barrels as she could get open. So far, nothing. As she edged her way closer to Makana at the front of the ship, voices drifted her way. Aviama extinguished the lantern and ducked between the stacks she'd come to know better over the past few weeks.

"Keep her quiet. Shiva doesn't want to hear a peep out of her, or he'll be holding you directly responsible."

Pretentious. Female. Durga. Aviama's stomach churned. But what had Makana been doing if she hadn't been staying quiet? Talking to the guards? Singing? Aviama hadn't heard anything, and she hadn't had a good enough reason to make it down to the cargo deck since their last meeting—until now.

"How are we supposed to keep her quiet if we have our ears plugged?"

Male. One of the guards.

Durga's tone was sharp as she answered him.

"One of you removes your ear plugs. You were instructed to have one guard listen and one stop up his ears. You've been disobedient cowards, and I'm here to set that straight."

"What if she sings the death lullaby?"

"Then the one of you with a sound mind, kill the other one if he tries to let her out. And then stop the siren."

Aviama's fingers dug into the sides of her tablet, the rough wood of its exterior pressing hard into her hand. She held her breath.

"Just ... stop the siren."

"That a problem, sailor?"

"No disrespect, but you don't know anything about sirens or what they can do."

"I've seen this one in action. Have you?"

Silence. Aviama shook her head. Durga would have only seen Makana *in action* in the arena, with Aviama and Chenzira. She knew Makana had refused to buckle to Queen Satya's blackmail and had instead linked arms with Aviama and taken out the guards on the sidelines to let Aviama and Chenzira get through to the next stage unharmed.

Durga knew Makana was more than a witless creature bent on destruction. She knew Makana had a soul.

Not that the value of life had stopped Durga's cruelty before. Aviama blanched at the callous tone she used now to break the stillness.

"I recommend using the harpoon we provided and staying at a distance. And if you don't have the stomach to kill your friend if the lullaby sucks him in, I'll have you reassigned."

Durga swept off down the deck, a lantern swaying from her fingers, casting an eerie light about her in all directions as she moved. Aviama flinched away from the light, crouching as low as she could as the girl marched past.

Hard eyes looked down Durga's sharp nose as if being a glorified piece of mail gave her the authority of the throne itself. Chin high, shoulders back, with a few new bangles adorning her wrists, the woman looked like she owned the *Wraithweaver*—and expected the rest of the world to be handed to her on a silver platter by sunrise.

Aviama's heartbeat doubled its pace, pulse throbbing in her temple as she waited for Durga to pass. She might have a reason to be on the cargo deck, but eavesdropping on Durga's conversation with Makana's guards, with an extinguished lantern, was unlikely to count.

The light of Durga's lantern rolled from side to side with

each cocky step she took. Darkness engulfed Aviama, and she slipped out of her hiding place. Aviama crept along the cargo deck, the wax tablet and stylus clutched to her chest, the extinguished lantern held out in front of her as she went. But she knew the space better than she had before, and her knuckles only bumped a few of the crates as she moved along the narrow corridor.

"Oh!"

Ahead, a dark figure strode toward Durga, blocking her way to the stairs. Durga gasped and staggered backward. Aviama dipped behind the thick pole of the mast and crouched down to peer around the pole at the figure. Durga cleared her throat.

"What are you doing down here?"

"Sand and sea, you're like a rat infestation nobody can rid themselves of. If you must know, I recently ran into someone I despise. I've dreamed of disposing of her body. Any recommendations on a method? Just so I'm prepared. When the time comes."

Aviama bit her lip. *Tally.* Apparently, Chenzira wasn't much better at holding his tongue than she was.

Confidence oozed back into Durga's body—not as the dictator she'd been to the guard, but this time in a way Aviama hadn't seen her use before. Her voice was slippery oil as she moved toward him. "I knew you'd grow tired of her. For a man of your station, to escape Keket and find peace in Radha, only to have it all upended by a princess who has done nothing but toss your life to the dogs."

Durga sidled up to Chenzira and looked up at him, slithering a hand up his chest. "I could help you regain your reputation. Rebuild your peace with Radha."

Aviama's mouth went dry. Her heart stopped. Was this Shiva's doing, or Durga's?

He swatted her away with a grimace, as if her touch carried disease. His jaw clenched, but he said nothing.

"Not in the mood, I see." Durga held her hands up innocently, then arched an eyebrow. "Even after she set you at odds with Darsh *and* Prince Shiva, dragging you into an avoidable battle that nearly cost you your life, and landing you in the brig? What is it about this princess that has such a hold on you?"

Chenzira slowly cocked his head. "Drowning would work, but strangulation would be more fitting for the dark places of the ship where there are no windows. Do you have a preference? I'm leaning toward strangulation."

Durga clucked her tongue. "Am I so repulsive? Or is she really so incredible?"

Chenzira clenched his jaw and looked Durga dead in the eyes. "Yes."

Warmth flooded Aviama's chest at his answer, solemn as the grave, without a moment's hesitation. But just as quickly, her stomach dropped—as the fingers of Durga's free hand uncurled, and a mighty gale of wind tore through the cargo hold, knocking Chenzira off his feet and slamming him into Durga, pressing him up against her body until they both slid together into the pole of the mast.

Aviama sucked in a breath and jerked back behind the mast. Durga's heel landed only a handsbreadth from Aviama's hiding place. Glancing up, Aviama could see Chenzira straining against the wind holding him to her. Durga laughed and snaked her arms up around Chenzira's neck, pulling him tighter to her.

"Oh, but what would your princess say?"

Bile flew up Aviama's throat. She leaned her back against the mast and slid to the opposite side of it from where Durga and Chenzira stood. Slowly, slowly, she set down her lantern, wax tablet, and stylus.

"Oh, Prince, I couldn't possibly," Durga crooned. "But I suppose if you convinced me..."

Chenzira braced himself against the mast, his arms straining against the wood on either side of Durga as he fought the wind holding them together. "You. Are. Repulsive."

"Don't be like that. I could be useful." Durga dropped her voice and whispered in Chenzira's ear, but as Aviama straightened, she caught every word. "I know where the magna is. I could keep you stocked and protected."

"Tell me, then."

"Kiss me, and I'll tell you everything you want to know."

Aviama stretched out her hand. Swirls of air pooled in her palm. She was free.

Chenzira laughed, but the sound was dark and hollow. "I'd rather have relations with a troll."

He grunted against a new onslaught of wind. Aviama's stylus skittered past her along the floor, away from Durga and Chenzira—but sound was like a hammer in the quiet of night. She froze. On the other side of the mast, Chenzira and Durga stilled.

"What was that?" Durga hissed. "If you tell a soul what's happened here tonight..."

A rush of wind slammed into something sturdy behind Aviama's head, and Chenzira stumbled back. Aviama whirled around the mast, hands outstretched, heat flooding her face as she called the wind to her will. A great gust seized Durga by the torso and threw her forward against a stack of barrels. Durga gasped, clutching her stomach, and as she straightened, the lantern cast orange-yellow light on a gash on her head, dripping with blood.

Durga slung her free arm and hit Chenzira's feet with

wind, shoving him back against her again. She wrapped her arm around his waist and kept him between her and Aviama. "Stay away from me! Or I'll do to him what you did to me!"

Aviama's lip curled. "You think I can't reach you where you stand?"

Aviama lifted her hands, but Chenzira spun and hit Durga on the chin with his elbow. She staggered backward, and Chenzira closed the distance, wrapping large hands around her dainty throat.

"You wanted me close, didn't you?" Chenzira growled.

Durga lifted her hand to fend him off, but Aviama sent whirling wind in tendrils like rope, crushing her palms to her sides. Her eyes widened, and a choking sound came from her throat as she desperately tried to pull in air.

Fear etched every inch of Durga's face. Aviama swallowed. Is this what her parents had felt when they lay dying? Had her mother even had time to be afraid? What about Sona, on his knees before Shiva? Her gut wrenched, and she shook her head. Her grip loosened on the wind binding Durga, but she kept the girl's hands down.

"Chenzira?"

"Just a minute. Durga was about to tell us where the magna is." Chenzira tightened his hold. "Blink twice if what I said is true."

Aviama released one of Durga's hands, and she clawed madly at Chenzira's steel grip. He was unmoved. Her face drained of color, her open mouth useless, lungs empty.

Aviama sucked in a breath. "Chenzira."

Chenzira didn't let up. And Durga's face was turning blue. Aviama lifted a hand. Would she have to? Would she be an idiot if she stopped him? Would she ever forgive herself if she didn't?

Durga blinked twice.

21

Chenzira loosened his grip, and a wave of relief washed over Aviama as air flooded Durga's lungs. The girl coughed and gasped in long, ragged drags. Aviama pressed Durga's hands to her sides again with a fresh wave of wind, and Chenzira scowled as he bore down on Durga. "I'm waiting."

"Prince Shiva's room. He keeps it in his room. Samud keeps some too, in his quarters."

Chenzira leaned in close, hovering over Durga's ear, and Aviama edged closer to listen. "I would never hit a lady. But you are not a lady. And the next time you touch me, I'll break whatever part of you makes contact."

Durga gaped at him. He released her out into the aisle, and Aviama pushed a wall of wind at Durga's feet until she skidded backward to the stairs. Hair mussed from the wind, gash decorating her temple, Durga picked up her skirt and fled up to the gun deck. Aviama's wind extinguished Durga's lantern, and a palpable darkness surrounded them the minute Durga's footsteps faded up the stairs.

Fingers gripped her wrist, and Aviama clapped a hand

over her mouth to stifle her squeal as Chenzira pulled her out of the main aisle of the cargo deck, several steps further into the belly of the ship, and tugged her down to a crouch.

"There's an opening … here." Chenzira placed her hand on the bottom of a suspended barrel, holding her hand delicately in his as he moved it from the barrel to the crates on either side, creating a low space to crawl through. Chenzira went first, and Aviama scrambled after him on hands and knees. Ridges in the oak planks of the deck stood out against her fingers as she lowered herself to avoid hitting her head on the barrels above her. The hem of her skirt snagged on something behind her, and she tugged it free.

She passed under the end of the barrel and sat up. Aviama pressed her hands on the planks before her in the dark, and something soft—a blanket—interrupted the wooden surface. She reached out to her left. A stack of crates walled her in on that side. He'd created a little room for himself on the cargo deck?

Turning, Aviama reached out to test the limits of the space on her right. Her hand bumped into cloth and skin. Chenzira's shirt and arm. Aviama snatched her hand back and tried again, this time unmistakably finding his chest.

Biscuits. Heat flushed her cheeks, and she began to pull away, but he captured her hand in the dark and pulled it back. A fluttering sensation battered her chest as Chenzira placed her palm over his heart and held it there. His heart beat bold and swift under her fingertips, and her own pulse raced to match.

He adjusted his position beside her, and she pulled her feet under her, sitting on her feet to get a little taller, a little closer to his height. He moved again, the rustle of his clothes and the sound of their breath the only interruption piercing the stillness of the night. His nose brushed hers, and she jolted with a sharp intake of breath. She hadn't realized he was so close. But when she recovered, she didn't pull away.

Chenzira dropped his hand from over hers, the back of his knuckles barely brushing the skin of her arm before he softly, tenderly, slipped his hand beneath her hair to the nape of her neck. A shiver rippled down her spine at his gentle touch. Aviama leaned toward him without thinking, noses brushing again in the night. Her lips grazed his.

She froze.

What if he thought she was using him somehow, the way Shiva had used her? What if he thought she would compare the two of them, as if she still held some sort of flame for the manipulative monster who had demanded her public displays of affection and kisses in the past? That she was moving through the motions?

But if she pulled away, he might think she didn't want him. And every fiber of her being told her that was a lie. Her stomach flopped.

Would he kiss her? Did he want to? Did he watch her the way she did him, the memory of the night he held her in his arms through the bars playing through her mind, the way his touch sent goosebumps along her skin?

Chenzira ran his free hand along her back, encircling her, his hand finally settling at her hip. "What do you think of me?"

Aviama's lips parted in surprise. Her mind clouded with the feel of his lips barely brushing hers as he spoke. "Um..."

She felt him smile. "Mhmm?"

"I think ... that I like you a lot." Aviama grimaced. *I like you a lot?*

Chenzira moved his hand from her hip to her wrist, flipped it over, and tested her pulse. Her heartbeat only rocked faster, and she could feel the throb of her heart in her chest, her wrist, her temple—like a dragon on the wing, plummeting through the air at a dizzying speed.

"Yes?" He was smiling. She could hear it. "What else?"

Her mouth went dry. "I think ... that it's hard for me to think when you're touching me."

"Hmm. That's problematic. Because I like hearing your thoughts. But I also like being close to you."

She laughed. "I also think ... that whenever I'm alone, you're the one I want to see. When I'm sad, you're the one I want to tell. And the good moments I hold on to—the ones I replay in my mind—you're in them."

Silence.

Aviama bit her lip. She'd gone too far. Been too forward. She sounded pathetic. He wouldn't feel the same. Would he?

"What is that emotion called?"

He was teasing her. But the moment she heard the warm, honey tenor tones of his voice, she knew he felt the same. She pressed her lips together, suppressing a smile.

"I don't know. Butterflies and sunshine. And something steadier. Like an anchor."

Biscuits, you're in love.

Chenzira leaned in and whispered in her ear, his breath tickling her neck. "It's okay. I won't make you say it. I don't want you to say it just because you think I want you to. But I've dreamed of nothing else these past weeks. Nothing else but you. What it would be like..."

He kissed her neck, and a shot of adrenaline flooded her body with tingles. Aviama slid her arm up to his neck, playing with the ends of his hair. He shifted and kissed her softly along her jaw line, and once more at the corner of her mouth.

Aviama's head swam. She was alive and dizzy all at once, both afraid to push in, and silently begging him to take her in his arms.

What if it didn't go well? What if she ruined it, and lost the only friend she was beginning not to bear to lose? Worse, what if, after this moment, nothing happened at all?

"I was always told my relationships mattered because of who I am. That they reflected on the crown, even as a second-born." Chenzira dodged her lips and kissed the corner of the other side of her mouth. Aviama tried to concentrate on what he was saying. "And here I am, renegade royal, entangling myself with a high-profile princess."

She tipped her chin up toward him in the dark. "I didn't think that's who I was to you."

"No, you're the girl who gets lost in hallways and lies about it."

"Hey!"

He laughed. The deep richness of it was a balm to her soul. "High profile isn't smart for runaways. But it wouldn't be the first time I did something stupid to be close to you."

"So you're saying this—this is stupid?" Aviama drew back. His tone hadn't changed, but he had to believe the words coming out of his mouth. At least some. "Wasn't ... wasn't this your idea?"

"First of all, I very much like being as close to you as you'll let me. So whatever I said to make you back away, I take it all back. And secondly, between the two of us, I think it would be *you* being with *me* that would be the poorer decision." His warm hand slipped from the back of her neck up to her face, brushing away a tendril of hair and twining it behind her ear.

Aviama traced the corded lines of his arm with her fingers. "And why is that?"

"I'd cause a problem with creating better diplomatic arrangements. And we might cause an international incident."

"I've been a living international incident everywhere I go since I left Jannemar."

"Then I'm running out of excuses."

"Good. I like doing stupid things."

Aviama leaned forward, and Chenzira tipped her face up toward him again.

"*Tally.*" He said it as a whisper, but it was the most delicious word she'd ever heard.

Aviama opened her mouth to respond, when his lips met hers like a wave meets the shore—sudden and surging, an urgency in his movements as though he could hold back the dam no longer. Butterflies exploded in her chest, and a shiver fled down her spine as he wrapped his arms tight around her and moved his mouth fervently against hers.

She reached for him and pulled him in, closer and closer, as if letting go would be the death of them both. His warmth surrounded her, his solid muscled chest and strong arms setting a stark contrast to her slender softness. Nothing felt so safe, so secure, as that place in the circle of his arms. And yet nothing felt so electrifying or exhilarating as his touch.

Shiva had never felt like this, even before she knew the truth about him. And her head had never spun so wildly, yet somehow agreeing with her heart, as it did in this moment.

Time escaped them there, in the secluded hole of the *Wraithweaver's* cargo deck. She didn't know how long they lost themselves to that kiss, or where one ended and another began. But when they parted, she reached for him again, and when at last they broke free, he took her face in his hands and kissed her once more—this time not as a surging wave, but tender as starlight kissing the surface of a glassy sea.

22

Aviama cringed at the creak of the wooden stairs as she crept from the cargo deck to the main deck. She could only make out the outlines of the first couple of rows of sailors in the moonlight filtering down from the hatch in the ceiling. No one moved. Aviama continued on from the main deck to the upper deck and back through the captain's kitchen to her room.

The feel of Chenzira's lips on hers clung to her as she pushed open her door. His strength surrounding her, his tender closeness. And the last words he'd said before they parted.

"If you stay any longer, I'll want to do things I shouldn't. But find me tomorrow. I have something to talk to you about." He'd paused then and drawn her into a long embrace. *"See you in the morning, Tally."*

Aviama smiled. It had happened not ten minutes ago, but she couldn't stop replaying it in her mind. She latched the door behind her, collapsed into bed, and slept more deeply and soundly than she had in weeks—dreaming of Chenzira.

Daylight streamed into her room by the time she awoke,

brighter than normal. Aviama sat up. How long had she slept? She rubbed her eyes and blinked. Had she missed prep for the morning meal? Her stomach burbled in complaint. She winced. Had she skipped breakfast entirely?

Aviama hopped out of bed, raked a comb through her hair, threw the door open, and—fell flat on her face in the hall. Her foot had caught on an object as she dashed out in her hurry. Her ankle hurt, and something metal rattled on the floor behind her. Aviama twisted around. Her heart stopped.

A silver meal tray and cover sat on the floor.

Aviama glanced at Shiva's door. It was shut, and he was nowhere to be seen. She tested her palms. Wind pooled in her hands at her command, then dissipated. No magna. No konnolan. She was free.

Her mouth went dry. No. No, something was wrong. She stared at the tray. Could Shiva be changing tactics? Sweetening her up with food and supposed freedom?

It didn't fit. It didn't make sense.

Her stomach dropped. Perhaps—perhaps for once, Shiva had kept his promise. A horrific promise. The oath of a murderous tyrant.

Aviama reached her hand out toward the cover. Once she lifted the lid, she would know for certain. Did she want to know?

She lifted the cover.

A scream ripped from her throat. She snatched her hand back as if she'd been burned, and the metal cover clattered to the floor. Blood dripped off the end of the plate. And on it, a severed head stared back at her with glassy, unseeing eyes frozen wide with fear. Bhumi.

Nausea swept through her. Bile burned the back of her throat as an involuntary shudder shook her whole body. Tears stung her eyes and streaked down her cheeks.

He'd really done it. He'd delivered someone's head to her door, without a word, without warning. She never thought— she didn't think—

Death. Death. Death.

Her heart beat in a stolen rhythm, like the drum of a funeral processional, the reminder of her own useless life causing friends to die again and again. On this voyage alone, Sona and Bhumi had died. And Shiva still had two more names on his list to kill. Sai and Chenzira.

Durga had squealed after last night. She must have. Which means she must have lied about where the magna was, or she'd never have owned up to Shiva that she disclosed it.

Unconscionable weight bore down on her chest. She couldn't breathe. She needed air. But she couldn't go through the captain's kitchen and face the upper deck.

If Shiva killed Bhumi for Aviama's involvement in stopping Durga last night, he must know she was with Chenzira. Her blood turned cold. Chenzira wasn't safe. Not with her. Not as long as Shiva was alive.

What had they done with Bhumi's body? What would they do with the head? Would they spin it somehow, as if Aviama had killed her, paint her in a bad light, make the crew hate her even more? Maybe they would wait for Aviama to leave her room and send someone in to find it...

Aviama grabbed the cover, slammed it back over Bhumi's ghost-white face, skidded it across the floor into her room, and shut the door behind her. Sweat beaded on her brow and slipped down the sides of her face. Pain built in her chest, the weight pulling her down, slowing time to a molasses slog. Her mind spun through a thousand scenarios but refused to slow long enough to grasp onto any of them.

She couldn't breathe.

Aviama leaned back against the door, spinning the rings

on her fingers at what felt like a hundred times a minute. She couldn't go to the kitchens now. She couldn't pretend nothing had happened, and she couldn't risk being close to Chenzira without a plan to keep him and Sai safe.

What would he think of her?

Tears poured down her face. In vain, Aviama gasped for air. Her lungs refused to fill. Her heart scorned all hope of slowing. And the pain in her chest escalated into an all-consuming agony.

Scourge, kill me now.

The thought frightened her. But wasn't she already dead?

Except that if she was dead, Shiva would have no reason to keep Chenzira and Sai alive. Though hope of their survival was plummeting by the second.

If she didn't get some air, she'd die here on the floor next to Bhumi's decapitated head.

Panic swelled in her belly, and her throat ached with the sting of bile. Aviama opened her mouth to breathe, but though wind swirled into the room, running along her skin, pooling in her palms, it would not enter her lungs. Dizziness washed over her, and she threw a hand out to steady herself.

She was dying. She would die. She was already good as dead.

Maybe it was for the best. Maybe then Chenzira would know she hadn't rejected him but had been killed instead. He'd never think she betrayed him or rejected him by staying away after the events of last night. She'd never get to explain, but she wouldn't cause more harm.

Power swirled through the air, currents sweeping up and down her arms and legs. Horror ripped her apart in the chest in a whirlwind of boiling torment.

Air. Air.

Freedom.

Wind seeped into the room from the door behind her leading to the hall, and from the cracks around the door across the room—the barricaded, blocked door leading out onto the forbidden balcony her room and Shiva's room shared.

Aviama hardly noticed. She blinked furiously against the tears blinding her, but fountains of weeping replaced every tear she wiped away. Gusts of wind licked at the oak boards of her room. Plank walls, plank floors, plank ceilings. The forecastle stood above her, and Sai's room would be situated beneath her.

Wind lifted her up off the floor, fighting against the lead-heavy weight on her heart. Shiva's despicable face, his slimy, silky words, floated through her mind. Images of Sona and Bhumi assaulted her.

"If your attitude steps one hair beyond my profound tolerance for your insolence, I will give no warning..."

What had she said to him, the day she betrothed herself to Shiva in exchange for her life and Chenzira's life? The day she sold her soul?

"You only want me for your menagerie."

His response came back to her clear as crystal, vivid as daylight.

"Nonsense ... I don't hide my collections for special occasions. I wear them. And I will wear you on my arm."

He'd always threatened her with their deaths. It had just taken this long to make good on them. They'd still been in the palace when he'd demanded she fake physical affections to keep them alive. Fear gripped her with an inescapable hold. A tremor rocked her body, and her hands shook.

"And if I get even a glimmer that I am not the apple of your eye —if you do not convince me that I am your greatest dream, that

you are obsessively, head over heels in love with me—I'll kill one of the women attending you."

Obscene. Despicable. And yet *he* would live, and *she* would die?

Magic rumbled through her, as natural to her body as lightning to the storm. Sai's bruises ran through her mind again. Living under the thumb of evil men was not living at all.

Aviama's heart shattered into a million pieces. She felt, rather than heard, the blood-curling, shrieking scream that racked her body and ripped her throat hoarse as she threw her hands out sideways, and a colossal gale of wind coursed through the room and struck the door to the balcony.

Crackkkkkk!

The door flew off its hinges and spun out to sea. Sunlight flooded the room, and her desk and chair rocketed backward, slamming into the door behind her. Aviama landed on the floorboards of her room with a thud and glided out to the balcony like a phantom, without soul or trace, expression, or agency.

She would die. Once she was dead, maybe they wouldn't bother killing Chenzira and Sai. But if the magna really was in Shiva's quarters, she'd destroy it first, so Shiva couldn't control anyone else with it. He'd be forced to use konnolan, but maybe he'd run out. Or maybe the others would find a way to get to it once she was gone...

Tabeun magic lit along her skin like fire. Someone would have heard the sound or seen her door flying off the ship into the open sea three decks below. She didn't care. If only she could destroy whatever was in Shiva's room first.

Aviama lifted both hands to Shiva's door. A gale wrenched it open, and the top hinge broke. The door swung limply in the wind. Rich decor, fine linens, and bottles of wine rolled back from her presence like a sheet as she swept into the room. Her power almost ... blinked? From one corner of the room. She stepped into the space, her windcalling essence roiling with rage and strength on three sides—but still she sensed a dampening in one corner.

The bed.

Aviama flicked her wrist, and the bed flipped on end, slamming into the wall. Feathers burst from the mattress, and sacks ripped free underneath. Durga *had* told the truth. Not only was the magna in his room, he was sleeping on it.

Coward. Did he think it would protect him? Just its nearness while he slept?

But she didn't have to touch it.

Aviama raised her hands again, stepped out of the doorway, and sent the sacks flying out the door, over the balcony, and overboard, where they plunged into the ocean in a flurry of white feathers.

The interior door shook, and she was faintly aware of shouting. The knob turned, but the table had slid against the edge of the door, and it didn't open.

Bam. Something heavy hit the door. *BAM.* Again. And again.

Aviama didn't care. She was going to find Shiva. And when she did...

Well, she didn't know what she'd do. But by the time she was done with him, he'd never hurt anyone again.

Rage fueled her muscles as the wind blew her hair back and she half-walked, half-glided back out onto the balcony. With a double twist of her wrists, she commanded a powerful gust and shot up into the air, up off the balcony, and over the rail of the level above.

Sailors shouted. Terrified faces drained of blood. An arrow whistled at her head, but she deflected it with a wave of her hand. And there—sprinting from the captain's kitchen out onto the upper deck—was Prince Shiva. The star of her night-mares. Murderer of every light in her life. Destroyer of hope, oppressor of souls.

Unspeakable fury filled her at the sight of him. Red-hot wrath overwhelmed her senses. She lifted her hand.

BOOM.

Cannon fire. The wind was gone. Aviama dropped like a sack of bricks.

23

Aviama hit the deck of the forecastle, the impact knocking the breath from her body. Pain reverberated through her, head to toe, as a wave of nausea and dizziness rocked her stomach. Out of the corner of her eye, a long teal coat and heavy boots marched up the stairs from the upper deck. Shining gold buttons emblazoned with the Radhan pakshi flashed in the sun from hem to collar.

Dread mixed with a sick satisfaction as she twisted up to look at Captain Samud, his perfectly wrapped teal turban and hat towering over her. The man glowered down at her, but the konnolan had taken its effect. Weakness riddled her every cord and sinew. She winced against the effort of looking up at him.

But she had done it. She'd destroyed the magna.

Samud seized her by the hair and dragged her across the forecastle and down the stairs. Aviama cried out as her scalp erupted with a burning sensation, as if her hair would rip from her head. She reached up and gripped his hands to lessen the pressure, but she was too weak to hold on. Bile lurched up her throat as another wave of nausea hit her. Her body went *bump, bump, bump* down the stairs like a rag doll, Samud's iron grip raking her across the deck. He threw her down by the rail, and she collapsed in a heap of aching, blazing fire, as if her insides were ripped to shreds and set to flame.

A man fell from the mast and landed with a smack on the oak planks, his arm cocked in an unnatural position. His hand was scarred on the palm. Melderblood. Weakness from the konnolan had taken him out on the rigging. He stared, unseeing, up at the sky, and blood pooled at his head.

Samud drew his sword and raised his voice, glancing somewhere beyond her. "Come see your woman, Prince. Is this the same woman you claimed to have such control over at the start of our voyage? The one you promised would be no trouble?"

Aviama groaned and tried to sit up, but her limbs failed her, and she slumped back to the floor. Shiva strode forward, chest heaving, face white. His usual confidence had utterly abandoned him. Behind him, other crewmen burst up the stairs to the upper deck, stopping in their tracks when they saw their captain standing over the limp body of the strange woman the Radhan prince had brought on board.

For an instant, she thought she saw Onkar slip from the shadows toward the aft of the ship, but she blinked, and he was gone. Laksh emerged from the quarterdeck, keeping a sharp eye on her—but he leaned heavily on the barrels, and his face was drained of color. No melder was free of the konnolan's reach.

Aviama's heart sank. If they didn't kill her soon, they might still decide to kill Chenzira and Sai instead. And she was too weak to do anything about it.

Samud drew the edge of his blade along her chin, then glared back at Shiva. "Their power is yours to command, is it not? You allow it or take it away, do you not? Tell me, if that is true, why my ship is blown to bits, in my captain's quarters, which you borrow?" The captain curled his lip and waved his sword in the direction of the corpse. "If I hadn't set off that cannon, you would be the one dead on the deck. She had murder on her mind and nearly succeeded."

Shiva straightened and snapped his fingers, and two men appeared—dragging Chenzira between them. Aviama's lips parted.

"And if *my* men hadn't found this man in your quarters, he might have destroyed a lot more than the stash of magna he dumped overboard through one of the gunports."

Samud pursed his lips. "They did this together. And you brought them here. Why did we need them for this mission, I ask?"

Shiva crossed his arms. "Captain. We are on the cusp of Ghosts' Gorge. Her utility was never for the voyage portion."

Samud's expression hardened. "If she murders everyone on board and blows my ship to pieces, I'd say her utility has run out."

The prince cocked his head and eyed Aviama. She gritted her teeth as another wave of dizziness tilted her world in circles. "She looks harmless enough."

"Don't play games with me, Highness. I did you a favor, but I'm the captain, and this is my ship. I will not have it destroyed by melderbloods who don't know their place."

Shiva shrugged. "Kill the big one, then. They'll not be any trouble once he's gone."

Aviama sucked in a breath and lurched forward, promptly falling again to the floor. She raised her eyes to Chenzira's. He offered her a sad smile and mouthed one word. *Tally.*

Her chest caved in. Excruciating torment ripped through her, adrenaline racing through her blood just as the stupid, useless breeze wafted harmlessly over her face. A guttural cry tore through her throat, and she lunged at Samud's feet, knocking the edge of his sword.

Samud kicked her back and sidestepped out of reach as if she were a misbehaving pet. Aviama shook her head to clear it and clawed her way up onto one elbow. "I'm the one who destroyed the magna and blew up your bedroom. I'm the one the Tanashai boy wanted on board. I'm the one he's obsessed with keeping alive, even when your crew drop like flies. He doesn't care about your sailors."

The captain's brows soared. "Tanashai boy?"

Aviama smirked. "He's not a man, Captain."

Shiva crossed the deck in two long strides and ripped Aviama up off the floor by the throat. She gasped for air as pressure crushed her windpipe. Black spots dotted her vision. A shout came from Chenzira's direction, and a blur of movement crossed her vision. Held fast by men on either side, Chenzira swung between them and kicked Shiva square in the torso with both feet, knocking him sideways.

The men holding him jerked him back, but he fought them through the muscle weakness and pain the konnolan must have been causing him. Aviama rubbed at her throat and caught the rail to steady herself. She turned to Chenzira. No, he didn't look impacted at all. He looked strong. Alive. Had he dosed himself with magna before dumping it?

Chenzira spun into the men at his sides and broke their hold. In one smooth motion, he slugged the first in the gut, drew the sword off the second man's belt, and kicked him backward. Chenzira moved into the momentum of the blow, struck Shiva in the shoulder with the butt of his sword, and snaked his arm round the Radhan prince's throat. "Does fighting women half your size make you feel like a man? How about now?"

Shiva slammed his elbow into Chenzira's midsection and tried to rotate into the elbow holding him, but Chenzira didn't budge. Shiva pulled at Chenzira's arm to get space for his windpipe and glared at Aviama. "Call off your dog, Lilac. You know I'll only kill him later if he doesn't comply."

Aviama tilted her head. "I thought you just said you would kill him anyway."

Samud gripped her by the hair again and yanked her head back. "Got a death wish, Princess?"

She smiled sweetly up at him. "I think I've proved I'd rather die than marry Shiva. He said he didn't need to marry me anymore, and you don't want me on board. So let's get on with it."

Samud's grip tightened. "I'm a sailor, and this is my ship. I will not have it destroyed by melderbloods who don't know their place."

"And I'm just an orphan girl whose parents were assassinated and whose life has been stolen by the man you work for. The man who killed Sona without your permission. You want to protect your own, do you not? Is it so wrong for me to protect mine?"

"You've been out of control since the day you boarded."

"Does it really count as *boarding* if you were kidnapped and carried onto the ship against your will?"

A shout from the quarterdeck interrupted them. "We found the fleet, Captain!"

Samud's grip loosened as he turned, and Aviama wrested free of his grasp. She clutched the rail as another wave of nausea hit her and cast her gaze out to sea. Sure enough, a fleet of warships dotted the horizon on their starboard side.

Aviama turned just in time to see one of the men toss a sword to Shiva. He caught it, flipped it in his hands and slashed back toward Chenzira's torso. Aviama screamed and lurched forward, but Samud caught her and threw her back against the rail. She spread her hands, but the wind mocked her, filling the sails of the *Wraithweaver*, but ignoring her call. The konnolan would be impacting her body for hours.

By then it would be too late.

Chenzira leaped back just in time and crossed swords with Shiva. Samud gave two sharp whistles, and sailors poured on deck. Shiva leaped forward, slashing at Chenzira's neck. Chenzira parried, whirled under Shiva's sword arm, and knocked him off balance from behind.

Aviama's chest tightened. She was worthless in combat. And though the two men were evenly matched, the crew would do as Samud commanded. And Samud wouldn't let Shiva die. Would he?

Aviama eyed Samud. His face was set, his eyes dark, as he watched the two young men dance in and out, swords flashing in the sun. The captain might wear patriotic buttons on his jacket, but he had no love for Shiva. What motivated him? Money? Promised power? The legend of Ghosts' Gorge?

Men pressed in around the two princes locked in combat, squeezing Aviama back and out of the forming circle. By the time she found a hole through which to watch, both men had lost their swords, and they were pummeling each other hand to hand. Chenzira struck Shiva with an uppercut to the jaw, and Shiva snapped back, grabbing Chenzira's head in both hands and smashing his own head down on his.

Crackkk!

Aviama winced. Chenzira stumbled back. Shiva dug his thumbs into Chenzira's eyes, but Chenzira wrenched free and pounded Shiva into the deck. Samud snapped his fingers, and three men jumped on Chenzira as he snatched up Shiva's sword and whirled it over the downed prince's head.

If Chenzira killed Shiva, he'd be dead in seconds. If he

didn't, he was dead already. Everyone was dead. Dead, dead, dead.

Aviama's mother. Aviama's father. Liben. Enzo. Sona. Bhumi.

Chenzira wouldn't want her to interfere. He'd look weak. But if he was going to die anyway, what was the difference?

Still, if the sailors could shove her out of the way to watch the show, how was she supposed to fight off multiple trained men? Dizziness knocked her off balance, and she rocked back on her heels, clutching the rail again. Pain rolled through every muscle, every joint. Two crew members hauled away the dead melderblood who'd fallen from the rigging, making space for combat.

Shiva's army was on the horizon, but the crown prince of Radha was busy slugging Chenzira in the stomach as four men held him in place. Chenzira spit blood at Shiva's face. Aviama's mouth went dry, and her stomach soured. Panic welled in her chest.

And then a voice cut through the chaos of her mind.

In a world of snores, be an artist, darlin'...

She blinked. An artist? Now, in the fight? When she could barely stand on two legs?

Be a chameleon.

An idea formed in her mind. If only she could make it down the stairs, it just might work. Aviama edged sideways along the rail, letting sailors fill in the gaps between her and Samud until all she saw was a sea of men. Unable to help herself, she stretched on her toes to look back one final time as the crew shifted and shouted.

Chenzira was staring right at her. His eyes were soft and sad, their fire slowly dying out. Her heart sank. Everything in her screamed at her to remain where she was, to root herself to the spot and refuse to leave his side. Her lips parted, and she gritted her teeth against another wave of konnolan-induced pain and nausea.

Shiva hit him again, and he grunted, but his eyes never left her face. Hurt flickered across his features.

I can't stay. If only he could understand. If only he could know that she was leaving *for* him, not abandoning him. Shiva turned to look in her direction, and Chenzira lunged, smashing his skull into Shiva's.

Aviama fled.

24

Aviama stumbled across the upper deck, Chenzira's hollow eyes and hurt expression haunting her every step. Tears streamed down her face. What if that was the last she ever saw of him? What if he was dead already on the deck behind her? What hope did she have?

Men angled away from her as she flew across the deck. Other melders dotted the ship, supporting themselves against the railings or masts to get through the aftereffects of the konnolan.

Be an artist, darlin'.

Onkar was right. She'd never win this fight like a ciraba. But maybe this moth could pick up a sword after all. Maybe she could be rash and stupid and still join the fight. And maybe she could do more damage and increase her leverage, even while konnolan dampened her magic.

Jignesh eyed her as she passed on the deck and reached out to catch her elbow as she tripped her way down the ship. His face was white, and he winced against the lurching movement to catch her. She patted his hand in wordless thanks, but her eyes were on the stairs.

Onkar appeared just beyond Jignesh, and she stumbled into him. She muttered an apology and pushed off him, doubling back behind the mast again so he'd lose her in the crowd before she made it to the stairs.

A mass of men moved past her to the fight. Face after face of sailors she'd served day after day in the kitchens. Face after face of men she'd come to recognize. And then one set of footsteps stopped and turned. She twisted to look back. The creepy sailor who'd waggled his eyebrows at her. He grinned. She blanched, whirled around, and plunged for the stairs.

The man surged after her, and she half-ran, half-fell down the steps to the main deck. Fingers wrapped around her biceps, and a shot of ice and pain ran up her arm.

"Going somewhere?"

Aviama turned and punched him in the face. He pulled back, but his grip only tightened. He laughed, revealing a missing tooth.

A thick fist crashed through the shadow then, connecting with the man's temple. "Not with you, moron."

The sailor dropped to the floor, and Aviama gaped into the gentle face of Umed. He looped his hands under the arms of the unconscious sailor and jerked his head down the hall. "Whatever you're doing down here, go do it."

Aviama swallowed and nodded. Her heart hammered in her chest. What would Chenzira say if he were with her? Surely this plan would get her at least one tally in her list of stupid ideas. Or a hundred.

But that was okay. Because she'd already planned on dying once today, and of all the acceptable conclusions to the day, being smart and surviving alone while Shiva killed everyone else on his list was not on the docket.

Familiar smokey smells hung in the air from the morning's

use of the furnace as she ricocheted off the doorway and into the main kitchen. Half-rolled balls of dough sat neglected on the worktable. Broken glass littered the floor where someone had dropped or knocked over one of the glasses in their haste to leave the kitchen, leaving a wet rag still wadded up by a bucket of clean glassware.

Aviama snatched up the rag and dug her fingers into the crevices of the furnace until a stone gave way under her touch. She pulled at the stone, and it fell out of its place. The clear container of liquid Onkar had used fell into her hands. She replaced the stone, fumbled her way to the box of cleaning supplies, and yanked out the second container.

It looked the same. Was it the same one?

The bottle was mostly empty. Aviama dumped half the liquid in the clear container from the furnace into the bottle and swirled it once. Only one more ingredient to activate the solution. Only one more piece to the puzzle, but in far greater quantities than before.

How delicate did the ratio of the two solutions have to be? Aviama shoved a crate under the shelf along the wall, stepped up on it, and grabbed the third jar. She ripped off the lid, dumped the spices out, and grabbed at the one at the bottom. The one that looked like myrrh but wasn't. The one with more cracks along the pebbles, and a whole lot more of a bang.

She didn't even remember what it was called. What would happen if she dropped too many rocks into the mixture? If the ratio of the two liquids mattered, and she got it wrong, could she blow her hand off her arm just by being near it?

There was no time to test it. Aviama covered the bottle in the rag and dumped a handful of the rocks into her pants pocket. She'd have to hope for the best. For the sake of them all...

Aviama turned, stabilizing herself on the worktable through another dizzy spell, and froze. Manan stood in the doorway. His face was drawn and pale, and his eyes were red.

"He killed Bhumi, didn't he?"

Fresh tears pricked her eyes, and a lump lodged in her throat. Aviama nodded.

Manan wavered on his feet and clenched his jaw. Sorrow etched the lines of his face, aging his young features by a decade. "What do you need?"

Aviama hesitated. If anyone was going to help her, it would be the melders from the kitchen crew. They were friends, weren't they? Friends and thieves. "I need to get to the helm."

Manan dipped his head and drew the dagger at his side. "I'll go first."

Aviama swept her hand in front of her to gesture him onward, and she fell in behind him as he pivoted to the hall and moved through the hallway and back up the stairs to the upper deck. Shouts crashed about her ears as they emerged under the quarterdeck, and Aviama quickened her pace to keep up with Manan's long strides. Jignesh was still positioned near the stairs. He straightened when he saw them coming but made no further acknowledgment he'd seen them. Umed appeared in the shadows of her peripheral vision among the crates and barrels, his hand on the hilt of the sword at his side, as Aviama stepped into broad daylight and angled for the stairs.

The mob on the upper deck was thick with jeering men making sport of the spectacle. Her stomach soured. But sport was good. If they were toying with Chenzira, he must still be alive to toy with.

The quarterdeck was abandoned, and two sailors manned the aftcastle. The first rushed forward as Manan moved to one side and Aviama stepped toward the wheel. Manan flipped him onto his back and spun toward the second man, but Aviama held up a hand. It was Peg, and the man only gave her a sad smile and slipped past them down the stairs. Manan lurched for the rail and vomited over the side.

Aviama reached into her pocket, pulled out two rocks, and set them on the smooth wood of the helm between two of the handles. The ship's wheel stood as high as her chin, nearly swallowing her behind it. She unwrapped the bottled mixture from the kitchen rag and yanked the cork free.

No one paid her any mind. No one even knew she was there.

Down on deck, a small circle in the swarm revealed the body of a man face up on the wooden planks. His shirt was in tatters, and scuffs and bruises covered every square inch of exposed skin. His eyes were half closed, fluttering as he struggled to stay awake. Chenzira.

Samud's teal coat and golden buttons caught the sunlight off to one side, a silent approval of any death or injury Chenzira might incur. And there in the center, Shiva paced, sword twirling in his hand with a flourish.

In a flash, Shiva's sword whirled overhead, and he clasped it with both hands for a fatal blow. Aviama's heart leaped to her throat. She lunged, snatched the knife from Manan's hand, and hurled the blade down into the fray—directly at Shiva's face.

She'd never had a better throw. The blade flew straight and true, silver glinting in the sun, its sharp edge begging for blood. Samud shouted, and Shiva pivoted at the last second, knocking the knife sideways with his sword.

The knife skittered harmlessly across the deck, and the mob turned as one to gape open-mouthed at Aviama. Terror gripped her chest. Sweat broke out on her brow. But she wasn't some helpless strumpet. She lifted her chin and poured several drops of the mixture onto the rocks set atop the ship's wheel.

Sparks crackled and embers flew in every direction. Smoke went up from the helm with a hiss, and purple liquid oozed down the sides of the wheel. When she glanced back down at the wheel, a hole half the size of her fist had been gouged out of the wood.

Screams and shouts erupted. Sailors tripped over themselves in their haste to surge toward the helm. But Aviama lifted up a handful of fresh rocks and the bottle of liquid solution, and the men skidded to a halt.

"Nobody moves! Nobody moves until I give the order!"

Samud spread his hands. "It's amazing how quickly you've moved from stupid to insane, Princess. Just what do you think you're doing?"

Aviama pulled her shoulders back. "Step away from Chenzira *now*. Clear the area, or I'll blow the wheel to pieces, and we'll be directionless in the sea at the gates of Ghosts' Gorge."

An electric horror rolled through the men like thunder. Sailors scattered, stumbling away from Chenzira until only Samud and Shiva stood near him.

Shiva whirled his sword again. "Getting rid of the magna does nothing. We have enormous quantities of konnolan. You think you did yourself a favor? How would you like konnolan set off every morning instead?"

A moaning rumble swept over the sailors, but Samud held up a hand, and they quieted.

Aviama shrugged. "Go ahead. Waste all your konnolan before we get to the Gorge. Incapacitate a tenth of your men when you need them the most. Destroy the last of their loyalty, as their opinion of you moves from incompetent, rash, and violent; to brainless, wild, and poisonous. Let them know you the way that I do—that anything you touch dies, or wishes it was dead. And that you do not care how many perish in the service of your selfish, bloodthirsty agendas."

Samud tilted his head. "What makes you think we won't just wait you out and kill him after you give up?"

"Because I have something you want. I acquired it just today, and no one will look at it except me." Aviama set a handful of stones on the helm and slipped her hand back into her pocket. She deposited the rest of the stones in her pocket and drew out a folded, painted cloth. Uncorked liquid still held over the wheel in one hand, Aviama lifted the cloth with the other.

Shiva's jaw dropped. Samud gasped and moved forward, but Aviama held up a finger.

"I wouldn't do that if I were you. I can drop the map over the rocks, and it all goes up at once."

Chenzira twisted to look up at her from his place on the deck, and his eyes widened. He grimaced against the pain and crawled on his elbows toward the mast.

Aviama lifted her chin, a new kind of power flooding her veins. Konnolan might be blocking her tabeun abilities, and the wind might not answer her call. But every eye on the *Wraithweaver* was fixed on *her* face. Every ear leaned in to hear *her* voice.

Onkar was right. Only a chameleon could have pulled this off. Running into Onkar on her way to the kitchens was just the stroke of luck she'd needed. The konnolan's waves of weakness and dizzy spells offered good cover for the best lift she'd ever dared accomplish.

"Counteroffer." Shiva strode forward three steps, and Aviama tilted the bottle over the wheel until the liquid lapped at the opening. The sailors shouted, and Shiva halted. He spread his hands, sword still firmly in his grasp. "You'll do as you're told, and I'll reward you with life. A life you clearly don't appreciate or deserve. Hand over the map, and I swear on my mother's life I'll let you live. After we make port, I'll let you go."

Aviama clucked her tongue and shook her head. She scanned the men. "How do you feel, men, that your navigator who swore to get you safely in and out of Ghosts' Gorge *doesn't have the map he needs*?" She turned back to Shiva. "I have no interest in being under your thumb again. You kill Chenzira, you kill Sai, and you'll find me dead by morning—and the map burnt to ash."

"My fleet joins us in an hour. You can hardly walk straight. And you think you can call the shots?"

"Depends. Do you want your fleet to see a woman at the helm, the woman you swore you could control, blowing the *Wraithweaver* to pieces? Do you want to lead them to the Gorge, or be dashed to pieces against the rocks, with no power to navigate?" Aviama eyed the map and glanced back up at Shiva. "The opening looks awfully narrow. Is it true that no other map has the details of its position?"

Samud crossed his arms. "Name your terms, girl."

"If a soul lays a hand on Chenzira or Sai, I destroy the map. If konnolan goes off, I destroy the map. The quarterdeck and aftcastle are mine for the next two hours. Medical supplies for Chenzira will be left at the base of the quarterdeck stairs. There." Aviama gestured to the stairs in front of her.

Samud glared daggers at her, as if by mere imagination he could incinerate her where she stood. "You aren't standing at my helm for two hours."

Aviama arched her eyebrows. "Then you won't *have* a helm, Captain."

She stuffed the map back into her pocket, snatched all but two of the rocks off the wheel, and dripped more of the solution onto them. The wood crackled, sizzled, and smoked, leaving the gaping hole in the wheel almost twice as deep as before. "The fleet can fall in around us. I don't want everyone to die, so I will consult at a distance regarding the position of the rocks. Make your preparations for the Gorge. This conversation is over."

25

As confident as she'd sounded when she made her demands, Aviama could hardly believe it when Shiva lurched for the quarterdeck and Samud dragged him back. Aviama scattered several more rocks on the wheel, and Chenzira slowly hauled himself up against the mast.

"Pssst."

Aviama glanced down at the base of the stairs. Umed and Peg stood side-by-side, Peg rolling an apple in his palm, and Umed taking a swig from his flask.

Peg looked out at the oncoming fleet and kept his voice low. "Your man looks like he's going to fall over. Tell us to go get him."

She squinted down the deck. Chenzira clutched at the mast, face drained of color, leaning his full body weight into the sail. Her heart ached. She nodded and lifted her voice a little higher. "You two. Bring him up here to me."

Sailors parted to let them through—the short, stocky fellow with a deep chest and broad shoulders, and the taller, slim, peg-legged man with graying hair and a scar down his face. A muscular melder still recovering from konnolan, and an unaffected sailor with half Umed's strength.

Aviama dug down in her pocket and pulled out the cloth map. Radha sat to the right of the map, its west coast split by a strip of sand on the northern side and the start of vegetation toward the south. The House of the Blessing Sun sat just inland, along with the thriving city of Rajaad. The dock where Aviama had been taken on board the *Wraithweaver* was positioned right at the meeting point of desert and plant life.

Curion and Tomos were too far east to show up on the map, which seemed to be only a small snapshot of the Aeian Sea and its borders. To the south, the Ghuma River fed into the Aeian Sea, which was in turn fed by other rivers. Aviama had traveled the Ghuma River from the Shalladin on her way to Radha. The northern-most portion of Jannemar was visible, along with markings of outposts on the northeast, and the Horon Mines—the destination Radha's army marched toward as they spoke.

Had they reached the mines yet? Aviama's throat constricted, and she swallowed. No, it was too soon. But if they took control of the mines and gathered wyronite, would they wait to make new weapons before continuing the onslaught, or move straight on to Qalea?

Batal stretched across the northern border of Radha and west across the upper edge of the Aeian Sea, only barely visible on the map before the sea rose up north and off the boundaries of the cloth. The island nation of Keket, with its surrounding islands and reefs, stood proudly in the northwest corner of the map.

And there, impeding Radha's fastest course toward Jannemar by sea, and again blocking the most efficient route toward Keket, was Ghosts' Gorge. No land surrounded the area, but rocks cropped up like cliffs rising straight out of the water. Underwater mountains were marked with a narrow pass between them on the Radhan side, opening up into a circular formation and branching out like long, clawing fingers in three possible exit routes.

Where was the nursery? What were they hoping to accomplish? Was this a slaughter of the Iolani, or a kidnapping mission to steal siren children? Did Shiva really want to strike a deal with the Iolani or destroy them once and for all to gain control of the passage?

A man called out to Samud from the rigging, and she looked up toward the horizon. They were coming up on Shiva's fleet. She could make out the silhouette of flags in the distance. She'd know his intentions soon enough.

Because, according to the map, they were only days away from the Gorge.

Peg and Umed each took one of Chenzira's arms around their shoulders and walked him back toward the quarterdeck. Aviama's stomach dropped, and she tapped the bottle in her hands as she watched their progress toward her. Laksh approached the stairs on her left, lifting a medical kit of some sort so she could see it, and setting it on the quarterdeck several paces to her left before receding back to the base of the steps.

Aviama moved toward it, but Manan reached out and gripped her wrist. "Stay back from the edge. And get down behind the helm. Samud just called archers to the forecastle, and they'll be waiting for a good shot."

Her mouth went dry. She hadn't thought about archers. Aviama nodded. "Tell Laksh to find Sai. I want her up here with me. And tell Umed to find out which melderbloods are on the side of freedom. We're going to need help. And we're going to need crestbreakers."

"I'm a crestbreaker. I'm not sure what Laksh is."

Aviama maneuvered herself behind the helm and gripped the bottle of solution with both hands, fingers digging into the glass as sailors stepped back to let Chenzira, Umed, and Peg through. "We'll need everybody we can find. How's your control?"

Manan grimaced. "Shaky, but better than t'was."

Umed and Peg helped Chenzira up the stairs, and Aviama rushed forward without thinking, abandoning the wheel. Manan pitched forward to cover her, standing between her and the forecastle as she reached for Chenzira.

A lump formed in Aviama's throat, and she swallowed against the guilt and sorrow threatening to overtake her in a tidal wave. Her rash decision had forced the men from the kitchen crew to choose a side—to out themselves as disloyal to Samud in order to protect her. The more they did for her, the more likely it was they'd be killed for their defection.

How could she protect them all? It was hard enough keeping Chenzira and Sai safe from Shiva. But with more numbers came greater responsibility. The last person charged with keeping her alive was her bodyguard, Enzo. Satya had killed him. A weak flame could easily be snuffed out with a puff of air. She had to strengthen their side so that the wind fueled the fire—enough to ward off an attack.

And if her allies consisted entirely of melderbloods, she had to destroy the konnolan, or they'd be a useless heap of dead meat the minute a cannon went off.

Aviama scanned the somber faces before her: Manan, Umed, Peg. Chenzira. Their eyes met, and her breath caught.

Chenzira's dark eyes pierced her through, lit with fire, solemn as the grave. "I'm fine. Set me down; I'll be fine. Get down, Tally."

"You're not fine." She blinked back tears as her gaze traveled down his body. Bruises were already forming, black and blue, across the exposed flesh under his shredded tunic where he'd been beaten to a pulp as four men held him fast. Blood oozed from a gash on his forearm, and another along his ribs. A swollen cut across his cheekbone completed the picture. "You can hardly stand."

"It's just the konnolan. It'll wear off. Move."

"It's not."

"Aviama. Get down behind the helm before you get shot."

Chenzira jerked his head at Manan, and Manan took her by the elbow and yanked her back behind the wheel without a word. Umed and Peg brought Chenzira down beside her behind the helm and leaned him against it.

"I can't see from here. I need to see the forecastle. He's got four men on the forecastle and two in the rigging. What weapons do they have in the rigging? If they get—"

Umed held up a hand. "You need to rest. I'll watch the rigging."

Manan scanned the rigging, forecastle, and upper deck. Peg took the medical kit from him and passed it to Chenzira. Manan let him take it and turned to Aviama. "What now?"

Aviama sucked in a deep breath and let it out, twisting the rings on the fingers of the hand still holding the bottle of explosive solution. "Lessons start tonight. Whoever wants to drown the fears of their Awakening, replacing the nightmares of unmitigated chaos with the confidence of mastery of their element, havoc with utility, helplessness with strength—tell them to be ready. Tell them to join me. Tell them that if they think konnolan will stop a civilization of sirens in their own home, they can think again. And if they don't start fighting like melderbloods, they'll die like dogs."

Manan stood up tall and offered her a stiff bow. "As you say, Your Highness."

Aviama blanched. "Please don't call me that."

He furrowed his brow. "Isn't it proper?"

She grimaced. "It feels wrong out here, somehow. I'm the same girl as I was rolling dough and practicing lifts in the kitchen between serving bread and ale. And everyone who calls me *Princess* or *Highness* either assumes I'm an idiot or wants to use me as their pawn."

Manan clasped his hands behind his back and pursed his lips. "I can't call you by your first name."

"Yes, you can. I'm just a girl out here trying not to die."

"Like it or not, ma'am, you're not *just* anything anymore."

Umed and Peg murmured their agreement. Aviama looked to Chenzira for help, but he only looked back at her expectantly. *Go on,* he seemed to say. *They're right. Deal with it.*

If they wouldn't call her Aviama, and she denied them the use of Highness, what *could* they call her? The famed sovereign Shamaran line would be twice as bad, emphasizing not just her royal status, but her connection with the kingdom that brought magic back into the world.

She bit her lip and spread her hands. "Then call me what you like, but if you aren't going to use my first name, I ask you not to use my last name either."

"As you say." Manan dipped his head and tapped the fingers of one hand to his chest. "Heartmeet."

Aviama swallowed hard and blinked back unshed tears stinging her eyes. "Heartmeet."

Manan slipped away down the stairs, and Aviama's gut wrenched to see him go. Would his head appear in a box by nightfall? She hadn't mentioned protection by name for anyone but Sai or Chenzira. Then again, was it really a good strategy to pick off sailors one by one this close to the Gorge?

Umed rapped his thumb on the hilt of his dagger and positioned himself by the starboard railing at the top of the stairs, and Peg moved to the opposite end, leaving Aviama and

Chenzira alone in the middle behind the ship's wheel. Aviama twisted on the floor toward Chenzira and gasped at the blood still seeping into the hem of his shirt from the open wound across his ribs.

Chenzira snorted, then coughed, wincing at the pain of the movement. "Sand and sea, Tally, it's not that bad."

She set her jaw. "Why did you do that? Why did you break into Samud's quarters? You could have been killed."

He drilled her with a cool stare. "You really want to lecture me on dangerous decisions? Would you like to tell me why you've been trying to die all day today?"

Aviama looked away. A sinking feeling pulled at her chest, and her breathing quickened. "I haven't been trying to die all day."

"Don't lie to me. I'm a forgiving man, Aviama, but never lie to me."

Aviama stared down at her hands, fiddling with the edge of the glass bottle. "If I didn't, you'd be dead."

"What are you talking about?"

"Shiva's threatened to kill you, Sai, and Bhumi all voyage. Sai and Bhumi are *my* maidservants, which means they're *my* responsibility. Mine to protect. No one else will. After last night—with Durga—"

Aviama swiped angrily at a runaway tear and swallowed hard.

Chenzira reached toward her, and she snatched her hand away.

"I'm fine." She set the bottle down between her legs, plucked the medical kit from his lap, and strained to rip it open.

"Clearly." The thin material of the kit gave way, and he watched her yank out ointments and bandages, then pursed his lips. "You could have just untied the bag. There's an opening on the other side."

"Of course there is." Aviama groaned and ran trembling fingers through her hair. She could feel Chenzira's gaze hot on her face as she dug through the supplies.

Chenzira cleared his throat. "Do you think if you don't look at me, you won't have to tell me why your solution this morning was a wild rampage that looked an awful lot like suicide?"

Aviama bit her lip and turned her face away again, letting her hair fall like a curtain between them as she rifled through small medicine bottles. Weight pulled at her heart, a crushing pressure suffocating her throat and chest. Chenzira was right, of course. And he'd just told her not to lie to him. But she couldn't say the words out loud, either.

Yes, I planned to die. It was the only way that I could see. It was the only way to keep you safe...

Aviama uncorked one of the little bottles and smelled it. Wine. She set down the cork and lifted a clean bandage in her free hand.

"Aviama, look at me."

"No."

"Aviama."

Aviama ignored him and reached across his body to pour half the contents of the wine over the gaping wound draping Chenzira's ribs. He slammed a fist into the deck and let out a stifled guttural sound as the alcohol hit the gash.

If he hadn't been probing, she might have felt sorry for him. But as it was, she doused the cut on his forearm next, before he could recover. Chenzira swore under his breath. She reached for his forehead, and he captured her wrist in a vise.

"Do you honestly expect me to believe you planned on surviving what you did today in Shiva's quarters?"

She winced. Tears welled in her eyes, but she blinked them back. "Chen..."

Chenzira shook his head, his grip tightening on her wrist. He took in a ragged breath. "I saw you come up over the stern. You looked—you looked like fury on wings. I've never seen anything like it. Like a song caught up in a storm, something captivating and deadly all at once. Shiva's men already had me, and they were dragging me up the steps. But I couldn't take my eyes off you."

He hesitated, examining her slender hand, and his thumb stroked the soft skin of the underside of her wrist. "I've taken life before, Aviama. And I've seen other men take it. This morning, you had death in your eyes. A resigned, determined look, like power melted into hopelessness. I imagine I'll dream of it for years to come. You were set on killing, and you were set on dying. Deny it."

Aviama's lips parted, and she turned to look at him. Her heart hammered in her chest, and a deep ache stirred inside her soul. She searched his endless, rich brown eyes, and any hope of escaping the truth evaporated.

He knew it. She knew it.

She took a breath to speak when another voice cut the tension.

"Plucky. Surprising. I'm impressed."

Aviama jumped and twisted toward the sound.

One man moved up the stairs to the quarterdeck, and Umed and Manan let him do it. Onkar Dhoka.

26

———

The cloth map in her pocket practically burned against her leg as Onkar glided up the steps carrying an open tray of food, dropped to a seated position on the edge of the deck's level, and popped his elbow up on his bent knee.

Aviama eyed the tray and clenched her jaw. Was the man never ruffled by anything? Did he just slink from conversation to conversation, oiling his way in to appear with his snide comments and affable attitudes while everybody else suffered?

Chenzira stiffened beside her, and somehow his reaction soothed her. He felt the same way. On the one hand, Aviama respected Onkar and thought they had become somewhat friendly. But on the other...

She steeled herself to keep from checking on the map in her pocket. It was there, safe and sound. No need to announce it to the ship's resident swindler.

Onkar slid the tray across the space between them and cocked his head. "Risky. Stupid." He grinned. "That's the best way to start the life of a cheat, little missy. The incapable die, and the survivors end up like me—or working for me."

Aviama ignored the tray, and her grumbling stomach, and reached for the bottle of oil instead. She gently doused the wounds on Chenzira's ribs and arm and dabbed lightly with a cloth. "Needed a good reason for a cook to come chat with me?"

"I'm nothing if not helpful. What kind of cook would I be if I didn't bring food?" He dropped his voice low and leaned toward her, his eyes suddenly steel. "I also thought congratulations were in order. Nice lift."

Aviama shrugged as she unwrapped a strip of clean cloth. "I must have a good teacher."

"You need to get rid of the konnolan."

Aviama leveled him with a dark glare. "Thanks, genius."

Onkar's brows soared, and he held up his hands. "Gold and gumption, Rookie's made one good lift, and she's saucy as my mother's cameline." He sucked his teeth. "You still need me."

Aviama opened a packet of herbs, smelled it, and gagged.

Chenzira plucked it from her fingers and replaced it with a different pack from the kit, then turned to Onkar. "I think it's high time you considered that you don't hold all the cards, Grigglor. It is Grigglor, isn't it? What do you go by, Griggy?"

Onkar's fingers froze halfway through running a hand through his hair. He completed the motion, examined his cuticles, and plucked at an invisible something on his shirt. "You've got the wrong gent, boy."

Aviama glanced between the men. Grigglor?

A muscle in Chenzira's neck tensed, and his eyes bored the swindler through. "No, I don't think I do. I think you're running from a cursed family name, and you take on any name but yours. I also think *Frizzletwerf* is such a ridiculous surname that no one would ever forget it, least of all one of such high status and scandal. And I think if either the prince *or* the captain discovered you were a Frizzletwerf—or that you were Onkar Dhoka, or any number of your aliases undermining the work of the Radhan crown and selling secrets like candies on the street—well, I don't think they'd take too kindly to it."

Aviama gaped at Chenzira.

Onkar's eyes narrowed. He waited a beat, then dismissed Chenzira with a wave of his hand and leaned in toward Aviama again. "If you've got half a brain—which I questioned at the beginning of this venture, but now have come to believe you have—you'll be training more melderbloods by nightfall and setting up a plan for getting off the quarterdeck without being murdered. Considering how many ships will be able to take you out an hour from now when we are surrounded, you haven't got time to spare. And your chameleon skin is improving, but could use finessing."

"I see." Aviama returned her focus to Chenzira's arm, crushing the herbs and placing them over the wound. "You have everything figured out. What do you recommend?"

Onkar—or Grigglor, or whatever his name was—let out an easy laugh. "I was born for the limelight, darlin', but I live for the shadows. Continue training with me out of the kitchens. I'll teach you to survive in the cracks, to hear through walls, not to rely on brawn or melder power. I'll train you individually in every spare moment between now and the Gorge."

Aviama shook her head. "We are *days* from the Gorge. And as much as I'd appreciate the tutelage, I can't afford to split my focus. I have other priorities first."

"I know where the konnolan is."

Aviama and Chenzira swiveled to look at him. "And?"

He held up one finger. "First, might I suggest controlling

rather than destroying it? After all, it's possible the Iolani will not appreciate our presence, and we can't hold a candle to them either with power or knowledge of the sea."

"Where is it?"

"I'll tell you as soon as I receive the second half of your payment for the voyage. And you agree to include me in the plan to get the konnolan."

Aviama groaned.

Chenzira balled one hand into a fist. "What if we forget the payment, and I forget your name?"

"You never knew my name, kid."

"I'm not your kid. You're not that old, and I'm not that young."

Aviama rolled her eyes at the chest-puffing, laid a hand on Chenzira's arm, and rotated to face Onkar. "Tomorrow morning you will bring me not only the location of the konnolan, but more hands, and a security plan for keeping us alive. After all, that's what we're paying you for. Safe passage. I'll pay you the rest, and you'll get us not only through the Gorge, but safely off this ship, or I will personally ensure that every snitch in Radha spreads the rumor that Grigglor Frizzletwerf is alive and well and looking to get back into the family business."

She had no idea what the family business was, or what would happen if people learned Onkar's real name. But all hints of his comfortable languid movements vanished at her words, and she knew in that moment that whatever Chenzira had uncovered about him was true.

"You need me."

Aviama shrugged. "And you need me. But for whatever reason, Shiva continues to want me alive. Can the same be said for you? Don't deceive yourself. To him and Samud, you are no more valuable than Sona."

"Bring payment, Rookie. Tomorrow morning. And as you gather people you think are allies, don't mistake friendliness for loyalty."

You mean the way you've been friendly to me?

Aviama dipped her head. "Leave the food. Tomorrow morning, we meet in the pantry opposite the kitchens. Make sure it's empty."

Onkar slithered back into his casual demeanor and offered her a smile she neither returned nor believed. "I always offer full service to my favorite maladroit customers. By the time you get off the *Wraithweaver,* you'll qualify for a higher level of service, and I'll drop that fee for any returning business you require."

Aviama pursed her lips. "Chivalrous."

Onkar winked and hopped off the edge of the quarterdeck, landed on the upper deck, and disappeared.

Chenzira clenched his jaw. "I don't like him. I don't trust him."

Aviama arched an eyebrow. "You don't *trust* the black market cheat you hired, who betrayed us, and then asked for more money?" She clutched at her chest dramatically. "Say it isn't so!"

He laughed. "You sound like my sister."

Aviama wrapped Chenzira's arm in clean cloth, tucked in the end, and set it down. A wave of emotion caught her by the throat. She had a family she missed and loved. How selfish she'd been not to have asked Chenzira about his. But he'd run away from his family...

"What happened?"

"My father wanted me to take on more responsibility in the family, but what he asked me to do ... I couldn't do it. I couldn't be part of it. My older brother hates me for it, and he and his mother wanted me gone."

"Wait. Your *brother's* mother hates you? You don't have the same mother?"

Chenzira shook his head. "My sister and I are the only children of our mother. My mother wasn't welcome at court. She wasn't welcome anywhere. She died before I could meet her."

Aviama's heart pinched, and an ache returned to her chest at the sorrow deep inside the faraway look in his eyes. What would it be like to have a mother she'd never met? To know that this figure everyone had in their lives was missing? Aviama had lost her mother. But she clung to memories of her like a child with a favorite blanket, replaying them at night to help her sleep.

She hesitated, then reached up with one hand and softly tilted his head back so the gash on his forehead faced the sky. He let her do it, and she poured the wine over the wound, catching the runoff in excess bits of cloth.

He winced, but made no sound. Aviama added the oil and poultice next. Her fingers lingered on his face, and he turned into her touch, his warm skin against her palm.

"Come to Keket with me."

Her stomach flopped. "What?"

He took her hand and squeezed it. "Not forever. Part of me doesn't want you anywhere near my family. Most of them are horrible people, and I never thought I'd go back. But with everything that's happened, and the way you keep fighting to protect your family and your people—there's someone I need to protect too. Maybe, when things calm down, I could get my sister out."

"She's at the palace in Keket?"

"No, I got my father to hide her from my brother in a village on the outskirts. She's safe, but ... it's not the life for her."

Aviama nodded. She'd been sequestered away herself, locked in castle rooms, and knew what it was like to be unable to do anything. Chenzira's sister was hidden in a village or on a farm in the middle of nowhere. It didn't seem like a fair life for anyone. Aviama had hated every minute of it.

"Is it safe for you to go back?"

The corner of Chenzira's mouth tipped up. "No."

She laughed. "Death-defying feats?"

"Always." He grinned. "Will you come with me?"

"Yes."

Her quick answer surprised her. It had rushed from her lips before she had the chance to think about it, and from the dumbstruck look on Chenzira's face, her ready response had surprised him just as much. Aviama opened her mouth, closed it, and bit her lip.

Chenzira leaned in and kissed her on the cheek. "Then you're going to have to stop trying to die, Tally. Because there's no one else I want with me."

Warmth flooded her body. Aviama reached for him, the memory of last night's closeness sending goosebumps along her skin—and then Manan cleared his throat from the stairs.

Aviama gasped and lurched backward. She'd totally forgotten herself. What was wrong with her? She was hiding behind the ship's wheel to avoid getting skewered by the arrows of her enemies, watched over by sailors who had betrayed their captain and their prince to keep her alive, and all she could focus on was the man beside her who spun her insides to goo?

Chenzira chuckled to himself as she turned, and she tried to ignore the way the pleasant sound sent a thrill through her.

Laksh had brought Sai, as requested, and the two of them moved up the stairs. Umed jerked his chin toward the front of the ship, and Aviama twisted to see Samud speaking quietly with Shiva and four of his senior sailors at the forecastle. To either side of the prow, the pakshi symbol of Radha was now visible on the flags of the oncoming fleet as they drew nearer and nearer.

Umed set his jaw. "We need you out of sight before those ships reach us."

Sai knelt on Aviama's other side so that Aviama was sandwiched between Chenzira and Sai. "But she's a sitting duck below deck too. We can't put her in an enclosed space with no exits."

Umed shook his head. "All it takes are a few archers in the rigging, or men with knives and a good arm, and we're all dead by morning."

"Another konnolan cannon would do it too." Chenzira shifted his position against the ship's wheel and stretched his legs out in front of him. "None of us will be able to move. If they're able to set one off when they believe Aviama won't or can't blow up the helm, we're done."

Aviama gathered her feet under her and pivoted, leaning over Sai to peer around the wheel. A dozen men crossed the upper deck, carrying a translucent box between them, sloshing water on either side as they moved. Makana gripped the bars over the opening with both hands to stabilize herself as they carried her. One of the men at the far corner tripped, and the men scrambled to recover the weight on that side as Makana's heavy tail slammed into the wall of her cage.

"Makana." Aviama's heart sank. Shiva still had one person Aviama cared about under his thumb. And even if he wanted her alive for whatever he had planned at the Gorge, she was confident he wasn't above torture.

Samud eyed the man in the rigging of the mainmast, and the man turned so his back was to her as he looked down at his captain. What was he gesturing to Samud? Did he have any distance weapons on him?

Makana dropped down into the water and pressed her hands against the glass-like walls, her lavender gaze sweeping the deck this way and that.

"We need to make a move for the konnolan tonight." Aviama stretched out her hand. The wind did not answer. "As soon as our abilities return."

Aviama looked over the crew assembled before her on the quarterdeck. Umed, Laksh, Manan, Chenzira, and Sai stared back at her. Five melders, four fighters, three sailors—all defectors risking their lives to follow her lead.

Only Jignesh was missing from the kitchen crew.

Manan shifted his weight. "But we won't know where it is until morning, ma'am."

Sai frowned. "You don't know where it is?"

Aviama gaped at her. "You do?"

"Yes. It's under—"

Aviama held up a hand. "Okay, stop right there. Before we get to that." She swallowed and turned to the five rebels arranged on the deck before her. Chenzira and Sai sat on either side of her. Umed and Manan flanked them, standing near enough to listen, but watching each of the steps leading up to the quarterdeck. And Laksh, crouching several paces in front of her, one hand on his dagger and the other sneaking a roll from the tray Onkar had brought.

What she was about to say could change everything about their little band. How many of them would stay when she made them choose? She steeled herself and spoke slowly, choosing her words carefully.

"I'm grateful to Onkar. He's a good tutor, and he brought us together. But Onkar doesn't want the konnolan gone. He wants it transferred from Samud and Shiva's control to *his* control. I'm tired of anyone using it for control at all. As long as it exists on board, we can be incapacitated and disposed of without any way to defend ourselves."

Manan grimaced, and Umed crossed his arms. Aviama took a breath.

"If anyone wants out, now is the time. I realize you've risked your lives to publicly join me. I didn't ask you to do that. But I'm grateful. If you do nothing else for me, if you walk away, know that I will not hold it against you. I will forever hold you in the highest esteem."

Aviama looked long and hard at each of them. Sai stared back at her with a firm, expectant expression. She was in. Umed was unreadable. Laksh adjusted his head wrap and eyed her skeptically from across the bridge of his crooked nose. They might be against Samud, but they hadn't expected to have to choose between Onkar and Aviama.

Her mouth went dry, and her breathing ticked up a notch. Chenzira extended his fingers in the smallest gesture toward her, small enough she might have been the only one to notice. *Calm,* he seemed to say. *Shhh. You got this.*

She looked into his eyes for a long moment, soaking up the confidence she found there. Aviama nodded and turned back to the rest of the group.

"Onkar brought you all to work with him. He knew he'd bring me on, and he knew melderbloods had more reason not to trust Shiva than any others on the crew. He was planning all this from the beginning. He wanted us together, and he wanted me to train melders. And I intend to. I just don't know his endgame." She spread her hands. "In short, I need to know —are you with me?"

Silence fell. Aviama squirmed, gripping the glass bottle of explosive solution between her hands and drumming her fingertips against it. The cloth map seemed to itch in her pocket, mocking her for stuffing her greatest leverage in a wad in the most obvious place imaginable.

Umed drew his dagger, and Chenzira lurched forward. Aviama's heart lodged in her throat as she surged to her feet, but Umed wasn't focused on Aviama. He was focused on the upper deck.

Aviama spun just as a man in the rigging lifted a bow and arrow into the air.

27

———————

A *dagger isn't going to do much against arrows.*

But then she saw the archer hadn't notched an arrow, but lifted his bow into the air in a sweeping gesture toward Shiva's fleet as they drew nearer. A shout went up from the closest of the ships as the men on deck of that vessel caught sight of the siren on board the *Wraithweaver.* Samud's crew whooped and hollered, thrusting their weapons in the air.

The sailors next to Makana began to taunt and jeer, pounding against the side of her cage. She lunged toward the walls, baring her teeth like a wild animal. The crew laughed, teaming up to pitch the cage this way and that, so the water level dropped, and her body was smashed into the sides of the narrow enclosure. Makana shoved up with her tail and seized the bars overhead, but one of the guards assigned to her whirled his harpoon, stabbing at her fingers as they clutched at the bars.

Aviama's chest tightened. She reached for the wind, and this time she could feel it bump up against her skin in answer, but her powers had not returned enough to use it. Heat flushed her face as Makana thrashed in the water and the men sneered at her through the glass. Aviama took a step toward the stairs.

Umed sidestepped, blocking her path. "You can't go out there, and you can't blow the helm. The minute you do, all leverage is lost."

Aviama stared at Makana, tears stinging her eyes as she turned back to Umed. "They can't do that."

He looked back at her, calm and steady. "They can. They will. And you don't just *want* us on your side, you need us. The truth is, we need you too. If you die, we die. We have tied our fates to yours, and we're betting on you. So I'll not be moving from this spot."

Aviama pressed her lips together, and her shoulders sagged. She looked back out on the deck. Makana hit the side of her cage, and this time, a daring sailor threw an apple into the water at her. How long before they added tar, or konnolan —or arrows?

Up on the forecastle, Shiva was laughing. The sight of him brought bile to her throat. He caught her eye, and his laughing lips curled into a sneering smile.

Samud had his eye on his long glass. Aviama turned to follow his gaze out into the open sea, but saw nothing. Did he expect to see the Gorge already? Or were they that lost without access to the map in her pocket?

A feral hissing screech emanated from Makana's cage on the upper deck. The men cackled and howled, and one slung the butt of his sword to hit her on the head. She lunged, seized the hilt, and nearly wrested it from his grasp. But three other men joined the struggle, and the edge of a guard's harpoon drew blood as it grazed her neck.

Where was the seamen's fear of sirens now? Where was

their respect for the ocean, of legends come to life, of the terror of Ghosts' Gorge?

If the thirst for blood prevailed over a healthy respect for the Iolani's power by the time they reached the Gorge, one of two things would happen. Either the konnolan would succeed in subduing the merpeople, and there would be a slaughter—and Iolani children stolen for menageries and exhibits and abuse—or the Iolani would crush the measly humans who invaded their territory once again, crushing them against the rocks and drowning them in the depths as they had for centuries.

The Iolani were undefeated for hundreds of years. What arrogance led Samud's crew now to taunt a siren? Having one single mermaid in their clutches? Did they think the Iolani would surrender their home, all their families, because one of them had been taken?

No, the konnolan needed to be destroyed. And the crew needed to remember to fear Makana. If they didn't, Radha's greeting to the Iolani might be the corpse of one of their own, strung up with the sails.

Aviama gritted her teeth. She moved back behind the helm, held the bottle on the wheel between her hands, and fixed her eyes on Makana. The siren thrashed against the sides of her narrow cage, the water level already lower than it had been when they brought her out. Aviama opened her mouth and sang.

The first notes were light and small, snatched away by the wind. But as resolve hardened in her chest, a wordless song spilled from her lips and flowed out over the deck, rising like the tide and filling the air.

At first, no one seemed to notice, but then one of the guards turned to look at her, and another sailor, and another. One of the crew had climbed up on the rowboat kept on the deck and halted mid-stroke over Makana's cage with a club in his fist. Makana turned at last, her impenetrable lavender gaze locking onto Aviama.

Sing with me. Remind them what sirens do.

There was no need for a death lullaby. Only a threatening reminder that she *could*.

Makana pressed her hands against the glass. And as Aviama dove into a new measure, Makana lifted her face above the surface of the water and joined her, weaving harmonies above and below Aviama's melody with a voice clear as crystal, soft as velvet, and bold as glittering gold.

Several of the men threw their hands over their ears, but most stilled to listen to the siren and the human, their duetting melody sweeping over the *Wraithweaver* and carrying out to sea. Aviama pulled herself up tall, tossed one rock in the air from the helm, and poured a drop of solution on it as it fell.

The song swelled, and Makana took over the melody as sparks crackled in the air. Aviama intertwined her music with that of the siren, dancing in and out of Makana's notes as the last of the explosion's embers floated toward the oak planks of the deck. A thrill ran through her at the magic of the sounds gracing her ear—the sound of a siren's song set to harmony.

Had any human heard a siren sing and lived to tell the tale?

Legends still carried memory of one or two seamen who had heard the death lullaby, tied to the mast, or locked in the brig, and had lived. But those days were hundreds of years past.

Until the arena. Until Aviama.

The song fell into a haunting minor key, and Makana rose up out of the water, gripping the bars overhead and daring the men around her cage to strike at her hands. But no one moved. No one dared.

How easy it would be for her to switch from one song to another—from life to death?

Aviama lifted one hand, and as the final note rolled out, long and powerful, she met Makana's eyes and closed her fist at the end of the beat, the two of them falling silent in an instant.

The other ships were nearer now, and their men gaped spellbound at the *Wraithweaver*.

Aviama raised the bottle of solution in one hand, placed her other hand on one of the handles of the ship's wheel, and drilled Shiva with a cool stare.

Nothing that she could say would be as terrifying as what the crew had just witnessed.

Not only did they recall every story, every tale of sirens and their death songs—not only did they edge away from Makana and cast her fearful glances—but the melderblood princess had commanded the siren, and the siren had listened.

Makana flashed Aviama a pearl-white smile, and she smiled back. Warmth warred with an ache in her chest. How beautiful to sing with a siren, how honored she was to have garnered the loyalty of the people beside her on the quarter-deck. But how many of them would survive until morning? How many of them would see the Gorge? Would any of them return home?

Shiva glared at her, but she only drilled him with a cool look before turning back to the crew. Shiva rang his sword free of its sheath, thrust it into the air, and raised a shout.

"To the Gorge!"

The men answered his cry, fists and weapons in the air, but as they returned to their duties, a disquieting sense of unease moved through the ether. Mist rolled in from the direction of their heading, and within minutes, the *Wraithweaver* and its supporting fleet were enveloped in fog.

A chill ran down Aviama's spine. She swallowed hard and turned to her companions.

Laksh opened his mouth, closed it again, and shook his head. "If you were wond'rin' where me loyalties lie, miss, they're with you."

Manan grinned, eyes wide in wonder, as he turned to look at Aviama. "She shouldn't be a miss. She's not a miss. Not after that."

Umed touched his fingers to his chest and dipped his head in a slight bow. "Heartmeet, Commander. We're with you."

Aviama pulled back in surprise. *Commander.*

Sai stepped into Aviama's side and nudged her arm. "We're with you."

Chenzira smiled and rubbed his hands together. "It's time to plan. Let's see the map."

28

———

Aviama stretched her hand out into the fog. It had only grown thicker in the hours since their planning began. She could see snatches of the masts and sails of the fleet around them through the gauzy blanket of white, hemming them in to starboard, to port, and to the aft of the *Wraithweaver*. But she saw Makana only through haze, and sometimes only barely. The forecastle was completely lost to her sight.

A spider scurried across the helm. Aviama snatched her hand out of its path.

Chenzira chuckled beside her. "Princes and murderers, no problem, but spiders?"

Aviama grimaced. "They're creepy. And they have too many legs."

Chenzira adjusted the bandage over the wound on his ribs. He'd managed to stand, against nearly everyone's better judgment, and had stood beside her at the helm for the last hour. Did he want to ensure the crew saw that he was strong? That he wasn't defeated? Or did he just want to be close to her?

Any reason would do. His quiet confidence was a welcome contrast to the incessant hammering of her own heart inside her chest.

Aviama held up a hand and reached for the wind. It leaped to her bidding, wafting around her fingers and dispelling a wave of fog in a tumbling swirl. She released it and dropped her hand. As grateful as she was to have her powers back, it meant Durga had hers back too. And any of the other melderbloods on board whom Shiva might have bribed or blackmailed to secure their allegiance.

A new thought dropped into her mind, and she turned to the men behind her. "Has anyone ever seen Onkar use melder abilities?"

Umed frowned. "No. But he might not want to reveal which power he has."

Laksh stroked his beard. "He ain't never looked peakish neither. Konnolan or no."

Aviama raised her eyebrows. She pivoted toward Manan.

He shook his head. "Never."

"Interesting."

Aviama chewed her lip. What did it mean? Was he melderblood, and playing his powers close to the vest in favor of his chameleon skillset? Or was he not a melderblood, but surrounding himself with powerful players and seeking the insurance of konnolan in his pocket?

Sai shifted her weight. "He's coming."

Aviama glanced down to see Shiva approaching the steps of the quarterdeck, gliding through the fog like a serpent through water. Parth, the sailor who'd done Shiva's bidding in the brig, flanked him on one side. Durga strode forward on his other side, face set, chin high.

Chenzira stiffened beside her. Aviama passed him the rocks and the solution and gave a nod. Chenzira shot Shiva a dirty look, but backed toward the second set of stairs. Manan and Chenzira manned one side, while Sai and Laksh manned the other. Umed positioned himself in the aftcastle, sweeping the rigging of the *Wraithweaver* and surrounding ships.

Durga sent a chill breeze wafting Aviama's hair back over her shoulders and sneered.

Aviama offered Shiva a mirthless smile. "I'm surprised you brought your lapdog with you, after she turned the captain's kitchen into a whirlwind, spilled secrets like a fountain, and dropped me in the sand at the dock. Her secret keeping is almost as bad as her tabeun control."

Durga bristled. Shiva glared. Both brought Aviama a measure of satisfaction.

"If you want this ship to avoid hitting the underwater portion of the rocks, it's time to share the map and give up the helm," Shiva said.

Aviama pulled the map from her pocket and dangled it in the air. "Share? I wouldn't dream of it. You can have it. But if we're going to give up the helm, you're going to ensure our safe passage to the kitchens."

Shiva swept up the steps, and Durga moved to follow.

Sai stepped forward and shook her head, palm out. "Just him."

Durga shot a blast of air at Sai, but Sai responded with a blast of her own. The blows met in the middle and dissipated to either side in a puff of churning fog.

Durga's lip curled. "I'm coming up."

Aviama spread her hands. "By all means, ignore our instructions. And we, in turn, will ignore our deal, keep the helm, turn the ship around, and destroy the map."

Shiva cut Durga a withering glare. She stopped halfway up the steps, scowled, and planted both hands on her hips. Parth rested one hand on the rail and the other on the hilt of his sword.

Aviama swallowed as Shiva approached. She spun the rings on her fingers. What if he put archers in position and Umed missed them? What if Durga was a distraction, and a horde of other melders waited to attack? How could they trust Shiva to hold to his end of the bargain if they gave up the helm?

Shiva glanced at Aviama's fiddling hands and grinned. "Nervous?"

She set her jaw and folded her hands. "Tell me, how much konnolan do you have? Do you have enough to set it off every hour, incapacitate a tenth of your crew, and still immobilize the Iolani? Do you even know how many of them there are?"

"Why don't you let me worry about that? Strategy is not your strong suit. Don't you remember who informed me about konnolan in the first place?"

Aviama's gut wrenched.

Shiva gestured toward the map. "Let's see it."

She eyed him, but swept the rocks back into her pocket and unrolled the map against the handles of the ship's wheel. Shiva moved closer, his arm brushing hers as he leaned in to examine it. Aviama flinched, and he leaned into her again with a soft laugh before looking at the cartography in earnest.

He ran a finger along the lines of the map, glancing up several times into the distance, and referring again to the map with its numbers and outline of the rock formations of Ghosts' Gorge. He glanced up and beckoned to Parth. "Long glass."

Parth fumbled along his belt for the long glass and tossed it up to Shiva. He caught it in one smooth motion and brought it up to his eye.

Aviama squinted, but she could barely even make out the rest of the fleet around them. Visibility was murky at best.

"There's no way you can see anything."

Shiva pulled down the long glass and shook his head. "Look here." He drew his finger across the tallest of the rock formations on the map, lining one side of the narrow passage, and then pointed out to the horizon. "There." He handed her the glass.

Aviama arched an eyebrow, but took it, and looked in the direction he indicated. White fog. A glimpse of glittering sea. More fog. She shrugged. "There's nothing there."

Shiva took the long glass back, searched the horizon with it, then held the glass in place and moved out of the way. "Look again."

She pursed her lips but did as he said. This time, dark gray rocks wet with sea spray rose from the ocean, just visible through a patch in the fog. It was far taller than she'd imagined. But then, the map didn't indicate the height of the rocks. Some numbers did mark the depth of the outermost rocks, the ones tall enough to rip up the hulls of ships, but too far underwater to see until right on top of them. But the portion above the surface was more like cliffs and walls than a few scattered rocks.

"How do you know which part of the formation it is? It's there, but how do you know you're on this side of it, rather than that side?"

"In fog this thick? We don't. If we wait for night, and the air is clear, we can navigate by the stars. But if the fog stays like this, there won't be much to go by."

"Is it really a good idea to go, then? Is this mission really worth the lives of all your men?"

Shiva took the long glass and gave her a long look. "We're going to the Gorge. And Radha will take back the sea."

No visibility. Cliffs on either side. Invisible enemies in the depths. Death lullabies waiting to pull every last sailor into the sea. And a prince willing to kill all his men.

Aviama's stomach dropped. No wonder the crew was nervous. They should never have come.

The only hope of stopping him now was to destroy the konnolan before reaching the Gorge. Which meant they were running out of time.

If they could decimate the konnolan supply before reaching the rocks, Shiva's best shot at success against the Iolani would be gone. They'd be defenseless except for untrained, chaotic melders. And even then, melderbloods had no defense against a siren's death lullaby.

Aviama looked out at the expanse of cloud and water ahead of them. She raised both hands, summoning the wind. Mist rolled out of the path of her work as she pushed it back like a blanket. But there was too much.

"Sai? Help me target the fog on the far side. Not anything near us. Only there, as far out as you can reach..."

Sai lifted her hands, and the two of them pushed at the fog. At first, nothing moved. Aviama strained in the effort, bending her focus to the patch of thickest fog she'd seen obscuring her view through the long glass. And then, slowly, thick white cloud began to roil this way and that at her interference.

Shiva gaped at the patch of fog. The thickest portion was too far to influence, but they'd managed to shift a large section between their ships and the rock formation. Aviama admired their work. She'd never done something like that before. But with Sai's help, they'd done it. Would he dare dispose of her now, knowing she could clear the way for the ship?

Shiva looked through the long glass again, then glanced down at the cloth map. "We're too far starboard. If you don't want us to crash, you might need to do that again." He turned the ship's wheel.

"I'll let you keep the map, and I'll consider helping again, but my terms remain. I need the main kitchen."

"You're not getting the kitchen."

Aviama crossed her arms. "The pantry, then."

Shiva peered at the horizon and adjusted the wheel without looking at her. "Last time you had access to the kitchen, you nearly blew up the ship, so I'm going to go with *no.* No to the kitchen, no to the pantry, and no to anything stuffed with ingredients you might use for anything other than bread."

Manan opened his mouth, but Aviama shot him a dark look, and he closed it. Aviama took a breath. "We need a place out of sight. With a door. And we won't take the brig."

"You can take Durga's room."

Durga's lips parted. "What if she—"

Shiva silenced her with a glare, and she snapped her mouth shut.

Aviama lifted her chin. "Deal. You will clear the path between here and there, and I will leave you the map and the helm."

"Done." Shiva jerked his head at the solution in Chenzira's hands. "But I take the bottle."

Aviama cocked her head and smiled sweetly. "You think I'm going to give up my greatest bargaining chip? I won't give you the map *and* the helm without keeping some measure of assurances. We keep the bottle. And you'll have meals delivered to Durga's room, enough for six."

Shiva hesitated, then gave a short nod. "Fine."

He turned to Parth and waved his hand. Parth disappeared.

Manan and Chenzira stood stock still at the top of the

stairs, boring daggers into Shiva's skull. Sai and Durga exchanged an icy stare. A muscle on Laksh's neck moved, and Umed moved in from the aftcastle.

Aviama's heart hammered in her chest. She spun her rings, caught Shiva watching her, and folded her arms instead. He didn't deserve to know if she was anxious.

He knew, but it wasn't a good idea to give him fodder to confirm his suspicions.

Parth reappeared and gave a short bow to Shiva. The route was ready.

It was time. The most unsteady part of their plan. If Shiva and Samud were going to take them out before hitting the Gorge, it would be now, once the helm was secure.

Chenzira passed the bottle to Aviama, and Sai fell in just behind him and slightly to the side. Aviama grimaced at the familiar protection formation for an important person. She'd had similar setups with bodyguards, both at home and in Radha.

Chenzira and Sai took the front, and Umed and Manan flanked her on either side, separating her from Shiva as Laksh brought up the rear. Shiva gave her a long look. Aviama's mouth went dry. A chill ran down her spine.

"Commander?"

Aviama jerked her head toward the sound. Manan swept his hand toward the opposite stairs from the ones where Parth and Durga were stationed.

"It's time."

She swallowed. Time to live, time to die. Time for whatever came next.

Umed's words came back to haunt her.

If you die, we die. We have tied our fates to yours...

Aviama lifted her chin and strode for the stairs.

29

———————

Footsteps on wood planks. The swish of her skirt wafting the loose pants she wore as the breeze tugged on the fabric. Sailors parted to give them a wide berth as they landed on the upper deck.

Two archers were in position in the rigging of the *Wraith-weaver*. Aviama glanced left. Two more stood on the deck on one of the fleet's neighboring ships. Each man had an arrow notched on the string, following her every move.

Aviama tested the air, sensing her surroundings for tabeun power, but felt none. She kept her voice low and turned her head just slightly toward Sai. "Are Durga's hands up?"

Sai glanced back once. "Yes, but I don't think she's doing anything."

"Good. Follow my lead."

Aviama flipped her hands, palm up, and stretched a barrier of air around the six of them like a bubble. Sai strengthened it with her own barrier just as a soft *thwick* sounded from overhead. Aviama glanced up just as an arrow aimed for her head plummeted toward her and glanced off the barrier at the last second.

A deep voice shouted a command half a second too late. "Hold!"

Aviama caught the arrow in her barrier and twisted it in a tight circle in the air until its tip faced the archer who had released it. The man's face went white, and Aviama let the arrow drop to the deck as she turned and followed Chenzira and Sai under the quarterdeck and out of sight.

Seamen armed with swords, daggers, bows, and harpoons lined the shadowed space under the quarterdeck. Aviama's heart lodged in her throat. But the stairs to the gun deck were clear.

She could feel Sai's power joining with hers as they bolstered the barrier around them. No one said a word as they progressed down the stairs. The passageway to the main kitchen was packed with men, silent as the grave, eyeing their progress with expressions ranging from disdain to curiosity to hatred.

A man's hand moved, palm out, in her direction, and Chenzira half-drew his sword as they walked. The man froze and dropped his hand. For a moment, Aviama thought she saw Onkar somewhere in the crowd, but by the time she thought she recognized him, he was gone.

One step in front of the other. Down the gun deck, past bed after empty bed of displaced sailors cleared from the space to make way for Aviama and her band of miscreant melderblood traitors.

Bronze cannons lined the sides of the ship, each with its gunport looking out over the water and the rest of Shiva's naval fleet. Jannemar's cannons back home were cast iron. Another reminder of the superiority of Radha's budget and military equipment.

Aviama took a deep breath. Was it really a good idea to lock themselves away in the belly of the ship? But the open air wouldn't be much better. Not with so many archers and eyes on them. But if Shiva or Samud had enough melders on their side...

She shook off the thought.

Stacks of crates and barrels lined the middle aisle. Someone's abandoned game of cards and dice lay strewn across an empty cot on her left, next to empty bottles of ale. And at the end, two doors waited for them. Sai's room on the right, and Durga's on the left.

Guarded by half a dozen men.

Aviama tested the strength of the barrier around them. It held.

The first guard moved his lips, and Aviama's stomach dropped. She couldn't hear well inside the barrier. She'd have to drop their protection to listen.

Sai exchanged glances with her, and Aviama gave her a nod. They dropped the barrier. The first guard hesitated, then spoke again.

"Only the princess is allowed inside. Your guards can take the other room, and we'll ensure your safety through the Gorge."

Chenzira snorted. Manan drew his dagger.

Aviama arched her eyebrows. "I beg your pardon. I think I misheard you. The only reasonable response you could have had was, 'Welcome, here is the room promised by Prince Shiva, and the privacy you were ensured by His Royal Highness in exchange for your kindness in not blowing up the helm.' I can only assume that is what you meant to say. Move aside and let us into the room we were promised, and I'll forgive your unfortunate word choice."

The guard winced, eyeing the six melders before him. One of the young men behind him visibly gulped. The first guard cleared his throat and offered a pathetically shallow, clumsy bow.

"Your Highness. Our instructions are to only allow you, the princess, into this room. But we assure you that you will be protected."

Manan whirled his dagger in a flourish. "And *we* can assure your tongue winds up outside your head."

All six guards raised their weapons, and Aviama held up a hand. "I would be happy to acquiesce, if only there was a princess present. Unfortunately, there is no such individual here."

The guard's eyes narrowed.

Aviama spread her hands, the fingers of one hand still wrapped tightly around the neck of the bottle of explosive. "You can call me Commander Shamaran. Please inform the slimeball you call a prince that we forfeit Durga's despicable quarters, since they are apparently reserved for princesses and amateur melderbloods who cannot think for themselves."

The first guard adjusted his grip on his sword handle and stepped forward. "Instruct your guard to retreat."

Chenzira spoke a word, and in an instant the four men at Aviama's side moved past her like flowing water. Manan's sword connected with the first guard at the same moment Chenzira's elbow clocked a second man in the jaw, knocking the man backward as Chenzira swung at a third.

Aviama flicked her wrist, and a blast of wind slammed two of the men into the wall. Umed rushed forward and raised his sword, but one of the guards raised a hand. A ball of fire appeared in his palm and shot toward Umed's face. Sai caught it in a ball of air, and Laksh sent a fireball of his own into the guard's face.

Or it was probably *meant* for the man's face. His control

was off, and it ended up hitting the fourth guard, to the side. Umed punched the fireblood in the gut and sent him sprawling to the deck. Aviama stepped through the tangle of bodies to Durga's door and raised her voice. "To me!"

Sai, Umed, Manan, Laksh, and Chenzira extracted themselves from their fights and stepped to Aviama as she gathered a gale into her hands, sucking fresh air from the gunports and pooling it in her hands. Sai threw her hands up and joined her, and together the two of them sent the guards sliding and tumbling over each other down the gun deck.

Aviama opened Durga's door and turned back to the aisle, raising her voice to the heap of bruised bodies picking themselves up from the deck halfway down the length of the ship. "And please tell Captain Samud that if he thinks one captive siren and a few untrained melders will turn the tide against the Iolani, his nescience knows no bounds."

Umed and Laksh stood sentry outside the door as Aviama swept inside the room, with Chenzira, Sai, and Manan close on her heels.

Manan shut the door and spun toward her, eyes glittering bright. He grinned. "You called yourself Commander Shamaran."

Aviama's stomach was a bundle of knots and nerves, but she couldn't help laughing at Manan's enthusiasm. "Don't get used to it. I won't be using that surname regularly, but I thought it appropriate today."

Chenzira wound an arm around her waist. "You did great."

His deep brown eyes sparkled, and a warmth filled her chest. "Thank you."

"Save it, lovebirds. We've got work to do." Sai ran to the bed, dropped to the floor, and rolled under it.

Aviama knelt on the floor to peer under the bed. "Is it there?"

Sai stared at the underside of her bed in disbelief. "They searched my room. In the last couple of hours."

Manan moaned. "It's not like that's the most brilliant hiding place ever."

Sai shot him a glare. "As if you would know anything about brilliance."

His brows shot up, but he said nothing. Aviama glanced at the door. How long did they have before Shiva or Samud received her insult and decided to drag them out or set off another round of konnolan?

Sai ran her fingers along the wooden frame. She pressed against a swirling knot in the wood, then pulled her hand back in a flowing motion as if tugging an invisible something free. The wood popped out of its place, and a narrow dagger fell into her palm. She rolled free of the bed and popped back up in an upright sitting position.

"They got the axe. This is all I have left."

Aviama grinned. Sai had done some stealing of her own. But just as a weird sense of pride swelled in her chest, Chenzira deflated her growing hope.

"That's not much of a saw."

Manan took the dagger and stabbed it into the floor, moving it back and forth, prying at the edges of the boards. He shook his head. "If it does any damage, it'll be to the blade."

Aviama stretched her hand out toward the floorboards. Wind whistled through the cracks to her fingertips, but the floor didn't move. She rocked back on her heels. Her stomach churned. So close, but so far...

Manan gestured to the bottle in Aviama's hands. "Can we blow it?"

"No. Too loud." Aviama drummed her fingers against the bottle and swirled its contents. "And we need to save it."

Sai bit her lip. "Do we have any firebloods?"

Aviama snapped her head up to meet Sai's gaze. "Laksh. He can do it."

Chenzira shook his head. "Too conspicuous. Too dangerous. What if he takes out the whole floor?"

They hadn't had time to test everyone's abilities or the level of their control. If they failed now, they would draw too much attention. Their one shot at taking out the konnolan would be gone.

The means by which he'd murdered countless melderbloods in the weeks before their voyage. The konnolan that she had told Shiva about in the first place.

They were so close she could almost taste it. If Sai's information was accurate, the main stash of konnolan lay just beneath their feet, in the cargo hold where Makana had been guarded. It made sense when she thought about it. The guards could watch over Makana and the konnolan at the same time, and if Makana caused any trouble, they could use konnolan if they couldn't manage to hit her with a harpoon.

Aviama closed her eyes and ran a hand over her face. She'd been reckless. If she didn't find a way to even the odds against Samud and Shiva, everyone with her would die. More blood on her hands.

Would it ever end? Would the deaths ever stop piling up? This morning, she was ready to die. But now...

Clink.

Aviama opened her eyes. A crooked iron nail lay in the center of the floor.

Creakkkk.

It was a tiny sound, only barely perceptible in the quiet room. But there, at the end of one of the boards, an iron nail head worked its way to freedom. The dull silver head bobbed this way and that, tugging as if drawn out by some invisible force.

Aviama glanced at Sai. She gaped open-mouthed at the nail. Manan leaned forward to get a closer look. But Chenzira lifted one finger in light jerking movements, calling the sliver of metal to him. The nail at last broke free and fell to the floor.

30

Aviama had almost forgotten Chenzira was a quakemaker. Weeks had gone by with no land in sight. How could he meld the elements of earth without any earth to meld? But she'd been wrong. So wrong.

Because ore held the ship together. Iron ore.

Could all melders access their element when it was isolated? The crestbreakers had manipulated water in the pool at the bathhouse. That was isolated, wasn't it? It hadn't been part of any ocean or river.

Aviama plucked one of the nails up off the floor, and it curled into a circle in her hand. She twirled it in her fingers and grinned up at Chenzira. "Do it again."

Chenzira's mouth turned upward, and he proceeded to pop out two more nails, curling the edges of the planks upward in the process. His movements were smooth and subtle, his focus entirely on the task before him.

A knock came at the door.

Aviama froze. The last nail in a third neighboring plank ripped free and flew to Chenzira's palm.

Umed's voice came through the door.

"Commander? It's the cook. He brought the food you ordered in person."

Of course he did. Aviama gritted her teeth and took a deep breath. "Tell him to leave it and go. We'll eat when we're ready."

Onkar's rumbling voice cut through the air. "Too busy for an old friend?"

"Is that what you are? And what will you be in the next hour?"

Manan stiffened, and Chenzira arched an eyebrow.

Aviama rolled her eyes and cleared her throat. "We'll meet in the morning as scheduled. I need more time to get your payment, and you need to focus on the intel I asked for."

Aviama lurched forward at the same time Chenzira leaned in from across the hole he'd made in the floor, the two of them bumping heads in their hurry to peer through the opening to the cargo deck below.

"Ow!"

Her heart dropped the second the sound escaped her lips. The other side of the door was silent.

After a moment's pause, Onkar's voice came again through the door. "You wouldn't ask me for something you already knew, would you?"

"You wouldn't ask cryptic questions as an excuse to stick around, would you?"

Aviama rubbed the spot on her head where she'd run into Chenzira's skull. She moved forward again, slower this time, to look through the hole. And stared directly into the faces of two men standing guard, staring up at her, harpoons in hand.

Chenzira swore and shoved Aviama out of the way just as the first guard drew his arm back to throw. Aviama dove for the wall of the small room, but there were few places to go.

Thud.

Aviama squealed as the sharp tip of the harpoon flew through the opening in the floor and lodged in the ceiling. Chenzira shot her a look, and she clapped a hand over her mouth. She held her hands up in silent defense.

She'd gotten a lot better about not screaming. Really, she had. But how was she *not* supposed to react to that? She'd nearly been skewered like a fish!

"Everything okay in there?" Onkar.

"Commander?" Laksh.

And if either of the guards in the cargo hold shouted for help, as they would at any moment, all hope would be lost.

Biscuits.

Sai leaped to her feet and held her hands up toward the door, summoning the wind to her palms. "Everything's fine. She's just feeling a little unsteady. It's been a long day."

"Yes, in my experience, exhaustion *does* cause sudden screams of panic."

Aviama could only imagine Onkar's sarcastic expression. His tone was dry as old crusty bread left out overnight.

Chenzira snatched the dagger from where it had been abandoned on the floor, darted into the opening, and threw it. Aviama leaned into the opening. The first guard spun out of the dagger's path, but with a flick of her wrist, Aviama altered its trajectory and sent the blade plunging into the man's neck.

Bile flew up the back of her throat as he dropped to the ground. The second man twisted toward the brig and opened his mouth to shout. He couldn't be allowed to raise the alarm.

Barely thinking, Aviama threw her hand out toward the man and instinctively closed her fist. He clutched at his throat, dropping the harpoon in his hands, eyes bulging as he stared up at her. She stared back in shock.

Had she stopped his windpipe? Did she control the air inside a person's body too?

A thrill ran through her at the power under her command. But just as suddenly, the thought revolted her. She released him, falling back onto the deck. What had she done?

Chenzira leaped to his feet and pried the boards back as far as he could manage. He reached a hand toward Aviama. "Give me the mixture. It's now or never."

Aviama handed him the bottle and dug in her pocket for the rocks. Chenzira dropped to the cargo deck, ripped the dagger out of the first guard's throat, and drove the blade through the second man's gut as he stood doubled over, gasping for breath.

The doorknob turned. Sai threw a blast at the door to keep it shut, and a blow came from the other side. Who'd hit who? Was Onkar down, or did Shiva send men for Umed and Laksh?

Aviama's mouth went dry. Two dead bodies, a snooping swindler, and still no konnolan destroyed. And Chenzira needed the rocks in her hands, or the solution was worthless.

She spun to Manan. "Whatever you do, don't let them in."

Aviama dropped through the opening. She slowed her descent only a hair with the wind around her, landing heavily and wavering on her feet. Chenzira was already searching through barrels, and Aviama turned to the stack of crates she'd climbed up on when she first came to find Makana in the hold. Two locks secured the lid from prying eyes. She sent wind to unlock the mechanism, but it didn't open.

She glanced up. "This one is built different. Can you get this open?"

Chenzira waved a hand in the direction of the lock, and the bracket holding it onto the crate pulled free from the wood, falling to the deck, locks and all.

She arched her eyebrows. "That'll do."

Aviama yanked the lid open. Konnolan. Chenzira pulled

the crate off the stack and opened the next one. More konnolan.

She pulled the rocks from her pocket and sprinkled some inside the first crate. This was it. They could destroy it.

Chenzira grabbed her wrist and shook his head. "We need to dump it. If you blow it up, it'll get in the air and incapacitate us all just as much as a cannon would."

"Impossible. There aren't any windows on the cargo deck. This is the only way to get rid of it."

"What if there isn't enough explosive? And what's to keep Shiva from dispatching us while we're down—or was this another of your suicide missions?"

Aviama winced. *Biscuits.*

But how could they destroy it without blowing it up? She bit her lip. The two dead guards stared unblinking, unseeing, at the ceiling. Above them, Onkar was still running his mouth to Umed and Laksh. What if he persuaded them to let him in?

She looked up through the hole. Manan peered down at her, hand on his weapon, worry etched in the lines of his face. Then it hit her.

Aviama reached into the crate and touched the powder. Nothing happened. The substance was totally inert without something to light it. And water would destroy any chance of being lit. Her pulse quickened. If only they could move it all fast enough.

"We need to get these up to Sai's room. Help me move them."

Chenzira glanced up at the small hole and back down to the large crates. "Are you serious?"

"Yes. Come on. We don't have much time."

Aviama lifted her hands and gathered the wind, and Chenzira threw his weight against the crate so that it scraped along the floor. He cast a glance behind them down the dark cargo deck toward the brig. No shouting. Not yet. Only Onkar making a scene on the gun deck above them.

Had he done it on purpose? Was he helping her or hurting her? She never quite knew for sure. If Onkar wanted to help, he could have caused a scene literally anywhere else on the ship but right outside their door.

Chenzira commanded the iron in the boards overhead and ripped the nails from three more planks. Manan let out a shout. Wind whipped through the air in the room above them. Aviama climbed up on the crate and Chenzira boosted her up into Sai's room without a word. Manan caught her arms and pulled her up, and Aviama tapped Sai on the shoulder.

Sai flinched and whirled, but Aviama held a finger to her lips. "We need Laksh. We need to let him in."

"How do we let him in and keep Onkar out?"

"Have Laksh and Chenzira work together to pull away the ship's side and burn a hole. Manan, you're fire control. Bring water up from the sea to douse it. We're dumping all the konnolan. Sai, create air currents to help bring the crates up. Lift the powder and send it overboard in gusts. I'll deal with Onkar."

Manan gaped at her. "I don't know if I'm good enough for that."

Aviama set a hand on his shoulder. "Breathe. Focus. The only precision job belongs to Sai, and she's pretty controlled. If you bring in more than you need, it's okay. Reach for the sea."

He swallowed and nodded.

A hissing whisper came from below her. Was it Chenzira? If it was, it didn't matter. They didn't have time to strategize.

He'd forgive her, right? She grimaced. If they'd had more

time, they could have figured out a better solution. But it was like Chenzira said. Now or never. And with two dead bodies in the hold, shouting on the gun deck, and a massive hole in Sai's room, the line crossing from now into *never* was fast approaching.

Aviama sucked in a breath and nodded at Sai. "Open the door."

Sai cut off the wind against the door, reached forward, and yanked it open. Laksh, who had apparently been leaning against the door, fell into the room with a yell. Aviama sent a gale of wind, knocking him sideways into the wall to stop him just short of tripping over the twisted boards and tumbling to the floor below.

Aviama swept out the door and pulled it shut behind her. Umed stood beside her with a drawn dagger, his gaze flicking back and forth between his inexperienced so-called commander, and the black market mentor he'd been baking bread with and learning lifts from for the past couple of months.

Six trays of food sat untouched on the floor near Durga's door. Half a dozen armed sailors stood watch at a distance, maybe a quarter of the way down the deck. And Onkar stood leaning against the pole of the mast toward the front of the ship, arms crossed, just a couple of paces off from Umed's position.

He raised an eyebrow. "Where is the bottle of chemistry you've been carrying around?"

Aviama shrugged. "Guess I lost it."

Onkar sucked his teeth. The sound grated. "That's unfortunate. If it goes off, you'll be dead as a doornail, with all that konnolan beneath our feet."

Ice ran down her spine. It hadn't occurred to her that the konnolan alone could kill her in high enough doses. Kill them all, even. And with a fireblood behind the door, anything could happen.

She spun one ring and clasped her hands tightly together. "I thought we agreed to meet in the morning. Is something pressing?"

The corner of his mouth twitched. "I've always been interested in construction. It looks like you're doing some renovations. Mind if I take a look?"

Aviama waved him off, matching his cavalier tone. "It's probably bad luck to look at a project before it's done. Considering how superstitious you are, it sounds like a bad idea."

Onkar's eyes narrowed. "I'm not superstitious."

"You believe in curses."

"Only the real ones."

Aviama pursed her lips. "Curses aren't real."

The man rolled his eyes. "Thank you. All my problems are solved now. If only someone had said that to me earlier! Decades of knowledge, experience, and magic expunged at your word. What power you hold."

Wow, he really believed it. This curse thing was a hot button for him. A pain point. Good to know.

Aviama sighed. "What do you want?"

Onkar unfolded his arms, strode forward, and jabbed a finger at her chest. "I want you up on deck or near a window, so that when trouble comes with the Iolani, you have a shot at keeping everyone alive."

Umed stiffened, but didn't move. Would he do what it took to protect her, if Onkar resorted to violence?

Onkar's icy glare penetrated with such intensity that the hair on the back of her neck stood on end at his next words. "Because if you're ridding us of Sunboy's plan for safety, we're going to need you more than ever."

Aviama swallowed, trying to keep her voice level. "Once he realizes the konnolan is gone, he won't dare enter the Gorge."

As if on cue, a shadow passed over the light coming in through the gunports in the sides of the ship and hatches in the ceiling down the deck. A chill breeze wafted through the cabin, sending goosebumps up and down her arms.

"We're already here, Rookie."

31

Aviama's heart lurched to her throat. Heavy boots thudded down the stairs at the far end of the ship. The sailors watching stiffened, hands flying to the hilts and handles of their weapons. Umed whirled the dagger in his hands, but Aviama put her hand on his arm.

"I'm not sure steel is our best bet against the entire crew."

Umed's expression hardened, but he did not move.

Onkar tilted his head. "Chameleon?"

Aviama pressed her lips together. "I think we're long past chameleon, don't you?"

"Indeed."

She spun her rings. Once, twice. Her stomach churned. Her heart threatened to beat out of her chest.

They were coming for her. And if they'd truly already reached the Gorge...

Aviama stepped backward against the door. "Chenzira?"

Her voice shook. A creak and sizzling sound escaped the room beyond before his voice came through.

"Tally?"

She blinked back tears. Telling him would give them the

best shot of protecting against what happened next. Of sealing the door shut, not letting anyone in or out. It would also be the kindest goodbye she could give him if she never saw him again.

But it also opened up the opportunity for him to follow her. And the konnolan *had* to be destroyed. Aviama bit her lip. "Hey, um, don't be mad. It's fine. But we may already be in the Gorge, and men are coming. I'll let them take me and draw attention away."

"No. No, Tally, that's a bad idea. They'll use you as bait for all of us. You're leverage for every melderblood on board and the only human link to the Iolani."

The footsteps toward the aft landed on the cargo deck. She looked up to find no fewer than a dozen men marching toward her. On her other side, the doorknob to Sai's room turned.

Aviama held up both hands almost on reflex, summoning the wind to keep the door shut. The door pressed against the barrier she made. They tried again to open it, and a *thud* from what could have been a man's shoulder slammed into the wood from the other side.

"Sai, this door has to stay closed. Help me. Chenzira..." Aviama blinked hard to keep tears from her eyes. "It's okay. It'll be fine. Just get the job done, or we're done for."

Onkar leveled her with a knowing look. "Without tools to fight against the Iolani, we're probably done for anyway, darlin'."

Of course. He still wanted control of the konnolan. Aviama sniffed and tossed him a glare. "You're not helping."

He shrugged. "Sometimes truth hurts."

A shout rang out from the aft of the ship, and the sailors watching adjusted their grip on swords and daggers and moved forward as one, joining with the new blood sweeping down the hold. Chenzira's voice cut through the door.

"Don't be stupid, Tally. Stop doing things without me. Don't you dare pull a stunt like you did this morning."

"Commander?" Manan.

Aviama backed away from the door. Umed followed, and she lifted up a hand. "If I am your commander, complete the task assigned. The best way to protect me, to protect us, is to get rid of it. Now."

Thud. The door shook, and nearly opened, as Chenzira rammed into it once again from the other side. "You're not my commander, Aviama. You're my—"

She never heard the end of his sentence. Aviama wiped tears from her eyes, ordered Umed to block the door, and backed away, hands still maintaining the barrier against the door to Sai's room.

Onkar stared at her, his face showing something between concern and fascination. Concern for her, or for the konnolan? For his own skin, if they'd really entered the territory of the Iolani? The domain of sirens. The final passage for any ship dumb enough to make the voyage. The watery grave of nearly every lost sailor in the region for hundreds of years.

When the seamen were only paces away, Aviama dropped the wind barrier on the door and spun to face the captain's henchmen. "Gentlemen! Welcome to our final moments. Does the captain request my assistance?"

Parth stepped forward and spit on the deck, tapping a club against his shoulder. "Request isn't quite how he put it."

She dipped her head. "Let's get on with it."

Parth jerked his head at a man behind him, who scurried forward with a snarl of rope. "Hands behind your back, Highness."

Aviama set her jaw. The longer she could occupy the men, the longer Chenzira, Manan, and Sai had to dispose of the konnolan. She put her hands behind her back. "If he's scared of me, and I'm only one person, how do you think that bodes for success against an entire civilization of sirens?"

Parth was unfazed, but a flicker of what might have been fear danced across the face of one of the men behind him. One of the sailors tied Aviama's hands behind her back, the coarse rope rough against her wrists.

How long would it take for the dead men on the cargo deck to be discovered? If they were already at the Gorge, when would Shiva try to prepare konnolan for use against the Iolani?

Parth barked an order to his men, and the group—nearly thirty armed sailors—filled in around her. Parth gripped her elbow and pulled her along with him back down the length of the ship toward the stairs.

"Aviama!"

She twisted back toward the voice as she walked, and her heart nearly ripped in two at the expression on Chenzira's face. Umed and Onkar still stood outside the door, neither stopping nor encouraging him, staring between Aviama and Chenzira as she was marched further and further from safety.

"It's okay," Aviama heard herself say. "I'm not as important. It'll be all right." She hoped he would understand what she meant. She was less of a priority than the konnolan. Nothing could stop that mission. And nothing else could turn the ship around faster than removing all temptation for Shiva and Samud to use it.

But if they were already at the Gorge, they didn't have much time before the ship would be unable to turn around. How close were the rocks? How many of the other fleet ships would file into the narrow space before the *Wraithweaver*?

Parth jerked his head in Chenzira's direction. "Bring him."

Six men split off from the group and broke into a run toward Chenzira. Umed seized him, pulled him into Sai's room, and slammed the door shut. Only Onkar was left standing outside the room, trays of abandoned lunchmeats spread at his feet.

The group reached the stairs, and Aviama was forced to look forward again. But why would they send sailors to get her? Had they learned nothing of melders so far? Where was Durga? Why not use her?

Maybe Shiva knew Aviama would give herself up. Or maybe he knew that if Durga fought Aviama, Durga would lose—and the ship could be blown apart in the process.

One foot after the other, the troop ascended the steps to the upper deck. Aviama had expected the light of day reflecting off the surrounding mist, but instead, dark clouds loomed over them. Dense fog swept over them in patches. Moisture in the air clung to her skin, and an eerie wind snapped at the sails.

Durga stood at the prow, hands lifted high, sweeping them this way and that to part the fog as best she could. Cloud rolled away from her fingers, piling up on either side of the ship before spinning this direction and that into the ether. Shiva stood beside Makana, one hand on the wall of her cage, the other on his drawn sword. Rocky cliffs hemmed them in on either side, soaring high above the crow's-nest of the *Wraithweaver* mast.

Aviama's heart stopped as she stumbled out from under the overhang of the quarterdeck. They weren't just *at* Ghosts' Gorge.

They were in it.

32

———

The *Wraithweaver* cut through the water like a serpent, its brass skull figurehead leading the charge against enemies unknown and unseen. Radha's flag curled about itself in the heightening wind overhead. Aviama scanned the cliffs. Mist and fog. Water lapping at the rocky walls. The whistle of a rising gale coursing through the narrow passage and whipping at her hair.

But no sirens. No Iolani. None but the one in a cage in the middle of their ship.

The men marched Aviama down the deck toward Shiva. He nodded at Parth, who gestured to the others, and they dispersed. Parth stayed beside her. Shiva jerked his head at Parth, and he released Aviama's arm and backed away, keeping an eye on her from several meters off.

The silence of the ship was tangible, like shackles of eerie emptiness no one dared to break. Men armed with swords, harpoons, and daggers lined the rail all the way around the ship, keeping vigil without a word between them. Looking closely, Aviama could see wax stuffed in their ears.

If the Iolani sang the death lullaby, everyone on the edges

would be safe. They could engage the threat and keep their companions from going overboard. That seemed to be the plan, anyway.

Aviama winced against the rough rope cutting into her wrists, bound tightly behind her back. She turned away from Shiva, looking instead at Makana. The siren rotated slowly in the water around her, peering at Aviama through the translucent wall with those intense lavender eyes of hers.

She looked sad. The fight and fire had gone out of her eyes. Aviama stepped forward until they were almost nose to nose—daughter of the land and daughter of the sea. Tabeun sisters.

Shiva shifted toward her, watching Makana and Aviama's silent exchange. "Am I so evil?" His hand gripped the handle of his sword. "To not want to be used, to not want to be someone else's pawn? To create a future for my kingdom?"

The softness of his voice took her aback. Was this really how he felt? Or was he only playing another game, trying to gain her sympathy on the eve of battle?

Aviama set her jaw, but forced a low, steady voice in response. "Who uses you?"

"My father. My mother. The court. Every kingdom this side of the Great Sea. You're royal. You know that no one breathes without a usefulness to someone."

Aviama considered this. Shiva wanted to make a name for himself on his own—not under his father's thumb or his mother's pernicious orchestrations. To fight back against the danger he believed melderbloods would bring.

"All people want to be free. I want all those things you mentioned, and you were the one using me as a pawn and destroying my kingdom's future. You're doing it even now. There is such a thing as right and wrong within our goals. You say there is freedom, but I see only bondage and intimidation."

Shiva let out a long sigh. He eyed Makana and angled his body toward Aviama. "Jannemar should never have brought magic back. Melderbloods are the greatest threat to the known universe. Without them, perhaps we wouldn't have pressed so hard for control of the Aeian Sea. As it is, we are not so secure as we once were. Radha fell to the temptation of tabeun power before, and it nearly wiped out all life. Never again."

A lump lodged in Aviama's throat. "You weren't there. You don't know. I was there, and I saw the housing artifacts killing the body and soul of anyone who used them. Tabeun power is like military power—it carries no morality of its own. How you use it is what matters. But housing artifacts are sifal magic. Dark magic. And it corrupts, always. You say you will never be tempted by tabeun power again, but you plan on mining our wyronite to make more artifacts. If you continue this obsession, this poison will not stop until it turns you inside out and you hardly recognize yourself."

Shiva shifted his weight and lifted his chin. "We need the Aeian Sea to protect our borders."

"Or to invade others' borders."

"Only if they pose a threat."

"As you see it."

"Yes."

Aviama set her jaw. He could not be reasoned with. "Get out of the Gorge at your first opportunity. Don't engage. Run up a white flag. The konnolan is gone."

Shiva's face slowly drained of color. "What?"

She shrugged. "It's gone. We destroyed it. In the cargo hold, beneath Sai's room. You have no weapons against the Iolani. Get out while you still can."

Shiva's hand shook as he ran a hand through his hair. He cast his eyes this way and that, scanning his men at the rail, the archers in the crow's-nest, Samud with his long glass at the helm. His breathing came quickly, and his eyes bulged as he turned on her. Nostrils flaring, Shiva ripped his sword from its sheath and shoved Aviama back up against the glass of the siren's cage.

Aviama gasped as he pressed the cold edge of his blade to her neck. His eyes bored into hers, and a vein pulsed like a drum in the side of his neck.

"Tell me you didn't. Tell me you weren't stupid enough to leave us defenseless in the belly of death."

Her throat burned, and she grimaced at the bite of steel. She tried to speak, but nothing came. The pressure on her neck lifted just a hair, and she swallowed.

"It's gone. I thought we'd have time to turn the ship around, that you'd realize the mission was hopeless and abandon course."

Shiva's face reddened. Every muscle tensed, and she stiffened in preparation for the blow. The prince dropped his sword and slapped her hard across the face. Aviama stumbled sideways, reaching up to her cheek where the pain flared along her skin.

A shout came from the aft, and Aviama spun to see Chenzira charging forward from the stairs. Sailors surged to cut him off. Her gut wrenched. She whirled back to Makana.

"If we run up a white flag, if Shiva releases you, would they let us go? If we say we're here for a peacekeeping mission, to make amends, to return Radha's hostage…"

The words stuck in her throat. Makana slowly shook her head.

Shiva's knuckles turned white on the hilt of his sword. His lip curled. "It's too late."

Aviama glanced up at Durga, still parting the fog in front of the ship. Nothing moved. No one seemed to so much as breathe. "But why don't they strike? What are they waiting for?"

Makana pushed up out of the water and looked down the deck to the aft of the ship, where the fleet filed one after the other into the heart of Ghosts' Gorge. She pointed a long finger as her crystalline voice answered in a hushed tone.

"They wait more ships enter Ipuka Akala."

Aviama glanced at Shiva.

"It's what they call the Gorge. They're waiting for more of the fleet to be trapped inside with no escape." His face turned to stone. "You've killed us all."

No sooner were the words out of his mouth than the clouds pooled together overhead and a mighty squall hit the ship like a sledgehammer. The *Wraithweaver* rose up on the crest of a wave that had no space to gather and plunged down again with a slap. Aviama fell to the deck, pain reverberating up her arm where she'd landed. Hands still tied, she rolled to one side, but could not gather her feet under her.

Wind ripped into the sails in mighty gusts, first this way, and then that, snapping at the cloth like hungry vermin. Up went the ship, and down again.

Whooosh. Slappp. A third of the men fell this time, the rest clinging to the rails or to each other. Swords and clubs clattered down the deck, abandoned in favor of free hands to cling to anything that might keep them upright. Aviama rolled and skidded down the deck, heart in her throat, unable to stop herself.

A hideous scraping sound tore through the air as one of the masts grated against the cliff at a sharp angle. Shiva lost his balance and slammed into the deck with a *thud,* skidding down the deck after her. Aviama knew nothing but oak planks, gray stone, clouded sky, and the spray of the sea as she tumbled meter after meter down the upper deck. Bumped and bruised, her back hit the stairs to the quarterdeck and stopped her with a jolt. Shiva landed on top of her with a grunt, knocking the wind from her lungs.

Aviama tried to cry out, but no sound came. In vain, she gasped for air, her chest burning like fire. The ship rocked again, and Aviama's stomach dropped. The quarterdeck climbed high into the air. They were about to roll in the other direction.

Just as she felt her weight shifting with the ship, Shiva hooked his arm through the loop of her tied hands and wrapped himself tight around the base of the stairs, holding her to him. Bodies flew past them, falling from the aftcastle, the quarterdeck, the rails. Barrels and crates scraped their way down the deck and fell free, smashing into the deck or the sides of Makana's cage or falling overboard.

Smash.

The ship landed again, and this time leveled out for a moment as the winds battered the ship sideways. Two masts now raked across the cliff. If the hull hit the rock, they'd be sunk.

Shiva pried at the rope around her hands, unlooping the excess and tying it instead around one of her wrists. He yanked it tight, added a knot, and tied the other end to his own wrist.

Aviama shook her head. "That's a terrible idea. We can hardly stand up straight with both hands free!"

Another gale swept through, and the ship soared once again. Shiva wound an arm tight around her waist as they clung to the base of the quarterdeck stairs. He leaned in to yell into her ear above the din. "If I die, you die. So keep us alive, Windcaller."

Aviama's lips parted. "You're a coward."

"I'm smart."

The ship tossed again, and a great *crackkkk* sounded above them as the tip of the foremost mast snapped and fell. A cascade of collapsing sail enveloped Durga in its folds, and she was lost to Aviama's sight. The cacophony of screams and splintering wood battled for prominence over the sound of the squall ripping through the rocky ravine.

Shiva's arm around her loosened as he refastened his hold on the stairs. Somewhere, Aviama heard her name. Chenzira? She twisted. The slight movement was all it took—her grip on the stairs slipped. The ship bucked and rolled, and the aft of the ship flew skyward.

The *Wraithweaver* dove, prow straight down, into the waves. Men clung to whatever they could find to secure their hold. And Aviama fell.

Her scream stuck in her throat as she plummeted from the aft toward the prow. The foaming waves of a hungry sea laughed up at her. Aviama's wrist yanked, and her body jolted in midair as the rope tethering her to Shiva held true. But her weight was more than his weak grip could manage. Aviama's chest caved in as the last of his sea-sprayed fingers slipped from the stairs.

Wrist tied to wrist, only half a meter of rope between them, Shiva and Aviama dropped like stones. Bodies, barrels, and an archer's bow tumbled end over end beside them. Wind ripped through her hair, stinging her eyes as she clawed for something to hold on to. Any moment, the ship would hit the water and rock in the other direction, and they'd be dashed to smithereens on the deck.

To her left, Parth reached toward her as he fell two meters opposite them, eyes wide and mouth open in silent terror. Aviama lifted one hand and called the wind. The ship hit the water and rocked in the other direction. Parth's head smashed into the rowboat secured to the upper deck, leaving a bloody stain on the wood before his limp body dashed against the rails and spun overboard.

Makana's cage slid down to the forecastle, tipping precariously before falling on its side and dumping water onto the deck. Shiva's arm encircled Aviama's waist as she raised both hands and shut her eyes against the swirling gale.

Come to me.

But hers was not the only tabeun power at work. Wind flooded her palms, leaking through resistance she felt in every direction. It wasn't enough. This was no ordinary storm.

Aviama bent her will, the last shreds of her focus, on one purpose.

To me.

At last, the air responded, stealing from the opposing torrent just enough to give her what she needed. Enough to survive. Wind encircled her and Shiva, cushioning them against the forecastle as the ship rocked again, threatening to spill them back to the aft.

Aviama hooked her arm around the railing of the forecastle, feet dangling over the upper deck and Makana's broken cage, as the ship leveled out horizontally once more. Shiva seized the railing beside her, sliding his wrist closer to her to give her more room to command the wind.

He leaned in toward her. "Sing!"

Aviama nearly dropped the wind she was sending up into the gale overhead. "Are you kidding me?"

Behind them, the ship following the *Wraithweaver* careened into the cliff face. The hull broke apart, and the third ship rammed into it so that the *Wraithweaver* continued alone into the heart of Iolani territory.

Shiva nodded. "Do it."

Up on the forecastle in front of them, Durga untangled herself from the broken sail. Eyes wide, hands trembling, she looked to Aviama. "What do you need?"

Aviama reached for the wind, testing the direction where it came easiest to her call. "We need to right the ship as it sails and protect the masts from the cliff. They're sending wind at the base and into the sails. Interrupt the gales."

Durga's gaze darted over the cliffs and over the rail. "Who is? I don't see anyone!"

Aviama raised her hands again, elbow still crooked around the railing, foot wedged against the base of the forecastle to support her weight. "The Iolani. They're there."

Durga lifted her hands, and the two of them pooled their strength together. The mainmast leaned dangerously close to the cliff, but Aviama sent a buffer of wind around it so that the mast seemed to bounce off an invisible force and stabilize in the water.

Shiva winced as he adjusted his grip and lifted his wrist in the air to follow her movements, allowing her more freedom as she moved her hands. "Now, Aviama."

How could she sing? No one would even hear her. Not in wind like this. Not with the sea crashing below. Her heart pounded, beat after beat of a life under threat. What did she have to lose?

Aviama looked down at Makana. The siren flopped helplessly in the empty cage, her pewter tail slapping against the last of the water, her pure white hair dripping saltwater down her back. What had Makana said? Sirens learned something about the heart through song. Some extraordinary magic...

She opened her mouth, but no sound came. She drew in a shaky breath, but nothing was left. No music, no song, no inspiration.

How could she sing in a moment like this?

Makana looked directly up at her then, eyes lit with violet fire. A long, unsteady note spilled from Aviama's lips. The note built upon itself before dropping into a mournful rising and falling, drifting in and out with somber, evocative microtones she felt rather than intended. Makana's gaze was fixed on Aviama's face, and she stared back at the siren, as if the sight of her gave her strength, permission, to sing in the heart of Ghosts' Gorge.

The ship rocked, and Makana fell. Aviama held up her hands, softening Makana's fall, and then created a tunnel of air to carry her voice out over the ship and through the mighty gales wailing against it.

How many must die? Not all humans were worthy of trust. Not even most of the men on board. But if a siren and a melderblood could be tabeun sisters, couldn't the Iolani come to accept some humans?

The song grew, amplified by the wind as she directed it out over the water—a call for help, a plea for mercy. The cry of the helpless, the anguish of a slave. Was that not what she was? Was that not what the Iolani feared, if they swam but a hair beyond the protection of their home?

Aviama thought of the Iolani children Makana had told her about. Of the captivity Makana herself had suffered, the arena she and Aviama had endured together. Melderbloods and merfolk were meant for more than a menagerie.

Come. Treat with me. Let us pass in peace...

The wind stopped. The rage of the water ceased, leaving the *Wraithweaver* heaving to and fro on a glassy sea. Silence fell.

Aviama's final note died off in an upward slide that begged the answer to a question.

Today they would live, or they would die. And their lives were in the hands of the Iolani.

She scanned the deck. No wind. No waves. No sirens.

And then she saw it. A metallic flash to her left. A woman climbed up the railing, peering up at one of the sailors still clinging to the side. Scales the color of brass graced her perfect skin, matching long, flowing hair. But at the waist her female form transitioned to a powerful marine tail, a golden-brass color like her scales and hair. She lifted a hand toward the sailor's face, and he gaped back at her.

Another siren appeared along the railing, and another, until the ship was surrounded by them. Stunning specimens with soft lips and piercing eyes. The seamen stared at them, taking in their supple, radiant skin and pleasing curves.

The brass-tailed siren gently pulled the sailor toward her, running her hand up his chest and around his neck. And then she plucked the wax from his ear and sang, soft and quiet, imperceptible, for him alone to hear. The man's eyes lit with longing, and as she drifted down, down the side of the ship, back to the water, he followed her—straight over the railing and into the water below.

33

———

Aviama stared open-mouthed at the gap in the seamen, where the brass-tailed siren had stolen the sailor from the crew. Shiva grabbed her hand and jumped with her from the railing of the forecastle down to the upper deck. Her shoes landed in the spilled water of Makana's broken cage, inches from her friend's tail.

Shiva barked an order to the men without wax stuffed in their ears, and they moved among the crew, tapping them on the shoulder. At each tap, the sailor adjusted his grip on his weapon and raised it toward the ethereal female vision before him. At least, they were supposed to. Only maybe half of them did so, the rest too enraptured to care.

Aviama knelt beside Makana. "Is there any way we survive this?"

Makana glanced down the railing, but her face showed no comfort at the sight of her sisters. Her brow furrowed. "My brothers. They come."

Shiva snatched up a fallen dagger, seized Makana by the hair, and yanked her head back. He ran the sharp edge of the blade along her alabaster throat and turned to the sirens along the ship's edge. "Safe passage, or we kill her!"

A mighty wall of water rose from the ocean and hit the side of the ship. A male Iolani rose in its crest. His hair was red streaked with gold, his tail striped with scarlet and shimmering gold to match, with long spines and fins gracing the sides. He wore golden forearm guards and a spotted sharkskin breastplate across his bare chest, an abalone shell marked with some sort of symbol in its center.

The merman gripped a long spear in one hand and tossed the waterlogged corpse of a man on the deck with the other. The body landed with an indelicate *thump* and half-rolled, exposing the lifeless glaze of frozen terror etched on the face of the sailor the brass-tailed siren had taken overboard just moments before.

"You think yourself strong? Radha man want fight?"

Shiva swallowed and shook his head. "I don't want to fight. I want to negotiate. How else was I to get your attention?"

Aviama's stomach twisted. Dread set into her bones with a hopeless chill. Her wrist was still tied to Shiva's, the hand he now had embedded in Makana's hair. If she saved Makana now, Shiva would have no leverage.

But Shiva couldn't afford to destroy their only leverage. Without the konnolan, his position was weak.

The merman jerked his chin at Aviama. "You. Singer?"

Her lips parted, but she only managed a nod.

"Why?"

Aviama's heart stopped in her chest. The merman's expression was dark, his features flint. She suddenly got the feeling that she had done something terribly, horribly wrong.

Down the deck, Captain Samud strolled for them. His heavy teal coat and turban were still in place, but he was soaked to the skin, and his boots squelched with water as he walked. He bowed low to the merman.

"It is our honor to treat with you. I am Captain Samud. Whom do we have the pleasure of—"

The merman whirled the spear in his hand, and two electric eels shot out from some place behind him, flying through the air and sinking their teeth into Samud's neck.

"Mola mola! You want negotiate, but know nothing! You have eyes like goblin shark and brain of jellyfish. Remora does not make demands of shark."

A soft hiss came from Makana, barely a breath against the steel at her neck. "Kneel."

Aviama knew it was meant for her. She knelt.

Beside her, Makana hissed again. "Never interrupt chieftain. When he speak you, call him *Most Excellent Chieftain*."

Shiva glanced at the siren and back at Aviama. He looked like he'd been slapped, his usual poise gone.

The merman turned back to Aviama. "Why you sing?"

Aviama swallowed. "Most Excellent Chieftain. The Iolani are known for their power and strength. Legendary for their ferocity..." She licked her lips. "But your powers surpass death, wind, and water, do they not?"

The merman's eyes narrowed. "Who are you?"

Her lips parted. Aviama looked to Makana, but the mermaid gave no hints of what to do next. She couldn't say she was part of Radha. Aviama wanted no association with that treacherous nation whatsoever. But what could she say?

Samud lay twitching on the deck, the eels still attached to his throat. Sirens faced off with sailors around the rim of the ship. The drowned sailor's empty gaze stared up at the endless sky above, and the narrow cliffs hemmed them in.

Shiva bowed his head, his blade still against Makana's

throat. "Most Excellent Chieftain. Forgive her. She is not used to diplomatic matters."

Aviama steeled herself against the glaring look she nearly shot in his direction. Not used to diplomatic matters?

"She is no one of consequence. A representative alongside myself, working with me for the good of both our people and yours. She assists me, but has no authority in international issues."

Aviama's cheeks flushed hot. She cast a sideways glance down the deck. The dead sailor from the crow's-nest still lay on the boards, catty-corner from Captain Samud, whose limbs rocked with intermittent tremors as the eels slowly detached themselves and slithered back to their master. Sailors and sirens still lined the railing around the perimeter of the ship. Under the shade of the quarterdeck, Chenzira, Sai, and Umed watched with bated breath.

She locked eyes with Chenzira, then swallowed and jerked her focus back to the chieftain. No one else needed any heat on them. No one but her and Shiva.

The merman followed her gaze and then scanned her position, kneeling beside Makana, and Shiva, dagger to the siren's throat. Aviama's wrist was still bound to Shiva's, the three of them making a strange sort of trio.

Aviama shifted her hand beside Makana's on the deck, the side of her little finger bumping into Makana's in silent solidarity. Her stomach dropped as she stared up at the chieftain.

The eels slithered through the railing and into the water below. The chieftain's eyes narrowed on Shiva's face.

"You lie."

A sickening hiss rolled through the listening sirens.

Shiva's lip curled, and he nicked Makana's neck. Blood trickled down the blade. "Excellency, if you do not negotiate with me for peace, I'll kill her."

The chieftain laughed. "She is disgraced. She will never sing among her people again. Do with her as you please."

Aviama's lips parted, head reeling. Makana stared down at the deck, saying nothing. What had they walked into?

The merman whirled his spear and let out a shout. Two other mermen rose on either side of the ship, lifted by great towers of water. Their vibrant tails swished back and forth in the water, holding them in place as they lifted their arms. A howling whirlwind whipped up directly over Shiva and Aviama, and the *Wraithweaver* tilted precariously in the water.

Biscuits. Not again.

The whirlwind descended around them until Aviama's vision was filled with snatches of pewter scales, Shiva's steel blade, droplets of blood flashing in the wind, and her own golden hair blown in front of her face. The prince, the siren, and the melderblood tumbled across the deck toward the chieftain.

Aviama threw her palms up to fight it, but the current trapping them was too strong. Her muscles strained as she pressed against the circling wind. Her feet left the deck as the three of them flew up into the air and over the side of the *Wraith-weaver*. The chieftain's eyes darkened with the same deadly quality Shiva's held moments before a kill. An icy chill ran down Aviama's spine.

And then they began to fall. Down, out of the ship. Down to the domain of the lethal Iolani. At the last moment, Aviama felt a weakness in the current as the wind began to drop away. It wasn't enough to free all three of them. But maybe it would be just enough...

She blasted a hole in the circulating air around them and threw Makana back onto the upper deck of the *Wraithweaver*, sending her flying on a mighty gust. Her last sight was of

Makana landing with a crash on the deck. And then she was plunged into the depths.

34

Spiraling water. Bubbles of air escaping her lungs. Screeching.

Aviama opened her eyes, squinting through the salt water as it burned her eyes. Above her, sirens threw themselves off the railing of the *Wraithweaver* and down into the sea. They moved with an ethereal elegance, cutting through the water with all the grace of a ray and the deadly beauty of oleander. Two of them angled straight for Aviama and Shiva.

Cold hands seized her by the arm. Her captor, a copper-haired, copper-tailed mermaid, made no expression either of hate or sympathy as she flicked her powerful tail and propelled them with a lurch down, down into the dark of the underwater ravine. Beside her, a silver-tailed siren did the same to Shiva, pulling him down with her into an ever-blackening deep.

Aviama's lungs burned. Panic welled up in her chest. Her upper arms were firmly in the grip of the copper mermaid, but the rope still connected her wrist to Shiva's. And there was clearly no intention of getting oxygen anytime soon.

She twisted in the mermaid's grip and spread open palms

to the sparkling, dwindling surface. Power flooded her veins. Her chest ached with the scorching burn of starved lungs.

Air pummeled the surface of the water in mighty blows, breaking through the swells and charging to her aid. A bubble three meters wide coursed through the ocean and alighted at her fingertips, enveloping her, Shiva, and the copper mermaid swimming with them.

Aviama and Shiva gasped for air, raking in long breaths. The copper mermaid shrieked in blood-curdling surprise as the water around her fled to make room for the air. She dipped low to escape the bubble, shooting Aviama a dark glare and shifting so Aviama and Shiva inhabited the bubble between the sirens, and the sirens could swim unencumbered in the water to either side.

Shiva sucked in another breath before rotating toward Aviama. "You couldn't have sent *us* back to the *Wraithweaver*?"

Aviama shot a sideways glance at the copper siren. Her focus was fixed ahead, but surely, she was listening. "I think he would have killed Makana. If we can separate them a little longer, maybe we can negotiate for all our lives. We don't mean anyone harm."

Shiva shot a pointed look at their surroundings. The water grew darker and darker against the black rock of the cliff. Sirens fell in on all sides now, blocking out the last rays of the sun filtering in from the surface. "You have ruined every opportunity for negotiation. When the time comes, keep your mouth shut."

Aviama stiffened. Her heartbeat ticked up a notch, pulse pounding in her temple at the bite of his words. *He* had brought her here. *He* had threatened the Iolani. And *he* was the one who had ruined her life, manipulating and black-mailing her, forcing her close to him while he plotted the destruction of her home.

Memories of his breath on her neck, his hands around her waist, Enzo's head on a platter, assaulted her mind. Tears stung at her eyes, and a lump lodged in her throat. Shiva slitting Sona's throat and leaving Aviama helpless on the floor of the brig. Shiva's lips on hers, tongue flicking into her open mouth. Sickening lilac purple dresses. Bhumi's decapitated head and lifeless eyes staring back at her.

Her lip curled into a snarl, and the roar in her ears had nothing to do with the waves. Bile shot up the back of her throat as hatred washed over her. With a light tug, Aviama pulled the bubble in tight around her, dumping Shiva back into the cold of the water.

Something twisted in her chest as she watched his face turn blue. His body jerked violently, his hands clawing toward her—but the siren's grip was iron, and his fingers fell short, only grazing the bubble. So close to life-saving air. So close to salvation.

Not close enough.

An icy cold wormed its way through her heart like a poisonous vine. But then Chenzira's soft eyes invaded her mind's eye.

Would you like to tell me why you've been trying to die all day today?

It was the same hatred she'd felt that morning. Had it only been that morning?

You looked like fury on wings. Like a song caught up in a storm...

What would Chenzira think of her if she killed Shiva? What would she think of herself? Is this what had happened to Shiva to twist him to such depraved evil?

Aviama let the bubble snap back into place. Shiva clutched at his throat, coughing and sputtering as the color slowly returned to his ashen face. She set her jaw and looked away, turning her attention instead to their surroundings.

Up ahead, brilliant luminescent blues and greens twinkled like underwater stars lighting the dark. The bright shimmer struck a stark contrast against the ebony black of the cliff, casting a soft glow on the sirens around them with every flick of their powerful tails driving downward through the dark and toward the light.

The lights seemed to grow along the cliff itself, with balls of glowing coral strung up across the two sides of the ravine. Schools of fish scattered at their coming, and beyond them, stone statues twice life size glared at them from their places carved into the face of the rock. As the light grew brighter, Aviama saw tunnels, holes, even pillars, weaving in and all throughout the cliff.

Aviama's lips parted in awe. She nearly forgot to sustain the bubble of air surrounding them. Somewhere in the back of her mind she wondered how long the air she'd brought down would last, and if she'd be strong enough to call for more from this deep down if she needed it.

Shadows of sunken ships lined the ocean floor far below— ship after ship, broken and splintered and stacked one vessel atop another, the mast of one piercing through the shattered hull of another. Various levels of ship model design and degradation decorated the floor of Ipuka Akala, the final resting place of hundreds, if not thousands, of seafarers through the ages.

A green eel peered its head out of the mouth of an abandoned cannon when a manta ray coursed through the water, its massive wingspan completely cutting off Aviama's view of the ship beneath as it passed. Sirens and mermen darted in and out of the openings in the cliff—the tails of the females shining in every metallic shade from brass to steel to copper, the males dazzling in markings of all the vibrant colors of the rainbow.

Across the ravine, two massive statues faced each other, perhaps five stories high and cut into the rock. A male and female Iolani each reached one hand out toward the other over an expanse of smaller ornate carvings Aviama couldn't make out. The figures' palms touched in the same gesture Makana always did toward Aviama when she said *tabeun sister*. In the male's right hand was a magnificent spear, and in the left hand of the female, a battle horn.

The copper siren banked right, pulling Aviama toward a large opening with two pillars on either side. Aviama's stomach wrenched. The pillars were built from skulls. Haunting luminescent-green light dotted the foreheads of each skull, graced a bone threshold, and lined what looked like a road made entirely of human femurs.

The sirens holding Aviama and Shiva dragged them through the water and into the dark opening cut into the rock. Over a floor of long bones, skulls embedded the walls and ceilings of the tunnel. Aviama's mouth went dry. How many corpses had been required to make this? How long had it taken to gather the bodies?

The tunnel split, and they took the wider road. The green glow transitioned slowly to blue as they approached a wider room, lit by more of the glowing blue substance. The room was shaped like a dome, three stories high, protected by two stone merman sentries at the entrance. In the center, four skull-formed pillars held up a rounded ceiling of bones beneath the dome overhead, a grand yet petrifying meeting place for rituals or courts or some other significant event.

Aviama winced as she pulled the air bubble along with her. How much longer could she hold it? How much longer would it last?

It would last longer for one person than for two.

The thought intruded in her mind, and she shot Shiva a dark look before she could stop herself. But it wasn't right. As evil as he was, right now, he was helpless. Aviama had seen what power did to people. She had no aspirations to join their wicked ranks.

But you already have, a voice seemed to whisper. *You have power. You enjoy using it. And he deserves to die.*

Aviama shook her head violently to clear it and shut her eyes against the onslaught. The thought receded, but not from defeat. It felt more like a calculated retreat—a mocking patience.

She welcomed its absence all the same.

A dozen sirens remained with them through the tunnel and into the meeting room. The mermaids surrounded them now, hovering in the water. Long fingers spread toward them like claws. The bubble around them vanished, drenching them in cold water once again, stealing the last of their air supply. Aviama held her remaining breath, pulse thundering in her temple. She had a minute, at best, before her lungs would give up the fight.

Mind spinning, muscles tense, Aviama watched helplessly as the sirens laid hold of her arms and clothes from all directions. An eternity seemed to pass for her starving lungs as the sirens tilted their heads, inspecting her. Then a single thought dropped into her consciousness that stopped her cold.

How long has it been since they've had a fresh human corpse to harvest?

Perhaps they needed new bones. Maybe it had been too long since they'd watched life pass from someone's eyes. Perhaps they thrived on it.

An inescapable compulsion swept over her, to suck in the water and drown her burning lungs. Anything to stop the blaze. Anything to fill her lungs. Her mind spun, but she couldn't catch a single thought to identify it. Unable to stop herself, Aviama opened her mouth.

Water entered her lungs.

The sirens moved as one, surging up through the water. Dark spots floated across her vision. Dizziness washed over her. They broke the surface of the water, and her body went airborne.

What surface?

Bones. Shimmering, candescent light. Seizing in her chest. Shiva's face.

Deep dark.

35

T ime did not exist. Dark prevailed.

And then pain exploded in her chest. Her heart was an anvil, and someone was beating on it with a hammer.

Pressure smothered her mouth and nose. Her chest heaved.

Aviama lurched, eyes snapping open to find Shiva's mouth leaving hers and his hands moving down toward her chest. Water spewed from her mouth, and her body racked with coughs. She swung an elbow at Shiva, clocking him in the jaw as she turned away in a hacking fit that shook her body from head to toe. Bile flew up her throat, and another shot of water escaped her lungs and spilled onto a rounded floor of bones.

"You're welcome. I just saved your life."

Aviama leaned heavily on her arms and drew her hair back, away from her face. Shiva's voice grated. The patronizing quality in it was even worse.

She glanced up. The top of the dome in the meeting room where the sirens had brought them had a large air pocket trapped near the ceiling. They'd been deposited on the top of the chamber held up by the skull pillars, so that her knees and elbows now dug into a floor that doubled as the ceiling of the structure below—made entirely of human bones.

Aviama wiped her mouth with a shaking hand and pulled her knees up to her chin. Her chest ached, and her throat still burned. She wrapped her arms around her legs.

"Next time, if saving my life means your mouth touches my mouth, leave me to die."

Shiva made a face. "That seems a little extreme."

"I'm surprised you would care. You're the one who treats life like currency. Some lives are worth more than others. And if you can't get something valuable in return for it, there's no use keeping it."

"I do what I have to do."

"You do plenty you don't have to do. Like kidnapping Iolani children. Like keeping Makana. Like orchestrating the deaths of countless melderbloods."

"We never took any Iolani children."

Aviama groaned. "You tried."

That's how they ended up with Makana in the first place. She tried to protect them.

Shiva shook his head. "My father tried. If you haven't noticed, *he* is king, not me. It's *his* menagerie, not mine. As for the melderbloods, I quelled a rebellion of dangerous criminals and am securing safety for my realm."

"Ahh, of course." Aviama gritted her teeth. "So it's your father's menagerie, but it's *your* realm."

Shiva leaned back against the bone, stretching out and crossing his legs in front of him. "I can't let what happened before The Crumbling happen again. I'll do anything to stop it, and I don't care if you hate me because of it."

Fury lit every fiber of her being. How was he so blind? Was there no right or wrong in the world? Did everyone just do whatever they thought was right based on their own warped standard? Where did it end?

She pursed her lips and glared off into the glowing water and carved rock walls surrounding them. "Touch me again, and I'll kill you."

Shiva's eyes narrowed, but he said nothing. Aviama glanced down at the rope still tied to her wrist and yanked at it. She summoned wind from the air pocket around her, but the rope was too flexible to be manipulated meaningfully. Aviama pried at it with her teeth and raked at it with her fingers.

Shiva arched an eyebrow. Aviama's cheeks flushed with heat. He could probably untie it, but she'd just told him not to touch her. *Biscuits.* She couldn't take it back now. Aviama dropped her arm back to hug her legs and rested her chin on her knee.

An hour passed, maybe two, before a silver flash in the water caught Aviama's eye. Shiva gathered his feet under him in a low crouch. Aviama sat up. The siren who had escorted Shiva broke the surface of the water, her platinum hair reflecting the glowing sapphire color splashed across the walls. Silver scales shimmered along her temples, and startling white irises rimmed with black scrutinized Aviama's face.

"Siren on boat. You sing with siren on boat?"

Aviama frowned. "Makana?"

"*Kokowai!* She give name!" The siren cast a furtive glance around her, ducked beneath the water, and reappeared. "Yes. Makana Mahina."

She bit her lip. Was Makana really disgraced like the chieftain had said? If so, was Aviama's connection with her a good thing or a bad thing? But this siren didn't seem to want others to see her here...

Aviama took a chance. "Yes. I have sung with Makana. She calls me tabeun sister."

The siren's eyes widened. "You save life Makana. Makana help you. I see, on ship."

"She's saved my life more than once. I do what I can to return the favor, but I'm afraid there's little I can do."

Shiva could have done something more. Bitterness rose in her chest, but she shoved it down. Now was not the time.

Shiva watched her, but for once he kept his mouth shut. The siren edged closer in the water, and Aviama leaned down toward her. The siren put a hand on the edge of the bone structure.

"More you can do, yes. More."

Aviama's breath quickened. She glanced at the prison walls around her. "What could I do?"

"No deal with Ali'i Limakau." The siren's lips pulled back in a snarl at the name. She dropped her voice to a hiss barely above a whisper. "Talk Ali'i Makuakan. Most Excellent Chieftain. Ali'i. Save Makana, save you."

Aviama gaped back at her. But as quickly as she'd come, she was gone. The water rippled in her absence, and Aviama stared open-mouthed at the space the siren had occupied.

How was she supposed to call the shots from here? What leverage did she have to make any deal at all?

"Yes!" Shiva pounded the air with a fist, yanking Aviama's arm in his direction. She grunted and jerked her arm back, pulling his arm down with it.

Aviama cut him a sharp glare. "What could you possibly be happy about right now?"

He grinned. "We're in a better position than I thought."

She threw her hands up. "You have no konnolan. We're kidnapped inside of a cliff. And we're sitting on the evidence of what they do to humans who enter their territory."

"They're divided. They're using us as the political issue to pull support to the side they want. We've walked into a coup."

Aviama shook her head. "I don't get it. Makana called the merman we saw *most excellent chieftain*. But he's the one who hates her. So which Ali'i is the merman we saw? The red-and-gold-tailed one?"

"She never called him most excellent chieftain. She told *you* to call him most excellent chieftain."

Aviama blinked back at him. "What?"

Shiva ran a hand through his damp hair and arched an eyebrow at her, as if she were a child missing the punchline of an obvious joke. "She wanted you to live. He has an ego. She told you to call him whatever gave you the best chance of survival."

Understanding dawned. She spun the rings on her fingers, thinking.

"So the other chieftain—Makuakan—he's the one who likes Makana. Who would save her."

"Probably."

Aviama groaned. How were they supposed to find a chieftain they didn't know, from the air bubble prison cell of an underwater civilization, with scores of powerful merfolk swimming around every corner?

Shiva cleared his throat. "Which means your relationship with Makana won't do you any favors with Limakau. If you want to live, you'll need to distance yourself from Makana. I can negotiate with him to keep you safe, but you'll have to agree to keep your mouth shut and let me do the talking."

He gave her a look, and her jaw dropped.

"Are you kidding? You have nothing to negotiate *with*. You're sunk. Like all those ships lining the bottom of the Gorge. If any other sirens come, we need to find out how to contact Makuakan. Makana can arrange for our freedom once she's safe."

Shiva pursed his lips. "I don't trust Makana to care much for my life."

"Yes, well, terrorizing people and threatening to murder their families certainly doesn't boost rapport. She and I had that in common—you held us both hostage."

Shiva scoffed. "Don't play that game. You came to Radha of your own free will. And when you betrayed us and conspired against us, you did that on your own, too."

Heat flooded her cheeks. She opened her mouth to retort, then closed it. He was right, of course. She *had* come of her own free will, with the express purpose of maintaining international relations and gathering intel for Jannemar. And she'd done it.

But she'd never expected to be trapped there. Or to accidentally give up critical intelligence on her own kingdom, putting all melderbloods in danger and handing Shiva the keys to a successful invasion. And it didn't make what he did okay.

"You didn't have to force my hand."

"You think I wanted to force you?" Shiva ripped his wrist backward, yanking Aviama off balance by the rope connecting them. He caught up the slack, pulling the rope and dragging Aviama across the bone beneath them. Aviama gasped, raking her fingers over the smooth surface for hand holds to slow her movement.

Shiva crouched low, the excess rope in his hands, leaning in toward her face. "Do you count yourself some hapless victim? Some innocent young maiden tossed into a sea of vipers? I cared for you."

Aviama pulled back. His tone was severe, his breathing ragged. What was happening?

He gritted his teeth. "I told you more than I should have, even when I knew you were dangerous. I did my best to make our arrangement livable. If you had tried, you could have come to love me. You could have worked alongside me. We could have been a team."

He was too close. Far too close. Her stomach twisted. How could he say they could have been a team? He silenced her, blackmailed her, and used her to mastermind the destruction of her home and family. And to think she'd ever cared for him.

Her throat constricted. Aviama shot a blast of air into Shiva's chest, and he fell back—but the rope still connected their wrists, and he still held the excess between them. With a cry, she tumbled after him, silently cursing herself for her stupidity.

Shiva rolled and slid across the stone structure, flinging out a hand to stop himself. He landed on his back just beyond the crest of the domed structure, milliseconds before Aviama slammed into him. Her momentum sent them skidding down the bone again, and they fell together, chest to chest.

His left arm wrapped around her instinctively, doubling her right arm behind her back with the tension of the rope. Aviama's heart battered her ribcage like the pounding of a drum as she threw out her free hand and summoned the wind to slow their descent. Shiva braced himself against the narrow ridge of raised bone around the edge of the structure, as Aviama formed a barrier to slow their progress.

They lurched to a halt right on the rim. Shiva's right foot and Aviama's left dangled in the water, their upper bodies pressed close together on higher ground. Shimmering blue light bounced across the water, reflecting off the walls and through the expanse below.

Fragments of human skeleton held them up over the domain of sirens, beautiful and deadly at once. Just like Shiva.

Aviama's stomach flopped uncomfortably as she tried to decide which was worse—planting her hand on the bones to lean away from Shiva, or allowing her full weight to remain on his chest. She glanced down to find a place for her left hand along the structure, but with her right arm still doubled back behind her, it did little. When she looked up, her nose grazed his, and he was staring at her.

He grinned. "You can't kill me for this. It was your fault."

Aviama's lips parted, but for the second time in as many minutes, she could think of no response. He was right. Again.

She could feel his heart beating fast through the damp tunic clinging to his chest. His gaze drifted down to her open mouth, and his arm around her waist tightened.

All it took was that small movement, and a fresh onslaught of memories filled her mind. Hot breath tickling her neck, fake smiles, and deep kisses fed by blackmail and victory. Aviama strained away from him, and her lip curled into a snarl.

"Murderer."

He laughed, the sound emanating through the hollow chamber in a deep rumble. "You didn't seem to think killing was so bad when you came flying over the bow after ripping my bedroom apart. Did you really think killing me would solve your problem?"

A ripple interrupted the smooth glass of the luminescent blue surrounding them. Aviama turned to see the crimson and gold merman from the *Wraithweaver* break the surface. Half a dozen sirens followed him, forming a semicircle behind their chieftain. The merman took in their compromising position at a glance and turned a sharp gaze on Shiva.

"Is this how the woman assists you?"

36

Bile shot up Aviama's throat at the revolting thought.

"Forgive us." Shiva smirked. "This is how we settle disagreements in our culture."

A disquieting chill ran down her spine, and she twisted violently in the prince's grip. His arm loosened around her waist, but just as Aviama moved to sit up, he pulled her in once more to whisper in her ear. "If they find out who you are, you're dead."

She jerked upright and as far over from him as their tether would allow and tilted her head in respect toward the chieftain. As if such a formal gesture could smother the shame of having just been found horizontal on top of Shiva. *Biscuits. No reason was strong enough to justify it.*

The merman tapped his fingers along the side of his spear, scrutinizing his prisoner pair. "Convince me not kill you."

Aviama lifted her chin, but Shiva spoke up before she could say a word.

"Most Excellent Chieftain, I come with good news and a desire to make peace." He spread his hands. "I am Prince

Shiva of Radha, and I represent the most powerful kingdom under the sun."

The chieftain's eyes narrowed. "So say you."

"Under the sea, no one compares to you. But on land, Excellency—and I say this with all sincerity—no one compares to Radha. We return Makana to you now at your discretion. Forgive us, we can't release her into your hands until after we make an agreement, so my assistant here returned her safely to our ship. But the moment we reach an accord, mark my words, Makana is yours to deal with as you please."

Aviama shot Shiva a dark glare, but Shiva ignored her.

The chieftain laughed. "Or I take entire ship, entire crew, and Makana. No need agreement."

Shiva ran a hand through his beard and tapped his index finger across his lips. "That's one option, Excellency. But a wise man would aspire to more than another pile of sunken lumber. What's another sack of human bones when you could freely roam the entirety of the Aeian Sea, unchallenged and unafraid, with the tabeun power you saw on display today fed into your own hands?" Shiva gestured at Aviama. "You saw that since The Return, the Iolani are not the only species with tabeun power. Mankind has regained elemental magic, and with it, your first real threat in hundreds of years has come. What is to stop them from banding together against you?"

Aviama held her breath. What was he doing? Would it work?

The chieftain studied him. Perhaps he pondered the same questions Aviama herself asked about Shiva. He pursed his lips. "More."

"With pleasure." Shiva bowed his head. "The Iolani have long been revered as legends. But with crestbreakers to manipulate the sea, and windcallers to try to tame your storms, who's to say they won't seek to discover for themselves if the mysterious merpeople live up to their fame? You need to act fast to secure the appropriate amount of fear. But how will word of you spread if you remain safely beneath the surface?"

Shiva leaned forward, eyes bright as he locked onto the chieftain's expressionless face. "Ally yourselves with us, and we will tell of your might. We will offer the resources of the land of the sun to the waters of the moon, we will give you wyronite to control tabeun powers of your own in addition to the immense power you already possess, so no one will be able to hold a candle to you."

Aviama's mouth went dry. Shiva bartered Jannemari resources as if they were already his. But he barreled on, as if the bomb he just dropped were nothing at all.

"No nation has a navy like ours. If you permit us to sail this region, we will protect your lands from foreign ships. And ... we will support *you* as Ali'i. You may think your hold on your throne is secure. But your kingdom is divided. The coup is not yet complete, and you have less support than you believe."

It was a gamble. A well-calculated guess, at best. But the merman stiffened at Shiva's words. Aviama's heart sank.

Biscuits. Shiva was right. Shiva pulled his shoulders back a little further, sat a little taller. The corner of his lips twitched. He'd seen it too.

Behind the merman, in the semicircle of sirens, Aviama spotted the silver-haired one who had come to speak with her earlier. She looked stricken. Much like Aviama felt, she imagined. Shiva had just put all his eggs in the basket of the chieftain who wanted Makana dead, and he'd promised to hand her over.

The siren drilled Shiva with a dark glare he never saw, as he and the chieftain exchanged a long, unblinking stare. But

Aviama saw it. Her gut wrenched. And then the siren turned that steely gaze on her.

Hatred lit a fire behind those pearl-white eyes. The siren blamed Aviama for this betrayal. She'd seen Aviama on top of Shiva just moments ago. What could she conclude but that they were working together? That Aviama was a liar?

Aviama cast a sideways glance at the chieftain. He was still examining Shiva. Aviama looked back at the silver siren and chanced a slight shake of her head.

No.

No, I am not part of this. No, I do not want this.

But what was she expected to do? She couldn't leave. If Shiva offered her a ticket out, didn't she have to take it? She had to admit, he was doing well. The chieftain was considering his offer, as despicable an offer as it may have been. And it was probably their only chance at survival. Maybe she'd find a way to save Makana on the way out.

Her stomach soured as soon as the thought crossed her mind. If the chieftain wanted Makana, he would secure the terms of his agreement before letting Shiva and Aviama out of the Gorge.

Was Aviama willing to risk the lives of everyone on board the *Wraithweaver* in a vain attempt to save Makana? The lives of Sai, Umed, Manan, Laksh. Chenzira's life.

She was going to be sick.

"Woman."

Aviama snapped out of her swirling thoughts and blinked back at the merman.

"Makana tell you name. You know me most excellent. Good faith, I tell you name. Me Ali'i Limakau. This man say you no one. He lies. Who you are?"

This was it. Shiva shifted beside her. Aviama grimaced. If she dismantled Shiva's plan now, the game was up. Limakau would kill them here and now. She sucked in a deep breath and lifted her chin.

"I am a servant, Most Excellent Chieftain."

"Radha people dark, friend of sun. You shark underbelly color."

Aviama pursed her lips to stifle a laugh. She had to admit, she'd never been described as looking like the underbelly of a shark before. But to Limakau's credit, he knew more about the land of the sun than Shiva had given him credit for. Hundreds of years without human contact, and still he knew Aviama was out of place and unlikely to be natural-born Radhan.

She bowed her head. "You are most knowledgeable, Chieftain. I am not Radhan. I come from Jannemar and was sent from my homeland as a peace offering to Radha. I have been there as a servant, in the House of the Blessing Sun, ever since."

Close enough. She *was* sent to keep the peace, since a refusal to compete for Shiva's hand could have insulted Radha beyond repair. And in the wake of the war with Belvidore, Jannemar's coffers were low. They couldn't afford another conflict on that scale. Which meant if the rich and powerful Radha invaded, any prolonged war effort would bleed Jannemar dry.

Limakau studied her, then jerked his chin at Shiva. "What you think of him?"

Aviama steeled herself and glanced at Shiva. Shiva smiled encouragingly. Sickly sweet, like the smell of konnolan on the air. Ugh. She shouldn't have looked.

She turned to Limakau and forced a small smile. He wasn't buying it. If she oversold Shiva, he'd see through it.

"Prince Shiva is an intelligent and influential man. He has many resources and the ambition and drive to do what it takes to accomplish his goals. A friendship with him is advantageous."

"You did not say he is good."

"Is goodness something you typically look for in political alliances?"

Limakau laughed. "You do not speak like a servant."

Aviama spread her hands. "In order to have gained your esteemed position, Most Excellent Chieftain, I believe you know from experience that people are more than they seem. A king can be a fool. A servant can be wise. And who sees more of the inner workings of a kingdom than the servants?"

Limakau scrutinized her for a long moment. Her skin pricked with goosebumps in the chill of the damp air and the icy stares of the Iolani in the water before her.

Say nothing. Let them speak first. Let him think.

Shiva smiled. "You see why I chose her to accompany me, no?"

Aviama could have punched him. Limakau's pensive look shifted to suspicion, then back to a neutral diplomacy in the blink of an eye. He'd broken the silence too soon. Overeager. Brash.

The Iolani weren't like any other royals Shiva had treated with, and they certainly weren't simpering delegates crawling to a kingdom more powerful than their own. Ali'i Limakau had the upper hand in every way. Shiva's accurate guesses and appeals to Limakau's ambition were the only things keeping them alive.

The merman tapped his fingers on the edge of his spear and smiled—but the smile didn't reach his eyes. Slowly, he disappeared into the water, and with a flick of red and gold was gone. The sirens followed him, metallic tails bouncing bright lights through the rippling water and vanishing deep down below.

Aviama stared into the sparkling blue glow of the water. Her heart sank, chest tightening as she replayed the conversation in her mind. She backed away from the edge and sat down again, plying at the rope biting into her wrist.

"You came to kill them all, and now you're striking alliances."

Shiva arched an eyebrow. "I don't remember you in any of my preparation meetings for this voyage. You have no idea what I came for."

She clenched her jaw. Power, control of the Aeian Sea, better access to the Jannemari coast. Fame in Ghosts' Gorge.

He'd wanted to use her to control melderbloods, to expose them in Radha and funnel their power to his command. She'd told him point blank when she boarded the *Wraithweaver* that she'd never go through with a wedding. What had he said?

It no longer matters. I'll get what I want by other means.

Now that she'd refused to marry him—and now that he had konnolan—he'd set his sights on the powers of the Iolani, moving up his timeline for the Gorge.

Aviama focused hard on the rope fastened around her wrist. She lifted her free hand and sent slender tendrils of air between the fibers. It didn't unravel, but it did loosen. Just a little.

"Promise me you'll free us if we survive. Me, Chenzira, and anyone who wants to come with us."

Shiva tilted his head. "Would that make you feel better about cooperating?"

The silken quality of his voice sent a chill down her spine. His word wasn't worth a single silver coin. She winced.

"No."

He spread his hands. "As you wish, then."

Aviama tugged at the edge of the rope, holding the knot in

her teeth and yanking on the end with her free hand. She groaned.

"Why did you bring me on board? I'm a liability. You should have killed me on the dock."

"And start an international incident?"

"Please. That ship sailed ages ago."

The edge of the rope slipped free of the first knot. Victory flooded her chest. She glanced up at Shiva.

He swallowed and looked down at his hands. "I don't know."

She made a face. "Yes, you do. You don't do anything without a calculated reason."

"Maybe I don't give up my prizes easily."

He looked up sharply then, intense umber eyes under a rim of thick lashes.

Breath left her body like a punch to the gut. Had she once craved this man's attention? Been jealous for his affections? Nothing was more dangerous than being the relentless fixation of a treacherous man.

She'd gotten what she wanted. And she hated it.

Aviama was a medal for Shiva's jacket, the head of a beast to hang on his wall. He loved her, but not the way a man loved a woman. Perhaps he loved her like a hunter loved the stag.

Heart in her throat, she loosened the last of the knot and tossed the end in Shiva's direction as if it burned.

Never again.

She lifted her hands to the walls, sending wind swirling through the air of the rocky dome overhead, feeling for cracks. Nothing. On one hand, their air supply was stable. On the other, their only way out was through the main thoroughfare of the Iolani civilization, in the full sight of all.

Aviama edged toward the rim of the bone structure, staring into the crystal blue water. Could she really risk her life—Chenzira's life, Sai's life—for the unlikely chance she could find this Makuakan? But then, she had no guarantees that Limakau liked Shiva's offer. They could easily be dead by sundown anyway.

"Don't do it."

Aviama pivoted at the sound of Shiva's voice.

His eyes were dark, his expression flint. "Limakau is our best chance at survival."

"Or maybe he's destroying the *Wraithweaver* as we speak, murdering everyone on board, and will be back with a new deal—you give him everything you offered, or he kills you."

A muscle in his neck twitched, but no surprise crossed his face. He'd already thought of that.

"He's curious. He'll be back. If you do something stupid, you'll muck it all up."

Aviama shook her head. A sad little smile crept over her face as she looked back out at the glassy surface of the water. "Stupid is my specialty."

She dove into the water.

37

Water engulfed her. Glowing luminescent blues flashed along the skull-stacked pillars under the surface. But only the statues guarded the entrance.

Were Aviama and Shiva so useless that they weren't worth guarding? Or were sirens assigned further down the tunnels?

Aviama swam down as far as she could without oxygen, hovering in the water at the entrance to the tunnel. How would a siren kill her if she was found?

Biscuits, what wishful thinking. It wasn't *if* she was found, but *when*. She was on another suicide mission. What would Chenzira say?

Aviama reached a hand back up toward the trapped air inside the dome and drew her palm sharply into a fist at her chest. Air blasted through the water, enveloping her in a larger bubble than last time, and lifting her up to the ceiling of the tunnel. Controlling her position in the water was easier with the bubble bumping up against a natural barrier ceiling.

Sploosh.

Startled, she turned to see Shiva swimming toward her

with long, graceful strokes. Aviama scooted the bubble further into the tunnel, but soon enough, Shiva broke the barrier and joined her, floating in the bubble beside her.

"You're an idiot."

Aviama rolled her eyes. "Thanks. Now shut up before I drown you."

He glared at her, but pressed his lips together.

She dipped one ear out of the bubble and into the water. All was quiet. She drew her arm forward, rolling the bubble through the water and along the tunnel in the direction they'd come. Glowing blue transitioned to luminescent greens, and still no sirens.

A shriek split the air, and a distant roar rocketed through the water. Aviama and Shiva exchanged a glance. Aviama threw them forward in the tunnel, past the fork, and over the skeleton road. Shiva seized her arm and placed a finger to his lips. Aviama stilled.

A series of whistles and clicks emanated through the water. Close. Aviama lifted the bubble and flattened it along the ceiling of the passage, pressing her and Shiva along the top of the rock just as two armed mermen darted across the opening. Three sirens burst by a moment later, a ululating war cry cutting through the depths as they flashed through the tunnel.

Aviama's mouth went dry. Something was happening. Something big.

Shiva tapped her on the shoulder, and she smacked his hand away. He lifted his hands defensively and gestured onward. *It's clear.*

She considered dunking him in the water again, but there was no point. Onward they must go. Aviama pushed the bubble along through the water, directing the air around them to the mouth of the prison tunnels. Ahead of them, the tails of the three sirens flicked out of sight as they rounded the last bend.

Aviama sucked in a breath as she took in the sight. Silhouettes of sailors hit the water above them, one after the other. Sirens screeched and lunged for each fallen man like sharks drawn to blood. Below, Limakau raised his spear toward four mermen, a shaft of swirling water shooting toward them in a spiral.

She didn't see the eels caught in the spear's current until Limakau's first victim stiffened and went limp, slowly sinking to the splintered ships on the ocean floor. Sirens shrieked above, and a pack of them dove toward the altercation, splitting off, some to Limakau and some to the fallen mermen. A coursing spear grazed Limakau's arm from some hidden niche in the far side of the Gorge, and he spun to face the new threat.

Aviama took the chance and shot out of the entrance and down, down, into the shadows of a broken ship. She burst through a cracked open, empty gunport of a barnacled vessel lying on its side. Shiva was close behind, but she didn't care. He couldn't afford to kill her. She was his air supply. As long as he didn't slow her down.

Another unearthly roar rolled through the deep. Aviama peered out of the gunport, every muscle tense, teeth set on edge. A dark gray missile shot into the heart of the ravine. At second glance, the missile was a living, breathing creature, surging through the water at lightning speed like a knife through butter.

Its body was long and flexible like an eel, but small fins accented the head behind the gills and the long muscular tail. The beast's head was triangular, almost serpentine, and when it opened its mouth, its death cry sent sirens shrieking into their holes. The thing opened its mouth to reveal hundreds of trident-like teeth in distinct rows from the lip of its jaw leading in toward its throat.

Spears and harpoons arced through the water toward the beast, but it thrashed forward with snake-like agility, weaving in and out of each weapon sent its way. A copper siren let a harpoon fly from just above the skull columns of the outside of the prison tunnels, and the tip of it drew blood along the creature's side.

In the blink of an eye, the beast's head swung round and plunged, sinking its teeth into the copper siren's tail. The siren screamed, a ghoulish squall that threatened Aviama's eardrums. She winced against the blood-curdling sound—and her jaw dropped. She hadn't noticed before. But now, as the long body of the monster, three times the length of any Iolani, arced through the ravine of the Gorge, she saw a metal ring embedded in its back and a powerful merman rippling with muscles bracing himself for the ride.

Burnt orange scales spotted with white shimmered on his tail at the waist, transitioning in a gradient to aquamarine with black spots down to the fins, exploding in a burst of sunset colors along the fins and spines. With one hand, he gripped the beast, and with the other, he aimed a splendid two-pronged ebony spear.

Aviama pushed away from the gunport and further into the recesses of the shattered ship. If she could move away from the conflict within the concealed safety of the ship ruins, maybe they had a chance at reaching the surface. But with sailors being tossed right and left, were they really any safer on the *Wraithweaver*? If they were, would there be enough men to maneuver the vessel clear of the Gorge?

She pushed off the side of the ship and rolled the air bubble across the splintered ship's remains. The mast rose a meter up from the floor of the gun deck before turning into wooden shards. Coral and algae carpeted the old planks, and a large hole two meters wide yawned up at her as she floated over the opening. A crab scurried away along a cannon through the hole in the deck below.

Sections of the upper deck still remained intact, hemming them in inside the gun deck and shielding them from Iolani eyes as Aviama moved toward the bow of the ship. The monster's roar rocked through the water again, followed by a *crash*. The sunken ship creaked and shuddered on impact, and a loose board shook free above her, sinking slowly through the water, hitting the air bubble, and plunging through it in freefall before hitting the water again with a splash.

Aviama froze. Her pulse pounded against her temple, heart beating out of her chest. A splash. Underwater. From inside a sunken ship.

Crackkkkk.

Aviama spun as the planks of the hull snapped inward, revealing a flash of gray hide and rows of ivory teeth. The monster's great serpentine head hit the side of the vessel like a battering ram, breaking the ship apart. Shiva moved in front of Aviama and snatched the broken-off plank that had fallen, holding it up like a shield in front of him as the beast dove through the new opening and stretched its jaws wide. Copper scales from the siren's tail still clung to one of the animal's rear rows of teeth.

The beast plowed into him, its nose splitting the board in half and driving Shiva backward. Shiva's body hit Aviama like a sledgehammer. Her head snapped back with the whiplash of the hit, and she flew through the air of her bubble—crashing into the water on the far side. The air escaped, rising through the sunken ship toward the surface in a great, conspicuous orb.

Pain shot through her body. Cold water swirled around

her. When she opened her eyes, blood drifted through the water across hundreds of triangular teeth. The mouth of the beast stretched wide and lunged at her head. She called to the wind, but there was no wind.

At the last second, the animal jerked sideways, its teeth sinking into the splintered mast instead. The mighty Iolani warrior on the monster's back leaned along the spine of the wriggling creature and whirled his spear. A current of water shot from the tip of his spear and encircled her, binding her hands to her sides as her lungs burned for air.

The warrior wrenched the monster around, and out they flew from the belly of the ship—out into the open water of the ravine. Aviama and Shiva tumbled after him, each trapped in the merman's current. A dozen sirens armed with harpoons descended on the warrior like vultures on carrion, and the swirling waters encircling Aviama and Shiva broke apart.

Aviama threw her hands up to the bubble of air shimmering through the water high above her, almost out of view. Would it answer in time to save her? Could she keep her focus on it long enough to maintain her hold?

A faint crackle and hiss caught her ear, and she rotated in the water. Beyond the mass of sirens and flash of harpoon spears and metallic scales, Limakau arced his spear over his head and thrust it at the warrior. The monster ripped into a brass-colored siren, and her shriek rippled through the water. The warrior whirled and sank his spear into the neck of a silver-tailed siren. He didn't see Limakau.

Two wriggling eels glinted in the crest of a sharp current, bursting from the tip of Limakau's spear and coursing through the water toward their unwitting victim.

Aviama's stomach dropped. Her lungs burned. She couldn't save them both, could she? Herself, and the warrior?

The one that had his monster attack her? But hadn't he also saved her life?

Biscuits.

With a sinking feeling in her gut and a burning in her chest, Aviama strained to pull at the air bubble overhead with all her strength. And it came, barreling through the water at her command—straight past her to intercept the deadly eels. In an instant, the air pocket enveloped the eels, and she spun her hands to redirect it, spinning Limakau's eels over the warrior's head and into the two remaining sirens attacking him.

The warrior spun, eyes wide, to take in the last of the sirens around him—ten killed by him or his monster, and two by the human girl he'd caught in his domain. The girl who'd saved his life from Limakau.

The one about to drown.

Aviama's chest hitched. Her head swam.

Shiva had tried to treat with Limakau, but if Limakau was operating in good faith, why were *Wraithweaver* sailors still plunging to their deaths over the rails of the galleon at the surface?

And if they were caught now, weren't they dead anyway?

It had made sense when she did it. But now, as the last air bubble escaped her lips and floated up toward the sunlight cascading through crystal waters, she wasn't so sure.

I'm sorry, Chenzira.

And for the second time that day, she began to sink.

38

Something wrapped around her body and pulled. Dark spots filled her vision, with snatches of shimmering orange and blue filtering in as if through a fog.

A rush filled her ears. Water spilled over and around her as she was whisked through the depths, but whether she went up or down, she could not tell.

Bright light burst around her, and she gasped for air. Blessed air filled her lungs, and Aviama revived to a flurry of activity in every direction. Choppy waters tossed the ships of Radha's fleet this way and that. The damaged ship behind the *Wraithweaver* had already begun to sink, and sirens still swarmed in the water.

The clang of steel rang out from the upper deck of the *Wraithweaver*, though none of the Iolani had boarded. A man in a teal coat shouted orders from the helm, and men turned, palms up, to engage the rest of the crew.

A lump choked Aviama's throat. Samud must have revived. He was killing melderbloods and tossing them to the Iolani to save his own skin.

"Air. Now."

Aviama turned to see the warrior holding Shiva by the back of the neck and drilling her with a cool stare. She blinked back at him. "What?"

"Bring air. Show me or die."

He raised his two-pronged spear, and down they went again into the churning water. Aviama reached up to the surface and drew down more air as the warrior drove the three of them along into a cleft in the rocky ravine to one side. The monster roared as the warrior released it. Aviama's mouth went dry as the merman's hand let go of the ring embedded in the creature's back, but it did not attack them. Instead, it surged into the ocean and was gone.

Aviama pulled the air pocket around her, and the merman entered it with Shiva, surrounding the bubble with swirling water from the end of his spear and positioning them where he wanted inside the cleft. The intensity of the merman's deep saffron eyes bore the same ferocity as Makana—the same lethal vigilance Aviama had seen in Makana moments before she'd nearly choked Aviama to death the day they'd first met in the menagerie.

The warrior tossed Shiva to the other side of the air pocket and glared at Aviama.

"Why Limakau keep you alive?"

Aviama bowed as best she could. "Most Excellent Chieftain. Ali'i Makuakan, I presume? I am Princess Aviama of Jannemar. I am friends with Makana."

Makuakan's eyes darkened. "Makana is dead."

"No, Excellency. Makana was taken captive as she protected the Iolani nursery from the Radhan invasion. She has been held hostage by this man and his family ever since." Aviama jabbed a long finger at Shiva.

Makuakan's nostrils flared as he turned his attention to Shiva.

Shiva's lips parted in shock, and he threw up his hands. "Excellency, we came on a diplomatic mission. Makana is safe and sound, and we will return her to you in a show of good faith in hopes of securing—"

Aviama cut him off. "This is Prince Shiva of Radha. He tried to cut a deal with Limakau to give him Jannemari resources to control tabeun melderblood powers and support Limakau's bid for the throne. He offered peace with Radha, Makana's life, and wyronite that he does not have. But you should know that he arrived with a fleet of warships and konnolan on board to control you, and only offered peace to Limakau after I destroyed the konnolan."

Makuakan's lip curled. "Mola mola. Why I believe you? You dare come to Ipuka Akala, when fight amongst yourselves?"

Shiva began to speak, but Aviama lifted her chin and raised her voice over him. "Ali'i, division exists in even the greatest of civilizations. Even among the Iolani, no? But I am not from Radha, and I did not come willingly. I was incapacitated when Prince Shiva dragged me on board the ship, and I did not know where we were going until the ship had left the harbor. But Shiva brought Makana in a cage."

Aviama edged forward. "If you want wyronite, Jannemar has it. If you want peace, I can broker it. But if you seek a trustworthy royal in Radha, I fear you will exhaust yourself in the search."

Makuakan let out a series of clicks and cocked his head. "And why I trust you?"

She bowed her head. "Excellency, I have sung with Makana, and she trusts me. We are friends. I saved your life from Limakau because I believe you care for her. I want nothing from you but my life and the lives of my friends."

Boom.

The familiar sound of cannons burst through the barrier around them, and Makuakan looked up. Ripping the currents free of the air pocket, he swam past them out of the cleft toward the firing of the guns. Shiva lunged for Aviama. Fury lit a devilish fire in his eyes as his fingers wrapped around her neck.

Aviama slugged him in the stomach, but his hold on her throat only tightened. She rolled them forward through the water and slammed them into the rock. Shiva's back hit the cliff, and the air around them burst and flew up to the surface.

The two of them kicked up toward the sun as the peal of ship cannons thundered through the sea. Aviama broke the surface and swam for a hold on the edge of the cliff where it soared up into the sky. She reached for the rock, but just as she neared it, pain exploded in her temple as Shiva struck her on the side of the head.

Aviama's head went under. Shiva's strong arms cinched tight around her, holding her down beneath the waves. Panic welled in her chest. She summoned the wind, but the air keeping the ocean at bay did no good—he'd blocked her windpipe.

In a desperate wrench, Aviama reached not to the air around her, not for the claws at her throat—but for the air in Shiva's lungs. If he would steal her airway, she would steal his breath.

Shiva's body around her jerked, and his fingers fell away. Aviama threw him backward and lunged for the cliff.

Her hands and feet searched for a hold along the clammy rock wall. Aviama's muscles screamed from exertion, and her chest felt as though it could cave in at any moment. The rough water splashed up against the side of the ravine, and she sputtered against the sea spray tossing up against the cliff and into her mouth.

Up and to her left, a piece of rock jutted out from the cliff. Her heart leaped, and she reached for it. But as her hands took hold, the rock itself seemed to grow up and out of the side of the cliff.

Aviama's stomach churned as she clung to the shifting rock. It wasn't fair. The Iolani could control wind, waves, storms, and rock? Was there anything they *couldn't* do?

But just as her hold began to slip, another piece of rock jutted out beneath her, and she dropped down onto it. Another segment pulled away from the rock, just above it and to the side, along the ravine toward the *Wraithweaver*. Aviama gathered her feet and jumped for it, and as she did, another step appeared before her.

She glanced around the frothing water for Makuakan or Limakau, but there was no sign of them. The *Wraithweaver* was pulling ahead now through the passage. Durga stood on the aftcastle, arms raised to fill the sails or knock the sirens from the railings. Other melders lined the sides of the ship, tossing the water into a foaming rage and knocking Samud's men overboard. The rest of Shiva's fleet was buffeted from one side of the narrow ravine to the other, blocked by the broken and sinking ship splintering to the rear of the *Wraithweaver*.

But then, there in the water between her and the *Wraithweaver*, Aviama caught the flash of a bright silver tail. Flowing white hair rippled behind the siren as she swam, and the closer she came, the more potent the shade of her lavender eyes. And beside her, holding on with one arm as the siren propelled them through the water, was Chenzira.

His face was caked with blood, his tunic torn to shreds. But his eyes were trained on the cliff, his free hand extended, palm outward, to the side of the ravine. At his command, slabs of rock rumbled from the cliff and jutted out at intervals like steps.

Aviama's heart leaped as she jumped from ledge to ledge. A scraping sound preceded each new step pulling free of its home in the rock as her quakemaker crafted new footing. Her foot slipped, and she teetered on the edge of a narrow rocky slab.

She twisted as she struggled to regain her balance. Behind her, Shiva followed in her footsteps, leaping to each new landing with a grace she wished she had for herself. Aviama whisked up a gust of wind to steady her as she began to fall, and moved forward again, picking up her pace as Shiva trailed close behind.

Makana and Chenzira swam hard toward the cliff as Aviama broke into a run along the cliff face, Chenzira forming each new step a fraction of a second before her foot connected with each one. Aviama's legs ached as her bare feet slapped against the cool, sea-sprayed rock. But if they had a prayer of getting out of Ghosts' Gorge alive, the Iolani coup had to be stopped.

"Makana! Makuakan needs to know you're alive, or we're dead. And I think he needs help—Limakau's support is too strong."

Makana glanced in both directions. "Where he go?"

"I don't know." Aviama pointed back to where she'd been. "He was there, but then he heard the cannons and took off."

Chenzira rotated his free hand, forming another landing for Aviama. "We need you on the *Wraithweaver*. Durga's sending melderbloods overboard, anyone who isn't loyal to Shiva. Sai is in trouble."

Aviama glanced up at the galleon ahead. Durga and Sai faced off on the upper deck, but Sai was holding up the bent figure of a man. Someone was hurt. Durga sent a mighty gale slamming into Sai as Aviama watched, knocking her off her feet and skidding down the deck. Aviama looked back at

Makana just in time to see a shadow spin up toward her through the water. A brass-colored siren reached for Chenzira and yanked him down into the depths.

Her stomach dropped. Aviama's foot extended for the next landing, but it never appeared. She fell.

Makana dove for Chenzira, and Aviama threw an air pocket down through the water toward his face, but she never saw if it reached him. Cannon fire ripped through the air, ringing in her ears. Iron fingers seized her by the wrist, halting her descent with a jolt.

Water crashed into her feet, a rogue wave sending her body swinging into the rough rock. Aviama glanced up at Shiva. He'd prevented her fall, but only ire filled her chest. Aviama hung there, making no move to alleviate her weight pulling at Shiva. Her arm smarted. But Chenzira was still underwater.

Aviama sent blasts of air down toward the murky shadows of figures beneath the surface. Silver and brass scales glinted in the water. Chenzira's silhouette came in and out of view through a tangle of limbs and fins.

"Hey!"

Aviama twisted to look back at Shiva. His hold on her arm slipped, and his grip tightened.

"Do you know what sirens do to humans? Didn't you see the tunnel we were just in? Don't be an idiot. Stay above water and help me, or you'll be next."

Aviama swung her feet toward the closest ledge back the way they had come and blasted Shiva in the face with a burst of air. He released her with a grunt, and she brought a burst of wind upward to send her up onto the ledge. "Leave me alone."

"You just painted me as Makuakan's greatest enemy. I'm not letting you out of my sight."

Ahhh, there it was. The real reason he was staying close to

her now. Because she might talk to Makuakan and cut an unfavorable deal regarding him.

Aviama's nostrils flared as she shot back at Shiva, "You sold my people's resources when you haven't even invaded! You killed Bhumi. You sold Makana. You deserve everything that's coming to you."

Shiva swung for her from his place one ledge higher than her position on the cliff, but she blocked his blow and leaned forward, drilling him with a cool glare. "And I'll make sure that it does."

He lunged, but the place she'd occupied a moment before was empty. Down, down into the water she went, plunging once more into the cold froth seething with blood and teeth. At her command, wind pounded through the surf to envelop the brass siren in air, breaking her contact with the sea. Aviama's lip curled as she sent the mermaid flying, her dagger-like nails leaving scratch marks on Chenzira's skin as Aviama ripped her off him.

Makana seized Chenzira and surged toward Aviama as she dragged down another air pocket, this time encircling herself and Chenzira as Makana propelled him through the water toward her. Aviama caught Chenzira around the waist as he sucked in blessed air to starving lungs.

Aviama wrapped her arms around him as he recovered and whirled to Makana. "What do you need from me?"

"Spear man take you ship. Me save Father."

Aviama blinked. "Father?"

Makana nodded. "Limakau half-brother. Hate me. Say not legitimate. Father favor me and prepare me lead Iolani."

Understanding dawned. "You're Makuakan's daughter."

She dipped her head. "I know where refugee Iolani hide. Not far. Can bring."

"Be safe. Go."

Makana dove out of the bubble and back into the water just as Aviama caught a glimpse of the great gray beast from earlier, surging toward them free and without a mount, mouth wide open. Chenzira ripped his fist sideways, pulling a segment of the cliff out like a shot and striking the monster in its side. It shook off the blow and roared, exposing each of its hundreds of hooked, barbed, triangular teeth.

Makana lurched in front of it, arms high, letting out a spectral shriek that transitioned into a series of clicks and a whistle. The beast lunged, and the siren launched forward to meet it, skirting its jaws by a hair and catching hold of the metal ring in its back. The animal roared again, but Makana wrested it into a zig-zag pattern and whirled its nose downward. In a flash, they were gone, leaving Aviama and Chenzira staring after them in shock.

Chenzira cleared his throat. "I think she'll be fine."

Aviama snort-laughed. *Understatement.* She turned toward him, and his eyes were roving over her face, her lips, her hair. Her stomach flopped, and the corner of her mouth quirked up.

He floated closer, dragging his knuckles along the skin of her arm and up to the nape of her neck. Aviama's mouth opened just slightly as she watched him, drinking him in. The tenderness of his touch sent chills down her spine, and the air pocket around them shuddered.

Chenzira bit his lip. "Come on. Let's get you to the ship."

She scrunched her nose in an embarrassed grimace and nodded. With a sweep of her hands, Aviama sent the bubble surging to the surface. The two of them broke the tension of the water, and Chenzira drew out a slab of rock from the cliff for them to climb onto. He pulled her to her feet and jerked his chin at the ship making its way further into the Gorge and further away from them with every passing moment.

"I'll get us to the *Wraithweaver,* and you can take out Durga. I'll get the others."

Ahead of them, Shiva still crouched on the ledge. He eyed Chenzira with a murderous dagger-like gaze sweeping over the two of them. Chenzira stiffened and pulled up to his full height, one hand wrapping around Aviama's waist, his fingers finding the curve of her hip as he glared back at his rival.

Aviama set her jaw as she locked eyes with Shiva. "Drop him."

39

———

Without hesitation, Chenzira flicked his wrist, and the ledge holding Shiva's weight tilted vertically, dumping him into the water. He plummeted to the surf with a cry.

A red and gold gleam caught the sun in the water to their left as another peal of cannon fire split the air. Limakau caught Shiva up in a current at the tip of his spear, raising him up in the water. "Stop cannons, or my sirens sing."

The death lullaby. Aviama's mouth went dry. A final song sweetly summoning every man to a watery grave.

Shiva set his jaw. "Get me to my ship, and I'll give you what you want. But let us leave in peace."

"Wyronite. Maps of all Aeian border rivers and regions. Makana."

"Done."

"Not everyone leave. Example make."

"Those of my crew you've already taken, I give you with pleasure." Shiva gestured at Aviama and Chenzira standing along the cliff face. "These two you can have also, as my parting gift. She's from Jannemar. The first of many Jannemari gifts."

Aviama's jaw dropped. Chenzira's fingers dug into her hip. He shot out another ledge before them and pulled her along beside him. A torrent of unnatural waves rose up behind Shiva, rising higher and higher as Limakau raised his arm.

Chenzira yelled in her ear as he yanked ledge after ledge out from the cliff. "Go, go, go!"

Limakau shot a great wave up at them from the water several meters below; Aviama threw up a hand and formed a barrier of air on that side as they ran. Surging sea hit the barrier and ran down it as if it had been glass. Chenzira pulled footstep after footstep from the side of the ravine, Aviama holding up a shield as Limakau struck them with blow after blow of ocean waves.

The *Wraithweaver* grew nearer and nearer, and as they approached, Limakau branched off from the ravine and tore away toward the ship with Shiva. Ahead, the narrow passage of the Gorge opened up into a larger space, the rock formation creating an eerily perfect circle and branching off into two more passages on the far side. If they didn't reach the ship by the time it left the ravine, they'd lose their chance to board.

Adrenaline coursed through her veins. The crow's-nest swayed high in the air, running dangerously close to the wall of the ravine as the water tossed the ship. The people on board were easier to make out now, and the action on board was a sight to behold. Durga blasted a gale into Manan's chest, and he tumbled overboard—and then the sea itself raised him up out of the water and spit him back out on deck.

Manan rolled to his feet and snatched his dagger from its sheath while sliding across the planks beneath another blast of wind. Up at the helm, the teal jacket Aviama knew so well caught her eye as the captain of the ship guided the vessel through the tight space. Jignesh threw a knife through the gut of an archer poised on the rigging. Behind him, a sailor stabbed a fireblood in the back as he shot a ball of flame across the deck at a siren climbing up the rail.

Aviama gaped at the chaos. "This is madness!"

Chenzira slipped on the slick rock, steadied himself, and drove forward two paces behind her on the cliff. The steps led higher and higher up the side of the ravine, rising up above the railing of the ship as they climbed.

"They need strong leadership, and a prayer of survival. We'll give them both."

Aviama's gaze swept the upper deck. Limakau drove forward on a wave of his own creation, supporting Shiva's weight with one arm, eyes fixed on the ship.

Her heart sank. "We might need Makana."

"No, we need her with Makuakan. Give her as much time as you can."

The ship began pulling away from the rock. Their window was growing short. Chenzira grabbed her hand as he caught up with her to run the final length of the ravine, pulling her forward with him and leaning into the wind as they closed in on their target. "The terrifying woman I saw flying over the bow of the ship—fire in her eyes and death in her hands—*that* is the woman we need right now. Don't hold back. We need you. You can do this."

Fire in her eyes. Death in her hands.

Was she ready to dole out death? To choose who lived and who did not?

But as a copper-colored mermaid leaped out of the water and threw a harpoon into Shiva's waiting hands, Limakau lifting the two of them higher and higher on the ever-growing crest of a powerful wave, resolve hardened in Aviama's heart.

Heat filled her chest, and her muscles tensed as she pushed off the final edge of the cliff.

Hadn't Shiva decided someone would die today by coming to Ghosts' Gorge stocked with konnolan hull to hull? Hadn't Limakau ensured it with his coup against Makuakan?

It was Shiva who had decided blood would spill. All that was left for Aviama to decide was whether she would stand idly by and let the slaughter happen, or if she would rise up to turn the tables. If he wanted blood to spill, let it spill—but let it be his. Not theirs. Not hers.

Never again.

Aviama's feet cycled in the air over nothing, nothing but air and wind and a freefall over crashing ocean waves colliding with the *Wraithweaver's* hull. Wind blew back her golden hair, flowing out behind her as she leaped from the cliff to the ship. The jump wouldn't be enough. And Limakau was almost to the ship.

Aviama swept her hand and summoned the air around them, pressing in on their backs and whisking them across the open space to the deck in a whooshing gale. Limakau thrust Shiva up and over the railing. Chenzira, Aviama, and Shiva landed on the *Wraithweaver* in the same instant, Shiva rolling to his feet and Aviama cushioning their landing with another wave of wind stabilizing them as their soles struck the landing.

Chenzira released Aviama's hand and was moving before she could blink. "Stop Durga first. I'll take Shiva."

Aviama set her jaw, but nodded. Chenzira's melder powers were less effective on the ship, and Shiva didn't have any—a more even match. But Durga was the greatest threat to melderbloods on board.

Fine.

She pivoted toward Durga and stalked toward her. Sea

spray tossed this way and that across the deck, catching in her lashes and hair as she walked toward the bow. Durga had Manan by the throat. Laksh sent a ball of fire toward her, but she blasted him backward off the steps of the forecastle.

An arrow whistled through the air toward Aviama's head. She caught it in an air current and brought it directly to her palm, snapping it in two and tossing aside the pieces. A crestbreaker had Sai around the throat, vines of water wrapping around her ankle and yanking her off balance. Sai sent a blast of air at her attacker, but missed as she fell.

Aviama ran forward to catch her as she fell, ripping the breath from the crestbreaker's lungs. He collapsed to the deck —breathing, but unconscious. How many melderbloods had turned against them? How many sided with Shiva and Durga? Did they realize they had signed their own death certificates?

Sai gripped her arm, staring up at Aviama. "You're back!"

"Yes, but if we don't get control of the ship, we're all going down. Stop the cannons, and if anyone gets in your way, reach for their lungs and pull."

Sai's lips parted. "What?"

"If you let go at the end of the pull, they'll live. But if you don't stop the cannons, the sirens sing, and we all die anyway. Go."

Her friend nodded and took off for the stairs. Laksh picked himself up from the deck, rubbing the back of his head where he'd fallen. He whirled his hands in a circular motion, a blaze leaping up between his palms.

Aviama laid a hand on his arm. "Bigger. Higher. Wind snuffs out a candle. Water extinguishes flame. Where should fire live?"

He blinked back at her.

She glanced across the deck. A pair of sailors had a barrel

of oil they were lifting to the rail to spill overboard. Oil helped calm choppy waters. Would it work on Iolani waves?

Aviama turned back to Laksh. "Oil. Set it on fire and burn any siren that gets close. Stop up your ears, and if any siren starts to sing, I want her thrashing in the waves to put out the flame before she sings a single bar."

Laksh's eyebrows soared. "Yes, Commander."

Durga turned on her heel, looking down at Aviama from the forecastle, hands around Manan's throat. Her lips curled into a wicked sneer.

Aviama threw up a shield just as Durga sent a blast of air toward her chest, but as Durga's hands extended outward, Aviama sent a swirling current at her ankles. Durga crashed to the deck, and Manan doubled over, coughing and sputtering. Aviama ran up the steps of the forecastle, but a wall of air from Durga's palm sent her careening backward into the mast.

Pain reverberated through her body. Aviama shot a blast at Durga just as the girl sent her next onslaught. A vortex of air swirled between them, currents meeting in the middle as Aviama strained to maintain her hold. Durga's strength had grown, and her control had increased. She was at her best in grand sweeping scenarios like this one, when raw power won the day.

But her weakness was in finesse.

Aviama rolled to one side, spinning under the gale before Durga could react, as the collision of air they'd created released in a gust of air thrown outward in every direction. Aviama whirled on top of Durga, dropping her knee onto the girl's chest. She extended trembling fingers over Durga's heart as she stared down into her enemy's eyes.

Durga's glare seethed with hatred. She flung a palm up toward Aviama's face, but Aviama was faster. Aviama pulled her hand in toward herself, drawing out the air from Durga's lungs. Slowly.

The girl's mouth opened, and her chest hitched.

Aviama shook her head. "I never wanted this for us. He uses you as much as he used me. I wish we could have been friends."

With a quick jerk, Aviama finished the motion, and Durga's head lolled back on the deck. Aviama dropped her head on Durga's chest. Her heartbeat was slow, but steady. Manan crouched beside her, dagger in hand.

Aviama gestured at Durga's limp body. "Put her in the brig. She can't do locks."

He nodded and hoisted her over his shoulder. "What if she wakes up?"

Her stomach twisted. "Do what you have to do before she comes to. And stop up your ears."

Aviama straightened as Manan ran toward the brig with Durga, washing a sailor overboard with a rogue wave when the man tried to stand in his way. His control wasn't perfect, but good enough. The seaman spun over the rail with a cry.

It was time. Aviama turned to find Chenzira and Shiva fighting hand to hand on the upper deck below. She leaped over the railing of the forecastle down to the deck a mere meter from their blows, but a crash of water knocked her sideways as she fell. Limakau lifted his spear, and wind began to gather at its tip. Dark clouds rolled in, and a rumble broke across the sky.

Her stomach dropped.

A storm was brewing.

40

Sirens spiraled in great arcs out of the water, flashes of silver and gold and copper in the shimmer of what sunlight remained through the darkening sky. One of them threw a harpoon, and Aviama barely saw it plunging toward her chest before she threw up a hand. The harpoon froze in midair, and Aviama snatched it.

Chenzira pounded Shiva to the deck, and Shiva lunged, dropping Chenzira to the ground and rolling on top of him. Shiva slugged Chenzira in the gut, and Chenzira reached up, grabbed Shiva by the face, and smashed their heads together. Shiva wavered, and Chenzira punched him across the jaw, laying him out across the rough wooden planks.

Aviama offered Chenzira her hand. He took it with a grin and gestured for the harpoon in her hand. "Come on, you don't really need that. I do."

She tossed him the harpoon, and he caught it just as the ship tilted hard into the driving rain. Aviama glanced down at Shiva, rolling to his side. Chenzira had things well in hand. He didn't need her. On the far side of the ship, two sirens clawed their way up the railing of the ship. Laksh lifted a ball of boiling, flaming oil from the barrel in front of him and hurled it at them. Their perfect skin splashed with angry red burns as they fell back to the waves with a screech.

Umed fought three men on deck, throwing one over his shoulder and off the ship. Aviama's gut wrenched. It wasn't safe to keep anyone on board who would serve Shiva. But with every seaman lost, they had fewer bodies to fight the Iolani or crew the *Wraithweaver*.

A scream caught Aviama's ear. Sai clung to the railing, her body dangling off the side into the water. Aviama sprinted toward her, but Chenzira caught her by the arm and yanked her backward.

"Manan's got her."

As if on cue, Manan hurtled at the railing from under the quarterdeck. He sent a copper siren flailing back into the sea with a crashing wave as she reached talon-like fingers up toward Sai.

Chenzira pivoted the two of them and pointed at the merman with a whirlwind growing ever wider, ever stronger, at the end of his weapon. "If you don't stop Limakau, we're all dead. I'll distract him, but you need to stop him."

Could she do it? Limakau was too dangerous to knock out once and imprison, like she'd done with Durga. All the vastness of the ocean spread before him to hide in, and he wasn't short on support. But if she didn't stop the threat, they were doomed.

Chenzira extended his palm to the deck, pulling nails out from the boards. They floated to his palm, and with a flick of his wrist, cut through the air at Limakau. The metal shards embedded in the merman's hide breastplate, and Limakau turned on him with a sneer. Chenzira swore. "I need something bigger."

Shiva dove for Chenzira's waist, but Aviama blasted him backward before he made contact. Limakau whirled his spear arm, the wave beneath him climbing higher still until he was higher than the *Wraithweaver* rail.

Cold rain pelted down, obscuring her vision and dripping down her spine. Laksh braced himself against the mast, stabilizing the barrel of oil in front of him as he sent a fresh volley of blazing oil at the sirens rising from the tossing waves. Steam sizzled from the surface of their skin as the sirens wailed and screeched, drawing Limakau's gaze. His lip curled, and the bulging muscles of his arms tensed as he drew the spear from the sky down toward Laksh.

Aviama threw a shield in front of Laksh, but Limakau's whirlwind shattered it like glass. The storm caught Laksh high up in its mighty tempest, snatching him off his feet and sending him slinging through the air in a twisting loop around the crow's-nest, the final coils of a noose about to drop.

Dread washed over her. Aviama's chest tightened as she rushed at Limakau, both palms trained on his lungs—beneath the impenetrable breastplate, beneath smooth skin and rolling musculature, to that which every air-breathing creature had in common.

Crackkk.

Out of the corner of her eye, the broad-shouldered form of a man plunged to the deck.

Energy flooded every artery, every vein of her blood. The tingling of unspent power called to her, begging for use. Indomitable rage filled her chest with an unquenchable burning.

Aviama ripped her hands in toward herself, hands clenched to fists trembling in exertion over her own heart— pulling from Limakau's chest, pulling, pulling.

The wind is mine. Your breath is mine.

A sickening splat marked the breaking of bones as Laksh's body hit the deck behind her, but she dared not look. Tears sprang to her eyes and a lump to her throat, chest heaving. Her nails dug into her palms as she felt for the last of the breath in the merman's body, calling it to her.

Limakau stiffened. Thunder rolled, but the whirlwind snapping at the sails began to break apart. His hand quivered on the spear, and his mouth opened as if to gasp for air—but no air was afforded him. His gaze darted wildly across the sea and over the deck, landing squarely on Aviama.

Aviama glared up at him, a red haze lining the edges of her vision. With a vicious jerk, she wrested the last of the air from his lungs. He fell to the waves, the water holding him up fleeing across the surface of the sea. Aviama rushed to the rail as the shadow of his silhouette sank deeper and deeper into the depths.

Was he dead? If the sirens got him to the surface fast enough, could he be revived? The deeper he sank, the further from her he got, the more impossible it was for her to maintain any control over his lungs.

Four sirens dove for him, disappearing under the hull of the ship as the *Wraithweaver* cut through the water and angled for a narrow channel exit on the far side. Lightning split the air, its peal of thunder sending a jolt through her bones. Rain continued to fall, a soft mournful patter mixing with the bloodstains smattered across the deck.

Aviama turned slowly, hardly daring to see the carnage behind her. Laksh's broken body lay strewn at an unnatural angle, staring up at the rain as it dripped down on his face and open eyes. The barrel of oil had been knocked sideways, spilling across the deck and soaking Laksh's feet. Chenzira delivered an uppercut to Shiva's jaw, then paused as he rotated through the motion and caught a glimpse of Aviama. Behind him, Shiva snatched a fallen harpoon from the ground, spun, and thrust it up toward Chenzira's back.

Her scream stuck in her throat as she threw up a hand in Shiva's direction. But as the last of Limakau's explosive whirlwind spun apart, her wind was caught up with it and whisked it away to the far corners of the sky.

Chenzira's deep brown eyes locked onto hers as the world seemed to slow. He hadn't seen Shiva. Perhaps he never would. Perhaps this, a final chance to look into each other's eyes at the end of things, was the last sight those beautiful eyes would behold before death took him.

Shiva's eyes lit with that lethal cruelty Aviama knew so well.

At the last moment, Shiva and Chenzira twisted as one, Shiva's harpoon missing its mark and breaking the skin in a shallow slit along Chenzira's side instead. A low, haunting hum danced across the water. Tingles shot up and down Aviama's skin, standing on end the hairs at the back of her neck.

Ethereal beauty surrounded the *Wraithweaver*. Visions of stunning female creatures broke the surface of the sea, long hair flowing in the ocean around them, their temples shimmering with silver and gold, as piercing eyes cut to the soul. Perfect lips parted, releasing heavenly notes, rising and falling in bewitching lilting song.

Mesmerizing lullaby descended on the ship like cloud. Shiva stumbled toward a rose-gold mermaid on the other side of the railing, her alluring voice smooth as silk. Gone was the ferocious murderer, the strategic prince bent on power and revenge. His face had gone slack, as if aware of nothing else but the siren. Aviama reached out reflexively to catch his arm, but he pulled free of her grasp with unseeing eyes.

Men walked like animated statues, without will, without agency, up from the stairs of the lower decks and over the side of the ship. Manan, Umed, and Sai drew together in the center of the upper deck, Manan and Umed's ears stopped up with wax. Aviama turned to look out across the ocean waves. A young Iolani girl, no older than eight, stared at her with large lavender eyes from behind the line of her sisters surrounding the galleon.

Someone brushed past her on the deck, and Aviama stumbled back. Chenzira.

His ears weren't stopped. The lullaby had struck him. Ice shot through her heart as Aviama shook off the captivating enchantment of the sound and clutched at Chenzira's arm. He shrugged free without looking at her, his gaze drawn to something in the water.

Aviama blinked hard against the rain washing her tears down her cheeks. Aviama threw up a wall of wind, and Chenzira bumped against it. He leaned into the barrier, and Aviama strained to hold him.

She twisted to Umed and Manan. "Help!"

They jerked to life, as if even without the sound of the lullaby they'd been rooted to the spot, the sound of Aviama's panicked voice awakening them from a deep sleep. The two men grasped Chenzira by the arms and pulled him back.

Shiva stared at the rose-gold siren, hanging over the railing to get closer to her. She drew her hand seductively along his face as she sang, toying with her prey.

Aviama walked up behind Shiva and lifted her palm to the siren. "Tabeun sister," she choked out. "Please. Tabeun sister."

The siren glanced at Aviama, tilting her head. The edge of her mouth twitched, but she turned her attention back to Shiva. *No. We are not sisters.*

Aviama's stomach churned. Nausea swept over her at the

enchanted control the Iolani sirens held over the men. Was there no way to break it?

She squinted up at the helm, but Samud wasn't there. The ship was unmanned. And they were headed straight for more cliffs.

"Sai." Aviama nodded at the quarterdeck. "Take the helm."

She blinked. "I don't know how to sail."

"I'm sure you'll do better than the nobody that's there right now."

Sai dipped her head and ran for the wheel. Aviama cast a sideways glance at Chenzira. Manan and Umed had a strong hold on him, and he wasn't moving. Shiva still draped halfway over the railing, along with several other men the sirens had chosen to play with on either side of the ship.

Aviama squeezed her eyes shut and took in a deep breath. Would it work? Would anyone hear? How far did her song have to go?

Softly, she lifted her voice, the whisper of a plea in the sorrow of a dirge. Higher and longer, she crafted the notes, swirling her hands to create a tunnel of air carrying her voice through the rain and out over the ocean. Aviama sang, an ache burning her chest, gradually turning in a circle so her song might go out in every direction—carried beyond the circle of sirens to anyone else who might hear her. Any other sirens with the tabeun magic to interpret the heart behind her song. The desperation of her plea. A final burning wick in the dark, about to be snuffed out.

But the sirens around the ship only sang out the more to the sailors, the men on the railing falling overboard into the waiting arms of death.

Aviama took in a shuddering breath. How many souls would be added to Ghosts' Gorge today? How many barrels of blood soaked Shiva's hands for leading them here?

The last siren fell away from the ship, drawing her victim to the waves. Shiva slipped overboard, and Aviama let him go. But as the last man splashed into the water, a new sound shattered the lullaby and the hold it had on the men.

A chorus of monstrous roars.

41

———

The cacophony of roars echoed the dissipating thunder, not from the sky, but from the deep. In a flash, the siren's lullaby cut short, and beauty was replaced by chaos, lilting harmony with blood-curdling shrieks. From the far side of the Gorge, gray hide after gray hide rippled along the surface of the water. Powerful tails of every imaginable color and pattern rocketed into view as a horde of male and female Iolani swept into view, a squadron pulled by the gray beasts like Makuakan's leading the charge.

In the water below, Shiva came to and skewered his siren with the harpoon in his hand. Hers was the first of a spine-chilling series of screeches cascading through the air as Makuakan's Iolani reinforcements broke into the heart of Ipuka Akala.

Aviama backed slowly toward the mainmast and threw up a barrier around herself, Chenzira, Manan, and Umed as the waters raged around them and the ship began to pitch this way and that. The four of them linked arms in a circle, backs to the mast, arm in arm. Chenzira was back, eyes no longer glassy, but sharp, if not a bit dazed. Aviama lifted the palms of her hands to smooth out the protective barrier against wind and waves on her side. Sai created a barrier of her own for herself up at the ship's wheel.

Out on the sea, at the forefront of the horde, a mighty Iolani chieftain and his formidable daughter led the charge. Each of them swept in on the incredible speed of the mysterious beasts decked with hundreds more teeth than Aviama wanted to think about. A thrill ran down her spine at the sight of them.

The first wave of Limakau's sirens fought tooth and nail, but weakened as they were already, they were no match for Makuakan's reinforcements. Makuakan whipped his beast through the water, the creature snatching up a siren in its jaws. Makuakan snatched the harpoon out of the dead siren's hands and tossed it to Makana, who caught it and sank it through into a merman's stomach in a single, powerful stroke.

Never did one leave the side of the other for longer than a minute, above or below the surface. Together, they swept through Ipuka Akala like a blight, leaving nothing but blood and victory in their wake.

Meanwhile, the *Wraithweaver* cut across the open space and entered the opposite ravine. To freedom. To peace. To open sea.

The ship tilted a little too far to starboard, and Aviama dropped their shield just long enough to bend wind at an angle into the sails. It wasn't enough for prolonged sailing, but it did tug the bow to where they needed it to be.

Thud.

Aviama snapped her attention back to the railing just in time to see Shiva topple over it to the deck, chest heaving in exhaustion. A shrieking siren swiped at him from below, but fell back to the waves as he collapsed on the safety of the ship.

Chenzira swore. "That man just doesn't know when to die."

Shiva pulled himself along the deck on both elbows before gathering his feet and stumbling for Aviama at the mast. "They could whip up another storm at any moment. Let me in."

Aviama stiffened.

Chenzira clenched his jaw. "Can I kill him? I'd really like to kill him."

Shiva glared at Chenzira, then returned his focus to Aviama's face. His intensity surprised her, as he softened the murderous rigidity of his face, the deepness of his frown, to allow a softness back to his features. "Come now, Aviama. Please."

But as she watched his expression morph from vengeful killer to terrorized victim in need of saving, she felt no pity—only disturbed by how quickly the man could fade from one state into another, one persona to the next. Shiva reached for her hand, and she snatched it back.

Behind him, Ali'i Makuakan rose in the water at eye level with the humans on board, his daughter Makana beside him. Aviama loosened her grip on Chenzira to her left, and Umed to her right, brushing past Shiva to approach the Iolani pair.

Aviama lifted her palm to Makana, and Makana mirrored her gesture. Their palms touched, and Makana smiled. Warmth spread through her chest at the openness of her friend's joy. She'd never seen such a smile on her face before. Aviama smiled back and looked at Makuakan.

"Is it done, then?"

Makuakan shook his head. "No. Much work do. But Limakau in prison, death sentence likely. Investigations remain, my warriors chasing more traitors."

Aviama bit her lip and nodded. Makana had been

returned to her people, safe and sound. She was free. But what of the humans?

She cleared her throat. "And the *Wraithweaver*?"

Makuakan hesitated, then exchanged a glance with his daughter. She arched her eyebrows and shot him a look. He laughed, then turned back to Aviama. "High unusual. But we do two thing today, that not done in hundreds years. First, let human ship see Ipuka Akala and live. You free to go."

One of the men at the mast behind her sucked in a breath, just as Aviama let out a long sigh of relief. Her shoulders sagged forward, and she nearly dropped to her aching knees. Instead, she yanked herself upright and dropped into a deep curtsy.

"Our deepest gratitude. And the second thing?"

Makuakan nudged Makana's arm, and she whistled. A copper siren flashed through the water to pass her something, and Makana held it out to Aviama.

"Gift to human. Friendship."

Aviama gaped at the object in the siren's hands. It was a large shell, perhaps a conch, carved all over and embedded with rubies along its edge. A woven tether draped from one end to the other, and a small hole had been made at the tip of the shell.

She swallowed, a lump lodging in her throat. "I—don't know what to say."

Makana laughed, and the music of it seemed to roll back the last of the storm clouds. "Not often you have no word."

Aviama snorted. "No, I suppose not."

Makana lifted the shell. "Take it. It is battle horn of Iolani people. We know it sound. If use proper, even far away, we hear."

Aviama took the horn in her hands, turning it over gently. The rain had stopped, and the sun reappeared to twinkle down on the glistening shell. The carvings were exquisite. Intricate patterns reminiscent of shells and waves lined the spiraling base of the shell, leading up to two carved Iolani—one male, one female—with their palms touching in the same manner the statues of the ravine itself had done. All manner of sea life swirled beneath the protective arc of their arms, a swirl of mother-of-pearl sheen gracing the two depicted figures.

"I've never seen anything like it. This honor is too deep to repay."

Makuakan's eyes narrowed. "For friendship be complete, must give us gift also."

Aviama blinked. She glanced back at the men. Shiva stood so still he might have been a statue himself. Umed's stoic face was stricken for once, and Manan's mouth was wide enough that he risked swallowing any passing bug. Chenzira glanced her way, then down at the deck. But his index finger tapped the ring finger of his opposite hand.

Her heart dropped. The only constant she had. The last physical reminders of her mother. Aviama stared down at her fingers, wrapped around the conch shell horn, and her eyes brimmed with tears.

A life for a life. Her mother would have wanted that, wouldn't she? Friendship with the Iolani? In a way, perhaps giving up her rings to Makuakan and Makana would honor the protection her mother had always had for Aviama. Perhaps the legacy of Queen Sharsi Shamaran would live on in this way—a final protection for her youngest child.

Aviama slipped the battle horn tether over her head so that the tether crossed her body and the conch, larger than her hand, rested on her hip. She took in a shuddering breath, and slowly worked two rings from her fingers and extended them to Makana.

Her mouth went dry, and she swallowed.

"If I were in Jannemar, I could give you much more valuable a gift. But these, to me, are priceless treasures. I would be honored if you would wear them."

Makana put out her hand and covered Aviama's open palm. She shook her head. "Not this."

Aviama frowned. What else did she have but a beaten-up ship and the torn clothes on her back?

"If I had something better…"

Makuakan jerked his chin at Shiva. "Liar man. Give us."

Her lips parted, and her stomach dropped. They didn't want trinkets or jewels. They wanted Shiva.

42

Aviama turned to Shiva. He gaped at her, eyes wide, casting furtive glances at Makuakan and Makana, and back to Aviama.

It was this or nothing. Life and friendship with Iolani or death to the small band of survivors from the hundreds of men who had come to the Gorge. Hundreds, across ship after ship of the Radhan fleet. She cocked her head as she regarded him. It was fitting somehow, wasn't it? He imprisoned Makana for years. Might he learn something from getting a taste of his own medicine?

No, perhaps not. Perhaps he would learn nothing. But maybe in lieu of life lessons, justice could still be served.

A flash of Makuakan and Makana driving harpoons and spears through their enemies just moments ago filtered through her mind. Were the Iolani just? They were quelling a rebellion. A rebellion by a leader who would have taken Jannemar's resources and cut a deal with Radha.

Powerful as it was, Radha could not be permitted to link with the might of the Iolani people. They would be unstoppable in the sea, and with wyronite added to both peoples, sifal magic would rise to unprecedented levels. The potential destruction was unthinkable.

Shiva stepped forward, hands up in a defensive posture. "Aviama. You have always preserved life. We've only done what was best for our kingdoms, you and I."

"What was best? What was *best*?" Heat flooded her chest, and her lip curled in disgust. "Was it *best* to slaughter your own people because you didn't understand them? To kill all melderbloods, whether or not they were rebellious, as you did with Sai's parents? Is it *best* to parade me around like a toy for your pleasure, a means toward an end—to control and dominate?"

Shiva shook his head, circling slowly away from the mast. Chenzira countered to head him off from the far side, but Aviama only rotated to watch Shiva's every movement as he slunk across the deck.

The silk-tongued prince of Radha oiled his way out from between his adversaries, looking more like a slithering snake than a royal. But then, had there ever been a difference? He held up a finger. "Darsh isn't just melderblood, Aviama. He's a criminal. He planned to kill the entire royal family. Would you really support him just because he has the same tainted blood as you?"

Aviama threw up a wall of air behind him as he moved, and he bumped into it. He turned and hesitated at the sight of Chenzira standing there.

"That's your problem, Shiva. You see melderbloods as tainted. Inherently evil. But the heart is what pumps blood through the body, and it is the heart that directs any power in our blood. It's not about what we can do, but how we choose to *use* our abilities. And you have great ability. As a charmer, a liar, and a man of wealth and resources."

Aviama grimaced. He'd fooled her too, at first. It was embarrassing, knowing all she knew now, but how could anyone know what they didn't know?

How many times had she sworn to herself *never again*? How many chances did a man get? Perhaps if she'd seen remorse. Perhaps if keeping him on board wouldn't almost certainly result in more deaths.

Aviama took a deep breath. "I didn't support Darsh. I refused to exchange one tyrant for another. But that is what you are. A tyrant. And I will not stand in the way of your right to consequences."

Shiva's pleading expression hardened. He stalked toward her. "You don't know a *thing* about consequences."

Oh, he knew about consequences all right. He killed Bhumi because Aviama and Chenzira had threatened Durga and got her to tell secrets about where the magna was stored. What had Shiva said to her?

If your attitude steps one hair beyond my profound tolerance for your insolence, I will give no warning. I will simply deliver someone's head to your door...

And that is precisely what he had done. Her chest ached, and she squeezed her eyes shut against the memory. Threats of death were the only time the man could be believed.

Aviama opened her eyes, lifted her chin, and flicked her wrist, stopping Shiva's approach with a sharp blast of air to the chest.

"It is best for my kingdom—and arguably for Radha as well—that you remain in Ipuka Akala. And it is fitting, after Makana endured so many years under your gracious hosting, that you now enjoy the hospitality of the Iolani."

Shiva's nostrils flared, and his eyes blazed. "Witch! Our armies march on Horon as we speak, and we will not stop until the last Shamaran burns!"

He lunged. Aviama's mouth went dry. She threw her hands into a mighty, sweeping arc, and the wind flew to her command—knocking Shiva clean off his feet. The gale hit him like a sledgehammer and threw him overboard like chaff.

Splash.

Scales and fins of every shade surged to the place where he'd hit the water. Sirens took hold of him and plunged downward into the belly of Ghosts' Gorge, drawing the prince toward the wreckage of uncountable ships and skeletons that had come before.

Aviama's pulse pounded in her ears. She stared blankly at the empty space where Shiva had stood. *Biscuits.* Had she really just done that? A pit formed in her stomach. Did her choice make her just, or vindictive?

Chenzira blinked, mouth agape, in the same direction. The corner of his mouth twitched, but he cleared his throat and came to her side as composed as he could manage. He slipped his hand in hers, and the warmth of his touch soothed her. He squeezed her hand. She squeezed back.

Makuakan inclined his head in a shallow bow and lifted his palm out toward her. "Tabeun sister."

Aviama swallowed, then reached out to mirror the gesture. "Tabeun brother."

"Much to do. Will leave you. May sea bear you well."

"Thank you."

Makuakan disappeared beneath the surface of the water, and Makana held onto the railing for a moment as her father's powerful wave holding her up dissipated. She smiled. "I home, tabeun sister. Thank you."

Aviama's eyes welled with tears, and she smiled back. "Thank *you*. I'd be dead without you. So would we all."

She sobered. "You lucky only Ali'i can order death lullaby.

Limakau too curious of you, then too busy with Makuakan to order. Gave you time."

Aviama considered this. If the sirens had started with the death lullaby, no one would have made it through the fog. "You are a good friend. I will miss you."

Makana dipped her head. "Miss you, sister. Be well."

The siren pushed off the ship and fell into the water below. With a flick of her pewter tail, the daughter of the chieftain was gone from the land of the sun, enveloped by the waters of the moon.

Aviama sniffed and ran the back of her hand across her nose. She turned around, surveying the *Wraithweaver.* Umed and Manan still stood by the mast, looking back at her expectantly. Sai guided the ship through the narrow passage, and already the walls of the ravine on either side were beginning to drop away. They'd survived the Gorge. They'd done it.

Shiva was gone. Makana was home. Makuakan had let them live.

One of the sails was down, a swath of battered cloth draped over the forecastle. The tip of its mast was missing, lost to the ravine. Bloodstains decorated the deck, and the barrel of spilled oil bumped up against the railing on the far side. The sun eased toward the horizon, casting glittering light across the calm of endless water.

Laksh's body had slid toward the quarterdeck, but remained there as a horrifying reminder of all they had lost. Aviama sank to her knees on the deck, staring at the corpse of her friend. The man may have looked surly, with his crooked nose and thick build, but it was Laksh who had comforted Manan over Sona's death. It was Laksh who had joined them in Onkar's lessons for lifts, laughing with them as they learned to steal this or that, and celebrating with Aviama as she met with success for the first time.

Chenzira knelt beside her and pulled her into a tight embrace. She could only stare at first, numb and empty even in the wake of victory in the Gorge. But what sort of victory was it, if there was more blood spilled in the sea than remained in the bodies of the survivors?

Her chest hitched, and a single sob caught in her throat. Enzo. The crestbreaker from the bathhouse, who met her in Waif's Garden as she escaped the palace. Sai's parents. Sona. Bhumi's head on a platter.

Had Murin made it out of Radha with Arjun? Were they safe? Had the army found them?

Shiva's final threat stuck in her mind—the threat that every Shamaran would burn. Few Shamarans were left, after the bloodbath led by the dragonlord of the black dragon. Her brother, Zephan. Her sister-in-law, Semra. Her older sister, Avaya, broken as she was. And Aviama.

Even when peace came, there was no peace. No one held a blade to her throat now, but she'd felt alive as she ran across the cliff with Chenzira at her side and death in the water. Yet as hope of survival dared settle over them, the surge of emotions she'd managed to keep at bay swept over her.

Her shoulders racked with sobs, and Chenzira pulled her in. She clung to him, burying her face in his neck, tears running down her cheeks, soaking his shirt with fresh salt water. Visions rolled through her mind of Laksh singing as they danced, and Bhumi clapping her hands. Her mother, again, in the pool of blood on the ballroom floor. Debris flying through the air as explosions rocked Shamaran Castle—the explosion that killed her father.

And of Liben, as always, glassy eyes staring up at the sky with the hammer by his temple.

Liben was her fault. Her first kill when the Awakening

came upon her. An accident, yes. But if not for her, he would still be alive. If not for her, they would all still be alive. Enzo, Bhumi, Sona. Even Shiva, evil as he was. She wouldn't miss him, but he was still a person. What now?

"Rookie?"

Aviama reeled back from Chenzira's chest, the shock of that voice pulling her from the dark swirl of her thoughts. Onkar knelt on the deck opposite her and Chenzira, brows furrowed in concern, eyes soft. Samud's fine teal jacket wrapped around Onkar's shoulders. He'd already filed off the emblem of the pakshi on the golden buttons.

Chenzira's eyes narrowed at the swindler. "Where have you been hiding?"

Onkar inclined his head in a gracious half-bow, as if Chenzira's question was complimentary. It wasn't. "I correctly assumed the siren song would come, and we would need a surviving crew to man the ship if you managed to keep the *Wraithweaver* afloat."

Aviama glanced down the deck. "We have a crew?"

"Yes, darlin'. We have a crew. Meager, but I could only fit so many of them in the brig. They had to be favorable to melders to qualify, and volunteer to be locked up indefinitely for the rest of the battle, with no promise that anyone would be alive to let them out again at the end. I'd say we have forty, maybe fifty, men."

Her jaw dropped. "You cowardly genius."

Onkar held up a finger. "I prefer *clever* genius. But then, I suppose that's assumed. I'll accept *exceptional* genius. And do you know what else this genius did? He kept a bulk of food supplies dry and ordered a couple of men to fire up the kitchens. Fighting always makes me hungry. You?"

Aviama's stomach growled. She hadn't eaten all day.

Chenzira nodded. "Get her some food. And we need to find a couple of large blankets. Laksh can't be left like that."

Onkar clapped and rubbed his hands together. "I'll get you all taken care of, never fear. Blankets and lunch. Or dinner, I suppose. In the meantime, let's get you off the upper deck." He surveyed the blood-spattered ship and scrunched his nose. "I'll have some of the men wash it down so we have fewer reminders of the day's events."

Aviama bit her lip. The thought of being enclosed in a small space again, of any darkness at all, made her nauseous.

"I think I need the sun. I'll head to the quarterdeck and get out of your way."

Onkar pursed his lips. "Below deck would be better. Lie down. Get some rest."

Chenzira glanced at Aviama and glared at Onkar. "She said she'd be on the quarterdeck. That's where you'll find us."

Onkar's brows soared, and Chenzira winced. He cleared his throat. "And thank you."

Onkar scurried off, and Chenzira walked her to the quarterdeck. Manan, Umed, and Sai met them there, and the five of them sat down.

Manan arched an eyebrow. "He's in Samud's coat."

Aviama shook her head and laughed. "I guess I shouldn't be surprised to see him claim captain, though."

"He's still acting like a cook. Serving, offering food." Sai examined a scrape on her arm, then leaned back against the side of the ship. "It's nice."

Chenzira grunted. "The *nice* part will run out. He'll still demand payment before we get off the ship."

Umed glanced up. "Payment?"

Chenzira nodded. "You didn't think he was a cook, did you? He's a black market cheat who promised us safe passage on a ship out of Radha."

"You call what we just did safe passage?" Umed snorted.

"That's what we said!" Aviama dropped her voice and leaned in. "Exactly. This is not what we were promised, though he swears it is. It's not a bad plan, I guess. If we die, we can't complain he didn't hold up his end of the bargain. If we don't die, well, we were safe enough, weren't we?"

Chenzira leaned his head back against the ship's wheel. "He runs an entire operation back in Radha. How do you think he taught you all those thievery techniques?"

Manan ran his hand over his face. "But why did he out himself and teach us?"

Chenzira shrugged. "I'm still trying to figure him out."

Aviama leaned into Chenzira and laid her head on his shoulder. "He's not the sort of man who does anything by accident."

"You know what else isn't an accident?"

The sing-song voice danced up to them from below as heavy boots thumped up the stairs to the upper deck. "The veritable *feast* I just prepared for you. Hurry up before it gets cold."

The group trooped down the stairs after Onkar and followed him under the quarterdeck and through the door to the captain's kitchen. Onkar swept his hand toward a table set with silverware and laden with bread, meat, cheese, and some kind of smoked fish steaming on plates. Aviama's mouth watered.

Several bedraggled, half-drowned sailors nodded to them in acknowledgment as they passed. Aviama gave a halfhearted smile and plunked down in the nearest seat. Onkar looked her up and down, then sighed.

"I'll find you some dry clothes. The kind without holes or blood. You don't look presentable at all."

Aviama snatched up a chunk of bread and stuffed it in her mouth. "Who am I supposed to impress?"

He pursed his lips, scanning the disheveled group. "A lady is *always* presentable. Any reasonable gentleman is too. Two of you are royals, and you don't know this? By the gallows, it's been nearly half an hour since any altercation, and you haven't cleaned up at all!"

Chenzira laughed and stuffed a piece of meat half the size of his fist into his mouth.

Onkar shook his head and left, muttering to himself under his breath. "Ungrateful idiots."

The food was good for the soul, as the five starving melders shoveled beef and cheese down their throats like there was no tomorrow. Onkar returned with dry clothes and ushered them into Aviama and Shiva's rooms.

Onkar apologized for the draft in Shiva's room. "Some crazy lady blew the wall out."

For Sai and Aviama, he provided simple white tunics and trousers. Aviama's tunic was a bit large, laced up at the chest, and had a ruffle detail on long, flowing sleeves. Despite the lack of embroidery, it was too fine a material for most of the sailors. Aviama suspected it must have come from Onkar's personal wardrobe. The trousers had a high waist and had stitching of a different color from the pants, cinching them at the waist. He'd had them tailored?

They fit perfectly. Onkar wouldn't have had time to sew in the brig, not to mention get her measurements. An uneasy feeling settled in her stomach. How long had he been preparing for this moment? What had he expected to happen? What had he known?

The boots were a little too big, but not as big as she would have expected. The trousers were comfortable, and she had to admit, as weird as it was to be without a skirt, it was wildly practical considering the type of activity she'd been involved in as of late. Aviama raked a comb through her hair, braided it, and slung the Iolani horn across her torso before rejoining Sai and the men in the hall.

Umed ran in through the captain's kitchen just as she stepped out. His eyes were dark, jaw set. "There's a ship on the horizon. It bears no flag. And it's heading straight for us."

43

No ship traveled this close to Ghosts' Gorge. Not unless they had a death wish. Aviama exchanged a glance with Chenzira, and the five of them, led by Umed, ran through the captain's kitchen and back out onto the upper deck.

Men scurried about in all directions, patching up the collapsed sail, washing the deck, or running up the rigging. Onkar stood at the helm, peering through a long glass out onto the horizon. Aviama followed his gaze and spotted a large ship angling toward them. It was bigger than the *Wraithweaver* by the looks of it, though she couldn't yet tell by how much.

Sai squinted into the sun at the approaching ship. "I thought you said it was on the horizon. This one is already halfway to us."

Umed shifted his weight. "It's possible I panicked. Didn't think about the distance."

Aviama pursed her lips. "*You* panicked?"

Chenzira waved his arms at Onkar. "Hey! Bear starboard!"

Onkar lowered the long glass and shook his head. "And pass up our great luck? What are the odds of getting supplies for repairs this close to the Gorge? No. We're going to meet them."

Aviama gaped at him. "They're not flying any flags. They could be anyone. They could be pirates."

He set down the long glass and turned toward her, striding down the steps with arms wide. "Look at you! You are a vision. What excellent fortune to have found these clothes in the bunks. We thankfully had a few scrawny men on board, and none of them are around to need them anymore. Free clothes, without the guilt! How wonderful!" Onkar grinned.

Aviama's stomach soured. She grimaced. "How fortunate."

"You're not pleased by the new clothes?" Onkar made a dramatic clutch at his heart and glanced around at the others. "I've been lied to, friends! I thought women liked new clothes."

Aviama set her jaw. "We need to sail for Jannemar. It's closer than any other land besides Radha, and I can guarantee they will receive us safely. You can repair the *Wraithweaver* there, and I can make sure my brother received word from Murin about the attack on the Horon Mines."

Onkar eyed her, the jovial look dropping from his face. He sucked his teeth. "Mmm, apologies, Highness, but that's not an option. This is a Radhan ship, and it *looks* Radhan. Jannemar might attack us before they realize you are on board. Not to mention Radha is planning on destroying Jannemar, and I'm rather tired of being in war zones. I'll ensure you reach dry land safely, but you'll need to leave the specifics to the experts." He mimicked tipping an invisible hat in her direction. "That would be me."

Aviama's chest tightened, and she stiffened. "If you don't want Radha's influence to spread, Jannemar is *exactly* where we should be going!"

Onkar sighed. "Look, Rookie, I like you. I don't know what

it's like to care much for family, but you seem preoccupied with yours. I get it, they're in danger, etcetera, etcetera, but if your brother is the warrior you seem to think he is, and your sister-in-law is the fierce dragonlord she is said to be, I'm sure they'll be just fine. She still has the dragon, yes? Beasty hasn't kicked the bucket?"

Her hands clenched into fists at her sides. "Zezura is fine."

"Fantastic." Onkar grinned. "Beasty, dragon lady, and brother dearest can deal with Radha while we hightail it to a land *not* embroiled in expensive, deadly wars. And we will start by meeting *that* ship"—he pointed a long finger in the direction of the strange vessel—"and see what we can barter for repair supplies. I'm not sure a spool of thread is going to cut it when it comes to getting that sail back in commission."

Chenzira drilled him with a cool stare. "What does your curse say about deadly wars?"

Onkar bristled. "It's not about the curse. It's about not being stupid. You maladroits might not be advanced enough for that, but I am. And if you haven't noticed, I'm captain of the ship." He dusted off the shoulder of his newly acquired teal jacket and lifted the long glass again.

Chenzira snatched the long glass from his fingers. "What do you plan to barter with?"

The man shrugged. "Whatever we've got on hand. I've kept a few valuable items in good condition, never fear. Now get below deck as we approach. Women are bad luck on ships in some regions, and if they see women on board, they might be suspicious."

Aviama crossed her arms. "I'm in trousers."

"Yes, and it completely detracts from the braid, the fair face, the curves. I almost forgot you were human at all." Onkar rolled his eyes. "Get below deck."

Chenzira ran a hand through his beard and cocked his

head at the man. "Maybe it's you that has such bad luck with women on board ships. Without this particular woman, you'd be dead."

"And without another particular woman, I'd be curse-free, but here we are." He shot Chenzira a withering glare and held his hand out for the long glass.

Chenzira pursed his lips, but handed it over.

Aviama clenched her jaw. "I'm not going below deck. I want to see who comes on the ship. They could be anyone."

"Lucky for you, I've never met a stranger." Onkar leaned in close, dropping his voice. "And unless you want to create a very extreme and very stupid scene for our coming guests, I suggest you do as I say, because I saved the life of every survivor on board. And they all swore allegiance to me if we made it out alive."

Of course they did. Biscuits. She couldn't incapacitate everyone on board and still expect the *Wraithweaver* to outmaneuver the approaching ship. They needed a crew. Especially if there were pirates.

Aviama bit her lip. She was *not* going below deck. Then she had an idea. "Okay. But ... how lucky is it to have a dead body on board?"

Onkar hesitated. "Not ideal. We'll have to get him overboard." He snapped his fingers, and four sailors came running.

"Stop! Don't touch him!" Chenzira ran down the steps to block the men from Laksh's body, but the four men hoisted Laksh's body, wrapped in blankets, up and over the railing before he reached them. Chenzira swore. He twisted back to Onkar. "Isn't this a man you invited on your team? Your exclusive kitchen crew? He fought and died while you ran and hid. He deserved better than getting dumped overboard like chum!"

Umed raced down the steps after Chenzira, landing flat on his feet and throwing a punch at one of the sailors. The man staggered back, and Onkar let out a sharp whistle and waved his hand at the rest of the crew. In an instant, seamen converged on Umed and Chenzira. Chenzira flipped one on his back and slugged another in the gut before five more yanked his arms back and held him fast. Aviama's heart lurched to her throat, danger prickling on the raised hairs on the back of her neck.

"All this *drama*." Onkar tossed his hands up and returned his attention to the long glass. "Gold and gumption, the dead man doesn't know the difference! I honor people who are alive. No need once they're gone. If you must grieve, do it, but not now. Have you noticed we have company?"

How dare he? Aviama strode toward him, teeth on edge. Her lip curled as she glared into Onkar's unconcerned face, knocking the long glass out of his hands. "Laksh was one of us."

Onkar's hands moved like lightning, catching her wrist with one hand, and the plummeting long glass with the other. A warning lit his eye. "Don't touch personal effects, darlin'."

On reflex, her fingers extended to reach for the wind. Nothing came. A dull tingle ran up and down her arms. Her stomach dropped as she stared down at her fingers.

No, no, no. The konnolan was gone. The magna was gone. There was no—

"What's the matter? Wind a little lazy today, Rookie?"

Aviama snapped her gaze up to Onkar's face. The meal he'd served them. He'd laced it with magna. Heat flushed her cheeks as she ripped her wrist free of his grasp. "I just saved your life, and this is how you treat me?"

A dozen more men ran up the steps and seized Aviama, Manan, and Sai. Aviama tried to rip free, but the wind refused to listen, and her aching muscles were no match for the burly man holding her back.

Onkar adjusted the cuff of his jacket. His eyes narrowed as he lifted his gaze to meet hers, threat undergirding his every word. "The truth is, darlin', that this ship needs a captain. I happen to be a seafaring man of considerable skill, and without *me,* this entire crew would have drowned themselves at the siren song while you gallivanted about with the breeze. We're grateful for your work, but your brazen impulsivity is as much a liability as it is an asset. I told you we might need konnolan to keep things manageable, and you didn't listen. Luckily, my life has not been filled with sweet trusting relationships, so I make my own assurances. Besides, you still haven't paid your final fee."

Aviama stiffened in her captor's arms. "Considering our deal was for *you* to give *us* safe passage out of Radha, and the only reason your body isn't at the bottom of Ghosts' Gorge right now is because of *me,* I'd say we're more than square. You broke your deal."

Onkar clucked his tongue and wagged a finger. "I never break a deal."

Chenzira snorted. "You're a crook. Your business is in broken deals."

Onkar's eyebrows soared. "Says the man who knew where to find me to cut a broken deal." He shook his head and turned back to Aviama. "No, you misunderstand. I am a businessman. Breaking deals is bad for business. And I *always* take care of my own. But I suppose your work in the Gorge did benefit me. I never liked Sunboy, and not having to deal with him anymore is a nice bonus. I'll sort out the final fee for you."

Aviama clenched her teeth. "Then release us. Why occupy the hands of the men with holding us when they may need their swords against the oncoming ship? We have no powers, thanks to you, and anybody crazy enough to sail out here has got to be up to no good."

Onkar turned the wheel just slightly and stepped back, satisfied. He tapped the long glass against his shoulder. "People who are up to no good are often the most fun. It won't be a problem."

"I thought you liked melderbloods. You stacked the kitchen with us."

Onkar smiled. "I like you fine, darlin'. Don't worry your little head. Now, if you don't mind, I could use a little breathing room."

He jerked his chin at the sailors holding them, and they pulled Aviama, Sai, and Manan away from the helm and down the stairs. Onkar let out a sigh, like a long-suffering, disappointed parent. "I told you to go below deck, but no, you had to stay on the upper deck. I'm a gracious man, Rookie. If you want a front seat, you'll get one."

Aviama glanced up through the sailors toward the oncoming vessel. It was bigger now, and she could see men swarming the deck. The ship was significantly larger than the *Wraithweaver*—both in length and width, and by an extra deck, by the looks of things. Still no flags.

Aviama's stomach squirmed. "You swore we'd get to land safely."

Onkar waved her off and answered without taking his eyes off the oncoming ship. "You'll get safely to land, all right, Rookie."

Chenzira tugged toward her through the sailors, three men still holding him back. He smashed his head into one, and the sailor dropped with a grunt. The other two let him move forward until he stood by her side and settled.

"Stay close," he whispered.

She looked pointedly at the sailors around them. "I'm not sure how much choice I've got."

"We just have to hold out long enough for our powers to return."

She pursed her lips. "You mean, through the entirety of any firefight we're about to have, and probably multiple hours after that?"

"Yes."

"With a pea-sized crew on a damaged ship, against a massive gang led by whatever insane person would sail near the Gorge without a flag?"

The corner of Chenzira's mouth twitched. "Yes."

"And both sides probably hate us."

"Probably."

She grimaced. "Biscuits."

44

____

The sun sank slowly to the west, casting warm light across the glistening glassy waters between the two ships. The larger vessel's figurehead depicted a young woman, long hair billowing out behind her, holding her hand out over the water—coiled air spilling out from her palm in carved brass. Letters on the side marked the ship *Raisa's Revenge.*

Aviama squinted at the ship's name again. Had she got it right? They named their ship after a melder from The Crumbling six hundred years ago—one of the four that had ended magic for good? If they had, and it was the same Raisa, did that mean they wanted magic, or hated magic?

The sails of the *Wraithweaver* were wrapped tight, the vessel carried along at the mercy of the current. Onkar stood at the helm, silently watching the approach of *Raisa's Revenge.* Aboard the *Wraithweaver,* the entirety of the meager fifty-person crew stood on the upper deck, stock still as statues.

Chenzira's arm brushed hers as he shifted his weight beside her. She leaned into him, and he looked down at her just as the man holding her tugged her upright. Aviama twisted to see Sai, Manan, or Umed held somewhere behind them, but only caught sight of Umed through the sea of sailors.

A sinking feeling soured her stomach as she watched the foreign ship. The real Raisa from history was originally from Radha. Could this ship be headed back there? Was it one of Shiva's?

A thick, gem-studded collar glinted from the nearly bare chest of a middle-aged man at the helm of *Raisa's Revenge*. Matching ornaments adorned his forearms, and a swath of white cloth crossed his torso at a diagonal up from his waist and over one shoulder. His crew wore a mix of shirtless and light tunic-based attire in white and beige, each armed with spears or an oddly curved sword, the blade bent like a sickle.

Both ships and crews stood silent as the grave as they drew nearer and nearer to one another. Aviama worried her lip. Shouldn't they be doing something? Running up a white flag, firing cannons? Shouting? *Something.*

At last, the man at the helm of the *Revenge* came abreast of Onkar on the *Wraithweaver*. He gave the signal, and his men launched grappling hooks across the open water. A murmur went through the men on the *Wraithweaver*.

Someone cleared their throat. "Captain?"

But Onkar only held up a hand. "Hold. Let them come."

The wood planks creaked as the ship rocked against the pull of the horde of men on the opposite ship hauling them in. Aviama tried to count the men on the upper deck, but lost count. To say they were outnumbered would be an understatement.

The captain of the opposite ship let out a sharp laugh as he left the wheel and marched down the steps of the quarterdeck to the railing of the upper deck. The upper deck of the *Revenge* was at eye level with the quarterdeck of the *Wraith-

weaver, and he leaned on the railing to look Onkar in the face.

"Sand and sea, you did it."

Aviama's lips parted. Chenzira stiffened. Whatever this was, it had all been part of Onkar's plan from the beginning. And she hadn't missed the captain's usage of the same phrase Chenzira so often used. Aviama glanced at Chenzira. His eyes hardened, and a muscle in his neck twitched.

"Abasi! What a pleasure to see your smiling face." Onkar gave a dramatic sweeping bow. "If we do more business, you'll learn I do everything I set my mind on, no matter the impossibility of the stunt."

Abasi chortled in a deep, resonating laugh that took over his whole upper body. "Your ship has seen a Gorge too many, I think. Is your stock better than your sails?"

Onkar spread his hands in a wide-open gesture and grinned ear to ear. "Inarguably. I think you'll be quite pleased with my selection."

Men in tunics and schentis, glittering in gold and jewels, leaped from the *Revenge* to the *Wraithweaver* with sickle blades and spears. Abasi beckoned with his hand, and Onkar nodded to one of his men. The men around the five melders pushed them forward. Aviama sucked in a breath as a tall Radhan seaman shoved her toward a tall shirtless man with a sickle sword longer than her arm.

The man caught her by the chin. Blazing fire erupted in her chest. She wrenched free and threw an uppercut at the man, but he caught her fist without so much as a flinch. A roar rocked the air as a blur wrested from the *Wraithweaver* crew and crashed into the tall man from the *Revenge*. Chenzira.

The man rocked back on his heels and swung his sickle. Chenzira whirled underneath it, popped it from the man's grasp, and sank his fist into his adversary's throat. The man caught his sickle again with his other hand before it hit the ground and struck Chenzira on the temple with the butt of his sword as half a dozen armed *Revenge* men swarmed him. The man curled his lip and turned away from Aviama to face Chenzira, arms yanked back by the fresh batch of fighters from the foreign vessel.

Aviama ran forward, slipping a dagger from the sheath of one of the *Wraithweaver* crew as she moved.

Chenzira spit in the man's face. "Touch her again and die where you stand."

Aviama spun the smooth blade in her hands and flew at the man's broad, bare back. She pulled back the dagger and drove into the motion.

An arm wrapped around her waist and yanked her back at the last moment, appearing as if from thin air. Onkar wrested the dagger from her grip and flipped it, pulled her body against him, and pressed the blade against Aviama's throat.

Aviama winced at the pressure of the dagger against the soft skin of her neck. Her pulse pounded in her ears. Chenzira strained against his captors. Their eyes locked.

Up on *Raisa's Revenge*, the newcomer captain gave a displeased hum.

"It's less than we agreed."

Aviama felt the vibration of Onkar's chest pressing against her back as he spoke. "I make up for it in quality. And I've increased the fee in goods to make up for the loss of ... other cargo offerings."

Two more of the *Wraithweaver* crew moved forward, setting a large chest down on the deck between them. Men from the *Revenge* took the chest up to their captain, and he took a moment to look through it. He arched an eyebrow.

"Acceptable substitutes, but not enough."

Onkar kept his voice light, but his knuckles whitened on

the hilt of the dagger. "I have another chest the same size for you after our business is complete."

Abasi's eyes widened, lit with greed. "Same size?"

"On my honor."

Abasi chortled again and shook his head. He wagged a finger at Onkar as if he were a naughty schoolboy, then gestured again to his men. Five large chests were passed down from the *Revenge* to the *Wraithweaver* and set in front of Onkar.

Onkar removed the blade from Aviama's throat, seized her by the braid instead, and pulled her down with him as he knelt to inspect the chests. He lowered his voice.

"I told you I'd get you safely to shore, and to shore you shall go. Stop causing trouble. Trust me."

Aviama could barely conceal the disgust that took over her face. "How stupid do you think I am?" she hissed.

"I'll not answer that, Rookie."

Onkar pawed through the contents—three chests of tar, cloth for sails, and other ship repair materials, and two of spices and coins she did not recognize. He ran his fingers through the coins with the relish of a beggar set before a feast. The swindler nodded, shut the chests, and stood. Aviama stood with him as he twined his hand tighter into her braid, pulling her head back.

Aviama stretched out her hands, calling to a lazy wind that no longer cared for her needs. Her heart sank. She knew it wouldn't work, but she couldn't help but try.

Her scalp burned like fire as Onkar yanked her closer by the hair. His fingers dug into her hip bone, tugging her into him. His breath tickled her neck as he whispered in her ear. "Telling them who the two of you are would be the quickest way to die. Right now, you're a moth. No swords."

Aviama clenched her jaw. Did he really expect her to trust

him? If she *did* say who she was, would the captain of the new ship have the good sense enough to ruin his deal with Onkar and sail away?

But then, what if he was telling the truth?

Onkar lifted his voice to Abasi once again. "You saw for yourself how much fire, how much spirit they have. They're strong. Good workers. Tame them a bit, and they'll be excellent for all sorts of work." He twisted Aviama's head in Abasi's direction so that she found herself staring into the leering dark eyes of the *Revenge* captain. "Not bad to look at either."

Aviama swallowed. Her lips parted, chest rising and falling with quick, shallow breaths. Her heartbeat battered against her ribcage, and she clenched her fists. Her stupid, magna-restrained fists. She dropped her voice to a whisper. "I'm going to kill you."

Onkar ignored her. "Beautiful singing voice, I might add. Excellent songbird. Looks great in a dress. Good for the elite settings where you're headed." His next words came out in a hiss against her ear, fraught with warning. "Shut up and act like the moth you are before he decides you're not worth keeping alive."

"Send her up."

Onkar released her braid, seized her by the waist in a far more intimate manner than was necessary, and gave her a hard shove that sent her hurtling across the deck toward the tall man with the sickle. Aviama's heart lurched to her throat as she stumbled her way through the air toward her latest nightmare.

Chenzira wrenched halfway out of his captors' hands and caught her arm as she whirled past him. The man with the sickle gripped her wrist on one side, and Chenzira yanked her toward him on the other. She staggered into him, and he caught her with his free arm around her waist, pressing his lips to her ear and dropping his voice to a dangerous rumble. "You're nobody interesting. Make up a new name. I will find you."

A ragdoll in a game of hot potato would have had an easier time of it than Aviama at that moment, as she went from Onkar to the man with the sickle to Chenzira, and back to the man with the sickle. The tall man ripped her free from Chenzira as the men holding him pried his fingers one by one from her waist and slugged him in the gut.

Aviama twisted back to reach for him, but it was too late. Chenzira was doubled over on the deck as the man with the sickle hoisted her over his shoulder, grabbed a rope from the *Revenge,* and scurried up the side like a rat with a prized piece of cheese.

The *Wraithweaver* dropped away below, and her feet swung helplessly in midair. Strong hands pulled her off the tall man's shoulder and set her on her feet with an unceremonious thud. Aviama barely had time to look up before a coil of rope wound around her wrists, lashing them together in front of her.

Abasi strode forward, dark eyes glittering, and slowly circled her. He looked her up and down and stepped toward her. Aviama leaned back, but he only smiled a crooked, unpleasant smile and reached one figure up her neck and under her chin. She snapped her head to one side, swallowing the bile that shot up the back of her burning throat.

He cocked his head, taking her in for a long moment, as if she were the only tall drink of water in a parched desert. An icy chill ran down her spine, and she couldn't help the grimace that took over her face. He dropped his finger and turned back to Onkar down on the upper deck of the *Wraithweaver.* "She'll do."

He cocked an eyebrow at the jewel-encrusted shell resting

on her hip. Aviama's mouth went dry. She'd nearly forgotten it was there, but now, forgetting about such a valuable thing seemed unconscionable. The gems and carvings marked it as something extraordinary, a high value trinket for any trader. Abasi gestured to a sailor, who seized her by the arm to keep her in place, and lifted Makana's token of friendship over her head. Pain wrenched in her heart as the horn left her side, like water wrung harshly from a rag. Aviama blinked back tears and set her jaw. *Don't show fear. Don't show pain.*

Abasi regarded her once more, then cast his gaze back to Onkar. "Send up the others."

Onkar whipped his finger in a small circle by his head, a gesture to the crew. Sailors bound Sai, Manan, and Umed at the wrists and shoved them into the waiting hands of the next crew. Chenzira stayed rooted to the deck of the *Wraithweaver,* held by *Revenge* seamen, as the man with the sickle whirled the curved blade in his face.

Someone passed him rope, and the man twisted the sickle and struck Chenzira in the ribs with the butt of his weapon before throwing him to the deck on his chest and dropping a knee on his spine. Half a dozen men held him in place as the tall man bent Chenzira's arms behind him and bound his wrists.

The sailors surrounding Aviama finished tying her and released her hands. Her wrists dropped in front of her—and bumped up against something small and solid inside her trousers. She sucked in a breath. It hadn't been there before. She was sure of it.

Four men tried to lift Chenzira up toward the *Revenge,* but with his arms behind him, he was dead weight falling in all the wrong directions. Finally, they slung two ropes around his torso and hauled him aboard, hitting his head against the hull of *Raisa's Revenge* twice in the process.

Aviama edged closer to Chenzira, the five new captives huddled together on a new ship with a new crew and a fresh danger on the horizon.

Abasi looked them over and gave a nod down toward Onkar. "And the other? You said there was one more."

"Oh, of course, my friend. By the gallows, I'm nothing if not fair! And in the interest of fairness, I've given you three men and three women. Just to round things out." Onkar snapped his fingers, and two sailors marched forward from the shadows of the quarterdeck, a woman held between them. Her hands were tied, and a sack over her head concealed her face. Dark hair spilled down her shoulders from beneath the sack.

Aviama bit back a moan. The girl still wore the same gypsy-like clothing from the voyage from Radha. Perhaps having Manan throw her in the brig had not been the best move.

The men tossed her up from the *Wraithweaver* to *Raisa's Revenge* like a barrel of apples. A scream ripped from her throat. Aviama winced as Abasi ripped off the sack over her head and stared into Durga's furious face.

Durga lunged for Abasi, bound though she was, and he caught her by the nape of the neck and threw her to the deck. She hit the rough boards hard, unable to catch herself. Onkar laughed.

"She may fight like a ciraba, Abasi, but believe me—she knows when to be a chameleon. Once she accepts her fate, she'll be smart enough to blend in."

Aviama jerked her head toward Onkar, but he was already drilling her with a cool, hard stare. There could be no misunderstanding that the statement was for her.

Chameleon. Not ciraba.

But was the cheat saying it for Aviama's sake? Or for his own?

Onkar sent a second small chest up to Abasi from the *Wraithweaver* and gave a dramatic bow as one of his men swept by the grapple hooks along the railing with an axe, chopping off the lines holding the two ships together.

"Gold and gumption, it's been a pleasure doing business! May the winds be favorable until you reach Keket's shores."

Aviama's jaw dropped. She glanced at Chenzira, and a flicker of fear passed over his face like a shadow before his features turned to flint. Barely restrained rage blazed behind the warm brown eyes she'd come to know so well.

But if the *Revenge* was headed to his country, why was he afraid? He was a Keket prince. He could get them out of whatever mess they were in, couldn't he? His people would be furious that he'd been taken captive—wouldn't they?

Chenzira met her gaze just once, and with that look, all her hopes of rescue sank to the bottom of the sea. He gave the slightest shake of his head.

45

The dark of Chenzira's eyes and the ghastly pallor creeping across his skin stood every hair of Aviama's body on end. Perhaps Onkar had told the truth, and if anyone found out who *either* of them were—not just Aviama, but Chenzira too—they'd be killed.

What had really happened to drive Chenzira from his kingdom? What had happened since he'd been home last? Her mouth went dry, each breath rocketing her pulse higher and higher. When he said he wanted to protect his sister, what exactly did she need protecting from?

Abasi shouted to the sailors in a language Aviama did not know, and the deck came alive with activity. Sails were let out, stations were manned, and one of the *Revenge* sailors seized each of the new captives on board. A man gripped Aviama by the elbow and half-pulled, half-dragged her down the deck away from Chenzira, Manan, and Umed.

Panic swelled in her chest, and she nearly screamed Chenzira's name, but the word stuck in her throat. No one could know who he was. She twisted back to catch a glimpse of him as more men descended on the male prisoners, tugging them in the opposite direction. Chenzira's eyes were scalding fire as he searched hers as they pulled him away.

"I'll find you!"

Aviama's stomach soured. He didn't know that. He couldn't promise that. But even as she thought it, she knew she'd do anything to get to Chenzira. And she only had to wait it out until the magna left her system and her powers returned.

The dim light of the sinking sun dwindled from view as Aviama, Sai, and Durga were marched down stair after stair. The thud of boots mixed with the pungent smell of urine and body odor, assaulting her nose more heavily with every step. The naked tail of a rat skittered across the floorboards at the bottom of the last set of stairs, disproving her growing doubts that living things might not be able to survive the filthy conditions in the intestines of this cursed ship.

But as they turned the corner, the air left Aviama's lungs in a whoosh. Women crammed into the small room, reeking of refuse and despair, as they huddled together like worms covered in dirt with nothing left to do but die. Apathetic, miserable faces blinked back at her, unmoved by new additions to their pigsty.

Aviama breathed in through her mouth, but the staleness of the air seemed to stick to her. None of them were bound, but these broken women didn't have enough life left to fight. The only unanswered question left to their wretched lives was whether they'd be snatched first by the weasel or the toad.

The sailors tossed her down to the straw-strewn floor like neglected livestock. Sai and Durga slammed into the wall beside her a moment later, and the men returned up the stairs without a word. Her chest tightened as the pounding boots receded. Pinpricks of light fell from the slats above them, slivers of flickering torchlight swaying with the ship.

Aviama sat up slowly. She exchanged a glance with Sai,

avoided Durga, and busied herself by staring at the floor and rubbing her arms in the chill until the women removed their hollow gazes from her face. Minutes passed, and dreary despondence filled the dank air like thick fog, threatening to choke her. Aviama waited until Durga's back was turned and carefully picked her way past a heap of three half-conscious women to the narrow space under the stairs. A wider slat in the boards overhead leaked a single stream of steady torchlight to the bottom of the ship.

Aviama felt along the waist of her trousers. Something hard and round. Her fingers moved along the band until she found an opening, hands still bound, both moving together. Digging one finger into it, she tugged at the object inside. Warm light glinted off three silver coins.

She stifled a gasp and shoved the coins back into their hidden compartment along her waistband. So. Onkar had tailored her trousers with measurements he had somehow gotten, and he'd added a secret compartment along the waist.

Her hands fell to the hard object she'd noticed earlier. It was almost round, with dull spikes jutting out. Not coins. Further down than her waist, bumping up against her leg, like a true pocket.

But there wasn't an opening. Nothing on the outside, nothing along the top of the waistband. Only the slit for the coins, along the seam at the top, and—

Aviama's fingers slipped across an exaggerated stitch on the inside of her waistband. The pocket wasn't open on the outside of the trousers, but on the inside, with the bulk of the small object swallowed up to any observer by the excess material of her blouse. She ran her finger along the stitch and tugged open the pocket.

A moment later, she was staring down at a wood-carved moth wielding a sword with its six little feet. A thin strip of parchment wrapped its belly. Aviama stretched it out and tilted it toward the whisper of light drifting down through the ceiling.

When the time is right, be Raisa.
—GF

AVIAMA BLINKED DOWN at the note. The moth, the sword, were clearly from Onkar. But who was...

Her lips parted. He'd signed it with his real name. His cursed name. Grigglor Frizzletwerf.

But what did it mean to be Raisa? To be revenge, like the ship's name? To be a windcaller, like she was? Was this the chameleon part or the ciraba part? How would she know when the time was right?

Aviama's mind swirled with a thousand different possibilities, each one more ridiculous than the last. She folded the parchment until it was even tinier than when she'd pulled it out and slipped it and the little whittled moth back into the hidden pocket. She pursed her lips. Maybe it didn't mean anything. Maybe Onkar was coy and mean and laughing at her.

Aviama didn't know who these people were, or why Onkar had done business with them. She didn't know why people in Keket wanted Chenzira dead—or wanted *her* dead. The urgency in Chenzira's voice haunted her as she replayed his words over and over in her mind.

You're nobody interesting. Make up a new name.

Thinking through all she didn't know was enough to turn her stomach inside out.

What she *did* know wasn't much better. She knew that Onkar's use of the term *stock,* paired with Abasi's inspection of the human cargo, implied that *Raisa's Revenge* was a slave ship. She also knew that Onkar had perfectly planned to survive Ghosts' Gorge with a crew that would be loyal exclusively to him, and earned their trust enough that they ate magna straight from his hand—just in time for him to sell them the moment they escaped the sirens, Shiva was dispatched, and with Samud's teal captain's jacket wrapped around Onkar's slimy shoulders.

She didn't know why he'd done it. Onkar knew the magna would wear off, and Abasi didn't know they were melders. The man had swindled Abasi nearly as badly as he'd cheated Aviama and her friends. Abasi and his crew would regret the day they purchased melderbloods like cattle.

But it was Chenzira's final words that kept a sprout of hope alive in the dark of the slave ship, as *Raisa's Revenge* turned into the wind and carried them off to new, unknown terrors. Aviama curled her hands into fists, resolve hardening her heart. She clenched her jaw.

Ragged breathing of sickly women scratched through the air, combining with the creak of the ship and the intolerable stench of muck and human waste. Aviama shook her head and leaned heavily against the underside of the stairs. She swallowed against the icy fingers of dread washing over her like a wave, threatening to choke her, and whispered softly to no one in particular—

"I will find you."

THANK YOU FOR READING!

Thank you so much for reading *Wraithweaver,* book 3 of *The Melderblood Chronicles*! I hope you enjoyed reading it as much as I enjoyed writing it.

If you did, would you be willing to leave a review? Reviews help enable authors to continue doing what they do, and help other readers to find books best suited to them.

If you'd like to leave a review on Amazon, scan the QR code.

THE BLOOD & FLAME SAGA

This explosive new dragons and assassins series is about to become your new addiction.

Are you ready to ride dragons and unravel the mysteries of a land steeped in magic and betrayal?

Scan the QR code to start reading.

Magical bargains, high-stakes heists, and lovers who could
kill each other just by falling in love...

Read on for a fast-paced romantic fantasy full of curses,
cons, and a love that could kill.

If he loves her, she'll die. If she loves him, he'll die. But only by
working together can they stop a vengeful mage from rising
again—and lift the curses that bind them both.

Scan the QR code to start reading.

ABOUT THE AUTHOR

Author of *The Forgotten Stone* and *The Blood and Flame Saga*, E.A. Winters loves pouring a hot chai tea latte and delving into creating epic fantasy worlds for you to enjoy.

Erin lives in Virginia with her husband and two boys. When she's not writing, she sees clients as a Licensed Professional Counselor, and spends time with her family. She loves playing board games and reading, whenever the elusive "free time" opportunity arises.

- Website and newsletter: eawinters.com
- Facebook: facebook.com/eawintersnovels
- TikTok: @eawinters
- Instagram: @e.a.winters

Also by E.A. Winters

Blood & Flame Saga

Raised by a dragonlord to kill without question, one girl discovers the truth—and risks everything to bring down the man that made her into a weapon.

Book 1: Dragon's Kiss

Book 2: Broken Bonds

Book 3: Noble Claims

Book 4: Crimson Queen

The Melderblood Chronicles

In a palace of gowns, secrets, and betrayal, one princess walks the tightrope between duty and death... while magic simmers beneath her skin.

Book 1: Melderblood

Book 2: Shadow Caste

Book 3: Wraithweaver

Book 4: Reaverbane

Heist of Hearts

If he loves her, she'll die. If she loves him, he'll die. But only by working together can they stop a vengeful mage from rising again—and lift the curses that bind them both.

Book 1: Heist of Hearts

Book 2: Oath of Odds

Stand Alones

The Forgotten Stone

When a tavern girl angers the realm's fiercest warrior, she flees straight into a legendary quest—and discovers that destiny doesn't wait for the qualified.

Browse All Titles by E.A. Winters by Scanning the QR Code Below

www.ingramcontent.com/pod-product-compliance
Lightning Source LLC
Chambersburg PA
CBHW051159190726
48288CB00006B/1714